THE MATCH FACTORY GIRLS

BOOK 1 IN THE MATCH FACTORY GIRLS SERIES

KAY BRELLEND

Boldwood

First published in Great Britain in 2026 by Boldwood Books Ltd.

Copyright © Kay Brellend, 2026

Cover Design by Colin Thomas

Cover Images: Colin Thomas

The moral right of Kay Brellend to be identified as the author of this work has been asserted in accordance with the Copyright, Designs and Patents Act 1988.

Every effort has been made to obtain the necessary permissions with reference to copyright material, both illustrative and quoted. We apologise for any omissions in this respect and will be pleased to make the appropriate acknowledgements in any future edition.

A CIP catalogue record for this book is available from the British Library.

Paperback ISBN 978-1-80658-410-9

Large Print ISBN 978-1-80658-412-3

Hardback ISBN 978-1-80658-409-3

Trade Paperback ISBN 978-1-80658-411-6

Ebook ISBN 978-1-80658-413-0

Kindle ISBN 978-1-80658-414-7

Audio CD ISBN 978-1-80658-404-8

MP3 CD ISBN 978-1-80658-405-5

Digital audio download ISBN 978-1-80658-408-6

This book is printed on certified sustainable paper. Boldwood Books is dedicated to putting sustainability at the heart of our business. For more information please visit https://www.boldwoodbooks.com/about-us/sustainability/

Boldwood Books Ltd, 23 Bowerdean Street, London, SW6 3TN

www.boldwoodbooks.com

For:
Mary Ann Nichols, Annie Chapman, Elizabeth Stride, Catherine Eddowes, Mary Jane Kelly

His attitude didn't bother her. She knew from past experience that West End men despised East End women. Still, they came to Whitechapel for the girls who listened for their carriages, then emerged from the shadows into gaslight, like moths drawn to flame.

1

EAST END OF LONDON

December 1887

A street lamp bracketed on a wall barely illuminated the spot in Fairfield Road where the girl had tucked herself out of sight. Twilight had long since been overtaken by a moonless night, yet still she waited. The blanketing gloom complicated the task of furtively studying passing females to find the right face. Her instinct was to bolt but Amelia Spencer had little choice other than to turn to her big sister for help.

Shoving her frozen fingers deeper into her pockets, she was tempted to stamp her feet to warm them. Making a noise wasn't wise though. A lone female loitering in an alley would be assumed to be up to no good.

Parents with a brood of children were to be found penned into a single room in Bow. Some properties were dosshouses where fourpence hired a wooden bunk for the night. Amelia had been informed of this by Sadie who had briefly set up home in a slum with her villainous husband.

A scurrying sound made Amelia jump and twitch her skirts

away from scavenging rodents... a timely reminder that human vermin were also about. She could be pounced upon and robbed but she held her nerve and stayed behind the gate leading to the backyards of the houses. The stench of over-flowing privies drifting on the mist was making her feel queasy but she forgot about that on hearing a clack of heeled boots on cobbles, alerting her to women approaching.

Peering around an edge of wall, she made out one tall and one short figure emerging from the factory gates in the distance. Bryant and May churned out matchsticks late into the evening and Amelia hoped to catch her sister at the end of her overtime shift. But Sadie wasn't one of these brunettes. Her sister's hair was as fair as her own. The match girls passed by, squabbling about a debt the shorter of the two insisted had been repaid.

The sound of hobnail boots clanging on cobbles came next. A hunched fellow in donkey jacket and cap was mean-dering drunkenly from kerb to wall. On the other side of the road somebody else was in sight. Her footsteps were light and quiet. A girl of about twelve with a tray hanging around her neck was crossing the road towards the fellow, having reacted to his whistle and beckoning finger. The child took his money and handed over a matchbox. Then off she set, padding bare-foot, her only protection against the frosty air a thin shawl over a ragged dress. The labourer she'd served struck a match to the dog end drooping between his lips before ambling onwards.

Amelia felt pity and anger at the little street seller's plight and hoped the girl was now on her way home for a warm drink and her bed. She certainly felt less sorry for herself than she had on arriving in this unsavoury place about an hour ago. Deciding she'd done enough loitering, she picked up her bag. She'd come from Mayfair and this neighbourhood was depressing and foreign to her, making her jumpy. A distant church bell warned her the hour was getting late.

As bad luck would have it, the drunk came to a halt abreast of her. She investigated the delay through a wormy hole in the wooden gate. He was only a yard away, facing the gutter. A steady flow of urine billowed steam in front of him as he sniffed and spat on the ground.

Her sigh of relief to see him go transformed into an alarmed squeak. A rat had run over her shoes, making her drop her bag. The noise drew his attention and he returned to peek at her, using the same ragged aperture through which she was spying on him.

'Wot yer hidin' in there for, miss?' He dropped his cigarette stub and smacked his thigh in enlightenment. 'You're noo and think the others'll claw yer face.' He wobbled a finger to his lips, miming secrecy. "S'alright, I won't tell Nell you're on her patch.'

The gate was creaked open and he continued grinning like a boy presented with a gift of sweets. Drunk, maybe, but he had enough strength to put her onto her toes while resisting his yank on her arm.

'How much?' Undeterred by her shoves, he fiddled inside his coat to find the trouser buttons he'd recently done up.

'I'm only waiting for somebody,' she hissed in nervous vexation.

'An' here I am, ducks. Four bob.' He used a foot on the battered gate to keep it open while she tried to shut him out. 'Other gels don't get so much but I reckon you've got class.' He winked and opened a hand to reveal a glint of silver. 'First, let's have a proper gander at yer.' His fingers snapped back over the florins. He wasn't too sozzled to have missed that she appeared cleaner and prettier than the regulars. He lifted a straggling tress of fair hair to appreciate a smooth complexion and youthful features. Her large glossy eyes sparked at him, but he continued smirking at his good fortune. Older women, raddled by years of rough living, plied their trade around here. This one was in her teens, he guessed, smelling of soap rather than gin, and had reacted to his hand on her like a scalded cat. Jolted out of happily imagining she was a virgin, he employed two fingers to warn off the nosy parker banging on her windowpane.

Amelia used the distraction to her advantage. She pushed the gate, sending her admirer reeling backwards. A strike of metal hitting stone was heard before he landed on his posterior in the gutter. Edging through the opening, she fled with her skirts gripped in one hand and her bag in the other. In her panic, she barely glanced at a youth dragging the irate fellow to his feet.

'Oi... watch where you're going, you clumsy thing. You nearly had me legs from under me.'

Amelia had careered around the corner and barged into somebody. She mumbled a breathless apology and in unison they bent to retrieve their bags, dropped to the cobbles. Their eyes met as they began to straighten up.

'Sadie?' Amelia gasped, winded from her dash. She spontaneously hugged her elder sister, squashing the feathered hat being raised towards its owner's head. 'I've been looking for you. I'm in trouble and could do with a place to stay.'

'Blimey, things must be bad. You said you'd have no more to do with me. So, what's happened?'

Despite her sister's spikiness Amelia hoped that past differences could be put aside now the man who'd caused the trouble was off the scene. Amelia had hero-worshipped her pretty, popular sister and had felt let down by Sadie, thinking her a fool to allow a wretch like Jimmy Burley to ruin her life. She was prepared to eat humble pie now she knew how easy it was to break your parents' hearts while unwisely losing your own to a deceitful swine.

'I'm sorry we fell out,' she said. 'I've missed you.'

'Likewise...' Sadie's attention was caught by the fellow blundering towards them, bawling about being robbed.

'We'd better go. I made him let go of me, and he dropped his money. If he's lost it in the gutter, it's his own fault for being a lecher.'

'Let go of you?' Sadie sounded concerned as well as curious to know more.

'I was hoping you'd be working late at the match factory and I'd catch you when you knocked off. He came by and saw me hanging about and thought... well I expect you know what he thought.'

'Dirty git. That's Bill Potts. He's a drayman at the Ind Coope brewery where Dad works.'

'No wonder he reeks of booze.' Their father was teetotal but he had spoken about men being sacked for stealing drink. 'Do you lodge close by, Sadie?'

'Close enough; we'd better make a run for it.' Sadie took her sister's hand, urging her along the street. 'I'm ready for a bite to eat and me bed, not a punch-up.'

Amelia did her best to keep up but the stitch in her side finally became unbearable. She slipped her fingers free and slowed down to take a breather.

'You never are?' Sadie demanded in shock as she noticed her sister supporting her abdomen. She unceremoniously yanked apart the edges of Amelia's cloak to study her figure.

Amelia closed her eyes, blocking out an unwanted reality. "Fraid I am.'

'Gawdawmighty! Amelia! You really are in trouble. Has he asked you to marry him?' Sadie sounded dubious.

'He's gone...' Amelia confirmed in a voice mingling many emotions, not least the shame she felt for having been such easy prey. Her innocence and affection had been thrown back in her face by her first proper love. She was no longer a gullible fool, but she was dismayed by Sadie's reaction. Her brash older sister would take this news in her stride, she'd thought. But Sadie had sounded alarmed, as though things might not be as easily solvable as hoped.

'Oh, Lia...' Sadie touched together their foreheads in comfort. 'You've picked up with a wrong 'un as well, have you? Us Spencer girls don't have much luck in love, do we?'

She sounded wistful, recalling the locked doors and punishments that hadn't stopped her creeping out of the house to meet Jimmy Burley. Finally her parents had come to the end of their tether and thrown her out. Defiantly, she'd marched off with a string-tied bundle of clothes and a warning to never return.

Amelia was also reflecting on her sister's bad choice of husband. As well as being a thief and a bully he was a lecher, as she knew to her cost. He'd tried to kiss her while his wife's back was turned. Sadie had accused her of misinterpreting his friendliness. Amelia had been saddened by the rift; they'd been friends as well as sisters before he came along. Now he'd gone there was a chance for a new beginning.

'Kicked you out, have they, love?'

'I haven't been back there,' said Amelia. 'I know Mum and Dad will find out sooner or later though.'

'Actually, I meant your employers. The Campbells sacked you, I suppose?' Sadie understood Amelia's reluctance to go home. Their parents were typical working-class folk, terrified of an unmarried daughter's swollen belly being spotted by neighbours.

'Mrs Campbell called me a disgrace before showing me the

door,' Amelia glumly informed her sister. 'I've got my wind back. Let's get going.' She didn't trust this area with its bad smells and shifty folk. She'd become accustomed to the elegant atmosphere of a West End townhouse, albeit she'd been housed in the servants' quarters in the attic. 'I'll tell you more about it when we reach your lodging.'

2

'I stopped off and bought some tea and jam at the end of my shift. The baker was closed but I banged on the door and he let me have a stale brown loaf, buckshee. The old goat fancies me.' Sadie was jabbering over a shoulder while leading the way, single file, through a door-less portal. The dank corridor was rumbling with domestic noises. Sadie unlocked her lodging and guided her sister inside with a warning to avoid bumping into the furniture. The strike of a match was heard, then a lamp was turned up until the musty gloom revealed its secrets.

'Pinched those from work. No decent wages at Bryant and May, so I take what I can.' The matchbox was lobbed onto the table, then Sadie produced from her bag a pot of jam and twist of paper containing tea leaves. 'Take the weight off your feet then.' A rickety chair was dragged out from under the table. 'I'll boil the kettle if I can stir this blighter into life.' She began loading torn newspaper and kindling onto the fire, employing the bellows until flames licked around the sticks. 'Ain't a palace, is it?' She had noticed her sister glancing around the poky room. 'Roof over me head, though, that's the main thing.'

She took off her hat and coat, pegging them up behind the door.

'At least you've somewhere to cook.' Actually Amelia was rather impressed; the room was only a few yards square but contained a hob grate set into the deep chimney breast. The black iron plate held a copper kettle and a long-handled pot. The table and pair of chairs looked serviceable. The iron bedstead was a single, Amelia noticed, and there was just enough wall space left over for a chest of drawers to support a china washing set. But it was a dwelling, and she was in no position to turn her nose up at that.

'We'll have to top and tail on it tonight.' Sadie jerked a nod at her sagging mattress then sniffed at the top of the milk bottle. 'On the turn but it'll do.'

Amelia used her foot to move her bag under the table so neither of them tripped up on it. She loosened her cloak then ran a few neatening fingers through her hair, dampened by December mist.

'Even got a couple of biscuits left.' Sadie had prised the top off a dented tin to display some digestives.

In spontaneous affection, Amelia got up to hug her sister, resting her head on Sadie's shoulder. 'I've really missed you. I'm sorry we fell out.'

"S'alright,' Sadie said gruffly. 'I wish I'd listened to you back then. You was only a kid but you had the measure of Jimmy. Anyway, how'd you find out I'd left him?'

'I had a weekend off in the summer and went to visit Mum and Dad.' Amelia seated herself again. 'Hadn't been there long when I overheard them arguing about Betty Logan spreading gossip.' She had loitered in the hallway long enough to learn that the neighbours knew Jimmy Burley was in Pentonville prison and his wife had come to her senses and left him.

After that it hadn't seemed the right time for Amelia to bring up her marriage plans. A blessing in disguise as it turned out; what a fool she would have felt, raising their hopes of having a decent son-in-law, simply to dash them when he revealed himself to be nothing of the sort.

'Betty Logan should mind her own business,' said Sadie. 'She knows Jimmy's mother so I expect they've been chinwagging about me.' Sadie had missed seeing her family, but guilt, and a fear of rejection, had kept her from making the first move to build bridges. 'How are they all?'

'Our brother had caught head lice off a classmate. He'd been shorn like a prison convict.' A reminder of Sadie's jailbird husband wasn't wise. Amelia pressed quickly on. 'Becky was angry in case she got nits and had to have all her hair cut off.' Their youngest sister was a moody adolescent. Amelia could remember being impatient to leave childhood behind for a first job. Being a grown-up wasn't all it was cracked up to be though, and being thirteen and able to start again was what she – and she suspected Sadie – would like to do. Their brother Thomas was nine years old and the apple of his doting mother's eye, nits or no nits. 'How do you afford this place on your own, Sadie?' Keeping even this modest place was quite an achievement for a Bryant and May match girl.

'I got made up to supervisor. I can pay the rent by penny pinching.' Sadie changed the subject. 'Thing is, Lia, I don't know how this is going to work out now you can't get a job 'cos of that...' She tipped a nod at her sister's belly. 'You can stay a day or two but I can't afford to feed both of us after that.'

Amelia found her purse, undid the string and emptied out a collection of coins onto the battered pine table. 'There's almost fifteen shillings to put in the kitty and once the baby's born I'll get full-time work straight away.'

'How'd you manage that?' An impressed and envious Sadie gawped at the assortment of copper and silver.

'Saved it. I've been putting a bit by since I left school to better meself. Thought I'd rent a little shop and sell haberdashery: lace and cottons and so on.' She finished on a self-mocking grimace. The idea of being her own boss had been forgotten when her dream of being a wife and mother took over.

'Would you be able to get me a job at Bryant and May? I can hide the bump for a while. I got rumbled when a colleague caught me.' She shrugged. 'I'd been undressing in the dark after I realised why I'd missed a couple of monthlies. A few days ago I spilled silver polish down my front and was changing my skirt when Lorna Smith barged in on me in my underclothes.' She sighed. 'I knew then I'd have to put in my notice but hoped to hang it out until after Christmas.'

'You've kept yourself trim.' Sadie gave her sister's figure a thorough inspection. 'You fooled me at first. This Lorna blabbed, did she?'

'She promised to keep quiet.' Amelia put her elbows on the table and rested her chin on her hands. 'Her sweetheart's a groom in the stable. She told him to keep his trousers buttoned in future 'cos she didn't want to end up like me. Thanks to his big mouth, gossip started. I couldn't lie when the mistress asked me outright, so that was that.'

'It's Christmas next week; Mum and Dad will expect to hear from you, Lia.'

'I wrote and told them I couldn't get time off as the Campbells are holding a big party, and that is the truth.' Amelia gave her sister's hands an encouraging squeeze. 'We'll be all right after the baby's born. About Easter time, I think it'll be. Once I'm back on my feet, a neighbour might mind the baby if I pay her out of those savings.'

'You're not planning to *keep* it are you?' spluttered Sadie, yanking her fingers free.

'What d'you mean, keep it?'

'Bloody hell, Amelia!' Sadie gestured her exasperation. 'I thought you'd leave it at the Foundling Hospital.' She crossed her arms. 'What about the father? Has he scarpered?'

'Oh, he's hiding under a stone somewhere.' Amelia defiantly met her sister's eyes. 'I'd never give up my baby.' The idea of it made anger burn in her chest. 'I can pay my way until spring. Afterwards we could do different factory shifts to take turns minding the baby...'

'No, we couldn't,' Sadie interrupted. 'I've got plans to better myself too, you know. I can't do that with your kid round me ankles, tying me down.' She paused. 'Jimmy got six months in gaol for affray and I've had a chance to move on. I want to quit Bryant and May before I get ill like some of my colleagues.' She unconsciously rubbed her face. 'Dreadful mess some of them look with their phossy chops.'

'What?' Amelia frowned.

'Phossy jaw,' Sadie explained, jerking her chin for emphasis. 'It's horrible. The white phosphorous that gives a match its flame can get into you and rot your teeth and bones.' Sadie tested her teeth with a probing finger. 'If you hang around these streets long enough you might see some wonky faces. Maura glows in the dark as well... poor ol' soul...'

'What? Don't be daft!' Amelia's amusement faded beneath Sadie's sharp frown.

'I wasn't larking, Amelia.' She shook her head. 'The stuff on the matchsticks gets breathed in and it sticks to your hands. We eat our dinners sitting at the work benches and that doesn't help.' She shuddered. 'So, if you don't want rotten gums and a phizog shining like a lantern, stay away from Bryant and May.'

Amelia smoothed her hands over her sister's face. 'You look fine, love,' she said although Sadie's talk of this 'phossy jaw' had alarmed her. 'You're still as pretty as ever.'

'I only started at Bryant and May when I came to Bow with Jimmy. Some of the old-timers have worked there for decades. I work hard, but that doesn't mean I'm happy with the way things are.' Sadie poured the boiling water into the teapot. 'The guvnors know people are getting sick but haven't improved conditions. I'm not waiting for changes to come about; I'm off before Jimmy's released and comes looking for me. He'll soon find out I've moved lodging.' She tipped what remained in the kettle into a tin bowl. 'I wash me hands a lot to clean off the factory muck. Some of the older women with kids' mouths to feed, can't afford luxuries like soap.' Sadie washed and dried her hands then started cutting the brown loaf.

Amelia had accepted that matchmaking would be badly paid drudgery, but hadn't dreamt, from her ivory tower in Mayfair, it could be hazardous. 'Buy some soap and put the rest in the kitty.' She pushed her jumble of silver and copper towards her sister. Sadie dredged the cash from the table into her palm then let it clatter into an old tobacco tin taken from the table drawer. Having put their suppers on the table, she took the seat opposite.

'We'll muddle through, won't we?' Amelia was hungry and immediately started eating. Her sister avoided meeting her eye, or answering her. Amelia pushed away her empty plate with a sense of dejection. 'What's wrong, Sadie?'

'Look... you're my sister and I'll do what I can, but you can't go into labour in secret. If you really want to keep the baby, you'll have to beg for Mum and Dad's help.'

Amelia knew her sister wasn't being unkind but practical in bringing to light that it would be dangerous to give birth in a place like this. Her savings wouldn't buy everything needed and a midwife's help.

'Buck up... once the shock wears off they might like having a first grandchild.'

'You were kicked out and weren't even expecting,' Amelia dolefully pointed out.

'You're Mum's blue-eyed girl,' said Sadie a trifle sourly. 'When you got that job in Mayfair she hoped you'd meet a toff and marry him.' She rolled her eyes at her sister's belly. 'Mr Campbell did that to you, I suppose?'

'Wasn't him; the master seemed a nice fellow... not that I ever saw much of him.' Amelia dropped her chin. 'It's my own stupid fault I'm in this mess. I fell in love and believed what he said about us having a future together.'

'Swine. Was he one of the servants?'

'Not really; he gave piano lessons to the children.' Amelia would sooner discover her sister's plans than talk about this. 'Will you divorce Jimmy?'

'Don't know what I'm going to do.' Sadie fiddled with her teaspoon.

'I thought you said you had plans.'

'I have... but...'

'Spit it out then. I can see something's up.'

'I've not told you everything yet,' Sadie said. 'I've met somebody. He knows about Jimmy and he's been good to me. He's looking for a room for us in north London so we can be together. First, he needs to sort some things out.'

'What sort of things?' Amelia asked, sensing there was more to this. 'Have you fallen in love again already? What's he like?'

'You might see for yourself that he's nice enough. I'm expecting him to call this evening.'

Nice enough didn't sound as though Sadie was embroiled in a passionate love affair, were Amelia's thoughts a second before she jumped out of her skin. Right on cue, a man bellowed her sister's name, then came a loud hammering at the door. If this was him, he didn't sound nice at all.

'Jimmy!' Sadie clumsily shot to her feet, rattling the crockery on the table. 'Oh, no! He's supposed to be locked up for weeks yet.'

3

'Not got a welcome-home kiss for the old man then?' Jimmy Burley flung off his donkey jacket and left the grimy garment where it landed on the floor. 'Anybody'd think you wasn't pleased to see me, gel.'

Sadie hadn't let him in; he'd not waited more than a few seconds before giving the door two hefty kicks, bursting open the lock and almost separating wood from hinges.

'What the bloody hell are you doing here?' Sadie confronted him, arms crossed. 'How'd you find out where I lived?' A factory colleague might have told him her new address. More worrying was the possibility he'd been spying on her.

The two empty cups on the table drew his suspicious eyes, making him wonder if she'd recently been with her fancy man.

'You got six months' hard labour, not five.' Sadie stabbed a finger at his bristly chin. 'Coppers'll be after you if you've absconded.' She hoped it was true and that they'd hurry up about it.

'No need to get in a tizz, dear,' he purred. 'Was let out early for good behaviour. Don't worry, we won't be interrupted.' His voice had a lustful pitch and he tickled his wife's cheek before slipping his fingers to girdle her throat. She knew it wasn't a tender caress. She'd had his rough hands on her like this before. After they'd tightened, she had to wind a scarf around her neck right up to her chin to cover the bruises.

'Clear off, Jimmy.' She shoved him. 'I told you before you got sent down that we're over.'

'You're my wife, and that ain't a very nice thing for a man to hear when he's just been let out of prison. I've been dreaming of you keeping me warm at night. Why didn't you come and visit me?' He nuzzled her cheek then ground his lips onto hers until she jerked her face aside. 'I reckon you've been missing me, haven't you, Sadie, with no man about the place?' He was watching for a sign of guilt and got it. 'That's what I thought,' he growled and started unbuttoning his shirt one-handed, imprisoning her squirming forearm with the other. 'After we've finished on that bed you can make me something to eat. Me belly needs satisfying 'n' all.' He withdrew a half bottle of rum from a pocket. 'Even thought to bring us summat to drink.'

The moment the door began shuddering beneath the onslaught of his boots, Amelia had concealed herself in the recess at the side of the chimney breast. Wrapped in her brown cloak with the hood drawn up, she was hard to spot crouching down in the shadows. She'd believed her sister must be confident of getting rid of Jimmy. But Sadie was already cowed. 'Leave her alone and bugger off,' Amelia cried, shooting upright.

Jimmy gave a rather comical, startled shout on hearing a command ring out close behind. Instinctively, he snatched a knife from a pocket and flicked it open. The blade disappeared whence it came after he realised he'd heard a familiar female voice. 'Well... if it ain't sweet Amelia.' He turned around to look at her with an insolent smile. 'Bit old to be playing peek-a-boo ain't yer, dear? No need to be shy with me, y'know.'

Despite her jitters at the sight of his knife, Amelia stepped boldly closer.

'Keeping your sister company, are you? Well, Sadie don't need you now she's got me back home.' His eyes veered between the women as he sensed a conspiracy. 'We've some catchin' up to do – as you can imagine.' He dropped a lewd wink but Amelia didn't react. She wouldn't give him the satisfaction of knowing she was scared.

Sadie jerked an urgent nod at the door. 'There's a tavern across the road. I'll look for you in the Anchor later, Lia.' She would go along with what he wanted for now in the hope he'd drink himself off to sleep. If her lover turned up as well, her pregnant sister might be caught up in a brawl. Word of Jimmy being on the loose would soon spread after the racket he'd made on arrival. The neighbours wouldn't call the police though; nobody had any truck with the peelers.

Jimmy had always considered Amelia prettier than his wife, but too slender. She seemed to have filled out. The outlines of her breasts and hips were visible beneath her cloak. He strolled closer for a better look. 'Last time we met we had a falling-out. Kiss and make up before you go, shall we?'

'You can leave Amelia alone.' Sadie knew her randy husband was thinking two women were better than one for a man who'd been celibate for months. 'My sister's having a baby and don't need your mauling.'

That surprised him; he jerked up Amelia's left hand. 'Tut tut; no wedding ring. Ain't so prim 'n' proper after all then.'

Amelia snatched herself free. 'I'm not leaving my sister alone with you. She's finished with you, so *you* should clear off.'

Deliberately, he pulled a chair towards him and sat down.

'Well, this is nice 'n' cosy, the three of us together.' He unstoppered the rum with his teeth, spat the cork and took a swig. 'We all squashing into that bed tonight?' He smacked his lips while giving Amelia another lewd stare. 'I don't mind, if you don't, love.'

'I said, leave her alone.' Sadie tried to drag him to his feet.

Without bothering to rise, he sent her stumbling to her knees. 'This is my home now. If you want to piss off with your sister, go right ahead. And when your fancy man turns up, I'll be waiting to give him a nice welcome.'

Amelia guessed he didn't yet know the whole story there or he would have named names. They couldn't force him out. He'd easily fight them off even though he looked thinner from hard labour.

Jimmy Burley was of medium height with a wiry build. What he lacked in brawn he made up for in vicious intent, and rarely gave up before winning a fight. He was quite handsome in a craggy way. He usually wore his mousy-coloured hair touching his ears. He'd been shorn in prison and his cropped stubble looked a similar shade to his deep brown eyes. Amelia had first known him when still a schoolgirl. Back then she had thought him roguishly charming with his naughty winks and easy smiles. Sadie had told her to keep quiet about the older man she was seeing and Amelia had gone along with it, thinking it exciting to be trusted with secrets. She'd envied her sister having a charismatic boyfriend who wore his flat cap at a jaunty angle and drove a horse and cart for his uncle's haulage business.

Then, after a while, her big sister would often look more anxious than happy following a clandestine rendezvous. But Sadie was caught in his web and at sixteen didn't know how to break free of a man eight years older.

Jimmy took another swig of rum and settled his back

comfortably into the chair. He hadn't followed them home, Sadie realised, or he would have been prepared for her sister's presence. He never liked witnesses when browbeating his wife; but he loved an audience when scrapping in the street. And he liked her watching him eying up other women. The sly glances he was sliding Amelia's way were stirring a prickle of jealousy. 'Off you go.' Sadie ushered her sister to the door. 'Me 'n' Jimmy need to sort things out by ourselves. Anyway, going home to Mum 'n' Dad's is your only hope now you're in this mess.'

Amelia felt utterly deflated. If luck had been with her, this could have worked. But wishing Jimmy was still in prison was pointless. 'It's too far to walk,' she said, accepting defeat. 'I need my money back so I can pay for a cab...'

Burley was on his feet before his sister-in-law had finished talking. He'd intercepted the look Sadie had darted to the tin she'd put on the shelf earlier. Before his wife reached for it, he elbowed her aside.

'Well... what have we here?' The tin got a shake, making the coins jingle, before he whipped off the lid. 'Now, where'd you get that lot from, sweet Amelia?'

'I saved it.'

Amelia lunged for the tin but his hand described a swift arc, taking it above his head. 'Buy yourself a glass o' porter while you wait in the pub. Once me 'n' Sadie's had words, you'll get anything else due.' He put a shilling onto the table.

'That's not enough! It's all mine!'

'I don't know it's *all* yourn,' he said, all wide-eyed innocence. 'Could be my wife's been giving you board and lodging here in my house for a month. Could be you owe me everything in the tin. And more besides.'

'Amelia's just arrived!' Sadie bellowed. 'Give her money back to her.'

'I'll get the law on you,' Amelia cried in a panic. Every penny she had was in his hand. 'You're a blasted crook and a bully. And it's not right the way you treat Sadie.'

'Husbands 'n' wives have tiffs. Just the way it is.' He lowered his face to whisper into Amelia's ear: 'While I was still in chokey I heard a woman got strangled only last week.' He patted her shoulder. 'So, don't go hanging around out there, eh? Whitechapel's a nasty place. Head back to Hackney and yer stuck-up folks.'

Jimmy wedged a foot against the door, which was sagging on loose hinges. With the money tin in one hand, he propelled Amelia outside with the other. 'Me 'n' the missus need privacy.' He gave her an aggravating wink. 'Cab fare.' He flicked a coin into the air before closing the door in her face.

'Lia! Wait in the pub.'

Amelia heard her sister's shout as the shilling hit her shoe. She crouched down in the solid darkness, luckily finding it by touch, inches from her toes. 'I want what's mine, you thief.' She rattled the handle, but the door wouldn't budge. 'I'll fetch a copper. He'll throw you back in prison after he's listened to what I have to say.' She put an ear against the panel and thought she detected his snigger. She couldn't prove that cash was hers and couldn't deny handing it over willingly to be put into the kitty. And he knew it.

'Woss all the racket abaht?' A neighbour had opened her door and stepped out into a puddle of light, thrown from a candle held aloft.

'Nothing... sorry to disturb you...' Amelia continued trudging towards the exit.

The woman wasn't satisfied with that; as the girl drew level she fastened a bony hand on her arm. 'And who might you be? Ah... now I can see a likeness.' She was playing the candlelight on Amelia's face, making her squint and turn aside from the glare. 'Sister, I reckon you are... younger than her.' She tipped a nod at Sadie's door.

'That's right; sorry about the noise.' Amelia removed the plucking fingers from her sleeve and swiftly carried on towards the street and fresher air. Staying to do battle with Jimmy would only make things worse. Sadie had tried to protect her, telling her to leave before a rumpus started. What had happened next was her own fault. She'd foolishly alerted Jimmy to the money in the tin.

'Burley's out of Pentonville sooner than expected then, is he?'

Amelia didn't respond but the crone seemed unwilling to give up on a gossip.

'Your sister wants to watch herself now. If the other feller comes back sniffing around, there'll be murders. It'll be a noose for Jimmy next time.'

4

Out on the frosty cobbles, Amelia felt chilled by more than the bitter night. Jimmy's warning of a strangler on the loose, and the old woman going on about a noose, seemed ominous. She glanced to left and right, unsure which way to take. This wasn't her London; she'd been brought up in a better neighbourhood, between Dalston and Hackney.

The mist had lifted, and from one end of the narrow road to the other, frozen surfaces sparkled beneath limey gaslight. Up above, between the rooftops and lines of limp washing criss-crossing from house to house, was a strip of twinkling sky. But the likelihood of snow hadn't kept everybody indoors.

People were congregating at the bottom end of the street, shouting rather than singing and punching the air with fists enclosing tankards. Sadie had mentioned the Anchor tavern. Amelia now knew its location, but wasn't in the mood to brave entering a rowdy house. Neither would she squander her precious shilling on drink. Even if her bullied sister managed to escape Jimmy to come to the pub, what help could she give? Sadie needed help herself. Amelia wanted to intervene, but fighting her own corner had proved too much. She'd have to recover her money and bag another time, and she hoped Burley wouldn't be about when she did.

Turning her back on the revellers, Amelia hastened in what she hoped was the direction of the High Road. Cab drivers didn't trawl backstreets for trade from people used to making do with Shanks's pony. She searched for a landmark to get her bearings, vaguely aware of somebody emerging from darkness on the opposite pavement. Having glimpsed a male silhouette, she instinctively pulled her hood forward and increased her pace. She wasn't unduly bothered about him until he bawled at her to stop. Startled, Amelia jerked up her face and froze as he broke into a purposeful run. Her instinct was to turn tail and dash back the way she'd come but she didn't because she'd done nothing wrong.

'Oi... you! I've been looking for you.'

Within seconds, a heavy hand was on her shoulder. The drunk who'd accosted her appeared to have sobered up.

'You give me back my money, you little cow,' he snarled. 'I know your game. You 'n' Spider was in it together. Well, it'll be a cold day in hell before Bill Potts falls foul of one of that tyke's cons.'

Amelia understood that he was angry to have lost his silver, but the rest of it made no sense whatsoever to her.

'I haven't got the money you dropped,' she angrily protested while struggling to free herself.

'Spider's still got it, has he? Where is the little runt?' He raised a meaty fist. 'He'll get a taste of this and you deserve a thumping too for being in on it.' He drove a searching hand into her cloak pocket. 'How many tricks you turned this evening?' He pulled out the shilling and grunted in disgust. His insolent fingers were soon inside her cloak to find another pocket. They encountered nothing but her swollen belly and he hissed an insult. Knowing she was pregnant didn't deter him from hunting between her legs in a decidedly lecherous manner.

'No more money, eh? Well you can pay me back that other way. You don't short-change Bill Potts.'

'Get off me!' Amelia kicked his shins, shaking her head to and fro to avoid his beer-breathed mouth slobbering on her. Her innocent baby was just inches from his mauling hands. She scratched his face and aimed a punch at his chest in an attempt to dislodge him. In response he swore at her and renewed his efforts to push her against the wall and yank up her skirts.

Abruptly he was gone, and when she opened her eyes, she saw he'd been flung back so forcefully that he was in a position she'd seen him in before: sitting on his backside in the gutter.

'The doxy robbed me,' Potts whined to a younger man standing with his arms crossed. 'She's in it with Spider. Turned a trick on me. I ain't going till I've got back me two florins. Or I'll have me money's worth that other way.'

'Four bob, eh?' The stranger's voice held a note of amusement. 'You was smitten then Bill, eh?' He glanced at Amelia in a way that made her control her panting and brush down her clothes. But he'd done her a huge favour, and she was grateful.

'Give him back his money,' the younger man said. 'Or he's entitled to have a crack at you and I won't stop him this time.'

Amelia had been about to thank him for what he'd done... but not now. 'Who do you think you're talking to like that?' She was incensed to be addressed as though she were a strumpet when she'd taken pains to keep to herself. The most she could be accused of was loitering and giving Bill Potts the wrong idea. She glared into a pair of narrowed eyes. 'I've been visiting a relative and was heading home when he attacked me. He must still be drunk to be talking rot about spiders.' She rubbed at her arm as though she felt something crawling upon her.

It was that small gesture rather than her protests of innocence that persuaded Nicholas Dupree she was telling the truth. She didn't seem to have a clue who Spider was, and she would know if she worked the streets round here. Then again, she could be new to the game because most of the working girls were known to him and he'd never seen her before. He would have remembered her if he had. She had a crisp tone better suited to the west side of town. Yet there was something familiar about her.

'So, you don't know Charlie Webb also known as Spider?' he cross-examined.

'No, I do not,' Amelia snapped, pulling up her hood with unsteady fingers. Potts's assault had rattled her.

'He's a lad who likes easy pickings and has a knack of knowing where they're to be had.' Nicholas watched her indignation falter. He guessed she'd remembered something after all.

'There was a boy... I didn't take much notice of him. He helped Mr Potts to his feet when he took a tumble.' Amelia turned to Bill, still slumped on the cobbles. 'You should be grateful, not go accusing the boy of things.'

'He wasn't *helping* me,' scoffed Bill. 'He was helping hisself. You lured me in and tripped me over and he swiped me cash. Oldest trick in the book, that is. In it together they was.' A finger wag emphasised his point to their referee.

Amelia had had enough of justifying her behaviour when she'd no case to plead. 'I'm going home, and you'd better leave me alone or I'll have the coppers on you.' She jutted her chin at Potts.

'Bleedin' cheek of it!' Bill scrambled to his feet in a paddy.

'I'll have 'em on you right back. Soliciting, you was, you dishonest little tart.'

'Enough!' The younger man got between them as Bill lunged for Amelia.

She knew the stranger's mind was working behind his slightly wearisome expression. So was her mind working... and coming up with an idea of how to recover her money and carpetbag and rescue Sadie at the same time. Something in this Thames-scented air obviously taught people to be sneaky, because she was learning fast to be so, she realised. If she could pull off this stunt, she'd put up with being called names by strangers. She'd never see them again, in any case.

'I'll tell you the truth,' she lied. 'The boy handed a coin to me after we did the trick.' Her cheeks burned and she lowered her chin to conceal her guilty expression. If Spider was innocent of theft she'd just dropped him right in it. 'A short while ago my brother-in-law stole all my cash then threw me out. So if you want your money back you'll have to go after him.'

'What's his name, this brother-in-law of yours?' Nicholas had corralled Amelia away from Bill, geeing himself up for a fight.

'Jimmy Burley. He's in there.' Amelia pointed to the house.

Bill Potts had been eavesdropping while rolling up his sleeves in preparation to do battle. He left his cuffs dangling and plunged his fists on his hips. 'Burley?' He spat a tsk of disbelief. 'He's doing porridge. You're lyin' again.'

'I am not,' declared an irate Amelia. 'He's been let out early.'

'She's telling the truth... he's out, all right.' Nicholas had heard gossip in the pub about sightings of Burley. He'd been on his way to warn Sadie, but it seemed he was too late.

Amelia instinctively inched closer to the fellow who seemed impartial and disinclined to wallop her. She slid surreptitious glances at him. He dressed like the bargees she'd seen on the Regent's canal: dark reefer jacket and peaked leather cap. She guessed he was about Jimmy's age, although he was taller and broader. His hair was much darker: quite black, she imagined, like his glittering eyes, though it was difficult to identify colours in dim light. He'd sensed her interest and quickly she looked elsewhere.

'You're Sadie's sister?' He tilted up her chin with a finger, the puzzle solved of why she seemed familiar.

Amelia moved out of his reach, having also put two and two together. She reckoned she knew who he was and seconds later had her suspicions confirmed.

'I was just on my way to see your sister.'

'Be prepared for an unpleasant welcome then,' Amelia retorted, pulling up her hood. 'Jimmy's expecting you.' Her warning flowed over her shoulder as she set off to find a safe spot to wait for the drama to play out.

'You can sort this out with Burley in the morning,' Nicholas told Potts. 'Clear off home to your wife and kids. Nobody wants a rumpus and the coppers sniffing around.' He had an axe to grind with Sadie in private. Jimmy unexpectedly turning up had complicated things.

'He's *married*?' Amelia sounded disgusted that a husband and father had tried to force himself on her.

As far as Nicholas Dupree was concerned, no further proof was required that she was innocent of all charges... apart from having lied about being in cahoots with Spider. His ironic grunt of laughter made her blush and elevate her chin.

Potts decided to ignore the younger man's warning as four bob was involved. 'That kid you're carrying'll be better off in the workhouse than reared by such as you.' He spat into the gutter then marched down the road, arms swinging belligerently.

'You're not fit to be a father, you... you dirty old man,' Amelia flung back though her eyes were burning with unshed tears.

'You're married with a nipper on the way?' Nicholas noticed her hand slipping protectively to her belly. Perhaps she'd be at home in Whitechapel after all and he was a worse judge of character than he'd thought.

Amelia was aware of receiving a thorough inspection and avoided answering him. 'Aren't you going with him? He'll start a fight.'

'Me? Why would I go?'

'Why *wouldn't* you? You must go and help her.' Amelia shoved at his bicep to stir him into action. Potts wouldn't care if Sadie got hurt in the crossfire. 'Jimmy threatened Sadie because of you. Her boyfriend should stand up for her.'

'Maybe... but he's not here. I am.' He gave her a half-amused smile. 'You're confusing me with somebody else. Your sister should stay away from the damned fool or she'll soon wish she had.' He looked Amelia up and down as though assessing the differences in the two women. 'She's bad news, your sister, and in that respect, her and Burley deserve one another.'

Amelia didn't care about his opinions. But she did care that her sister had no protection from a bruiser. Burley would first save his own hide – and the windfall money that had dropped into his lap – now he knew his wife was on the verge of leaving him.

'When he finds out you're lying he'll be back.'

'Why d'you think I'm lying?'

'You're not in league with Spider. You don't even know him, do you?'

'I'm not lying... not about all of it, anyway.' She avoided his mocking eyes. 'Jimmy has stolen my money... fifteen shillings.

Well fourteen as Bill Potts took one shilling and I want that back, too.'

'That's a lot of cash to be carrying around. Do you work at the match factory?'

'No... I'm in service.' *Not any more you're not*, she miserably reminded herself and started to walk away again.

'You had a run-in with Potts earlier though?'

'It's not what you think!' She swung around to face him. 'I was hanging about by Bryant and May, looking for Sadie. He was drunk and got the wrong idea. I pushed him off and he tripped over his own feet.' She gestured in frustration. 'I should never have come to the East End. I've just made things worse all round.' She didn't want his pity but was curious to know his name. She didn't ask in case he thought she'd an interest in getting to know him. 'Sadie will return my cash and I'll take a cab home.' *If you knew where home was, you wouldn't have ended up here in the first place*, she grimly reminded herself. Four shillings was a lot to give up on. She wouldn't challenge Potts over what he believed was rightfully his. Having said she'd set out to cheat him it was too late to go back on it. If her plan worked, she should consider the lost money well spent for her sister's freedom from Jimmy.

'Come and wait in the warm. Sadie will guess you've gone to the pub.'

'Thank you, but I want to quickly get going.'

'Where are you going?'

'Hackney.'

'Will your husband be wondering where you are, Mrs...?'

'That's no concern of yours.' He was fishing but she'd not reveal anything personal.

'I reckon you owe me something for protecting your virtue.'

There wasn't time to return him some sarcasm. A sudden

commotion had been expected; nevertheless, it startled Amelia when it came. Two men had tumbled out of a doorway onto the cobbles. Sadie had dashed out and was thumping Potts on the back to make him let go of Jimmy's throat. Amelia hastened down the road and her sister gave up trying to separate the grappling men and dashed to meet her.

'Look what you've done!' Sadie gestured wildly at the wrestling match. Folk were appearing from doorways to watch the spectacle, like mice emerging from rotten wainscoting. 'Why couldn't you bloody well do as you were told and wait in the pub? I would've brought you some money if you'd been patient.'

Amelia was shocked by her sister's angry accusation. By the time she was ready to speak up for herself Sadie had elbowed past to confront the fellow strolling to join them.

'You'd better warn Lenny that Jimmy's back,' she said. 'He's found out I've been seeing someone.'

'Lenny already knows Burley's back. Mary's wise to what you've been up to 'n' all. If you want to keep that pretty face of yours you'd better move on. My sister will scratch out your eyes first chance she gets.' He drove his hands into his pockets and set off down the road. 'I'm done with the whole damn lot of you.' After a few yards he swung around. 'If you don't get your money back and need a bed for the night... come down to the pub. I'll find you somewhere.'

'Find her a bed, will you?' Sadie's jeering followed him. 'That's good of you! Wouldn't be your bed, would it, Nick?' He didn't turn around and Sadie flung a look at Amelia. 'Should've warned you about him. Nick Dupree is the landlord of the Anchor tavern. Way he carries on makes my Jimmy look like a saint by comparison.'

Amelia paid scant attention; she was more concerned by the way her sister had said 'my Jimmy', and by the way she'd tried to protect him from a thumping. 'This is your chance to escape and come with me. It sounds like there's only trouble waiting round here for you. Let's go home together. We can talk to Mum and Dad... tell them we're both sorry and want a fresh start.'

'I'm not going back there to get bawled at all over again.' Sadie freed her arm from her sister's urgent fingers. 'I'm not a kid; I'm a married woman.'

'You wanted to separate from Jimmy and have a new life,' Amelia quickly reminded her. 'He's a vile bully.'

'Jimmy says he's changed and is staying out of trouble.' Sadie threw a distracted glance at him, now on his feet and getting the better of Bill Potts.

'And you trust him to keep to his word when you've just seen him fighting and stealing?'

'You can get off your high horse! You trusted the fellow who knocked you up and you weren't even engaged to him. I've got a duty to the man who put a wedding ring on my finger.'

'He hits you though, doesn't he?' Amelia shook Sadie's arm to bring her to her senses.

'He's promised no more of that from now on.'

'And you believe him? After what he *did* in there?'

'I've been unfaithful. 'S'me own fault. Anyway, I didn't ask you to come here and poke your nose in.'

'I'm sorry I did, and that's the truth.' With a defeated sigh Amelia let go of her sister's arm. All Jimmy Burley needed was a short while in his wife's company to weasel his way back into her good books. 'This Lenny you've been seeing? Is he married as well?'

'So what if he is?' Sadie shot back. 'The affair weren't my idea. The second he knew Jimmy was off the scene he was chasing after me, turning my head by promising me this 'n' that.'

'And now his wife's found out.'

'Lenny was going to tell Mary he was leaving her. He'd had enough of that family and wanted us to run a pub. He said he was sick of being his brother-in-law's sidekick.'

'His wife sounds like trouble.' Amelia glanced down the road, expecting to see an angry harpy thundering towards them. She didn't spot a woman but did notice that Jimmy was aiming a kick at Potts's backside as the older man limped off, to ridicule from the dispersing spectators.

'I'll give Mary Tanner as good as I get. Anyway, we're not hanging around here for much longer.' Sadie gave Amelia a challenging look. 'Jimmy's asked for a second chance, and I might as well tell you that I've agreed to it.' She ignored her sister's despairing gesture. 'My Jimmy got released early by behaving himself so we could spend Christmas together. Then I'm packing up work at Bryant and May and we're going to run a little business together. Jimmy wants to buy his own horse and cart and set up his own haulage company. He reckons his uncle will invest in it.'

Sadie's breathless account and shining eyes made it obvious her sister believed in this pipe dream. Amelia hugged her, knowing there was no point in reasoning with her. 'Hope it all comes true for you. I really do.' She turned her thoughts to her own predicament. 'I want my bag and my money... whatever's left of it. I can pay Mum my keep until the baby's born.' She hoped her sensible thrift might start her off on the right foot with her parents.

'You'll have to make do with the shilling Jimmy's already given you.' Sadie started edging away. 'Potts slung a crafty punch at Jimmy and grabbed the cash off the table before I could stop him.'

'There must be something left!'

Jimmy had lumbered up, and Amelia dodged past her sister

to confront him. He wouldn't have allowed Potts to get away with his windfall.

'Give me back my money. I know you intended to steal it, you thief.'

Jimmy stabbed a dirty finger close to her face, making her shrink back. 'You watch yer mouth, you interferin' cow.'

'What're you going to do? Pull a knife on me like before?' Amelia was too enraged to be frightened.

'I said shut up!' He slung a look around, hoping nobody had overheard that accusation. He had nearly pulled the blade on Bill but had controlled himself rather than be dragged back to gaol. 'Every time you show up, you bring trouble with yer,' he snarled. 'I don't owe you a penny and we don't want you back round here again.' He gave Amelia a shove. 'Go on... sling yer 'ook.' He took his wife's arm and started propelling her down the street.

Sadie went with him without a fuss, and only glanced back once before disappearing inside the house.

5

In a short while the lane was deserted. The revellers had either gone home or inside the Anchor tavern, and the spectators had melted away the moment the entertainment was over.

Amelia guessed several hours had passed since listening to a church bell toll. The lights behind ragged curtains were disappearing one by one as people settled down to sleep. The night was darker and the cold sharper, numbing her fingers and toes. She had never felt so miserable or so alone, stranded without a penny to her name in sinful Whitechapel.

A glimmer of a brighter future had emerged as she and Sadie had talked and shared memories. Then Jimmy Burley had barged in and extinguished hope for them both.

With an inkling of how badly things would go, she would have headed straight to her parents and presented herself at a respectable time at least.

She hadn't broken down yet but was on her own now with nobody to see her tears. In seconds, unstoppable sobs were heaving her chest as she vented her disappointment and frustration.

A long, low whistle split the silence and brought her head up in a jerk. She peered into the distance through blurry vision.

Nicholas Dupree was standing in a sliver of light leaking from the half-open doors of the Anchor tavern. He raised a beckoning hand. In the other showed the intermittent red glow of a cigarette. She stayed where she was and dried her eyes on the edge of her hood.

After a stand-off lasting about a minute, he pitched down his cigarette stub and started towards her. Amelia went to meet him, stopping beneath a gas lamp. By the time he'd strolled up she was considering finding the cheek to ask him for her cab fare. Sadie wouldn't hesitate in holding out her hand, but Sadie's ways weren't hers. Amelia had just received a hard reminder of that.

'No luck getting your money?' He propped his back on the lamp post and pulled a tobacco tin from his pocket.

'Sadie said Potts took it all. Don't know if I believe it though, knowing Jimmy.'

His half-smile hinted that he knew Sadie was pinned beneath her husband's thumb and capable of lying on his say-so. He rolled the cigarette and lit it before slanting a gaze her way. 'You look frozen. You coming with me?' The tavern was indicated with a nod, and he pocketed the tobacco then held out a hand invitingly.

'I'm going home,' said Amelia.

Earlier he'd had a jacket and cap but was without the benefit of either now. His waistcoat and rolled-up shirtsleeves would do little to protect against the December frost but the cold didn't seem to bother him.

'Long walk, Hackney. It's late for a girl to be out on her own tramping the streets.'

There was no denying that. Turning up at midnight would

start her parents panicking about calamities before she'd confessed to the mess she was in. Tears were prickling her eyes again but she'd not cry in front of him. 'Well... no point dawdling,' she said briskly. 'Best get cracking.'

'Pub's closed now. There's a spare bed if you need it.'

'Would you lend me my cab fare?' she blurted. 'I'll pay it back, promise.'

A coin was produced from his waistcoat pocket as though he'd anticipated the request. 'Whatever your big sister's said about me...' He shrugged. 'Not necessarily true, is it?'

Amelia flashed him a look. 'Sadie's not that much older than I am. Anyway, I don't need her to tell me about what's staring me in the face.'

'And what is?' His fingers closed over the silver on his palm.

'You don't know me. Why would you bother to put yourself out for me after I lied and Bill Potts called me those names? You said that boy Spider likes easy pickings... perhaps you do too.'

She was getting used to seeing his sardonic smile. 'Cards on the table then,' he said. 'You look out of your depth round here. And on the whole I actually believed your story over Bill's. As for sleeping arrangements... space in my bed's already taken. Clear enough for you?'

Amelia felt well and truly put in her place. When he opened his hand and offered the coin again she hesitated and it disappeared inside his waistcoat.

'I might not know you, but I do know you're not like your sister; apart from the two of you landing yourselves in a heap of trouble, that is.'

'I could be married to a decent man, for all you know.'

He snorted smoke along with derision. 'If you are married he can't be much use, letting his pregnant wife wander around in a dive like this.'

Bristling, Amelia nodded at his pocket. 'I'll pay it back.'

'Who lives in Hackney? Your folks?' The shilling remained where it was.

'Mmm...' was the sum of her answer.

'So, tell me if I've got this right: you're in the family way and approached your sister for help. She's been a dead loss so you're going home to your mum and dad instead.'

He'd easily summed up her predicament – not that it was hard to do. Hers was a run-of-the-mill tale; nevertheless, she felt niggled and tempted to tell him to mind his own business. She could ill afford her stubborn pride so managed a grudging nod.

'Best o' luck knocking them up to break that news.' He didn't pretend ignorance of her suffocated sob; he brushed his knuckles on her jaw in comfort. 'Things could be worse. You're young and got pluck enough for you and Sadie, that's for sure. And at least the snow's held off.'

'Could do with a few more small mercies.' A fragrance of tobacco remained on her chin from his touch. The smell reminded her of childhood, and her father's similarly scented fingers. He had been a pipe smoker before his wife had put a stop to it for being costly and smelly. 'Why're you offering to help me then?' she asked.

'You're a pretty gel with a sob story, and I'm a sucker for both of those.'

Amelia suppressed a smile. 'Not sure I believe you.'

'You should... I think it might be true.' He dropped his half-smoked cigarette and ground it out while chuckling in self-mockery. 'An introduction's overdue, don't you think? Pleased to make your acquaintance, Miss...?'

'Amelia Spencer.' She shook his outstretched hand.

'Take it Sadie told you my name, but I'd sooner have done it myself. Nicholas Dupree, at your service.' He gave her an ironic bow. 'Right, final offer, Amelia Spencer...' He set off for the pub. 'If you don't want to catch your death, and need a place to kip, follow me.' He turned and walked backwards. 'Sleep on it, is my advice. Problems sometimes seem better in the morning.'

* * *

Mr Dupree was right.

After a dreamless slumber, so cosy was Amelia, snuggled beneath a puffy eiderdown that she burrowed lower in the bed, hoping to doze off again. Her eyes were determinedly closed against pale infiltrating light but her ears strained for the noise that had stolen her sweet oblivion. It was muted by distance – she was up under the eaves – but identifiable as pots and pans being put to use. An aroma of frying bacon tempted her to pull the cover away from her nose to appreciate it. Her belly gurgled a reminder that she'd not eaten much yesterday. Sitting down to regular meals at the Campbells had been taken for granted. That luxury was lost along with her employment.

Her mind was buzzing with unhappy memories but she refused to feel sorry for herself. Having allowed her heart to rule her head, she must face up to the consequences of her seduction like every other silly girl whose dreams had disappeared along with the man she'd trusted.

Twisting onto her back on the mattress, she finally opened her eyes. A cobweb that had been invisible by last night's candle-light was strung across the black beams above her head. A huge spider emerged from a crack and sprang aboard, making the dusty lace swing. Fearing the great hairy thing might fall on her, she folded upright, flung off the covers, and was soon on her feet. Having slept in her underclothes she hastily grabbed her folded dress from the chair and stepped into it, doing up buttons. Next, her stockings were rolled on and gartered, then she plunged her feet into her low-heeled boots, fumbling with the hooks. She'd received an unpleasant reminder of last night's antics, in the shape of eight spindly legs. Charlie Webb, or Spider, as he was known, had started it all by running off with Bill Potts's cash.

There was a toilet set on a dressing chest along with a towel that looked and smelled clean. She'd sluiced her face and hands before huddling into bed last night. She poured what remained of the ice-cold water from the pitcher into the bowl. She commenced splashing, gasping as it shocked her fully awake, then dried her face.

On entering the Anchor tavern she had declined an offer of a nightcap and a bite to eat. She'd been conscious of her empty purse and that testing Mr Dupree's generosity wasn't wise. Candlestick in hand, he'd led the way up two flights of stairs to this low-ceilinged, wonky-beamed attic. The drinkers might have all gone but the place wasn't empty. She'd heard people moving around behind several doors, glimpsed in the shadows. They'd exchanged 'goodnights', and he'd handed her the candle and a key, then departed. Amelia had briefly pondered on who slept beside him while undressing. Sadie had hinted he was a womaniser, so it was unlikely he was married... but then you never could tell. Sadie had been sharing her marital bed on the sly.

A tap on the door brought Amelia to the dressing stand for the key to open up. She was surprised and disappointed to be confronted by a girl of about eleven years old. This wasn't the person she'd wanted to see.

'Me uncle says there's breakfast in the back parlour for you.'

'That's good of him, but please tell him I have to set off now. Your uncle is Mr Dupree?'

The girl nodded. 'Can't tell him anything. He's gone out.'

'Is Mary Tanner your mother?'

'That's right; she's downstairs with me little brother, Teddy.'

So, Sadie had been prepared to break up a family as well as a marriage. Amelia felt ashamed about that, and awkward, being here with Lenny Tanner's family, knowing what she did. 'What's your name?'

'Pearl. I'd better give Mum a hand. There's guests waiting to be served.'

The girl trotted off and Amelia closed the door. She had no reason to stay, other than to delay the meeting with her parents. She checked her appearance in the spotted wall mirror. Her hair could do with neatening but her brush and comb were packed in her carpetbag. She had to retrieve her belongings and wouldn't take no for an answer from Jimmy Burley. She'd create merry hell in front of his neighbours, if necessary.

After scraping some neatening fingers through her tangled locks, she took a final glance about. Plain pine furniture stood on bare boards around the perimeter of the room and a colourful rag rug filled the space between. The divan bed spanned one wall and a dressing chest holding the bowl and pitcher was opposite. The rush-seated chair under the window had come in handy for her clothes. She unfolded her cloak, giving it a shake before putting it on. The bed had been cramped and the mattress lumpy. Up under the eaves was the draughtiest place to be; she knew that from her sleeping quarters at Campbell House.

She wanted to forget all about that rotten place but she'd always remember this little sanctuary, and Nicholas Dupree.

The steep stairs necessitated a firm grip to be taken on the handrail when descending them. At the bottom, a side door was shedding colourful sunbeams through a stained-glass panel.

There was nobody about in the passageway. She could quickly use that exit but hesitated, reluctant to leave without a word to anybody. Steam leaking from the kitchen had created a humid atmosphere heavy with cooking smells. She glanced over her shoulder to where a cosy clattering of cutlery and rumble of conversation escaped through a half-closed door.

Suddenly, a woman bellowed for Pearl to take plates to the tables. Mary Tanner sounded harassed and unlikely to appreciate being asked to pass on messages to her brother. Especially by Sadie's sister. If brought face to face, Amelia would be tempted to apologise to Lenny's wife. She didn't fancy having her sympathy thrown back in her face because of who she was.

'Hold on a moment. This is yours, I believe.'

Amelia had pushed open the door but swung around to find a woman in a grubby pinafore behind her. The carpetbag Mary Tanner was holding hit the flagged floor and she crossed her arms over her bloated abdomen. 'Skipping off without paying, eh?'

'I'm not! Mr Dupree said I could have a bed.'

'Oh, I was just having a joke with you, Miss Spencer,' said Mary. 'My brother put me in the picture. I know you had trouble last night and needed a place to stay.' She put the toe of her slipper against the carpetbag, pushing it with her as she approached Amelia. 'Your sister stopped Pearl in the street this morning and gave her this. Shame I wasn't around; I've got something to say to that one.' Mary cocked her head. 'No need for you to look scared of me, though. Can't choose our sisters, can we, so I won't hold it against you... being kin of that tart.'

Amelia refused to take the bait and play a game of insults. Family loyalty was important, and if Sadie's version of events was to be believed, Mary's husband had instigated the affair. Perhaps the woman knew that but had decided to turn a blind eye to protect her children. She wasn't the battleaxe Amelia had been expecting, being in her early thirties and small-boned and pretty. Mary Tanner was as hard as nails for all of that, Amelia reckoned, despite her very pregnant belly.

'Thanks for returning this.' She picked up her bag. 'Please pass on my thanks and tell your brother I'll settle up with him as soon as I can.'

'You should tell him that yourself.' Mary snorted in amusement.

'Your daughter said he'd gone out.'

'Perhaps he'll come back to see you.' Mary poked her tongue into her cheek and arched an eyebrow. 'Nick ain't given to being sentimental as a rule. I'd say he's taken a shine to you, Miss Spencer. And that's not even his. Or is it?'

Amelia blushed while defending herself and him. 'I'd never met him before last night.' She'd hoped her own belly – tiny in comparison to Mary's – had gone unnoticed.

Pearl appeared, balancing a grizzly toddler on one bony hip. 'The old fellow wants another egg, 'cos it's off,' she reported.

'I'll give him off! That was fresh laid in me own chicken coop. If the greedy git wants another he can pay fer it.' Mary took her fretful son and rocked him to and fro.

'I can see you've got your hands full.' Amelia hastily opened the door, stepping outside.

'Don't want no breakfast then? Bacon and *fresh* eggs and fried bread 'n' onions? On the house, Nick said.' Mary wedged a foot against the door to prevent it swinging shut while tempting Amelia with food.

'Thank you, but I have to get going.' Amelia felt she should add something. She didn't know Mary Tanner, yet sensed she could come to like her, given a chance. 'Good luck to you and I hope everything goes well with the new baby. Not long to wait, have you?'

'Overdue, I reckon. Hope the little blighter hangs on till me husband's around, though. Lenny's doing a shift down the Sunday market in Middlesex Street today.'

The two women would have liked to carry on talking; perhaps confide their worries about what the future held for themselves and their children. A shout from Pearl about the complaining customer drew an exasperated sigh from Mary. 'Good luck yourself, Miss Spencer. I'll let Nick know what you said.' Mary let the door swing shut.

Amelia took a heartening lungful of crisp air, straightening her shoulders for what lay ahead. A lengthy walk was the least of her worries. Bag in hand, she carried on up the road, intending to say goodbye to Sadie before heading for her child-hood home.

6

In daylight Sadie's neighbour appeared younger – perhaps in her fifties – but thinner and uglier. Her sallow complexion and missing teeth hadn't shown up in the candlelit gloom. Neither had the tattered state of her attire been so obvious. Her shawl – if the holey wool could be described as such – was wrapped over her head, revealing tufts of coarse colourless hair. The rag's edges were gripped together at her breastbone by grimy hands that were virtually indistinguishable from her fingerless brown gloves.

'Your sister ain't in and neither's he,' the woman sent over her shoulder. 'Be wasting yer time banging on their door, love. You won't get no answer.'

Amelia's thanks went unacknowledged as the sprightly woman carried on tramping away from her in a pair of men's boots.

Amelia dodged bristles as beefy-armed women worked brooms towards the gutter. She proceeded up the road receiving little attention, and neither did the slow sonority of a church bell. These folk didn't look as though they possessed a set of

Sunday best, or wanted a sermon. Her reflection was curtailed by a sighting of her sister in the distance. Eager to speak to her, Amelia hurried onwards.

'You're still hanging around here, are you?' Sadie sauntered over.

'I overslept.'

'I bet you did. Wore you out, did he?'

Amelia ignored that and said, 'I couldn't risk walking to Hackney in the dark.'

'Took a chance on Nick Dupree instead, eh?' Sadie gave an arch smile. 'Bit crowded was it, the three of you snuggled up?'

'Three of us?'

'Polly Mayhew. She keeps her eye on him. S'pose she couldn't have been about though or you'd be sporting a shiner this morning.'

Amelia felt a twinge of disappointment on hearing confirmed that he had a girl. 'I slept in the attic. Anyway, how did you know I'd stayed at the pub?'

'Made it me business to find out so I could get your bag back to you.'

'Thanks.' Amelia dropped the bag and embraced Sadie. 'I hope things turn out right for you.'

'I hope the same for you.' Sadie's good wishes were rushed and she was already edging away.

'Where's Jimmy?' Amelia longed to hear he'd been carted back to prison.

'Catching up with some pals. He's taking me out later for dinner.'

'You two sound flush.' Hints about her stolen savings wouldn't get them returned. 'I want my money, Sadie,' she bluntly said.

'Oh, not this again. I told you Bill took the cash.'

That explanation wasn't any more convincing the second time around. Without proof, though, Amelia would rather not call her sister a liar.

'Nick told you all about his family, did he?'

'He's not told me anything. I met Mary this morning when she gave me this.' Amelia picked up the bag.

'S'pose she had something choice to say about me, didn't she?'

'She made it clear she knows about you and her husband.' Amelia felt compelled to add, 'You knew he'd got a family, and another baby due any minute.'

'I didn't when I hooked up with him. It was weeks before he owned up to being a family man.'

Last night Sadie had spoken of running off with Lenny but not a word of consideration for his wife and kids. Amelia felt disappointed in her sister but wouldn't lecture after making a mess of her own life.

Her baby's father was spoken for. Not that she'd known about it until he laughed at her naïve belief that he'd marry a housemaid, and revealed he had a fiancée. Amelia pushed his memory aside, acknowledging with a pang that it was becoming easier to do.

'You found her then, love?' A gravelly voice drowned out Sadie's claim to have no money to spare for Amelia's cab fare.

'I did... thank you.' Amelia raised a hand to the ragged neighbour. 'She told me I wouldn't find you at home,' was explained for Sadie's benefit.

'Daisy's always spying and gossiping.' Sadie slung the woman a dirty look.

'Daisy?' Amelia smiled. The pretty name hardly suited somebody who looked like a tramp.

'She's Doris Root but people call her Daisy Root 'cos she

always wears boots.' Sadie smirked on using the cockney rhyming slang and twirled a finger by her temple. 'You're a bit barmy, ain't yer, Ma?'

'Ain't too barmy to have your number. Ain't blind neither. I saw you again with Mary Tanner's husband.'

'You'd better stop making up stories about me, Ma, or you'll be sorry.'

'I'm Mrs Root, to the likes of you, you troublemaking trollop.' The older woman set off down the road and it became clear Sadie was itching to follow for round two.

Despite feeling ashamed of her sister, Amelia pecked her cheek, said a final goodbye then continued on her way. Before turning the corner, she stopped to wave. But Sadie didn't look back.

Amelia walked along, keeping herself occupied by browsing the shops she was passing. She halted by a haberdashery. Beribboned bootees and mittens in pastel-coloured wool were displayed behind glass. She strolled further into the deep recess that led to the shuttered doorway, enjoying window-shopping. Delaying the meeting with her parents was all very well, but no last-minute miracle was likely to happen. She should stop dithering and face up to it, she brutally told herself.

She retraced her steps but before emerging onto the pavement, spotted her sister by the kerb. Sadie had company, but it wasn't Jimmy she was arguing with. Amelia hurriedly took a step back, unwilling to barge into this business.

In height and breadth, Lenny Tanner – she'd guessed the man's identity – was Jimmy's equal, but there was no other similarity. Lenny had sparse fair hair and a pleasant rather than handsome face. He appeared intimidated by Sadie's tongue-lashing and so vociferous was it that Amelia learned its cause whether she wanted to or not.

'If you don't help me out I'll have to tell him, Lenny,' stormed Sadie. 'And I'll warn you, he's carrying a knife.'

'I already know Jimmy Burley's a vicious brute,' said Lenny, attempting to slip past.

'Just you hang on.' Sadie grabbed his arm. 'We have to sort this out.'

'I've told you to leave me alone. I ain't choosing you over me wife and kids.'

'That's nice! Seem to recall you wanted to leave her and run a pub with me.'

'That's a lie! I want me and Mary to set up in business.'

'Well, I need money to get rid of it before Jimmy wises up. He'll know straight away it can't be his kid.'

'Might not be mine either. Actually, I don't reckon it is.' Lenny seemed to have found his backbone and threatened Sadie with a jabbing finger. 'I'm a blasted fool getting involved with you.' He raked his fingers through his thinning hair. 'Stop pestering me for money I haven't got.'

'You wanted this affair more than me,' protested an indignant Sadie.

'It wasn't an affair,' scoffed Lenny. 'I thought we was friends though as well as...' He left the rest unsaid. 'Seems I was wrong. I was just a punter, paying for your time, like the others.' With that parting shot, he dodged past her and jogged across the road.

By the time Amelia had overcome her astonishment and decided to make her presence known, Sadie was marching away.

Lenny's unsubtle accusation that her sister was a prostitute had deeply shocked Amelia. Protecting pride came into it on both sides, she suspected. She knew how raw she'd felt when cast aside, having entrusted another person with her heart and body.

His adultery had been exposed, and Lenny was regretful. But

he was the guiltier in Amelia's opinion. Sadie didn't have children to abandon, as he did, and her spouse was vile. On the other hand Mary seemed a loyal, hardworking wife and mother.

There was no denying that Jimmy Burley and the slums of Whitechapel had changed her sister. Sadie was beautiful, but her manner and speech could be vulgar. She seemed a harder character, too. It had been mean of her to goad Mrs Root.

Since their reunion, Amelia had only briefly glimpsed the girl she'd grown up with and loved. She couldn't contemplate her big sister sinking into vice, though. Sadie didn't need to street-walk when she had a supervisor's job at the match factory. She might hate it and want to leave but she'd stuck it out and got a place of her own through hard work.

Amelia resumed her journey towards Hackney having persuaded herself that Jimmy Burley was the only bad company her sister kept.

7

A tune had been fluting in Amelia's head since last night. The sound had started to intrude on her indecision over having things out with Sadie.

The whistle came again, louder and less melodic and was accompanied by the rattle of an approaching horse and cart. She dropped her luggage, the start of a smile lifting a corner of her mouth as she pivoted about, wishing and hoping.

She'd not realised how much she'd longed to see him again until her heart did a joyful somersault. Thanking him wasn't the half of it. She'd craved his company. He'd been kinder to her than anybody else recently despite their short acquaintance.

Gaslight could deceive and she wanted to see if she'd been correct judging him at about thirty years old, with black hair and brown eyes.

The image didn't quite fit, although he was dressed as before in navy reefer jacket and leather cap. He was younger for a start, perhaps twenty-six. His hair was black and longish, and his jaw lean and unshaven but as he jumped down from the cart and started towards her she found herself gazing into eyes, not brown, but grey.

With every lithe stride that brought him closer she was reminded of him sending Bill Potts into the gutter with no trouble at all. She pushed back her hood and tucked her windswept blonde locks behind her ears. He'd called her pretty and she was woman enough to hope he'd not be disappointed when seeing her in daylight.

'Mr Dupree,' she said lightly, stepping up to him. 'This is a nice surprise. I wasn't expecting to see you again. I'm glad I have though. I felt uncomfortable leaving without saying thank you.' She quickly explained, 'I did ask your sister to pass on a message.'

'I got it.'

'Oh... good.'

'You left without eating.'

'I wanted to make an early start.'

'You weren't otherwise uncomfortable?'

'Beg pardon?'

'Did you sleep well?'

'Oh, yes. Like a log, actually. I liked that little room.'

'I'll find you somewhere warmer next time.'

She whipped her gaze from middle distance back to him, glimpsing sultriness at the backs of his eyes before his lashes descended and he concentrated on counting out some coins.

'I've been looking for you to give you this before you reached Hackney. Bill Potts did have some of your money. He grabbed four bob off the table and said Jimmy pocketed the rest.' He took one of her hands to tip money into her palm. 'I would've got all of it back, but wasn't sure you'd want me to, being as family's involved.'

'I'm glad you didn't,' she said with some emphasis. 'Please steer clear of him. He carries a knife.'

'I expect he knows I do, too.'

Amelia was unsure how to react to that information. Her mind was jogged to Sadie's warning that Nick Dupree made her Jimmy seem like a saint by comparison. For now, she'd judge as she found.

'Thanks very much for this.' She was grateful to no longer be penniless. 'I'll hail a cab. I was getting tired.'

'In your condition, you should take it easy.'

She wished he'd not brought that up. He had though, and to prove she wasn't ashamed, or a weakling in need of his pity, she patted her abdomen. 'I'm quite well, thanks.' She found a change of subject. 'I met your sister and niece and nephew this morning. And I just saw your brother-in-law along the road.'

'You recognised Lenny?'

'I did after I overheard him and Sadie arguing.'

'Your sister's still stirring things up, is she?'

'I don't see that this is all Sadie's fault,' she retorted.

'You're a prickly kid, aren't you, Amelia Spencer.'

She flashed him an indignant glance. 'I'm not a kid, Mr Dupree. I would have thought that was obvious.'

'Just a figure o' speech. You look about sixteen.'

'I certainly do not! I'm eighteen... almost...'

'Right... that's me told. Seventeen it is.'

A silence followed but he seemed more amused than peeved by her jumping down his throat.

'Didn't mean to snap. I'm a bit on edge. I'll be meeting my parents shortly.' A grimace displayed her apprehension. 'Eventually, I will come back and settle up for my night's lodging, I promise. Anyway, I should get going.' She picked up her bag and stepped away but he kept pace with her, so she continued in reverse rather than turn her back on him.

'I'll give you a lift to Hackney. Save your legs and the fare.' He squinted up at the gathering clouds blocking the sun. 'Reckon snow's on its way.' He beckoned for her bag.

She could also sense the change in the air and keeping warm – and keeping his company for a while longer – was appealing. 'Thanks, but I wouldn't want you to be drawn into this.'

He could work out the rest for himself. A conclusion would be jumped to if a man dropped off an unmarried woman at her parents' house to break the news that she was pregnant. Being as the side of his cart had *Nicholas Dupree, Esq., Lighterman & Warehouseman* stencilled on it, he wouldn't be hard to track down. Not that her mild-mannered father would go after him until her mother pushed him into it. Inwardly, she squirmed with embarrassment imagining that clash. She'd not see Nicholas Dupree come under suspicion, after all he'd done to help her.

'I know you don't need me complicating matters. It'll be a tough afternoon for you, I expect.'

She halted to hear him out and his knuckles brushed her cheek, more as an encouragement than a caress.

'I'll let you down a street away so nobody sees me.'

After a brief hesitation, she nodded acceptance. He lifted her onto the cart and nimbly alighted on the opposite side. The mare had barely settled into a sedate trot when drawn to a halt.

'Stay put. I'll be right back.' He threw down the reins, vaulting to the ground.

She swivelled on the bench to watch him sprint across the road, dodging traffic. Minutes passed and she became aware of a snuffling and scratching somewhere close behind. She jerked around to investigate the cart's load, lifting a tarpaulin and a heavy loop of tarred rope that was as thick as a man's fist. Its scratchy sticky weight made the rope slip from her hold onto a barrel that had a brand of rum stencilled across its planks. The ensuing thud provoked a growl of complaint. Tilting sideways she saw a salt-and-pepper-coloured dog, muzzle resting on its front paws. The beast slowly uncurled, raising his rear end and flexing his front legs. Having displayed his impressive size he shook himself before sinking down to guard his cargo.

Feeling increasingly nervous to have been abandoned to the mercies of a wolfhound, Amelia shifted to the edge of the cart. She yanked her skirts to her knees and gingerly lowered one booted foot then the other over the side. While preparing to slither to the ground she spotted Nicholas Dupree coming back, dragging along a boy dressed in shoeblack brigade uniform. Curious to find out what this was about, she resettled on the bench.

'Sorry about that,' said Nick, tipping his cap back on his head. 'Thought you might like to meet Spider. He's got something to say, and to give to you.' He kept hold of the scowling lad trying to wriggle free. 'Speak up – no need to be shy with Miss Spencer.'

The youngster glanced up at Amelia with one hazel eye. The other was closed against a sunbeam leaking from between the leaden clouds. 'Didn't mean to cause no trouble for you, miss, honest.' The apology emerged as a sullen mumble. 'Wouldn't have copped them florins if I'd known it'd land you in it with Bill Potts.' He cuffed his nose on the sleeve of his blue Guernsey top.

Nick gave him a mocking pat on the shoulder. 'Well done. But forgotten something, haven't you?'

The lad grimaced then reluctantly pulled a coin from his pocket. He reached up and with a heavy sigh placed the solitary florin on the seat. "S'all I've got left, swear it. Me mum grabbed t'other one. She *did* – you can ask her,' he whined as his captor's fingers tightened.

'I believe you,' said Amelia, although she didn't. Spider was being crafty but she didn't want him to receive a thick ear from Mr Dupree for having spent half of the ill-gotten gains. In the dark she'd only caught a brief glimpse of the thief and had assumed him to be in his mid-teens. She could see now this sandy-haired scamp was younger. 'Thank you for returning this, Spider, or should I call you Charlie Webb?'

'Spider's all right by me.' He smirked, proud of his nick-name. 'Can I go now, Mr Dupree? I'll lose me best pitch. Me pal's watching me brushes 'n' polish. If he buggers off, somebody'll pinch me stuff and I'll lose me job.'

'Yeah, clear off and try to stay outta trouble.'

The boy muttered something beneath his breath as he loped off.

'I heard that, you rude tyke...'

The lad grinned over a shoulder and gave a flourish of his cap before disappearing around a corner.

'You seem quite familiar with that scallywag.'

'Know his family. His older brother drinks in the Anchor,' Nick said as they set off towards Hackney.

'So... do you work at the pub or on the river?' Her father would talk about the lightermen who relieved the ships at anchor on the river Thames of their loads. The cargoes were then brought ashore on flat-bottomed boats called lighters. Her father had said the job was skilled, requiring physical strength and knowledge of river tides. Amelia was keen to know more about Nicholas Dupree and how he made his living. He seemed to be doing all right for himself.

'Turn me hand to both, and more besides. No use having a single string to a bow.'

'I see...' She sounded thoughtful.

He sent her a sideways glance. 'You're wishing you'd paid more attention to your sister's warning about me now.'

Amelia blushed and took an interest in the pedestrians. She *had* just mulled over Sadie's description of him. 'I can make up my own mind about people. If I hadn't decided to trust you, I wouldn't be sitting here beside you now.'

'I wanted to sleep with you last night. Got halfway up the attic stairs in the early hours. Still trust me?'

His truthfulness was startling, but what he'd said wasn't a shock. She'd sensed from the start that he fancied her. She couldn't kid herself that she didn't find him attractive in return. His brutal honesty was better than lies in Amelia's book. Her baby's father and her brother-in-law had stolen from her through deceit. 'You didn't knock on my door though. When you stop being nice, so will I, Mr Dupree.'

'You trust too easily, Amelia Spencer.'

'Why d'you say that? Because I'm in trouble and should have known better than to believe a gentleman would marry me once he'd got what he wanted?'

'Who is he apart from a... gentleman?'

There was contemptuous stress on his final word that she found reassuring rather than insulting. He despised the man who'd seduced and abandoned her. She didn't reply though, feeling bewildered and saddened by the change in him. She'd believed she'd found a friend in Nicholas Dupree.

'You're not going to answer me then.'

'If you think I'd tell you something as personal as that, you're the gullible one.' She pointed to the kerb. 'Pull over and let me off this thing. I don't want help that comes with strings attached. I'd rather walk the rest of the way.'

'I don't expect anything; if I did, I'd've made the top of the stairs. Just saying you're too innocent for your own good – that's all.'

'Not any more I'm not.' Her words hung in the bitter air for some minutes before he broke the silence.

'Will you give the money to your mum? It might sweeten things a bit for you.'

'I will.' She knew he was being conciliatory, so added, 'I appreciate you returning it to me.'

'You're welcome.' He turned his head to meet her stare.

'Oh... take the next turning please. We're almost there. I'd be obliged if you would put me down at the end of the lane.' The journey had passed quickly... too quickly for Amelia, despite their disagreement. She had relaxed after a little harmony was restored.

He didn't want them to go separate ways either. He slowed the horse down to draw out their final minutes together.

'Mary said she wished you'd stayed to eat and talk a while. She doesn't get a lot of female company; watermen or ships' crews are the pub's regulars.'

'You look alike. I think Mary's the eldest though.'

'She is. By seven years.'

'She looks too young to have a child Pearl's age.'

'Mary married young... at sixteen. She's a grafter and a good wife and mother.'

'Lenny Tanner's a lucky man.'

'Lenny Tanner's a damn idiot. And I've told him so. My sister deserves better. It's time she up and left him.'

'He's her children's father... I expect that's more important than pride or anything else.'

Amelia understood how difficult it must be for a woman to walk away from a man she'd loved and shared a family with even if he behaved badly. If Andrew Bowman had come back to propose, she would have married him for their unborn child's sake. And she would have hoped that in time the hurt would go away and forgiveness would come and with it the affection she'd once felt for him. None of that was possible now he was married to somebody else.

'That's how you see it, is it? You're bound to a man because of the baby he's given you?'

'I suppose so... but he won't give me or his child a second thought.' She added briskly, 'Don't need him anyway. I'll manage alone if my parents kick me out.'

The mare's hooves were clopping more lazily but before they said goodbye she had a question to ask. It was too late to go back and find this out for herself. Besides, he knew more about what went on in her sister's life than she did. 'Can I ask you something?'

'Ask away.'

'Before Jimmy barged in last night, Sadie told me she was running off with Lenny. Just now I heard him deny it. And he said he's not taking the blame for making her pregnant as she sees other men. For money.' Amelia blushed to be discussing this with a man she barely knew. But there was nobody else to ask about it. 'I don't believe she's been doing that. He's lying, isn't he?' The long pause that followed was enlightening.

'He's letting his mouth run away with him instead of sorting out his own mess. I'm sorry you've been dragged into it.'

'You don't think Sadie's only doing match factory work either then?'

'That's about the size of it.'

'People get the wrong idea because she's popular and pretty,'

Amelia said heatedly, unwilling to believe this could be true. 'It's not her fault men like her.'

He didn't reply but steered the mare to a halt in front of a terrace of drab houses.

'My sister's done some stupid things, the worst being getting involved with Jimmy Burley. But she's not a tart.' His silence pricked her into further defence. 'I don't know why she said she's pregnant. I'm sure she would have told me something as important as that.' But if Sadie was expecting, their babies would be close in age and cousins. How bittersweet it was that those children wouldn't have doting grandparents. Blanche and Wilfred Spencer would deny their existence, and Rebecca and Tom would be kept in ignorance of becoming an aunt and uncle.

Nick let the reins fall and turned towards her on the seat. 'For what it's worth, here's my theory: she's not pregnant. Jimmy's out of gaol with nothing in his pocket other than what he's stolen from you. Swindling a few quid, and getting revenge rolled into one, is just his style. From what I know of Sadie, I'd say she'd go along with it.' Nick glanced up as the first delicate flakes of snow drifted down. He brushed melting ice off Amelia's rosy cheek. 'I know you're gonna stick up for her... say she's not crooked. She's lucky to have a sister like you... maybe you aren't so lucky in return where loyalty's concerned.'

Amelia bit her lip, knowing he was right about that. She'd been ditched by Sadie on her rotten husband's say-so.

'Let that lot stew and concentrate on your own battles,' he gently said.

The snow fell faster. Still she didn't want to say goodbye just yet. 'What's his name?' She jerked a nod at the dog.

Nick peered over a shoulder. 'Jet. As a pup he was completely black.'

The animal had heard its name and stood up, tail wagging.

'He's well behaved.'

'Takes after his master.'

She rolled her laughing eyes and mocked him with a headshake.

'He does as he's told most of the time... apart from when he sneaks upstairs and onto the bed. He did last night.' He half-smiled. 'Not the company I was hoping for.'

He was letting her know that the space in his bed had been commandeered by his dog. It was an amusing tale that she didn't disbelieve. But a tall dark handsome man wouldn't lack female company if he wanted it. Perhaps Polly Mayhew had been indisposed, leaving him at a loose end. Nicholas Dupree could be more like his fickle brother-in-law than he cared to admit. The idea bothered Amelia but she wasn't about to question him and appear jealous.

'You'll get fleas on your sheets,' she said lightly.

'He gets washed down regular. He's in his kennel most of the time, or Mary lets him stretch out in front of the fire in the back parlour for everybody to stub their toes on.' Nick flicked a hand gesture at the animal and he obediently sank down and rolled over before adopting his customary pose, muzzle atop huge, shaggy paws.

Amelia mockingly applauded and he doffed his cap in acknowledgement. A surge of affection warmed her but she stopped herself reaching out to touch him. She'd discovered he wasn't much different to the rest of the cheats out there who chased after women behind their other halves' backs.

If things had been different though... if she'd visited Sadie in Whitechapel sooner... met Nicholas Dupree sooner... never fallen for a lying rotter... She pulled herself up short. Nicholas Dupree was no more than a charming stranger who'd shown her kindness and made her laugh.

She'd no idea where she'd be by springtime. She'd like to think it would be here with her family and her new-born baby, but the scandalised neighbours would put paid to that. Her gaze had been flitting along the street but suddenly she ducked her chin. Two women had emerged from a house and stood chatting on the step. Amelia knew one of them and had been recognised in return.

'You should get going now, Mr Dupree. A neighbour has seen us. Thank you for the lift... for everything.'

He sprang down and, after helping her alight, kept his hands on her forearms.

'I won't forget you, or what you did for me,' she said.

'I won't forget you either, Amelia.'

'Goodbye, Mr Dupree...' She slipped from his hold.

'If I'd got to the top of the stairs would you have opened the door last night?'

She occupied herself in positioning her bag in a double-handed clutch in front of her belly. 'I don't know.' Fleetingly she met his silvery eyes.

'Well, if your father can't find him, and things turn bad at home, you know where you'll get a bed for the night.'

'It's nice of you to offer, though Polly Mayhew might not see it that way.' She'd done it then, betrayed herself.

'Reckon I know who to thank for telling you that.' He darted a rueful glance at their audience. 'Why didn't you say something sooner if it's been on your mind?'

'It hasn't. It's none of my business.'

'Yeah... same as he's none of mine. You didn't find a gentleman in Mayfair, Amelia. Could be you're looking in the wrong place. Anyhow, best o' luck.' He shifted position, shielding her from inquisitive eyes as he touched her cheek. 'I really mean that. Whatever you want, I hope you get it. Be happy.'

He pulled up his coat collar to frame his stubbly jaw while watching her set off home. He was soon back on the cart, passing her with a tug on his cap brim. Then he had reached the junction and turned the corner without looking back.

8

'Mum! Look who's home for Christmas, after all.' Rebecca Spencer had whooped in delight then flung her arms around her big sister. 'You're getting fat,' she complained as Amelia tried to squeeze past into the hallway.

'It's my bag... see, you've squashed it.' She gave Rebecca a one-armed hug.

The younger girl was poking and prodding to find outlines of parcels. 'Have you brought us Christmas presents?'

'Not this year... sorry... couldn't afford to.' An apologetic kiss was planted on her sister's forehead. Rebecca had altered in the months they'd been apart. The child was a fully-fledged adolescent with a spot on her chin and buds of breasts beneath her blouse. Her hair looked greasy at the crown but her childish giggles were just the same. 'You've shot up since I last saw you, Becky.'

The girl beamed and tucked a wisp of fair hair behind an ear.

Tom had heard the commotion and dashed down the stairs. He grinned, swinging on the newel post before landing on the carpet runner. Mrs Spencer emerged from the kitchen, drying her hands on her pinafore. 'I thought I could feel a draught. This is unexpected, Amelia.' She used the back of her wrist to rub her perspiring forehead.

'Something smells good. Been baking, Mum?' Amelia was striving to sound happy as she normally would. Her mother's dear, harassed face only made her feel more wretched. She already regretted coming home. She'd been wrapped up in herself and had overlooked that her family would be busy preparing for their annual feast. The house felt warm, and the air was heavily scented with cinnamon and the fresh holly sprigs pinned to the wall. She could sense her mother's suspicion, and knew her bag couldn't serve as a shield forever. Mothers were programmed to spot a worrying thickening in a daughter's waistline.

'Me and Tom are making paper chains upstairs,' said Rebecca. 'We're hanging them up tomorrow.'

'Tom and I...' Mrs Spencer corrected. 'How many times do I have to remind you to speak properly, Rebecca?'

'That is properly round here, Mum,' her daughter patiently pointed out.

'I'm going to play snowballs with me pals now it's settling. You can finish the decorations, Becky.' Tom kicked off his slippers and grabbed his boots from the hallstand.

'Let your sister get right inside the door, Rebecca; you're letting the heat out.' Mrs Spencer beckoned them forward.

Amelia had barely felt the cold around her ankles. She pushed the door shut then turned around to find her mother was looking increasingly thoughtful.

'Come into the kitchen to warm up,' said Blanche. 'Tom can fetch in some kindling from the shed before the snow gets too thick out there.' She tapped her son's fair head to gain his attention. 'I'll put the kettle on for tea. Some cinnamon buns are just out of the oven. I was putting them by for tomorrow but we'll have a few now. I can make more for Christmas Eve.'

'The cake's in the oven,' Rebecca piped up. 'I helped make it, didn't I, Mum?'

'You did, dear. Normally I'd have had it iced by now but what with your father being laid up last week...' She tailed off into a sigh.

'Dad's had bronchitis again?' Amelia frowned in concern, following the others into the kitchen.

'I didn't write, as I didn't want to worry you about it, Amelia.' Blanche started setting out cups. 'I thought you'd be flat out at work with preparations for the Campbells' big party. It's been cancelled then, has it?'

Amelia was spared finding a reply.

'Me pals'll be expecting me to knock for them.' Her brother butted in. 'Becky can fetch the wood.'

'You'll do as you're told,' his mother contradicted. 'How long have you got off, Amelia? Will you stay until Boxing Day?'

'Oh, you must stay till Boxing Day, at least. You will, won't you?' Rebecca helped herself to a cinnamon bun from the cooling rack.

'Where's Dad?' Amelia parried the questions and quickly seated herself. She pulled the chair up close to the kitchen table so little of her body was visible behind her elbows propped on the scrubbed pine top. Normally, she'd offer to make the tea or stoke the fire but her mother didn't remark upon it. Neither did she ask why Amelia had kept her distance, when the first thing she'd usually do on arriving home was give her mother a hug.

'Your father's fetching some parsnips from the allotment. I told him not to go as it had started to snow. A chill won't do that chest of his any good whatsoever. He'll be as surprised as I am to see you.'

An unspoken question hung in the air, alerting Amelia that her mother was done with beating about the bush.

Tom rushed inside from the garden, creating another distraction. His wet soles slipped on the stone floor, earning him a reprimand for dropping the wood. Once a large splinter had been extracted from the boy's finger, Tom and Rebecca started to bicker.

'You two can stop that.' Blanche was stirring the teapot, standing in a steamy haze from the boiled kettle.

Tom grabbed a bun then disappeared before his mother found him another chore.

'You look fuller in the face, Amelia. The Campbells have been feeding you up then.'

'Everybody eats well.' The aroma of the spiced buns had caused Amelia's empty stomach to grumble. She should have stayed for breakfast at the Anchor tavern... She should have stayed with Nicholas Dupree. Instead she was waiting with her heart anxiously pounding for the moment these Christmas celebrations would turn to ashes. Because of her.

A glimpse of the unwashed mixing bowl with its dark treacly residue drew her wistful gaze. Stir the pudding, make a wish... Amelia pressed her lips together to stop them quivering.

'Nip to the shops and get some biscuits and a loaf, would you, Becky? We'll need a bit more on the table at supper time now Amelia's here. And wrap yourself up.'

The girl curled a sulky top lip at being sent out rather than staying to talk with the grown-ups.

'I didn't have time to warn you I was coming, Mum. Last-minute thing. I've brought some housekeeping money.' Amelia emptied her trembling fist of coins withdrawn from her pocket.

They clattered onto the table as cold air whistled down the passage. Then Rebecca left the house and a short silence ensued. Amelia knew what was coming, and why her mother was glad to have the two younger ones out of the way rather than let them hear this.

'You've been sacked, haven't you?' She plonked down a cup of tea and a cinnamon bun in front of Amelia then crossed her arms. 'You never come back with your belongings. You've been sent home for good, haven't you?'

Amelia nodded in defeat and her chin touched her chest.

'In God's name, why?' Blanche gasped. 'You haven't stolen anything, have you?' She dismissed the idea a second after uttering it. She wouldn't put that sort of behaviour past her eldest, now she'd turned rotten, but her Amelia was a different girl. 'Have the Campbells got wind of our bad problems? Are we all tarred with the same brush as her?'

'It's nothing to do with Sadie, Mum,' Amelia croaked.

Blanche planted her fists on the table and leaned forward to study her daughter's lowered expression. 'You've not been in touch with her again, have you?'

'I have seen Sadie...'

'I warned you to keep your distance or you'd be sorry.' Blanche banged the table with a flat palm before straightening up with an angry sigh. 'They gave you a reference, I hope? They can't deny you that because your sister's shameful.' Blanche seemed to have made her mind up on the reason for Amelia's dismissal. 'You'll need to quickly seek a position to start in the New Year.'

'I wasn't sacked because of Sadie.' Amelia got to her feet. 'None of this is her fault.' She took a deep breath and blurted, 'Mrs Campbell found out I'm pregnant.'

Blanche took a few seconds to digest the enormity of what

she'd heard. Then, white-faced and mouth agape, she tottered around. 'What's that?' she whispered, although she didn't need the awful news to be repeated.

Amelia was no longer hiding herself and it was obvious not only her face looked fuller. 'No... not you.' Blanche determinedly shook her head. 'Are you sure? There's nothing much there. You must be bloated with colic. Are your bowels regular?'

Amelia nodded and tears started to drip onto her cheeks. 'My monthlies aren't regular, Mum. I've felt the baby moving. I think about springtime...'

Blanche covered her mouth with a shaking hand. 'Is he going to marry you?' she squeaked with pathetic optimism.

Amelia shook her drooping head. 'I'm sorry, Mum. I never wanted to hurt you and Dad.' She tried to hold her mother's hands but was shaken off.

'You've broken my heart, and you promised me you wouldn't. Not after what your sister did to this family. What have we done to deserve such wicked girls?'

'Please don't say that.'

'What shall I say then, miss?' Blanche Spencer hissed. 'Three daughters and two of them have disgraced us before turning twenty. What hope is there for Rebecca when she is at such an impressionable age?'

Blanche was forty-six years old with a trace of the beauty she'd had in her youth. At present, her distress had splotched her complexion and her bun of fair hair was messy from her fingers having been dragged through it. She had married into the working class, yet had tried to instil some of her middle-class ways into her daughters in the hope they'd attract decent husbands and these sort of calamities wouldn't occur.

Blanche knuckled tears from her eyes. 'Who is he? One of

those swaggering hounds that hang around in the marketplace, I suppose. I thought you'd better sense.'

'He's not a local man; he's somebody I met at work.'

At fifteen, Amelia had quit her first job in a Hackney drapery and moved to Mayfair, pleasing her mother no end. She was too good for an East End flash Harry, her mother had told her, and would mix with a better class of people working in service for the Campbells. Amelia had trusted Andrew Bowman because she trusted her mother knew best about these things. Yet one of those despised Flash Harrys had treated her far better than a posh fellow. She'd been ruined by an altogether more sly seduction than a whistle and a shout from a man who'd stopped halfway up the stairs to her bedroom.

'Your father will go after him. The rotten pig might be persuaded to do right by you. Is he one of the Campbells' servants?'

'He isn't, and he's gone so there's no point sending Dad to look for him.'

'Are you sure it's due in spring?' Blanche scrutinised her daughter's figure. 'Summer more like, by the look of you. I could find a handywoman… if we can scrape together her fee.'

'I think the baby's due in April. I know when it happened…' Amelia fell silent, unable to describe the summer trip to the seaside or the cottage or the wine she'd drunk or the phonograph tunes that she'd danced to or the lies he'd spouted leading her to the bedroom that there was nothing to worry about because soon they'd be married…

She felt more ashamed of falling for such a character than she did of the innocent child growing inside her.

'Did he force himself on you? Your father can have him arrested. A magistrate will *make* him do his duty.'

'It wasn't like that; I fell in love, and believed we were going to get married.'

'It's his word against yours. You're from a good family... well we were once,' Blanche amended bitterly. 'Not well off, but respectable people all the same.'

'I won't accuse him of anything. I'd be as bad as him with his lies.'

'You'd sooner save your deceit for your parents, is that it?' Blanche wilted onto the chair by the table.

'I didn't tell you earlier because I thought there was a chance it might come to nothing.'

'A miscarriage, you mean? We should be so lucky.' Blanche dropped her face into her palms and howled.

Mother and daughter were jerked to attention by the sound of somebody in the hallway. Blanche scrambled to shut the door and compose herself before her youngest daughter saw her. But it wasn't Rebecca.

A cough and a clatter of boots being discarded onto the floor let them know that Wilfred Spencer was home. He burst in, bringing the clean scent of snow with him, and a bag of parsnips and groceries. 'Becky gave me these to fetch back.' He put the bread and biscuits on the table. 'She's playing snowballs with the boys up the road.' He beamed. 'She said I'd get a lovely surprise when I got home...' Finally he noticed the atmosphere indoors was icier than that outside and his wife and newly arrived daughter had been weeping.

'What's the matter?' Bewildered, he turned to Blanche then stooped to peer at Amelia's sad face.

She gave him a wan smile. 'Hello, Dad.'

'What's up?' Wilfred stroked his daughter's tear-stained cheek with a callused finger.

'Go on! Tell your father what brings you home!' Blanche said. 'After that you deserve to be put out on the street.'

9

The shock of hearing the bad news had started Wilfred barking, sending his wife into a panic. Amelia had fled from the kitchen to seek refuge in the bedroom she shared with Rebecca.

Downstairs, the coughing had stopped and the arguing had started about fifteen minutes ago. Amelia was huddled on her side on the bed, with the pillow over her ears to muffle the commotion she'd caused. After some minutes of staring sightlessly into space she realised the noise had abated. A warning signal from a creaking floorboard brought her upright on the bed.

Mr and Mrs Spencer filed in without knocking, Blanche leading the way. Their daughter got to her feet for their verdict, darting anxious glances from one bleak face to the other. Her father avoided her eyes as though embarrassed to look at her. Wilfred couldn't meet his wife's eyes either as she waited for him to speak up. His lack of leadership drew from her a heavy sigh.

'In my opinion you should go immediately,' Blanche announced into the awful silence. 'The children aren't back yet and that's a blessing. You can slip away quietly, without them seeing you again.'

'The Campbells won't have me. I've nowhere to go.'

'You should have thought about that, miss!' Blanche stifled a sob. 'You could have met fine people through the Campbells. Bettered yourself.'

'The girl can stop here until after the holiday.' Wilfred sounded wearily adamant. 'She's not being put out in the snow at Christmas, without food in her belly. That's my final word on it. In the New Year, the Salvation Army home in Mare Street might take her in...'

'She can't go there!' Blanche interrupted, aghast. 'It's much too close. She'll be seen and the neighbours will be gossiping about us all over again.'

Local people had petitioned to get the Salvation Army's mother and baby home closed before it lowered the tone of the neighbourhood. Yet, the same folk would purposely take a diversion past it to watch the comings and goings.

'I won't go there,' Amelia hastily reassured her mother.

'You won't enter a workhouse either,' stated Wilfred. 'You've misbehaved, but I wouldn't put a dog of mine behind such walls.' He grasped his wife's arm to stop her prowling and whimpering. 'I agree with your mother that you can't stay here beyond a week. The younger children mustn't suffer again after the other business.' He cleared his throat. 'You can apply to a different rescue home.'

'There's a refuge for deserted mothers and infants in Bloomsbury.' Blanche had made it her business to investigate those sorts of establishments the moment Sadie became besotted with a thug. The girl was sure to need a place like that situated at a safe distance from Hackney, she had thought. But her eldest had stayed child-free, proving she was shrewder, if not brighter than Amelia.

'That will have to do then,' said Wilfred. 'After the holiday you must go there for assistance.'

'They might refuse to have me.' Amelia swung a wide-eyed look between her parents.

'You must make your own way as best you can,' Blanche butted in before her husband caved in. 'You must never come back here again.'

Amelia sank onto the edge of the mattress, feeling wretched for hurting them both. But protecting her baby was still the most important thing of all. If she was given a place at this home, she imagined her life would be strict rules and hard work. And what then? No orphanage or foster mother for her son or daughter, she'd vowed. But she couldn't earn a living with a baby in her arms.

'We'll do it your father's way then,' said Blanche. 'Think yourself lucky. Your sister wasn't shown leniency and her shame was less severe.'

Amelia knew her mother would change her tune if she found out Sadie was rumoured to be a prostitute.

'You will remain in here and eat meals on a tray.' Blanche set out conditions while rubbing her coughing husband's back. 'The younger two will be told to stay away from you as you're unwell. Rebecca can share the small bedroom with Tom until you've gone.'

'I'm truly sorry...' Amelia said.

Her mother hesitated, not to acknowledge her daughter's tearful apology, but because another pitfall had occurred to her. 'Don't talk to any of the neighbours when you leave.' She quit the room without waiting for her husband to accompany her.

Wilfred Spencer was a tall thin man who had been exceptionally good-looking in his youth, according to his wife. As a toddler Amelia would grab handfuls of his springy brown locks as he carried her in his arms. He was completely grey now although his hair was still abundant. There was little of the handsome man recognisable in the lined face of the brewery worker who had bowled over Blanche Gooding and caused her to fall out with her family. When they married on her twenty-second birthday, none of her relatives had attended.

Amelia had long wondered if that lowering in status was what made her mother seem perpetually discontented. Blanche had never said as much to her children, but her husband no doubt knew that drudgery and penny pinching had made her regret what she'd done for love. They maintained a united front and bore life's disappointments stoically, but Blanche's ambition to regain ground through her children had floundered.

On impulse, Amelia rushed to hold her father. He straightened up, looking like a man far older than his forty-nine years. He emitted a muffled sob as his sinewy arms enclosed her. He smelled of yeasty beer as he always did, even on his day off from the brewery. Her father had always been the sentimental one; their mother kept discipline. Amelia had heard him crying after the business with Sadie even though his eldest hadn't pleaded to stay. She'd raced off up the road to meet Jimmy Burley, eager to start being an adult.

'I'm sorry, Dad...'

'I know you are.' He clumsily patted her back. 'But you must go – you understand that, don't you?' he said gruffly to the girl who'd always been the apple of his eye. 'It wouldn't be fair on the others, you see.'

'Have you seen a doctor about your cough?'

He shook his head. 'It comes and goes... nothing much to worry about.'

'You should get some medicine.'

He stroked her hair with a gentle hand. 'You've enough to fret over. Don't bother yourself about me. The dust off the hops and barley flies about and clogs our throats, that's all.' With children still at school and bills to pay, bad lungs seemed a fair price to pay to keep hearth and home ticking over.

In almost twenty-five years of marriage Wilfred Spencer prided himself in never having been late with a rent payment. A decade ago they'd only occupied the downstairs of this house. Now he had a tenancy on the whole of it. Not for him spending his wages boozing in pubs with pals, or gambling at the weekends. He'd done his utmost to uphold his wife's standards and replicate the middle-class home she had been brought up in. He'd done his best to protect his children and to make Blanche happy. And he'd failed miserably.

'Who is he?' Wilfred suddenly demanded. 'You're not a fool, Amelia. He told lies, and gave promises, didn't he?' Wilfred fidgeted in her embrace. 'Your mother said you met him at the Campbells' but he's not a servant. Is he a relative of theirs... a friend?'

'It doesn't matter now, Dad.' She didn't want him doing anything rash when he was unable to beat an affluent man half his age in a physical or a legal battle.

'It does matter!' he thundered. 'I'll take it up with the swine. Tell me his name. What does he do? I'll go to his employer and have him sacked.' Wilfred started to cough and extricated himself from her arms.

To calm him, she revealed some of it. 'Andrew Bowman visited the house to teach the children to play the piano. After I told him I was pregnant he stopped coming and moved away.'

'This Bowman thought himself as grand as the Campbells, did he?' her father said contemptuously. 'He should think himself lucky to have a girl as lovely as you for his wife. I'll find him, never fear.'

'He couldn't legally marry me, Dad,' Amelia hastily said. 'He owned up to being betrothed. The Campbells sent him a wedding gift in the autumn.' Amelia had overheard the house-keeper and the cook debating whether a silver-topped claret jug would have been more fitting than the crystal whisky decanter presented to the couple.

It had started in the music room when he'd taught her to play a tune on the piano after the children finished their lesson. He'd urged her to put down the dusters and sit beside him on the stool. He was pleasant-looking rather than handsome. Friendly but a bit shy, she'd thought. She'd remained snared in his web until the day he hadn't been shy or friendly when snarling at her that she'd never hook him with a baby. He'd spoken to her as though she were a scheming trollop instead of a seventeen-year-old whose virginity he'd taken at his uncle's seaside cottage. Of course, that probably wasn't true either. The rich uncle was doubtless a figment of his imagination and Andrew Bowman rented such places as required. She could see now that she'd not been special; she'd been naïve. She wasn't the first, neither would she be the last of his conquests, married though he was.

'I pity his wife,' said Wilfred, thinking along similar lines. 'The woman will never be happy saddled with a man like that...' He broke off mid-sentence. Footsteps were heard running up the stairs. 'Tom's home. Do as your mother says, and stay in this room.' He hung his head, ashamed of himself for being ashamed of her. 'It's best for the children, you see, Amelia. Too many awkward questions.'

Through the closed door she could hear him talking to his son as they descended the stairs. Within a few minutes a hum of conversation was ebbing and flowing in the kitchen below. She imagined her parents were attempting to explain her quarantine with white lies. Then she could be treated as a leper rather than a disgrace.

Feeling restless, Amelia went to the window to gaze over the quiet whiteness in the back garden. The sound of the door clicking brought her quickly around.

'What have you done?'

Rebecca, pink-faced from being outdoors, was looking at her strangely. She'd not yet taken off her coat and the chill that clung to the wool drifted across the room.

'You shouldn't be in here,' Amelia whispered.

'Don't care.' Rebecca sounded unusually belligerent. 'What's going on? Mum said you're not well but you were all right before.' She took a step forward. 'Why's she been crying? I know it's not 'cos the cake's ruined.'

'The cake's ruined?' Amelia longed to hug her sister and say not to worry, everything would come right. But well-meaning lies would only make matters worse.

'It's burned and she's thrown it into the garden for the birds, though Dad said not to. He was going to scrape the black off it. Now it's in bits and it took ages to weigh out all the currants and so on.'

Rebecca's eyes were brimming with disillusionment. It was a look to revive a memory of how Amelia had felt herself when Sadie fell from the pedestal she'd put her on.

'Everybody's upset and it's all your fault. You're not ill; you've done something bad. Like Sadie did. You've come home and spoiled our Christmas.' Rebecca turned to go. 'We were all happy before you turned up.'

The girl skittered back to avoid being knocked over as the door was swung open. A wild-eyed Blanche entered and dragged her out onto the landing. Before the door was slammed Amelia glimpsed Tom's white face. Then Wilfred's shout and pounding feet were heard as he puffed up the stairs.

Amelia sank onto the edge of the bed and wept for the trouble she had caused to the people she loved, and for being made to feel she was incubating a fiend rather than a child.

She accepted there was no hope for forgiveness and a place to call home. She'd wait until it was dark then go; delaying would only worsen matters.

* * *

Her mother had given her a brimming dish of mutton stew to fill her up. A final loving act for a daughter who might not eat again for some while. Amelia left the used crockery on the dressing table. Usually she'd clear up after herself, but they'd all gone to bed and she wouldn't make a noise in the kitchen.

By candlelight, she descended the stairs and went to find her things. Her savings were still on the table, left untouched for her to pick up and take with her. She dropped the cash into her pocket and eased out her carpetbag from between the table legs. She proceeded along the hallway and before blowing out the flame turned and looked back, wondering if she was seeing this beloved place for the last time. The smoking candle was left on the hallstand and quietly she let herself out of the house. Sparkling snow crunched beneath her feet as she went down the path. The gate hinges didn't squeak but she glanced up anyway.

Mrs Spencer had waited up, standing sentry at the bedroom window, to see her daughter leave. She had known Amelia would do the right thing and go away so they could pick up the pieces of Christmas for the younger ones. Blanche felt as though her heart were splitting in two, but she swallowed her sobs to keep from waking her husband. He was snoring... oblivious to the fact he had already seen his favourite child for the last time. Wilfred wasn't one to read anybody's thoughts or to anticipate a next move. He saw things plainly and had no subtlety to his nature that Blanche had ever been able to find.

Why didn't you tell me sooner so I'd time to help...? was her silent shout to the girl in the snow. But she knew why her daughters kept things from her: they were like her. She had concealed her behaviour from her parents when sneaking off to meet a man she knew they wouldn't approve of. Love wasn't logical, and avoiding a foolish choice wasn't taught but learned. And for beautiful Amelia this was a hard lesson indeed.

10

'We've no room in here, miss.' The mob-capped matron swayed an oil lamp to illuminate the pregnant girl on the front step. Pale wisps of hair were drooping about her cheeks; apart from that it was hard for Mrs Grubb to see much of her face. Her hood had been pulled forward as protection from the elements and beneath the cloak her figure appeared reasonably trim. The shivering wretch had said her name was Amelia Spencer and she wanted admission. But she didn't look too far gone. She wasn't about to drop like those already inside. 'The St Pancras workhouse might take you in if you tell the right tale, m'dear.' Mrs Grubb retreated into the hallway, shielding the lamp's flickering flame from the draught. She'd done her duty and wasn't catching her death. 'Hurry along now,' she called, closing the door. 'They'll be queuing up at St Pancras on such a night as this.'

'I shan't go there.' Amelia jerked up her chin, losing the protection of her hood. 'I have some money to pay for my board and lodging until the baby's born. Please let me in.' A paralysing chill had been shaken off, and she thrust out her fistful of coins.

Mrs Grubb glimpsed a glint of silver. Schoolgirls... middle-aged spinsters... educated merchants' daughters and coarsely spoken drabs: they all turned up on her doorstep. She guessed Amelia Spencer fell somewhere in between in age and status, but she was the prettiest of the lot, despite her limp fair hair and a complexion as white as the snow on the ground. 'Where d'you hail from, miss?'

'Hackney.'

'The Salvation Army is right on your doorstep, ducks.'

'I know... but I won't go back there.'

'Ah... I see...' Mrs Grubb did see. Some girls took such a beating from their fathers before being banished that they were barely able to walk. This girl looked healthy; maybe she'd no wish to go back and test her father's patience. 'I'm already over-crowded and watering down porridge to go around. You have enough cash to pay for a lodging room. These girls haven't got small bellies like you and can't hide what they are.'

Amelia hadn't considered herself fortunate; in fact she'd begun to pity herself. But the matron wasn't being cruel or exaggerating about the place being full. A medley of sounds was coming from within at this late hour: creaks and bangs and a hum of female voices that altered in volume and pitch.

A sudden scream startled Amelia into dropping her carpetbag. Mrs Grubb seemed to have been expecting it, though, and rolled her eyes. 'I must go. A girl's in labour and my assistance is required. Make haste to the workhouse, my dear.'

'I won't...' Amelia cried to an abruptly closed door. A bolt was slid home and she banged the knocker in protest. There was no response and she sighed in defeat, unsure where to head next. She perched on the carpetbag with her clasped hands hugging her knees and her chin resting atop them. Away in the distance a church bell chimed midnight.

Christmas Eve had broken on a magical sight. The snow had stopped and left a crystal blanket on the cobbles and rooftops. Up above, the brilliance of a thousand stars studded a clear sky that seemed to stretch beyond any horizon. None of it impressed Amelia, though. She was oblivious to pretty Christmas. But she was aware her boots and the hem of her skirt were soaked through with slush and the freezing air felt like glass shards attacking her throat.

Dithering here, wishing to be let in, would do her no good, she told herself. She refused to admit to being frightened; she clung to the thought of girls worse off than she was. She should feel grateful for the little she had and find a lodging and a job. Then when her pains started she'd come back and bang on the door again.

The railings to one side of her came in useful in assisting her to her feet. She was shaking her carpetbag to dislodge ice from its underside when she heard the bolts being drawn and a rumble of female voices. The door wasn't fully opened but a sliver of light leaked out. The conversation became clearer and Amelia stood quite still straining to listen to it.

'There is no need to involve the authorities, Mrs Grubb.'

'Very well, Sister. I'll clean the wicked girl up and make sure the stillborn is decently buried. I expected to have both to lay out, so it's a better outcome than might have been, thanks to you.'

'I will check on her after Christmas. She has made a mess of herself and might get an infection. If you suspect she needs my attention sooner, send a message with John Wolff. He'll be by tomorrow afternoon with meat and vegetables.'

'I will keep an eye on her, Sister. I hope the wretch feels ashamed of herself. What a dreadful thing to do.'

'All these girls should feel ashamed of themselves, Mrs Grubb. And pray for salvation.'

'Indeed, Sister. I believe most of them do.'

'Merry Christmas to you, Mrs Grubb.'

'And to you, Sister.'

Amelia jerked to attention the moment the women finished talking. She guessed the sister was a midwife, on her way home. Rather than be caught eavesdropping, Amelia hastened down the steps with her bag. A newborn hadn't survived, and the mother was described as wicked and at risk of an infection because she was in a mess. If things went wrong during her own labour, she might be discussed in that cold-blooded manner.

A figure dressed in long black garments appeared on the top step then began smartly descending, carrying a medical case. The sister wasn't a nurse but a nun. Amelia slipped behind the railings to wait for her to pass by. She'd made a soundless scramble for cover, but it seemed the sister had been alerted to her presence nonetheless. A pale oval face edged by cloth had turned in her direction.

'What are you doing, child?'

'I'm... I'm waiting to speak to Mrs Grubb again.' Amelia recalled the matron's name from the overheard conversation.

'You're another fallen girl, are you?'

Amelia put up her chin and jerked a defiant nod. The nun's eyes had lowered to find a tell-tale swelling behind the carpetbag.

'Surely Mrs Grubb told you there is no room in there?'

A lie... even a white one... didn't seem right in this company so Amelia owned up. 'She did, but I thought I'd try again.' She wished the nun would get going so she could whip back up the steps, but the woman seemed in no hurry to leave.

'What is your name, child?'

'Amelia Spencer.'

'Well, Amelia Spencer, I am Sister Evangeline. I can find you somewhere to shelter from the cold, and I expect some hot soup would be welcome.'

Amelia's stomach growled its own response to the offer of food. But she didn't immediately answer. She was now wise to the importance of careful consideration before acting. 'Is it a convent?' She'd feel uneasy in a place like that.

'It isn't a convent, Miss Spencer.'

Amelia detected a smile in the woman's tone. 'You're not taking me to the workhouse?' she challenged.

'No, child, I am not. If you come along you'll be in a place similar to this one. Our Saviour's Mission is a rescue home for fallen girls wishing to lead a better life. Is this your first fall?'

'Beg pardon? Oh, I see... yes, it is.' Amelia cottoned on and answered although she found the question impertinent.

'And what caused this fall?'

Again, Amelia hesitated in speaking up, believing this to be for her alone to know. 'I thought I was to be married,' she said stiltedly. 'But he...' Her explanation tailed off as annoyance took over. She should have realised this wasn't unconditional help, and she would be interrogated to see if she was suitably contrite and grateful for her soup.

'He abandoned you. Yes, I understand. I only accept girls ready to repent and embrace righteousness.' The nun cocked her head. 'If you are such a girl, you may stay with us and you will be looked after until your baby is born.'

'I'm definitely sorry for the turn my life has taken.' A stronger note of bitterness than guilt was in the statement, but the nun didn't insist on having a better vow to reform.

'I charge ten shillings to keep a woman through her confinement. Afterwards, I will help you to secure decent employment to stop you from straying again into sin.'

'I have eight shillings and thruppence, if that will do.' Amelia regretted having hailed a cab to get here, for she would have had more money left. Trusting fate to put a roof over her head and wages in her hand until spring, was a pipe dream. She had no option but to snatch at this chance of shelter for her unborn baby's sake.

'Eight shillings and thruppence will do on this occasion.' Sister Evangeline didn't count the jumble of copper and silver that landed on her palm. Briskly she deposited it in her case then crooked a finger, inviting Amelia to follow. 'Come along, child. It isn't weather to idle in,' was sent over a shoulder as she set off.

Billowing robes flapped at Amelia, tempting her to latch on to the black cloth to assist her over the snow. The nun seemed steady of foot in her sturdy boots, more serviceable than Amelia's daintier ones that slipped and slithered. Sister Evangeline proceeded to traverse a deserted road, the slushy surface criss-crossed by cartwheels. She hadn't lost speed and the medical case continued oscillating at her side. Then she led the way along a seemingly endless avenue that Amelia tackled from one glistening oasis beneath a gas lamp to the next while her laboured breaths formed clouds before her face.

Then they were in an unlit lane that soon terminated in a narrow track. Sister Evangeline plunged along the bumpy path. Amelia hastened in her wake, stumbling between parallel hedgerows as the rock-hard ruts dug into her thin soles. Brambles showered her with their snowy load as she yanked her clothes free of their thorns. The street lamps had been left far behind now and only starlight and the spectral landscape could show the way. The sister seemed to know where she was heading and Amelia kept the moving shadow in her sights, conscious that if left behind she'd remain lost and frozen until dawn.

There were no visible pinpricks of light to reveal a nearby property and she imagined a shortcut to another street was being taken. They proceeded deeper into a dark tunnel where the ground remained black, sheltered from the elements by an impenetrable canopy of ivy-bound branches. Amelia began to peer over her shoulder. Animal instinct was urging her to flee back to familiar territory while she still could.

The trek was abruptly over. Sister Evangeline had stopped by a gated entrance. A man emerged from the darkness, lighting the way with a lantern that painted a yellow oval on the ground in front of him and the animal padding at his side. Amelia gazed at the dog's glittering amber eyes. It wasn't shaggy-coated like a wolfhound but it was large: its head as high as the man's thighs. The padlock was dealt with efficiently and the gate was soon swinging inwards. The clang of iron on iron as the chain was released sent a shrieking owl flapping upwards in a streak of silver. Sister Evangeline ushered Amelia through the opening and onto frosted gravel.

'I have met another friendless soul, Jack. Miss Amelia Spencer will be staying with us.'

Amelia was aware of him shifting the shotgun resting on his shoulder to get a better look at her. But his features remained hidden behind blinding light as he raised the lamp.

'My Jack of all trades.' Sister Evangeline sounded proud of her manservant. 'John Wolff is a fine gamekeeper and carpenter. We are never short of infants' cribs or rabbit and hare for supper. Venison, too, when he hunts further afield.' Introductions done, the sister set off along the drive. 'The house is close now. Follow me, Miss Spencer, and we will soon have you warm and comfortable.'

Amelia imagined the mission sat behind the white skeletons of the trees. Her heart was still pounding and a wave of giddiness buckled her knees. She had never swooned in her life and had no intention of doing so now. She dropped her bag to gain support from the gate but it creaked away from her. John Wolff got a thank you for holding her up and she hoped he didn't know his own strength rather than was intentionally hurting her arm. Her brief glance at him told her he was cruel. His full beard was daubed yellow by the lantern and within its bushiness hid mean lips.

Being alone at midnight with a stranger brought a stark reminder of Mr Dupree. The men weren't alike. John Wolff was older, and shorter and stockier than the landlord of the Anchor tavern. Nicholas Dupree hadn't sneered at her, but he had warned her she trusted too easily.

She wished she'd not come here. She wished she'd followed her heart rather than her parents' orders and headed to Whitechapel for shelter. She'd been too eager to agree to their wishes after distressing them.

Fighting Polly Mayhew for Nicholas Dupree had little chance of success. But she'd risk it and live with him for as long as he'd have her. She'd lied to Sister Evangeline about repenting and embracing a life of righteousness.

And if he didn't want her, she'd apply to the match factory. The phossy jaw Sadie had warned her about hadn't disturbed her as much as the feeling of dread she got from this place. At least at Bryant and May she'd earn wages and have her sister's friendship while Sadie remained in Whitechapel. Amelia surfaced from her daze to find the nun was already lost from view.

She called Sister Evangeline's name but it was drowned out
by the clang of the chain being swung against the gate. Wolff
inserted a huge key into the padlock, then the chunk of heart-
shaped metal was tested with a jerk. Amelia glimpsed his nasty
smile as he turned to her. He was pleased to have thwarted her
attempt to escape.

'Heel.' His eyes remained on Amelia, but the hound obeyed
the command.

A sick sensation churned her stomach as the dog growled at
a creature rustling in the undergrowth.

'Hurry along, Miss Spencer,' said John Wolff with deceitful
softness. He retrieved the shotgun he had rested against the gate
and shouldered it. Then he swooped on her bag and thrust it at
her. 'Sister Evangeline shouldn't be kept waiting by the likes of
you.'

11

'Bloomin' heck. You're up and dressed at last, are you? I gave you a shake to wake you before I went down for breakfast, but you was out for the count.'

A jovial greeting drew Amelia away from the window and an entrancing view of a frozen landscape, iridescent with dawn light. A young woman was in the process of using her posterior to bump shut the door. She was carrying a food tray upon which sat a candle stump. The light assisted Amelia in getting a good look at her smiling roommate's snub nose and lively eyes set in a freckled complexion.

'Sister Evangeline said you could have something brought up as you was late getting to bed.' The tray was deposited on the washstand. 'You'll soon learn the rules. We take our meals in the refectory. Breakfast: six thirty sharp or go without. That's number one.' The girl displayed a thumb as though she might carry on counting off rules on her fingers. Instead, she crossed her arms over her pinafore and said, 'S'pose as you're new, and it's Christmas Eve, Sister Evangeline is making an exception.

She's all right on the whole, although she's a stickler and has some funny ways.'

'Thanks for telling me and for bringing my breakfast,' Amelia finally got a word in edgeways.

Last night, the nun had shown Amelia where she was to sleep. She'd been left with a candle and an instruction to bed down quietly to avoid disturbing her roommate. Amelia had nodded off not long after dousing the flame and pulling the blanket up over herself. On waking she had found the bed opposite had the covers flung back on an empty mattress.

'You're Amelia Spencer, aren't you? The sister told us your name. I'm Katherine Wheeler. Or Kitty to me friends.'

'I'll call you Kitty then, if that's all right. And I'm pleased to meet you.'

'I'll call you Amelia, if that's all right. And I'm pleased to meet you, too.' Kitty clasped the hands extended to her in friendship. 'I reckon we'll get on just fine.' She winked an eye that glinted green between sandy lashes. 'I expect you'll want to scarper back into the real world as soon as you can, same as me.'

Amelia was keen to hear more about what she'd let herself in for. On arrival she'd eaten alone at a long table in the kitchen while the sister disappeared to speak to her manservant. It had been a relief to discover that John Wolff lived in a neighbouring cottage rather than in the house. He gave her the creeps.

She had tucked into her chicken broth while taking in her surroundings. The black-leaded stove spanned half of one wall and contained a range of ovens and hobs. Above those were shelves holding polished copper pots. By the time she'd wiped the soup bowl clean with a crust of bread, her frozen feet were beginning to thaw and the homely aroma wafting from the stockpot was making her feel drowsy. Every thought of humbling herself and heading to Whitechapel, in the hope Mr

Dupree would take her in, had been forgotten. She had liked him too much to allow him to consider her – and eventually her baby – a nuisance in his life. With the peaceful thought lulling her that she'd not made of herself a burden on family or friends, she'd dozed off until roused by the nun's hand on her shoulder.

Amelia wasn't hungry after her midnight feast, but she tucked in, in case there was a long wait until the next meal. She perched on the edge of her bed with the tray on her lap and tasted the porridge. It was rather good: not thin but creamy. 'What's it like living here, Kitty?' she asked.

Her roommate settled on the mattress opposite with her brush in one hand and hairpins in the other. 'Beds are clean. Food's regular and we get just about enough of it.' Kitty carried on skilfully winding her auburn hair into a bun. 'There's five of us girls here... six now you've turned up. We have to skivvy to keep the place going. No servants, see, apart from the cook. Mrs Baxter is getting on a bit. A gamekeeper does all the odd jobs. Us girls do the cleaning and washing. In the evening we knit and crochet. The things we make are sold to fund the mission's work, the sister says. She also says the devil makes work for idle hands and so we can't be idle or we'll sin again.' Kitty jabbed the final hairpin into place and rolled her green eyes. 'Chance 'ud be a fine thing with no men about.'

'I met John Wolff last night. I thought him intimidating and sullen.'

'He's that all right,' said Kitty. 'I don't like him, but some girls do.' She smirked, having read Amelia's astonishment. 'Hard to believe anybody swooning over him, I know. He's a bit too rough and ready for me. Anyhow he's probably old enough to be me dad.'

'How old is Sister Evangeline, do you think? I couldn't make up my mind.'

'About his age I reckon. Forty... something like that. He's devoted to her and she seems to like him.' Kitty wrinkled her nose. 'He kills the chickens and rabbits and keeps the cooking pot filled. Does jobs in the house and garden as well. Sister Evangeline has a lot of time for people who work hard so perhaps that's why she keeps him around.'

'I don't mind working hard while I'm here,' Amelia said.

'You've turned up at the right time then.' Kitty chuckled. 'There'll be plenty to do over Christmas. I'm on kitchen rota. Best job of the lot that is. I have a crafty nibble when Cook's not watching. We've been promised roast saddle of venison for Christmas Day, courtesy of our friend John Wolff. And a plum pudding. Then there's a proper Christmas cake for tea. I helped Mrs Baxter ice it.' Kitty patted her stomach in anticipation.

Talk of Christmas cake had jolted a poignant reminder of her family. Amelia hoped they'd celebrate the holiday but feared her surprise visit had caused too much damage for much to be salvaged or enjoyed.

'Hits you at this time of year, don't it?' Kitty had noticed her new friend's dewy eyes. 'You'll soon settle into the routine, though.' She got up and kindly rubbed Amelia's shoulder.

'I'd hoped to spend Christmas with my family.'

'My lot's washed their hands of me. My married sister might come round in time but don't reckon me mum will ever speak to me again.' Kitty sat back down. 'How about you? Black sheep of the family like me, are you?'

Amelia nodded. 'I've got a married sister. Sadie knows I'm in trouble but she's got problems of her own.'

'Ah, well... never mind,' Kitty said. 'At least we've got a roof over our heads and aren't freezing to death in the snow. The worst part of being here is the Bible bashing, and that's not only at Christmas. I'm not that way inclined. Only been inside church for me dad's funeral.'

'I'm sorry to hear that.' Amelia put down her spoon in the empty bowl.

'Oh, it was years ago when I was a schoolkid. Then me mum hooked up with somebody else. Never liked him so got a live-in domestic job and left home at thirteen.' Kitty propped her elbows on her pinafored lap and jerked a nod at Amelia's belly. 'When are you due?'

'About April, I think.' She looked at the other girl's slender figure. 'How about you?'

'Already had my daughter, three weeks ago,' said Kitty. 'She was a month premature, Sister reckons. So, it was a good job I came here when I did. I'd only just settled in when me pains started. She was underweight but she's almost six pounds now.'

Amelia was surprised to hear Kitty was a mother. She was a chatterbox, yet had hardly mentioned her baby. 'Where is your daughter?' Amelia put the tray on the washstand then reseated herself on the bed.

'In the nursery. I feed her but don't see much of her other-wise. Sister Evangeline looks after the babies and Mrs Baxter helps when needed. My girl's being boarded out to foster parents in a few months so I can get a job and turn over a new leaf.'

'What did you call your daughter?'

Kitty studied her clasped hands. 'Sister Evangeline says Baby Wheeler is enough for now, as the new people will choose her name. She doesn't like us getting too fond of the children. She's my baby, though, and I love her so I've got her name up here.' She tapped her temple. 'Louise,' she whispered.

'That's a lovely name.'

Kitty dropped her chin to her chest. 'Sister Evangeline said it's my Christian duty to let the child go to a decent family.'

'I'm keeping my baby.'

Kitty jerked up her head. 'Are you getting married when you get out of here?' In her book that was the only way to bring about a happy ending.

'I'll go it alone.'

'You're brave,' said Kitty. 'One of me mother's neighbours pretended her daughter's baby was hers. We all knew it wasn't, though.' Kitty's chuckle faded away. 'Be nice to have a mum like that.' She glanced at Amelia. 'Will you try to persuade your folks to help out when the baby's born?'

'They would help if they could,' Amelia said loyally. 'They can't though with younger kids at home.' She didn't need to spell out that her family could expect abuse from neighbours. 'I'll manage and do whatever I have to.'

'Don't let Sister Evangeline hear you say that.' Kitty hissed the warning. 'She'll take it to mean you'll go on the game, then she'll send your baby away to a wet nurse as soon as it's born. You'll never see it again.'

'She wouldn't!' Amelia followed Kitty's lead in shooting a glance at the door, fearing being overheard.

'The sister did it to another girl,' Kitty whispered. 'I think she was a prossie though. The girl wanted to keep her baby 'cos she'd already put one in the Foundling Hospital. Sister Evangeline had the second baby fostered without telling her, then she was chucked out for lying about it being her first fall.' Kitty paused. 'You're the only one of us to speak about keeping the baby rather than making a fresh start.'

'Well, that's what I'm doing,' said Amelia fiercely.

'I wish I was as strong as you, Amelia. I bet I'm older than you, 'n' all. I'm turned nineteen.'

'I'm eighteen next month,' Amelia said. 'And I reckon you're stronger than you think. If you want to keep Louise, then you should.'

'A baby and no wedding ring means you're treated like muck and can't get a job.'

'We should stick together and help each other out.'

The two girls were cautious about speaking too soon when they'd only just met. Inwardly, they calculated the benefits of joining forces, taking turns with childminding and working shifts. If they pooled their wages they might be able to afford a shared lodging.

'My sister Sadie is a match girl. Bryant and May don't pay good wages and it's not nice work, but I'd do it to keep my baby with me when I leave here.'

'I've heard you get phossy jaw if you work making matches,' Kitty cautioned.

'Sadie told me about some of her colleagues getting sick after working there for a long time. I'd be careful and wash the phosphorous off my hands like she does. Anyway, I'd get other employment as soon as I could. But it's a start. And that's all I want.'

'It is a start,' said Kitty thoughtfully. 'Sister Evangeline said I could stop here as Cook's assistant then take over when Mrs Baxter retires. I intended to escape as soon as I could but now you've arrived, and we've hit it off, I might hang on. Then maybe we could get jobs at Bryant and May.'

Amelia gave a vigorous nod. 'Will Louise's father help you, or want to see her?'

'Him?' Kitty curled her lip. 'He's no good. I found out he had a family he never told me about.' Kitty mocked herself with a headshake. 'He said he'd do his duty, but when it came to it, he just borrowed ten bob and told me to get rid of it.' She paused.

'Glad I didn't listen to him. Louise looks like me; she's got a head of lovely thick hair.'

'Can we visit the nursery and see her?' Amelia said eagerly.

'Against the rules. Sister Evangeline don't like us getting fond of them. We're only let in there to feed and change nappies.' Kitty grimaced. 'This place is like a prison.'

'It looks nice from outside.' Amelia reflected on her first sight of the house.

The mission had revealed itself to be far more substantial than was the shabby townhouse run by Mrs Grubb. The property was like a smaller version of the Campbells' country house. She had dusted the picture frames of paintings of her employers' elegant mansion.

'Did you fall for a bad sort, like me?' Kitty had expected Amelia to return the favour and offer up her tale of woe.

"Fraid so.' Amelia continued to reflect on last night's events. 'I got turned away from Mrs Grubb's refuge before I came here. Sister Evangeline was delivering a baby there. I overheard them talking about it.' Amelia bit her lip, remembering the scream that had frightened her. 'What's it like giving birth, Kitty?'

'Bloody hurts,' came the blunt reply. 'Worth it though when you get to hold them. Thought I'd burst I was so proud of meself afterwards.' She added some reassurance. 'Sister Evangeline is a good midwife; everybody says so. You look strong 'n' healthy. And too pretty for your own good.'

'The girl they spoke about lost her baby.' Amelia was unable to shake off her disquiet. 'They called her wicked because her baby died.'

Kitty's eyes widened in shock. 'Sister Evangeline missed supper 'cos she had to go and help with Nell Yates. She did a flit from here even though she'd paid her ten bob. I noticed she'd taken some knitting needles with her.' Kitty wrinkled her nose in disgust. 'If Nell's done what I think she's done, and then expected Mrs Grubb to patch her up... she *is* bloody wicked.'

'What d'you think she's done?' Amelia sounded perplexed.

'Stuck the needles up herself to make sure she has a miscarriage.' Kitty sounded angry.

Amelia felt sick but was glad to learn more about the sordid world she'd landed herself in. 'Why would she do that if Sister Evangeline could foster her baby?'

'Gawd knows. Nell seemed a restless sort. Always talking about finding a man to be her ticket out of here...'

'What's going on? There's no time to idle on Christmas Eve. And we don't waste candles at the mission during daytime.' Unseen and unheard by the two young women, Sister Evangeline had entered the bedchamber.

Both girls shot to their feet, looking nervous as the nun pinched out the candle flame. They had been engrossed in their conversation and hadn't noticed that the dawn had brightened into pale sunshine.

'It seems you're rested and fed, Miss Spencer.' The nun gave the empty bowl and milk beaker a glance. 'Tomorrow is Christmas Day. Our saviour's birthday. A fitting time for you to embark on your journey to a better life.' She turned to Kitty. 'You know your duties for the day, Miss Wheeler?'

'I do, Sister.'

'And yet I see your bed isn't made.'

'Sorry, Sister. I was talking to Amelia... Miss Spencer about rules and prayers and so on.' Kitty started straightening the sheet and tucking it in.

'Very good. Put on your cap and go about your day. I will explain to Miss Spencer what is expected of her.' After Kitty had retrieved the plain white mob cap from the washstand and pulled it on, she quit the room with a subtle wink for Amelia.

'Your dress is acceptable attire.' Sister Evangeline ran her eye over the grey cotton. 'You need a pinafore and a cap; and your hair should be worn in a plait, or a bun.' A disapproving glance settled on the wavy flaxen tresses loose about Amelia's shoulders. 'Have you got a pinafore and cap in your bag?'

'No, Sister.' Amelia had returned most of her uniform to the housekeeper on the day she'd been sacked. Rather than delay her departure she'd been allowed to leave in the dress. As far as Amelia was concerned, if they were mean enough to want it back, they could come and get it.

'I'll fetch the garments you lack from the linen cupboard. While I'm gone, please neaten your hair. And make your bed. Then you will be presentable and ready to be introduced to the other girls.'

'Thank you, Sister. May I ask you something?'

'You may.' The nun had turned to go but faced Amelia again, her black habit swishing about her thin figure.

'Did Nell Yates have a stillborn baby at Mrs Grubb's yesterday? Did she harm herself?' Amelia noticed a flash of annoyance in the sister's brown eyes and the fine lines deepened around her compressed lips.

A lengthy silence followed; Amelia guessed her question was deemed impertinent. She had hoped for reassurance that Nell had done nothing wrong and stillbirths were rare.

'Your answer on both counts is yes, although I'm not sure why you trouble yourself with another woman's disgrace when you have your own to attend to.' Sister Evangeline paused to allow her rebuke to take effect. 'Nell Yates committed a mortal sin and the Lord will punish her for it. Some of those who fall are weak characters and cannot be saved.' She cocked her head. 'Are you such a girl, Miss Spencer? Are you weak?'

'No, I'm strong,' declared Amelia. 'And when my baby comes

I'll do whatever it takes to protect us both.' She turned away. In her passion she'd forgotten Kitty's warning to choose her words carefully in the sister's hearing.

Amelia started to make her bed while listening intently for the sound of the nun leaving the room. She'd not realised she'd been holding her breath until the door clicked shut and she exhaled.

12

'I've hardly seen my son.' Amelia fastened her bodice and stood up. 'You never let me hold Joey for long after he's been fed. And you don't answer when I ask how soon we can leave here.'

'I will answer you now then.' Sister Evangeline sounded impatient. 'Leave tomorrow if you wish. But I shall continue to care for this innocent child and protect him from harm.'

'He's coming home with me,' Amelia shouted. For all the cleanliness and godliness in Our Saviour's Mission, she sensed a darkness at its heart she felt compelled to escape.

'You have no home, Miss Spencer. You will struggle to keep yourself, without straying into vice. This boy's spiritual and physical welfare is my concern, not yours.'

'Don't dare talk to me as though I'm of no consequence in my son's life,' Amelia cried. 'He's *my* child. He's eight weeks old, healthy and thriving.'

This confrontation had been building up for weeks. At first, gratitude for the safe delivery of her baby had kept her arguments timid. He had been premature and forceps had been required to help him into the world. But he was perfectly beautiful to her with his fair hair, soft pink skin and eyes of deepest blue. She had fallen in love with her tiny son from the first moment she cradled him in her arms and breathed in his scent. The pain was all forgotten and she had paid her dues to Sister Evangeline, toiling uncomplainingly in the mission's laundry, and knitting and crocheting garments during the evenings.

The nun had a point about her lack of means, but a primal maternal instinct overruled those practicalities. For some weeks Amelia had feared Sister Evangeline might spirit Joey away to a foster home under cover of darkness and he would be lost to her forever.

'Go and join the other girls. Do your knitting until bedtime. Then pray for the Lord's help to control your selfishness.'

Amelia evaded the nun's attempts to usher her towards the door. She could identify Joey's contented snuffling in among the murmurings of the other children in the nursery. Since Amelia had been here she had made, and said goodbye, to several friends as they went to jobs procured by Sister Evangeline. Their babies also disappeared to foster homes.

Sister Evangeline positioned herself in front of the hewn wooden cot. With arms outstretched, the wings of her black habit made her resemble a crow protecting its nest. 'You should leave the mission,' she said coldly. 'Your rebellious attitude is not wanted here. You upset the other girls and the babies.'

'I will go... and so will my son. And I'm not ashamed to say that the other girls should keep their children if they want to.'

'You are insolent, and I have been too lenient allowing you to remain here. The boy will be entrusted to a wet nurse and I will bind you to stop the milk.'

'You won't,' Amelia shouted while her fists tightened at her sides.

'Go away now – your presence is distressing me.'

'Give me my son and I will go! You'll never see us again.' Amelia was in a panic. She either won this battle or faced losing Joey by the morning.

A bang on the door preceded a male voice booming, 'Do you need assistance, Sister?'

'You may enter.' The nun sounded relieved to have backup.

John Wolff had been refixing a door's hinges when the commotion started. He hadn't been the only one to hear it. Whispering girls had congregated on the threshold of the common room, to gawp up the stairs. A glaring look from beneath his thick eyebrows had soon sent them scuttling back inside, gripping their knitting. He had then mounted the treads two at a time and marched to the nursery.

'Miss Spencer is overwrought. Kindly escort her back to her room to rest.'

John Wolff stared viciously at Amelia for several long seconds before summoning her with a jerk of his head.

Her heart was beating so erratically she felt faint. She wouldn't give either of them the satisfaction of seeing her collapse.

She gazed at her son's crib. His wails were tearing a hole in her heart but she turned away, making him a silent promise to return.

'Goodnight, Miss Spencer. You will feel more yourself in the morning, I hope.'

Amelia didn't reply or bestow a glance on the nun; she didn't give a damn if she was being rude. She hurried through the corridors towards her dormitory, conscious of John Wolff close behind.

Winter had turned to spring and she'd become a mother since he and his hound had dogged her footsteps to the mission house on Christmas Eve. In the ensuing months she had scarcely spoken to him although he was often about the place, occupied with odd jobs. Mumbled 'good mornings' on passing were the only conversation they'd shared. Her brother-in-law was unpleasant but Jimmy Burley could be amiable when it suited him. If John Wolff had a spark of charm he kept it hidden.

Amelia opened the door and stepped inside the room, closing it in his face. She stood the other side of the panels with her ribcage heaving over her racing heart.

* * *

'Is the boy asleep?'

'He is. Look how he is thriving.' Sister Evangeline pulled the shawl back from a small face so John Wolff could gaze upon its rosy features.

'He still has the marks... just here.' The sister delicately traced the boy's forehead. 'And his hip bears the wound. I shan't undress him to show you again. He mustn't get a chill.' She tucked the blanket firmly around the child in the cot.

'She won't give him up easily.'

'I know. Her dormitory door must be locked at night from now on. She can't be trusted. She might try to abscond with him.' Sister Evangeline agitatedly rubbed her palms together. 'Mrs Baxter doesn't always heed the children's cries. I should say prayers here and sleep in the nursery, to watch over him.'

'There's no need for that if Spencer's locked in,' John Wolff said gruffly. 'I would miss it if you didn't meet me in the chapel.'

Her pale cheeks took on a faint blush. 'Amelia Spencer's roommate is picking up her bad habits and should leave as well.' Sister Evangeline sighed. 'A pity as Katherine Wheeler showed promise as Mrs Baxter's replacement.'

'Whatever you decide, you can trust me to help you, Evie. None of these creatures will defy me.'

'Don't address me like that.' It was a reprimand delivered with a hint of a coy smile. 'I know I can count on you to watch out for any mischief, Jack.' Sister Evangeline often reverted to using the pet name for the boy she'd grown up with in Essex. He'd been banned from using hers since the day she took vows.

'I could see the bad in the Spencer girl when you brought her here.'

'In her mind perhaps. But her belly was full of love and hope for us all. It was my destiny to meet her when I did.'

'She'll fight to keep her son.' He touched her arm tentatively, prepared to be rebuffed.

Sister Evangeline impatiently crossed her arms and his fingers fell away. 'Spencer was a housemaid before her fall. A similar position outside London would be suitable. She is a strong young woman and recovered quickly from her confinement.'

John Wolff's eyes roved the infant's sleeping face. All he saw was a baby with instrument digs on its forehead from a laboured entry into the world. He'd seen the patch of white skin on the boy's hip. It was similar to a birthmark he had himself on a shoulder. Evangeline saw what she wanted to see because she had been looking for it for so long. 'What if the Spencer girl is no better than the rest? This boy could be a strumpet's spawn. It might be best to let her have him, Evie.'

'Don't call me that.' She snapped at him this time. 'You are disrespectful and forget yourself, John Wolff.'

He inclined his head. 'Forgive me, Sister Evangeline.'

'This child bears the signs of the cross. The crown of thorns and the spear.' She unfurled the baby's minute fingers, seeking a scar on his palm. In time... in time... the scars will emerge,' she murmured to herself as she moved her thumb on clear pink skin. 'On Christmas Eve his mother was turned away when seeking shelter for herself and her unborn baby. He came into the world on Easter Day and she named him Joseph of her own accord. A divine intervention I think. She is too dull to see what I see but that is not a complaint, rather something to be thankful for or she might be more of a nuisance to deal with.' Her fidgeting fingers neatened the cot covers. 'How many more signs do we need? He must stay here and be educated in the scriptures. I will guard him with my life.' She paused. 'You can teach him too, Jack. Carpentry.' She bent to watch the sleeping infant, a look of wonder shining in her eyes. 'He is our saviour. As he grows you will see it as clearly as I do.'

* * *

'Where will you go?' Kitty asked. 'Will you return home to your parents?'

'I can't.' A long pause followed, then Amelia raised her lowered face. 'I'm going to Whitechapel.'

Both girls kept their voices low. They'd heard heavy foot-steps stop outside their door before moving off along the corridor. They had concluded that John Wolff was still prowling about in the mission. Usually, he had gone by lights out.

A burning candle was on the floor between the bunks they perched upon. It was positioned so its glow couldn't leak beneath the door and betray their disobedience. Kitty had listened in disbelief to Amelia's report of what happened in the nursery. Every girl was pressed to agree to fostering, but she'd never heard of downright refusal to let a baby go.

'I should have held my temper. I'll be watched now.'

'It's not your fault, love. Sister Evangeline seems very weird since you gave birth.'

'I'm taking Joey and leaving tonight,' Amelia suddenly announced. 'They won't expect me to act straight away.'

Decision made, she found her carpetbag and started packing her things before her courage failed. She had knitted Joey a shawl and some clothing from scraps of leftover wool. She arranged the garments into a soft nest. It would be easier to carry him like that and warmer for him on a cold spring night.

Kitty was watching her friend's frantic preparations. 'Are you going to Whitechapel to find your sister, Sadie?'

About to answer, Amelia sank swiftly onto the edge of the bed, shielding the candle's brightness with her hands. The sound of footsteps outside was followed by the scrape of a key being turned in the lock.

'Wolffs locked us in,' Kitty hissed as the footsteps retreated.

'That won't stop me.' Amelia knew the nun had given the orders for her incarceration. She took off her pinafore and her mob cap, tossing those onto the bed. 'Sadie showed me how to do it.' She withdrew a hairpin from her bun. 'Dad would lock her in. Didn't stop her though. Jimmy Burley taught her how to pick a lock so they could meet.'

She inserted the hairpin into the keyhole. If this worked, she'd have something to thank rotten Jimmy Burley for. While twisting the metal to and fro she thought of Sadie. She'd not forgotten about Nicholas Dupree either, but had stopped herself yearning for him and things past while at the mission, and she simply tackled each day as it came.

'I want to come with you.' Kitty materialised at her friend's side with an admiring grin as the door was opened inwards an inch. 'I don't want to stay here without you.'

'What about Louise?'

'She's coming with me. I've got a bag like yours to carry her in. I've changed me mind about stopping here to cook. I don't want my daughter fostered. If you can be a proper mum, so can I.' Kitty frowned at Amelia for reassurance. 'We'll manage somehow, won't we?'

"Course we will!' Amelia gave Kitty a hug. 'We'll get a room to share and jobs at Bryant and May. Then when we've saved a bit, we'll find better work and a better lodging.'

'I'm ready for all of that.' Kitty shoved her arms into her coat and grabbed her bag, packed with her belongings.

'So am I,' said Amelia. They exchanged a jubilant, if slightly terrified smile before slipping quietly into the corridor.

13

The nursery was peaceful, the only sound a sporadic snore. A night light should have been burning on the mantelpiece but the candle flame had extinguished in molten wax. A chink between the closed curtains had allowed a thin moonbeam to slant silver across the row of cots. Other than that this room... and the whole house... was dark and still.

While the sister was praying in the chapel Mrs Baxter willingly supervised the nursery. After the bustle and heat of the kitchen the cook liked the peacefulness of being with sleeping babies. If they did wake, she often didn't hear, having glugged from the gin bottle in her pocket. On the sister's return, Mrs Baxter found her own bed in the annexe situated behind the kitchen. The middle-aged widow was dead to the world now, in her comfy chair, jaw sagging onto her shoulder.

Amelia settled her slumbering son into his knitted cocoon. Kitty nipped past to collect Louise. The children remained asleep, emitting only snuffles on being disturbed. Their mothers worked efficiently, making them comfortable for the journey while darting anxious glances at Mrs Baxter, who might jerk herself awake with a snore.

Within a minute, the runaways were descending the stairs in single file, gripping the banister rail in one hand and their precious burdens in the other. They'd left the candle in their room, aware its glow and its encumbrance could be their downfall. They had their hands full as it was. The hallway was unlit but they knew the layout by now and crept to the side exit without mishap. Soon they were out on the path that led to the kitchen garden with a misshapen moon lighting their way. The cold night air sharpened their senses as they walked swiftly along the gravel. They were both straining their ears and eyes for any sign of trouble. It was too soon to feel victorious. They had a distance to go before they were outside the mission's grounds.

They set off towards the avenue of oaks, keeping close to the tree trunks for cover. In a few months the boughs would be lower, weighted down with an abundance of foliage yet to unfurl. They were both dressed in dark clothes, and shadows assisted in their camouflage.

'Here... let me help.' Amelia had noticed Kitty struggling with her bag. They shared the heavier burden of the bigger baby by taking a handle each. Then, on they hurried, over the frost-stiff blades of grass towards the mud track that led to the road, then freedom.

'What will we do if the gate's locked?' Kitty hissed.

'Climb over it. We'll manage,' Amelia reassured her friend on seeing her face drop. 'I can give you a leg up and we can hand the children over the top—' Amelia broke off, her attention caught by a weak light in the darkness. 'Sister Evangeline's in the chapel.' The stained-glass window was giving off a rainbow glow. 'I'd forgotten her routine.'

Kitty grimaced. 'She could come out and spot us.'

'We're almost there.' Amelia knew there was a risk to these rushed plans but she was prepared to take it.

'Hush... hush...' Kitty crooned. Her daughter had begun to protest at the bumpy ride. 'Slow down a moment, I'll have to hold her,' Kitty said as the cries grew louder and an owl shrieked a response. She took the baby out of the bag to nurse her.

Amelia was keeping an anxious eye on the chapel and cursed when two figures appeared in its doorway. 'Sister Evangeline and John Wolff! We must go. Hurry.' Amelia carried the two bags while Kitty concentrated on quietening Louise. They immediately set off with the howling child bumping against her mother's body.

'It's no good.' Kitty shook her head in despair. 'I can't go any further.'

Amelia could hear her son whimpering, but the idea of stopping and going back to the mission to certain punishment and a life without him... she couldn't. She'd go down fighting to keep Joey.

Amelia peered around a tree trunk and urgently reported back. 'Sister Evangeline is still at the chapel. She's pacing back and forth on her own...' The crack of twigs being shattered by heavy feet was explanation enough for John Wolff's absence. 'He's coming after us.' She hurried to Kitty. 'Let me take Louise and you can hold Joey, he doesn't weigh as much,' she babbled. 'Quick! He'll catch us up.'

'I can't.' Kitty sighed in defeat. 'Leave me behind. Sister Evangeline only wants Joey. We'll only slow you down. They'll kick me out after this and I'll come and find you in Whitechapel.'

'We can both escape now.' Amelia cupped her friend's solemn face in her hands.

'I'm too tired. I won't be able to climb over the gate.' Kitty pushed Amelia away. 'Go on! I'll hold Wolff up for as long as I can. I'll say this was my idea and you headed back to the mission when you knew the game was up.'

Amelia hated leaving her friend behind, but knew she was right. Joey was the child in peril and Amelia would do anything to protect him. Including being selfish.

'I'll wait in Whitechapel for you. Meet me at…' The rest of Amelia's farewell was drowned out as a shotgun was discharged and nesting crows flapped and cawed at the disturbance.

Kitty jumped on the spot and started to cry. 'He's warning us to stop.'

'I won't.' Amelia turned and ran, her bag clutched to her chest. She had never felt such terror, yet was determined to get away. John Wolff would expect her to head for the gate and get trapped behind those padlocked iron bars.

She veered off to the left and hurtled along the thicket that edged the boundary of the estate. Her head bobbed up and down as she searched for a patch of hedge that might provide a way through onto the track. Every yard of hawthorn was tangled up in impenetrable ivy and if she attempted to scramble through it she'd fail and injure herself and Joey, too.

She kept going, aware of her son's muffled cries coming from the carpetbag. He was fully awake now and to quieten him she would need to stop and put him to her breast.

The shrubbery came to an end and the boundary line became a brick wall, lofty enough to continue blocking her in. She slowed down, slinging a glance over her shoulder, praying Kitty had managed to stall Wolff. But he'd come after her again. She was certain of that.

She'd need assistance to get over the wall and a tree stump close by drew her eyes. The flat top could provide a stepping stone from which to launch herself. But she needed to get Joey safely up there as well.

A branch overhanging her head was low enough to reach if she went onto tiptoes. With no time to hum and hah she hung Joey's crib on the bough. She pulled the bag, testing its safety. Even when sure it wouldn't fall she went back again and held her arms beneath it... just in case. The rocking motion had lulled her son and she gave the bag another gentle swing.

A dog started barking in the distance; she knew it was now or never if the animal had picked up her scent. Amelia steadied herself on the tree stump then launched herself at the wall. She heard her cloak tear as it caught on a jagged brick, but with her thin arms shaking in protest, up she crawled, skinning her hands in the process until she straddled the top. The coping was digging into her buttocks but she hardly felt the pain and tensed when a woman's scream shattered the quiet. Wolff had caught up with Kitty. Then the gun was fired again and Amelia knew he was talking to her now.

She gulped a ragged breath and stretched out a hand for the bag's handles while praying to any God who'd listen to be merciful to her and her innocent son. Once free of the bough, the momentum of her swinging arm might either take her back the way she'd come or straight over the wall and onto the track the other side.

'It's all right,' she whispered. 'I'll always look after you, Joey. Swear I will.' Bracing one hand on the brick to steady herself, she used her other to yank the handles upwards. The bough flexed then bounced the bag free, dislodging Amelia at the same time. She fell without emitting a sound, twisting in the air to cushion her son as he landed on top of her.

* * *

'The Spencer girl is heading to Whitechapel.'

Sister Evangeline scrambled up off her knees. She was ready for bed and her white nightdress floated about her thin limbs with the quickness of her movement. She had been praying, elbows resting on her mattress and head bowed to her clasped hands. 'Is Kitty Wheeler still lying to protect her friend?'

'That one won't lie to me again,' he said. 'Not since I've put the fear of God into her.'

'Where is the wretch now?'

'Locked in the chapel. She can stay there and say her prayers until morning. If I don't find Spencer hiding in the grounds I'll go to Whitechapel.'

'That's an iniquitous place, is it not?' Sister Evangeline's smooth brow became furrowed.

'The dregs live there. Whores and thieves. The likes of these immoral creatures...' He rolled his eyes to encompass the mission's inhabitants. 'You might find any of them congregating in hovels and alleys in Whitechapel. Gin and fornication is all they know.'

'Not all our girls are without hope. Some embrace right-eousness and lead better lives.'

'You're a good woman, Evie, and do your best for them.' He gripped her hands. 'But they're no good and their offspring turn out the same.'

'That's why my work is so important,' she insisted. 'The children must be saved from damnation. It is possible, if they enter good Christian homes at a young age, before the devil can do his work.'

'Shall we pray together now?' John Wolff rested a paw of a hand on the crown of her short hair. 'I will need His strength and yours to help me succeed in this.'

'It is vital work. Can you do it, Jack? For me?'

Sister Evangeline sank down facing the bed and John Wolff came to his knees behind her. His trembling fingers fastened on the mattress either side of her then came together to clasp the cross lying on her bosom.

'I'll do it. I'll rescue him from the abyss and bring him back to you, Evie. I swear.'

14

'Put down the knife and turn around. You deserve a hiding, so don't do anything stupid or so might I.'

Amelia had almost jumped out of her skin on hearing that growled threat. The loaf she'd been sawing at was abandoned on the table with the knife and she drew her carpetbag towards her, taking care not to disturb the sleeping infant that only she was aware of.

'I said turn around.'

Slowly, she faced him, wishing she'd not been caught scavenging.

It was understandable that Nicholas Dupree would be angry. She'd just broken into his pub while it was still pitch-black outside and was helping herself to his food. Muffled in her hooded cloak with her back to him, she could have been any old thief.

He remained quiet while studying a willowy silhouette that seemed familiar. He struck a match to get a better look before deciding if his eyes were deceiving him. The flame lit up a tress of pale blonde hair before her small fingers pushed it out of sight. It was enough of a clue. The match was shaken out, and two swift strides brought him close enough to pull back her hood.

'Amelia Spencer,' he said hoarsely.

'You remember me.' She sounded relieved.

''Course I do. What the... How did you get in?'

'Broke in... well... The kitchen window wasn't properly shut so I managed to climb through. Sorry. I was hungry... Didn't think you'd mind if I...' She gestured at the loaf while backing against the table to support herself. She felt too exhausted to stay on her feet or carry on making excuses when blocking his view of her son's makeshift cot seemed more important. She'd enough of a problem explaining her own presence for now.

She had walked – or rather limped – to Whitechapel after her fall from the mission's boundary wall had gone her way. A thick mat of brambles had cushioned her drop. Joey's howls of protest at his rough treatment had penetrated her daze and she'd scrambled to her feet. Frantically she'd tested his little limbs, sobbing with relief to find him unscathed in his woolly layers. She'd bolted, travelling behind hedges and hiding in doorways, fearful that Wolff was already in pursuit each time she heard a horse and cart. She had rested her weary and battered body in any useful nook encountered, putting her son to her breast to quieten him, before hobbling towards the East End.

Rather than bang on the tavern door and rouse the household, she'd headed to Sadie's lodging, in the hope of finding her still there. She'd been prepared to humble herself and ask her brother-in-law for temporary shelter, but they'd gone away. An old fellow had opened up, peering a sleepy eye at her while cussing about being disturbed at an ungodly hour. He'd never heard of Sadie Burley he'd muttered when slamming the door in her face.

She'd gone back to perch alongside empty milk churns on the tavern step with Joey snuggled beneath her cloak. As dawn began to brighten the sky, the dairyman appeared at the top of the road. Amelia had made herself scarce to avoid any questions when his horse and cart reached the Anchor tavern. Prowling the perimeter of the building she'd spotted an ill-fitting casement ripe for prising open. She'd hung over the sill to place her son's bed carefully onto the seat of a rocking chair. Expending the last of her energy she'd heaved herself up and over, landing clumsily and making the chair squeak to and fro.

'Your father said you'd gone to a women's refuge.' His astonishment conquered, Nick was ready for some answers. 'I went there to find you. The matron said she'd sent you to St Pancras workhouse. You didn't go there though – I checked.'

'You've spoken to my dad?' Amelia kept her voice down, conscious of those asleep upstairs. 'Why did you go there? They'll think I've lied to them and you're the man involved.'

'Seems I am the man involved, or you wouldn't have come here, would you?' He turned away and lit a lamp, then found the kettle and put it onto the hob.

While he was occupied loading fuel into the range, Amelia studied him. The brightness of burning wood revealed he was barefoot and only wearing an unbuttoned vest and long johns. His breadth of chest and muscled arms were on show, and beneath thin cotton the shape of his strong buttocks and thighs was evident. He didn't seem bothered to be seen like this and perhaps was aware his athletic body and dishevelled black hair looked roguishly attractive to a woman. For no reason she could fathom, other than recalling he worked on a boat, he reminded her of pictures of pirates she'd seen in books. Seeing him in his underclothes reminded her that she was too. Joey had wet her dress and she'd removed it. Beneath her cloak she stood in her petticoats.

'What did my mum say to you?' She forgot about their state of undress by attending briskly to practicalities. She hoped her mother hadn't insulted him.

'Didn't see your mum. Didn't go there.' He turned around. 'Sadie told me your father worked at Ind Coope brewery. I waited for him outside at knocking-off time.' He paused. 'Don't worry, I said I'd met you through your sister and had some money from them to give to you.' He paused. 'He seems a nice fellow, your dad.'

'He is nice. How was he?' Amelia asked earnestly. 'At Christmas he wasn't at all well.' The memory of her father's distress at knowing nothing could be done to mend a second family calamity made her eyes sting with tears.

'He coughed a bit. It was a cold day, just after the New Year.'

So, Nicholas Dupree had soon returned after their parting in the snow. 'Why'd you go looking for me, Mr Dupree?'

'I did have some money for you. Got it off Burley, so I didn't lie to your dad. I know Jimmy's your brother-in-law but it didn't seem right him doing what he did. I went after him... thought if I gave it to your dad it might make things easier for you at home. So, that's what I did. He said he'd put the money by. Could tell he was choked up about you so I kept quiet about Burley stealing it, in case it made things worse.' Nick took the steaming kettle off the hob before it whistled. 'Cut some bread,' he said over a shoulder. 'I'll toast it. We'll have an early breakfast.'

She sawed at the loaf again, handing him the slices to stick on brass forks that were balanced on a stool by the range. Her son had whimpered and, attuned to his every need, she'd detected the sound immediately. Mr Dupree hadn't heard it over the crackle of the fire. He didn't appear to have noticed her dress drying over the back of a chair, either.

She knew she couldn't conceal Joey forever and, itching to comfort him, she lifted him up. Her lips were on her son's forehead when Nicholas Dupree turned around.

'That's some trick,' he said after a long moment.

'Couldn't find a rabbit... you knew I was going to have a baby.'

'Indeed I did.' He came closer to study the boy's fragile profile and wispy fair hair. 'Takes after you.'

'He does.' She smiled for the first time in what seemed a long while. 'He's soaked through. Do you mind if I change his nappy? It was too cold to uncover him outside.'

'Help yourself,' Nick said and drew a chair from beneath the table for her to sit down.

She did so, carefully arranging her cloak on her lap to disguise her petticoats.

'What's his name?' Nick asked, watching the wet nappy being removed.

'Joseph... Joey... after granddad Joe. My dad's dad. He was a lovely man.'

'Where've you been, Amelia?' He took the seat opposite.

'Nowhere nice. Couldn't stand it any longer so I ran away. I remembered you said I could come here, if I needed somewhere to stay.' Amelia concentrated on folding a replacement rag from her bag. She patted dry her son's bottom with it then deftly fastened it, all the while fearing she was about to hear that his offer had been made a long while ago and things had changed since then.

'Where'd you run away from?' he asked, watching four tiny wriggling limbs.

'Our Saviour's Mission. It's a mother and baby home set up

by a nun and she's got a horrible man helping her run the place. They don't want us mothers to keep our babies. They try to take them away to be fostered. I said no. Joey's mine and he stays with me.' She paused. 'My friend was going to come with me and bring her baby. But they tried to stop us leaving and she didn't manage to get away after all. She'll join me soon though; we've plans to find a lodging and start work at Bryant and May. I won't be in your way for long, Mr Dupree, promise.'

'You're not in my way...'

'What the bleedin' hell is going on here then?' The question was snapped out by a woman framed in the doorway.

While they'd been talking, the morning had gained a pale pink light that allowed Amelia to get a look at an attractive brunette.

'Mind telling me who this is?' The woman crossed her arms over her bosom and jerked a nod at Amelia.

'Go back to bed, Polly.' Nick had risen from his chair and started to propel her from the kitchen. 'It doesn't concern you.'

'I say it does.' Polly wrenched herself free, lunging at Amelia to drag her to her feet. Too late, she noticed the baby in danger of sliding off her rival's lap. That came as a shock, but it was the knife pointed at her seconds later that sent her skittering backwards.

'Get away from me and don't dare hurt my baby or I'll hurt you.' Joey was secured tightly in one arm and Amelia continued brandishing the knife.

'You cow... I'll stripe you right back. Coming 'ere, bold as you like, with yer bastard.'

Amelia hated that word but she discarded the knife onto the table, feeling ashamed of her behaviour. Having now revealed how little she had on beneath her cloak she'd got two people staring at her petticoated figure. With different glints in their eyes.

'You've been at it down here. With her!' Polly spat, her pretty face contorting in fury. 'And you kept bleedin' quiet about havin' a kid.'

Nick ducked her swipe and her nails sailed past his cheek.

'Well, if he does have a child, it isn't this one.' Amelia jumped to his defence. She didn't want to cause trouble for him. Yet, had known she would. Her sister had warned her months ago about Polly Mayhew's temper.

Amelia put her son in his cot. 'Don't worry... I'm going. Sorry to bother you, Mr Dupree.' With her dress bundled beneath an arm she made for the door, feeling heartbroken that their reunion had been interrupted. But the fact was, Polly Mayhew wasn't the interloper here, she was.

'Damn right you'll go, you trollop,' Polly shouted.

'Sit down, Amelia. We've not finished talking...' The smell of burning distracted Nick from urging her towards the chair. Cursing, he grabbed the smoking toasting forks just as his brother-in-law propped an elbow on the doorjamb.

'What's all the racket about?' Still half asleep, Lenny Tanner had been sent by his wife to investigate.

While he was rubbing his eyes, Amelia slipped past him into the corridor and headed for the exit.

Lenny followed her, yawning. 'You must be Amelia Spencer. Me wife told me you looked like your sister.' Obligingly, he unlocked the top bolt Amelia was stretching for. 'What brings you back here?' he asked, but not nastily.

'Pleased to meet you, Mr Tanner,' she rattled off, keen to get going. 'I went to see Sadie over the road; she's gone away though. S'pect you already know that. Any idea where I might find her?'

'Islington.' His downturned mouth let Amelia know nothing was forgiven there.

'Was she pregnant?'

He shrugged. 'Nothing to me either way. Me wife sent them both packing; threatened to tell everyone they was trying to blackmail us.' He sounded proud of his wife but Lenny had said all he wanted to on the subject. 'Had your baby then.' He'd heard a distinctive little sound and noticed Amelia's hand disappear into the open bag to quieten it.

She nodded. 'A boy. Did your wife have a boy?'

His chin sagged towards his chest and he rubbed a finger beneath his nose. 'A girl... stillborn.'

'Oh... I'm so sorry. What a terrible shame for you...' From the kitchen came a crash; Amelia imagined Polly Mayhew was hurling crockery. But she hadn't heard Mr Dupree raise his voice.

Amelia guessed Mary Tanner would be next on the scene. Being spotted in a huddle with Lenny – who was in undergarments like his brother-in-law – wasn't a good idea when her dress was under her arm.

Mumbling a farewell, she made her escape. Amelia hurried away up the road, feeling wretched at being thwarted by her own pride rather than by Polly Mayhew.

It wasn't Amelia's way to fight over a man. Andrew Bowman had flaunted in her face his fiancée and she'd wanted to set about him, not the woman who'd also been lied to. This time the man in the triangle was blameless. People like Nicholas Dupree were to be cherished, not used. It would be understandable if he didn't want to remain friends and invite more trouble for himself.

'You won't find yer sister in there, love. Don't waste yer time going inside.'

Amelia raised a hand, shielding her eyes from a rising sun. She'd recognised that gruff voice and knew who was clumping towards her in a pair of old boots. Daisy Root was wearing her grimy clothes and her hair was as wild as Amelia remembered.

'Hello, Mrs Root.' Amelia had taken to this odd individual. Feeling in need of a friend, she stopped to talk to her.

'Didn't that gel tell you she was moving to Islington?' Daisy's tsk of disgust followed. 'Ain't surprised. Inconsiderate some folk.'

'I did know.' Amelia defended her sister. 'Did she tell you her new address?'

'Well, if she did, I weren't listening,' Daisy flatly replied. 'Was glad to see the back of the pair of 'em.' She sniffed. 'Not that the bloke wot's moved in is much better. Miserable ol' git, he is.' Daisy was blunt in her opinions and knew she rubbed people up the wrong way. Sometimes on purpose. This girl she'd taken to. Polite and pretty, she was like a breath of fresh air in this swamp of a neighbourhood. 'You're up and about early, miss, if I may say so.'

'So are you,' Amelia returned with a smile.

'Needed me breakfast. Can't do without me early morning cuppa char 'n' slice o' toast.' Daisy shook the bag she was holding that contained a few groceries. 'Didn't think to see you back here. You 'n' yer sister look alike but nothing else matches up. You're too classy for us. You should get back where you belong.' Daisy patted her arm in farewell and moved past.

Amelia recalled Bill Potts telling her she had class. He'd soon changed his opinion. Mrs Root might too if she knew more about what had happened since they'd last spoken. Joey let out a gurgling sound, drawing back a curious Daisy. She gawped at the bag altering shape then gave a cackle. 'Got a ferret in there, have yer, dear?'

Amelia thought she was joking at first.

'I'd give me ferrets a ride in me bag when me 'n' the ol' man went rabbiting over Hackney marshes. Then after he died I kept a few chickens and a cat for company. Bag came in handy again when I moved lodging. Didn't put all of them in together; there would've been feathers 'n' fur flying all over the place.'

Once Amelia started laughing she couldn't stop.

'The mice are a problem here. I had a real good mouser once. Had him from a kitten but he got in a fight with another tomcat and that was the end of him... Oh, what's up, love?' Daisy's anecdotes tailed off; she could tell the girl's tears had turned from happy to sad. 'You needed to see yer sister urgent, is that it?' She patted Amelia's arm. 'Want to come in fer a cup o' tea? I'd like it if you did.' It was a tentative offer. Daisy was aware most people avoided her company.

With nowhere else to go Amelia didn't hesitate in accepting. Her body still hurt from falling off the mission wall, and lack of sleep was catching up on her. She also needed somewhere private to put her dress back on. 'I'd like that, thanks.'

Daisy tramped inside but the sound of a whistle stopped Amelia following immediately. She turned to see Mr Dupree striding in her direction, beckoning to her.

She answered him with a headshake and that prompted him into a run. Amelia hurried after Daisy, suddenly feeling embarrassed. He'd made it clear months ago that he'd wanted to sleep with her and she'd not had a chance to explain why she'd taken off her dress. Maybe he thought it was to sway him into being nice to her and letting her stay.

Amelia was relieved that Daisy's lodging appeared less ramshackle than anticipated. The woman moved a pile of old newspapers on the settee with an apologetic, 'Keep meaning to have a tidy-up but when you live on yer own, don't seem important.' She gestured for her guest to sit down. Amelia did so with a sigh as the saggy cushion moulded around her aching back. She carefully placed her carpetbag beside her.

'That's it. Take the weight off and I'll make the tea.' Daisy suddenly whipped off her glove and stuck out an equally grimy hand. 'I know you know who I am, but we should be properly introduced. I'm Mrs Root but please call me Daisy.'

'I'll call you Doris, if you like; Sadie told me that's your real name.' Amelia shook hands.

'Oh, I know they take the micky calling me Daisy Root 'cos of these.' The woman elevated a foot encased in cracked leather. 'Actually, I don't mind 'cos I never liked the name Doris and Daisy's pretty and suits me.' She winked in self-mockery. 'But I don't let on to that lot.'

'I'm Amelia Spencer.'

'Pretty name that suits you. Now... fancy a bite o' toast 'n' jam?' Daisy took off her overcoat and, on her best behaviour, shook the rag she used as a tea towel before wiping two cups with it and polishing a teaspoon.

'I would, thank you,' said Amelia. The smoky aroma of burnt toast had clung to her cloak, reminding her of the fracas she'd started and walked away from. Her son suddenly gave a lusty yell that sounded nothing like a cat meowing.

'I've had a baby, Mrs Root.' Amelia lifted Joey, cradling him on her lap while his little pink gums attacked his fist.

Daisy was gazing over her shoulder and there was only a brief, shocked hesitation before she rallied and carried on making their breakfast. 'Ooh... you lucky gel! Babies are better company than a cat, any day.'

Having filled the teapot from the boiling kettle Daisy came over and sat beside her visitor. She took Amelia's bare left hand. 'So, no husband and nowhere to stay, is that it?'

Her quietly sympathetic tone was Amelia's undoing. She

closed her eyes but the tears dribbled through onto her cheeks. 'D'you want me to go?'

'No! I want you stay. For as long as you like.' Daisy dug a hand into her pinafore pocket and drew out an assortment of bits and pieces. Having sorted through some washers and nails she found a brass curtain ring. She slipped it onto Amelia's finger. 'There y'are, Widder Spencer. Shame your husband come a cropper and you so young with this little beauty.' She rubbed the back of her finger against the child's cheek. The hardware on her lap was returned to her pocket and Amelia's shoulder received a pat as she got up. 'It's a cruel world out there, love. I know. You should protect yourself and your baby as best you can. Now let's have that breakfast.'

By the time the tea was poured and the toast spread with jam, Amelia had nodded off with her head lolling on her shoulder.

'Poor lamb...' said Daisy, holding the plateful of toast she'd been about to serve to her guest. She looked at the baby, mewling on his mother's lap. 'Both of you poor lambs.' Daisy picked up the little boy. She laid him beside his mother then found a colourful crocheted blanket and tucked it around the sleeping girl.

Gathering up the child, she began rocking him in one arm, and tucked into the toast before it went cold.

15

'Have you any news for me, my dear?'

Ivy Bowman met her husband's eyes in the dressing table mirror and gave him an apologetic smile. 'Another false alarm, I'm afraid, darling.' She put down her hairbrush, turning on the stool to face him.

'Well... I suppose I should have known it would be. It is hardly surprising that you're barren at your age.'

'I'm thirty-seven,' came her indignant response. 'There is still time for us to have a family.'

'I suppose we must try again then and hope for better luck next time.'

At just after ten o'clock in the morning, Andrew Bowman was ready to leave the house. He breakfasted early, in the hope his wife would laze in bed, and fail to join him.

'I'm off to my club and will eat there. I expect you have your own plans for today.'

'I shall be at home. Next week I thought we could visit my mother for her birthday.' Ivy pushed herself to her feet and tightened her dressing gown belt. She'd no waist to speak of and her bosom and belly almost merged, giving a false impression she might be carrying. Her best feature was her dark brown hair sprinkled lightly with grey. But Andrew wasn't a fan of brunettes or voluptuous females. Blondes with slender curves were his choice.

'I've made other arrangements for next week. You go, my dear, and enjoy yourself.'

'A day hasn't been set. Surely you could keep a few hours free for us to go together.'

'Yes... perhaps.' Andrew glanced at his watch, then at his frump of a wife. Those regular walks along the landing to his wife's bedchamber always necessitated him fantasising about a far sweeter face and body than hers to help him rise to the occasion. He wanted a son and heir to inherit the assets he had sacrificed his freedom to obtain.

He hadn't seen Amelia Spencer for a long while, but hadn't forgotten her. He'd bedded her once and she'd sprouted with his seed. Since his wife was turning out to be a dead loss at reproducing, the Campbells' pretty servant was constantly on his mind, as was discovering whether she had kept or destroyed his child. In the beginning, it hadn't mattered to him what she did. Now he found himself quite obsessed about it. She might have his boy. If the little parlourmaid had let his child grow to a noticeable size she would have been dismissed. By now she'd have given birth.

It was unfortunate the girl had been of no consequence. A minor pedigree and dowry would have been enough for him to propose to her.

His wife knew by now that he'd only married her for her fortune. So what? The deed was done and her inheritance was keeping him in style. The youngest son of a baronet who'd been kicked out of medical school when his father went bankrupt, he'd needed to quickly learn tricks to get ahead. Music had been his hobby and he'd been able to scrape a living teaching brats to play the piano. In the end, he'd achieved greater standing and wealth than his older brother, which was gratifying. He'd no more time for his own kin than he had for Ivy's lot.

Gamblers and whores were his associates of choice. And pretty housemaids, though he was parsimonious and employed only an elderly couple to keep house.

Ivy had been watching her husband's gleaming eyes as he ruminated on things he'd never tell her about. Before the honeymoon was over, she had guessed he was false, but she couldn't forget how special he'd made her feel during their courtship. If she could give him his longed-for heir, she would be special to him again.

Rumours of a divorce wouldn't suit either of them. It had taken Ivy two decades to get off the shelf, but marriage wasn't the idyll she'd expected it to be.

'I'll be off, mustn't let people down,' he said chirpily.

'You let me down all the time, Andrew,' Ivy said to a closed door.

* * *

A commanding whistle from the far end of the bar caught the attention of the landlord of the Prospect of Whitby public house. He frowned and bawled, 'I saw yer. Just wait a minute, damn yer. Got me hands full up here.' He raised two plates of steaming beef and oyster pies before clattering them in front of his diners.

John Wolff drummed some impatient fingers on the bar. By nightfall he wanted to be back at the mission with good news for Evangeline. So far, he'd made no headway in finding the

Spencer girl and her son. If she was here in the East End he'd winkle her out eventually though.

'Right... what you after?' The testy landlord wiped his gravy-stained hands on his pinafore.

John Wolff didn't like to be snapped at. It made his temper rise. He controlled an urge to grab the fellow by the throat and remind him of his manners. 'Half of light ale.'

'Thought you must be after a pint and a whisky chaser the way you was going on.'

The dig was wasted on John Wolff; he turned his back and studied the other patrons. The landlord pulled on the pump and watched the big man whose heavily fuzzed face and pair of mean black eyes were memorable. He wasn't a regular but he'd been in before and hadn't spent much on that occasion either, although he'd had company. Landlords tended to remember tight-fists and flash Harrys. It was the mob in between that merged into the background. 'She's not been in today. If you're looking for Nell Yates, that is.'

John Wolff shot the fellow a sharp glance.

'Saw you with her. You sat over there.' A jab of his head indicated the corner nook. 'Bought her a gin. Just the one.'

'Good memory, you've got.'

The landlord smirked. 'Pays to be observant in this game. Spot troublemakers early that way.' He sniffed and slid another sideways glance.

'Not seen Nell in a while. Any idea where to find her?'

'Gawd knows with that one. An alley... a street corner...' The landlord plonked down the beer. 'She was up the spout – I do know that. But she's not got a kid with her. Poor mite's probably been dumped in an orphanage so she could get up to her old tricks.' He slapped a hand down on the bar, making the beer slops jump. 'Now, can I interest you in a bite to eat? Pies are fresh out o' the oven. Help soak up all that beer you've got there.'

John Wolff grimaced a refusal, letting the man's sarcasm wash over him. He wouldn't mention that Nell's pregnancy had come to nothing at Mrs Grubb's place. He never told anybody everything. Evangeline was the only person he'd ever loved and trusted in his life. Yet even she didn't know all John Wolff's secrets.

'Nell's friend might know where she's hiding.' Wolff started a crafty interrogation. 'No idea where to find her though. Nice-looking girl with fair hair.' He sipped beer. 'About eighteen. Got a baby.'

The landlord's headshake and grimace indicated that description didn't ring any bells.

Wolff finished his drink in two swallows and banged down the empty glass, ready to leave. Then he remembered something else extracted from Kitty Wheeler: Amelia Spencer was heading to Whitechapel in the hope of hooking up with an older sister. 'Nell's other friend's called Sadie. She's married and lodging round here somewhere.'

'Only Sadie that sticks in me mind is Sadie Burley,' said the landlord. 'Pretty blonde, about twenty, I'd say. Not seen her in a while though. Heard talk they'd gone to Islington.' He wagged a finger. 'If you're thinking of looking her up, I'll warn you her husband's got a short fuse.'

John Wolff rubbed a hand over his mouth to conceal a smirk. He never lost fights. 'I'll tread carefully if I cross Burley's path.'

'Be seeing you then... come back when you've got more of a thirst.' The landlord's jaundiced eye fell on the coppers that had been thrown down for the beer. With a mutter, he swiped them up.

* * *

'Why, it's Miss Smith, isn't it? How are you? And how is your friend? I've something important to say to Amelia Spencer. Do you know where I might find her?'

Andrew Bowman was pretending this was a chance meeting but he had been twiddling his thumbs, sitting on a bench in the square, for almost half an hour in the hope she might pass by. The housekeeper had first emerged from the house, causing him to pull down his hat brim and retie his shoelaces until Mrs Liversey had gone. Then Amelia's friend had appeared and he'd quickly sprung up to intercept her.

Lorna Smith couldn't believe he had the brass neck to show his face, let alone ask after the girl whose life he'd ruined. 'Amelia was dismissed,' she said coldly. 'I can't say how she is, as I haven't seen her since.' She edged past with a glare.

Amelia had been popular with her colleagues and bad feeling had started – especially among the female staff – over the closing of ranks by their superiors to protect the man's reputation while the woman's was shredded.

'Just a moment.'

Lorna gave a startled squeak when Bowman barged in front of her again.

'Miss Spencer will benefit when I catch up with her.' He bestowed on Lorna one of his charming smiles. 'Has she returned to her parents' house? They live somewhere in Hackney, I believe.'

Lorna stopped trying to dodge past when it occurred to her he might intend offering to support the child. 'She's not in Hackney.'

'How do you know?' he demanded. He'd convinced himself he had a son. If the boy was in an orphanage then he could claim him. Even if Amelia still had the child he would claim him and make her his mistress. But he needed to act quickly or she might marry and present him with complications. Squaring up to a common labourer wasn't Andrew Bowman's style, but finding his child had become an obsession. Even a daughter might do. In time a grandson would surely arrive to carry on his lineage.

'I went to Hackney to tell her I thought she'd had the dirty done on her.' Lorna looked him up and down in disgust. With his silver-topped cane and gold pocket watch, he had done all right for himself after marrying an heiress.

Andrew ignored her insolence. 'Did her mother tell you her whereabouts?'

Lorna hadn't actually banged on the door. A younger version of Amelia had been talking to a friend by the gate. Having discovered what Lorna wanted, the girl had nervously said both her sisters were likely to be found in Whitechapel, then she'd hurried inside.

'Answer me, damn you! Did her mother tell you her whereabouts?' Andrew barked, forgetting to be charming.

Lorna backed away, fearful of the sudden change in him. 'Whitechapel. That's all I know.' She stepped off the kerb to avoid him and trotted away.

'Impudent hussy,' Andrew called loudly enough for her to hear him. With an imperious shake of his cane, an approaching Hackney cab drew to the kerb and he climbed in.

16

'Please sit down, Mrs...'

'Spencer. Amelia Spencer.' She perched on the hard-backed chair with her heart sinking. She wasn't going to like this place or him.

Ten minutes earlier, when approaching the red-brick premises, its striking clock had reassured her she was on time as she passed by a wall stone embossed with the fancy initials of the Bryant and May proprietors. This area remained foreign to her, but Mrs Root had said a high water tower was the landmark to look for. It had been hard to miss; it loomed over the rooftops in reinforcement of the claim that Bryant and May's match works was the largest factory in London.

Once inside, the noise and smell were so unpleasant Amelia had almost turned tail. But she badly needed a job and an unmarried mother couldn't be choosy. Not that she could admit to the truth of what she was; even in this dismal place they might turn their noses up at a fallen woman.

'You remind me of somebody, Mrs Spencer. I can't quite put

my finger on who.' The manager eyed her up and down as he settled his broad rump in his chair.

'My sister, I expect.' Amelia folded her hands neatly in her lap. 'Mrs Burley's her name. She worked here as a supervisor.'

'Ah... Sadie...' he purred and tapped a hand on his desk. 'I do remember her very well. I can't think why she said she was a supervisor though. Dear me no; she was a frame filler – and an efficient one. Might Sadie want her old job back, do you think?'

'I doubt it, Mr Lomax; she and her husband have moved to another part of London.'

'Well, never mind. You might fill her shoes very nicely. To start, you will pack boxes. The rate is one and ninepence for one hundred boxes.' Lomax paused to hear her agreement.

The pay was even worse than expected but without a penny to her name, Amelia wasn't in a position to turn it down. She jerked a nod.

'Hard workers can soon earn more. Frame fillers get a better rate.'

'I'll do that instead then, Mr Lomax,' she immediately said, determined to have the best pay possible.

He looked taken aback, as though he might tell her she was insolent in her demands. 'I'll give you a trial then and see if you're capable.' He cast an eye towards her written application. 'You're a very young widow.'

'I'd like to work afternoons only as I have somebody to mind my boy then.' She ignored his insinuations. He might not believe she was married but he didn't look the sort to put himself out and investigate.

'Afternoons? Would you indeed?' he scoffed. 'Employees work a ten-hour day. Most people want those hours and over-time. Fourteen hours for some is not unheard of.'

'I can't leave my son for that long.' Amelia rose from her

chair, feeling quite relieved to be rejected. The manager's cultured accent was similar to Andrew Bowman's and she wanted no reminders of him.

Lomax pushed himself out of his chair and approached her, brushing her waist in a way that might have been accidental, but she knew wasn't. Andrew had mastered those subtle strokes, too. His fingers would collide with hers on the piano keys and his hip would nudge against her on the stool as he turned the music. Exciting little tingles had hurtled through her, making her long for more of his touch. What a fool she'd been.

'I'm prepared to oblige you. You're like your sister and that's a point in your favour.' She didn't react to his flirtation and he became officious. 'You must abide by company rules. We pride ourselves on our efficiency in turning out three hundred million matches a day. Slackers aren't welcome at Bryant and May.'

'I understand,' Amelia said, although she didn't. She believed he was grossly exaggerating, unable to comprehend such a number of anything being produced in one day.

He seemed a braggart, not only in what he said, but in his manner. He was a youngish man – late twenties she guessed – with dirty blond hair and a pockmarked complexion. His plump cheeks and straining waistcoat buttons indicated he was doing far better for himself than the pasty-faced match workers. When walking the corridors to this office she'd seen people – mostly women and girls – scurrying to and fro in the distance. Some had been barefoot and balancing crates on their heads that she imagined were crammed with matchboxes. She'd looked for a sign of the horrible 'phossy jaw' disease that Sadie had warned her about and had been dismayed to spot a woman with an oddly shaped chin.

'You can start a trial now and if I have a favourable report you may begin a permanent job on Monday,' he said, beckoning her to follow him.

Out in the corridor the acidic smell and clatter of machinery from the factory floor again assailed her, making her want to turn tail not experience more of it.

'That way...' He pointed in the direction of the noise. 'Tell them Mr Lomax sent you.' He crossed his arms and watched her. When she hesitated he flicked his finger and smiled, aware of her reluctance.

Amelia felt tempted to bolt. But this was the only job she was likely to get and she had an opportunity to discover what she'd let herself in for. If Kitty turned up soon, it wouldn't be so bad, she told herself. She'd have a friend as a workmate.

From the gaping metal doorway of a large warehouse-like room she regarded a factory space crammed with people standing at benches. She noticed a few men were also stationed among the women and girls in here. All had their fingers flying over frames that they were filling with slivers of wood. Between the benches were marching foremen and one of them had spotted her hovering on the threshold. He began weaving between the tables in her direction.

'If yer considering joining us lot, my advice is don't,' said a woman toiling at the closest bench.

Amelia had been aware of this person because she recognised her as the sickly-looking woman she'd seen earlier. Her jaw appeared misaligned and she had sunken eyes set in a pallid complexion.

'You won't want that pretty face ending up like this.' She jutted her chin. 'Phossy jaw... that's what us matchstick gels get. And all fer ten bob a week. If you're lucky and keep yer teeth, you might lose yer fingers instead.' She grimaced in disgust. 'Young gel was told off by the foreman and fined a shilling for saving her fingers and letting the web catch in the machinery. Nice, eh?'

Amelia's heart sank on hearing that but she moved closer to the bench to study the work being done. The woman's movements were too fast to follow, yet she continued staring at Amelia, able to continue toiling without watching what her hands were up to.

'Have you been employed here for long?'

'Too bleedin' long.' The woman grunted a sour laugh that displayed some missing teeth. 'Eleven years. No offence, but you don't look like you'd fit in.'

The woman working opposite at the same bench chipped in, 'She's right, miss. Another girl weren't so lucky. She lost one of her fingers 'cos she did what the foreman said and never minded her hands but saved the machinery. She didn't get no help.' She sent a wary glance at the approaching foreman. 'You're pretty and speak nice,' she gabbled. 'Why d'you want to work in a place like this?'

Amelia couldn't answer that other than to say, 'I need a job. My sister was a frame filler so I thought I'd give it a try.'

'Who's that then?' asked the woman with phossy jaw.

'What are you doing standing there?' barked the foremen striding up to her. 'If you're new and have clocked on, fetch your pinafore and I'll find you a bench space.'

'Mr Lomax sent me for a trial at frame filling,' Amelia blurted. She didn't like the look of this fellow with his piggy eyes and greasy hair. He had his hands stuffed into the pockets of his brown overall and although barely an inch taller than her, he'd tilted back his head to peer down his nose at her.

'Don't dawdle.' He pushed Amelia in front of him then turned back to the women who'd warned her off. 'You can both expect to be docked pay for talking during your shift.'

'That ain't fair!' shouted the woman with phossy jaw.

'No, it bleedin' ain't,' added her bench companion. 'The new gel was asking directions: where to go and start work. We was only being polite and obliging.'

'That's right,' Amelia quickly said. 'That's what happened. They were helping me.' She couldn't believe that workers could be treated so harshly. Losing wages for talking to a newcomer – even if the conversation wasn't as innocent as described – seemed inhumane.

Feeling he was being ganged up on, the foreman again pushed Amelia in the shoulder to make her walk on. She dug her heels in and turned around. 'This is a factory isn't it? Not a monastery where we all take a vow of silence.'

He turned florid and his eyes narrowed on her as the women started tittering. The news of what was happening up by the doorway was spreading. Soon the whole vast space was buzzing with whispers and a hundred pairs of eyes were on her. Not everybody appeared amused or friendly. Amelia guessed that some of these people simply wanted to buckle down, keep their noses clean and go home as soon as they could.

But the woman with phossy jaw gave her a nod and a wink of appreciation. Amelia felt a swell of camaraderie as she fleetingly met the laughing eyes of other girls signalling their support.

The foreman looked her up and down. 'I'll give you the benefit of the doubt as you don't yet know the rules. Soon you will understand that insolence won't be tolerated either, Miss...'

'Mrs Spencer,' she said.

'Married are you, indeed?'

'Widowed,' she contradicted and with her head high she allowed him to propel her by the shoulder to a space at the end of a bench that was situated in the middle of the factory floor.

With the entertainment over, the match girls settled down to work, and the only sound was that of people coughing and the interminable grind of machinery.

The foreman demonstrated how to fill the frames by pushing the slivers of wood into the prepared holes. Dexterity was required and Amelia realised she hadn't yet got it. She received several splinters and sucked her finger.

The woman next to her pulled her hand down from her mouth. 'Don't do that, love. Ever. You'll take in phosphorous.' She extracted the splinter with tweezers kept in her pocket. 'Like that, see.' She showed Amelia how to insert the sticks at a slight angle.

Amelia nodded, miming her thanks having noticed she'd once more gained the attention of the foreman. She continued to fill the frame, finding she was becoming faster and more accurate. The moment one was filled another was pushed in her direction by her neighbour at the bench. She glanced around at her colleagues. They ranged in age from school leavers of about fourteen, to women who looked at least sixty and should be spending time with their grandchildren, not supporting themselves against a wooden bench for ten hours a day.

After an hour the foreman told her the trial was over and she could go. She was glad to make her getaway, feeling suffocated by the noxious atmosphere she'd been breathing in. She emerged into the sunshine and took a gulp of sweet summer air before starting homewards to tell Mrs Root she'd got a job.

As she walked she thought about her unexpected toil this afternoon. Frame filling was unpleasant and boring but the women weren't. Being a Bryant and May match girl might not be as bad as she'd thought. Nonetheless, she knew she would begin looking for other work straight away.

17

'He's back again, dear. I told him to wait outside in case you didn't want to see him.' Daisy Root winked. 'Reckon you might this time, though, judging from the colour in your cheeks.'

Amelia had been rubbing her son's back in the hope he'd burp out his discomfort. She handed him over to Daisy and went to see her visitor. The front door remained ajar but Nicholas Dupree had done as he was told and stayed outside in the corridor. He appeared deep in thought but raised his head as the hinges squeaked. He removed his hands, propped either side of the narrow opening, and plunged them into his pockets.

'This is daft, Amelia. You can't stay here any longer.'

'I can.' She sounded calm yet her heart had started to race the moment she knew he'd come back. This was the fourth time he'd called since she'd moved in with Mrs Root last week. Previously she'd been feeling too jealous of Polly Mayhew to speak to him. But she'd no right to be that way over a woman who'd greater claim on him than she had. She'd missed him, and having his friendship was better than nothing at all.

'The place is a dump. I wouldn't kennel my dog in there.'

Amelia slipped into the passageway, pulling the door to behind her. 'It's a roof over our heads until I can afford something better, and I'm very grateful to Mrs Root for letting us stay,' she said quietly. 'Anyway, we've tidied up the rooms and there's more space now.'

Daisy hadn't been offended by Amelia's suggestion of a spring clean. The woman had pitched in as well and had even scrubbed the windowpanes. Amelia had offered to do the washing. Every scrap of grubby cotton and linen she could find had gone into the laundry copper stationed in the outhouse. Half a bar of Sunlight soap had landed in the steaming water and the dolly had been plunged up and down until her arms ached. It was a communal wash house and the neighbours who'd turned up with baskets of laundry had goggled at the sight of a baby's nappies, and Daisy Root's clothes and sheets, pegged out on the line before theirs that morning.

Since Amelia started lodging here she'd discovered the woman's tough exterior was a protection against bullies. She'd seen the way people – her sister included – took against Daisy Root's eccentricity. She liked to hoard things and was reluctant to part with old newspapers or boxes of rags and old crockery.

A silence had developed between Amelia and her visitor but neither seemed in a hurry to part company. They'd only spoken a handful of times, yet she felt as comfortable with Nicholas Dupree as with her family. Perhaps more so now troubles were tearing the Spencers apart.

He withdrew cigarettes from his pocket without breaking eye contact. 'Where are you all sleeping in there?' He struck a match dipping his head to the flame.

'Daisy's given us the box room and she's using the settee.' Amelia sighed. 'I felt guilty about that but she's adamant Joey and I should have the bed.'

'What work have you found?' he asked, settling his back against the wall and exhaling smoke.

'I start at the match factory on Monday.' She shrugged. 'It'll do for now so I can pay my way. Daisy's been very generous to me.'

He raised her hand to examine the brass ring.

'Daisy's idea. To stop the gossips and to help me get a job.' Amelia withdrew her fingers curling them into her palm. 'I'm an army widow. Don't suppose anybody believes it though.'

'I certainly don't,' he said dryly.

'Well, you know the truth,' she said. 'Anyway, women shouldn't need to be forced into lying to earn a living.' She'd been conscious of her son's little squeaks turning to proper wails. 'I'll have to go now. Thanks for coming to see me.'

'I want you to stay with me over the road. Polly's gone.'

Amelia gave him a sharp glance. 'You didn't throw her out, did you? Because of me?'

'She doesn't live at the pub. She just stays sometimes...'

'Does she?' Amelia said sourly.

He reached past and closed the door she'd opened. 'Polly's been working shifts as a barmaid while Mary's been bad.'

'Mary's not well?'

'She's been suffering ever since she lost the baby. Lenny says it's her nerves playing her up.'

'Must've been dreadful for them. And for Pearl – she's old enough to understand what's happened.'

'Poor kid cried her eyes out.' He sighed, rubbed the back of his neck. 'Anyway Polly's been helping out behind the bar while Mary was laid up.'

'I see...'

'Don't think you do... not really. I'll explain... I want to... if you'll let me.' He touched her face and she noticed his fingers bore tar stains as though he'd come straight to see her after work. She reflected on the morning after they met when his wolfhound was concealed behind tarred rope and barrels of rum on his cart. The memory brought with it a wistful smile.

'Is that a yes?' He glanced past her as her son's crying became shrill.

'Ain't nobody gonna shut that kid up?' Daisy's cantankerous neighbour had poked his head outside. Spotting Nicholas Dupree pushing himself off the wall as though to remonstrate he withdrew, tortoise-like behind his door.

Amelia could understand the fellow being fed up. Her ears were ringing too. 'Joey's never usually like this.'

'Come over to the pub after he's settled down. We can have supper and talk some more: cards on the table about everything.' He dragged on the cigarette then dropped the butt and put a toe on it.

'Thank you... I'd like that.'

He seemed about to lean in and kiss her but with a rather diffident smile he walked away.

Amelia watched him taking off his reefer jacket and pegging it over his shoulder on a finger. His cap stayed tilted back on his dark hair. She felt an urge to call to him to wait because she'd fetch Joey and her belongings and go with him now into that glimmer of midsummer light at the end of the passageway.

Her son was still wailing and she hurried inside, closing the door. Daisy had laid Joey on his back on the divan and he was punching and kicking at air while screaming fit to burst. He was ten weeks old now and gaining weight. She had believed him to be doing fine. So far, he had been a placid little chap but had certainly found his lungs today and she'd no idea what she'd done wrong. She followed a routine, feeding him at the same times as she had at the mission.

'Nappy rash,' explained Daisy. 'It's driving the little lad mad.' She continued stirring a mixture in a bowl. 'This might help: castor oil and oat mash.' She carried the potion to the settee and gently held Joey's thrashing legs in one of her hands then smeared it on his red bottom. 'No leave that off, love.' Amelia had made to put a clean nappy on him. 'The air needs to get to him.' She smiled as the little boy hiccoughed and quietened as the soothing lotion did its work. 'Mother would make this oat mixture for my baby sister. Poor kid had rashes on her arms and legs. She'd scratch till she bled.'

It was the first time Daisy had spoken about her family. When Amelia had asked if she had children of her own she'd not got a straight answer and had taken the hint to mind her own business. 'How is your sister now?' Amelia asked.

'No idea... we lost touch. I was about eleven when Mother remarried and had another baby. She lost her first husband early, like I did.' Daisy paused. 'One husband was enough for me. His were big shoes to fill.' She seemed disinclined to say more about her one and only love, and turned her attention to Joey. 'We'll put a bit more jollop on him later. Next thing he'll need is a teething ring.'

'You seem to have the magic touch, Mrs. Root.'

'Didn't teach you much about caring for kids at that mission, did they?'

'That's because we were all supposed to give up our children.' Amelia impulsively gave Daisy a grateful hug as her son fell asleep. The woman smelled fresher since her clothes had been washed.

'He's lucky to have a mum like you. You could've walked away... most would've.' Daisy busied herself with her sewing box, finding needles and thread to continue repairing a blue dress.

Amelia had been surprised to discover Daisy ran a small business, selling goods from a hired barrow. She had been a seamstress, and now earned a living giving torn clothes a new lease of life. The local totter collected from posh houses, but to him damaged dresses were only fit for rags. Daisy Root thought differently and bought items off him for pennies, then, having worked a miracle, sold them for a profit to working-class women eager to own a classy outfit at a bargain price. The blue brocade dress with a Harrods label that Daisy had been working on had been proudly displayed for Amelia's approval. The stitching was beautifully neat and the patch repair, made with material taken from the hem, almost invisible. In Amelia's opinion, it was a wondrous skill for a woman who dressed like a tramp to have perfected.

She sat on the floor by the settee, with her knees drawn up and her chin resting on them, and watched the weaving needle. 'You don't think I'm selfish, keeping Joey? He could have had a better life... might even have grown up in a rich family.'

'Ain't no better life for a baby than having a mother's love.' Daisy gazed at Amelia. 'I bet Nicholas Dupree would tell you the same about that. Have you and him had a proper talk about things?'

Amelia shook her head. 'I'd like to get to know him better. He invited me to supper.' She got up, taking care not to disturb her sleeping boy.

'Not taking Joey with you?'

'He's comfortable at last and I don't want to upset Mary Tanner.' Amelia frowned. 'I just found out Mary's not been well since she lost her baby. Seeing Joey might rub salt in the wound.'

'That's thoughtful of you. I've no quibble with Mary. But I will say that she's too good for the man she married.' Daisy refrained from commenting on Sadie Burley's part in Mary's problems. 'Losing your baby right at the end must be hard. I miscarried twice about midway and that was bad enough.' Daisy pulled blue cotton tight then stabbed the needle back into brocade.

'Did you have any children afterwards?' Amelia was pleased Daisy trusted her enough to open up about her heartbreak.

'Weren't to be for us to have a family. But we had each other from when we was schoolkids. Happy we was right up until me husband died eight years ago. Pneumonia. He was forty-four but went quickly so that was a blessing for us both.' Daisy pulled herself together with a brisk sniff. 'Off you go then. I'm not going out for a couple of hours. I've this sewing to finish. Then it needs a press. The customer in Poplar can see it later. She'll suit this colour so I hope she takes it.'

'I won't be gone long.'

'Enjoy yourself, love. Me 'n' the lad will be just fine on our own.' Daisy cocked her head. 'That man likes you, y'know.'

Amelia nodded that she did know.

'You're thinking that the baby's dad told you he liked you then buggered off after he'd had his fun.'

Another nod from Amelia.

'This ain't Nicholas Dupree's boy, and lots of women like him so he needn't bother with you,' said Daisy. 'Unless he can't help himself 'cos he knows you're the one for him.' She paused. 'Not everybody's got a good word for him. Those sorts are jealous in my opinion; he's handsome and he's done well, even if he did have a bad start.' Daisy used her teeth to snap cotton. 'If I need you to come and see to Joey, I'll pop over to the pub.'

'What sort of bad start?'

'Not for me to say, love.'

Amelia wasn't satisfied with that. 'Did you know his mum and dad?'

Daisy took a while threading her needle. 'Duprees have been running that pub on and off since I moved to this road. Nicholas was just a toddler then. I've been here more than two decades and seen lots of people come 'n' go. But Duprees have always been at the Anchor.'

'What happened to his parents?'

'I can't say for sure. Victor Dupree had the pub with his wife but I hardly knew him. He was a merchant seaman, away a lot of the time. Disease got him... suppose Mary would've been about nine then. His wife's name was Hannah. She was a hardworking woman. Brought up those kids virtually single-handed even before her husband passed away. She ran that pub. I can see her in Mary. Same type of character... tough, and straight-talking.'

Amelia perched on the arm of the settee to listen to this interesting tale.

'Didn't Mrs Dupree have older children or relatives to help out?' Amelia was thinking of Lenny's role as barman at the tavern. And Pearl seemed to be a good help to her mother.

'They were pretty much on their own. Hannah had an older daughter; I never knew her. She'd made her own way before I moved here.'

'I thought Mary was the oldest. I've not heard another sister mentioned. D'you think there was a falling-out?' Amelia knew how easy it was for a family to break apart over a daughter's scandal.

'I couldn't say, love. Go and have your supper and your talk with Nicholas Dupree. Could be you'll find some answers.'

18

While strolling down the road, Amelia continued to mull over her talk with Mrs Root. The woman was right to say Nicholas Dupree should be the one to disclose his background. He knew a good deal about the Spencers but all Amelia knew about him was he worked on a boat and in a pub.

Her only experience of being on the water was a cherished memory of their dad juggling the oars while she and Sadie waved excitedly. Their mother had been pushing Rebecca in a pram along the bank of a boating lake. As for pubs, she'd never stepped inside one before Nicholas took her home with him.

Probably, Mrs Root believed him to be a reformed tearaway. Sadie had hinted that he was a villain. He'd returned her stolen money after fighting Jimmy. She didn't hold that against him; she would have battled for it herself. But until they knew each other better, she'd proceed slowly. Joey's real father had already turned his back on him; she didn't want her beautiful boy to be rejected again. Better it was just the two of them than to have a man around who found her son a nuisance...

'Oh, sorry, miss, I thought you was somebody else.' The woman stepped back then hurried away.

Amelia had been jolted out of brooding by somebody grabbing her arm. She continued towards the Anchor, enticed by an aroma of meat pies. Seconds later, she recalled the factory manager remarking on her resemblance to Sadie. Turning around she saw the stranger had also come to a halt and was staring at her.

The woman's brown hair was styled in old-fashioned ringlets and her clothes and sensible shoes were of the type an older person might wear. Yet her features put her age at about mid-twenties and her hat sported a jaunty feather. They started towards one another.

'Are you Sadie Burley's sister: Amelia?'

'Yes, I am. I want to find Sadie myself. Do you know if she's still living in Islington?'

'Islington? Last time I saw her she was working at Bryant and May and living in Whitechapel, but I've not been about much lately. Anyway, it don't matter 'cos I only wanted to find her to find you.' She chuckled, making the plumage on her head dance.

'Me?' Amelia's felt a prickle of unease. Had Sister Evangeline sent somebody to search for her?

'Sorry... should've introduced meself. I'm Nell Yates and Kitty Wheeler's been lodging with me. She reckoned you might be stopping with Sadie so I offered to come and find out. She wants to see you.'

'Kitty?' Amelia excitedly clasped Nell's arms. 'Oh, I've been longing to see her. Why didn't she come herself? How is she?'

'Not good.' Nell sighed. 'She'll feel better for seeing you, though.'

'Hasn't she got Louise with her?'

'The nun sent her baby away,' said Nell grimly. 'I think that was the final straw for Kitty. Even worse than—' She broke off. 'She'll tell you all about it herself. Come on, it's not far.'

'I was on my way to visit somebody. Would you wait while I nip and tell him I'll see him later?'

'Oh, well hurry up then. I can't hang about for long,' said Nell grudgingly, and cast a look at the gathering clouds.

Amelia had only covered a yard or two when she came to a halt. Polly Mayhew was approaching from the opposite direction and disappeared inside the Anchor tavern.

'Let's not waste time then, Nell,' Amelia said, retracing her steps. She felt betrayed, having been told Polly Mayhew had gone from there.

Their brisk march through the darkening streets passed too speedily for Amelia to get much out of Nell. The woman had spent the short journey complaining that her lodging wasn't big enough for two and Kitty must find her own place.

'Right, this is it.' Nell turned into an alleyway lined with tall terraces that faced one another across a dirt-filled ditch. She proceeded into a court then pulled an iron key from a pocket and unlocked a squat door to an outhouse.

Once she'd ducked inside, Amelia realised Nell hadn't been moaning over nothing. This stifling space made Daisy Root's home seem palatial in comparison.

'Visitor to see you,' Nell announced, putting a match to the candle on a shelf. She closed the door behind them as drizzle began spattering the cobbles.

'Oh, Kitty!' Amelia rushed over to the bunk beneath the single grimy window. Dropping to her knees, she gave her friend a hug but released her when she gasped.

'Take it easy with her,' Nell warned. 'Poor cow's had a battering.'

'What's happened to you?' Amelia gently cupped Kitty's face. Despite the poor light, she could see several bruises.

Again Nell answered. 'John Wolff set about her after you ran away. Took it out on her more than once.'

There was an intentional note of blame directed at Amelia. She knew she deserved it. If she'd not put the thought of absconding into Kitty's head, her friend would still be at the mission, employed in the kitchen doing a job she'd liked, and with her baby daughter close by.

'I'm so sorry, love.' Amelia sounded wretchedly guilty.

"S'alright,' Kitty whispered. 'Was me own choice to give it a go. Thanks for coming. I wasn't sure Nell would manage to find you.'

'She thought I was Sadie...'

Kitty's smile had soon gone and she shifted on the mattress to ease her aches. 'Where's Joey?'

'Somebody's minding him for me.' Amelia hadn't forgotten her son for a second since she'd left him. He was safe and sound and yet Kitty had lost her daughter, possibly for good. 'Do you know where Louise is?'

Kitty pushed herself into a seated position. 'Sister Evangeline wouldn't tell me. She said I wasn't fit to keep her.'

'Well, she weren't wrong about that, was she?' Nell abruptly butted in. 'You can't even keep yerself and Gawd knows how we would've coped if you'd showed up with a babe in arms.' She put down the candle and turned to Amelia. 'Will you take Kitty to live with you now? I've got me rent to pay so need to work. I can't lose this place 'cos you two have acted bloody daft.'

Amelia felt her temper rising. 'I don't think we were daft wanting to keep our children.'

'I say different,' snapped Nell. 'Sister Evangeline knows good

Christian people who'll bring your kids up right. The likes of us shouldn't have them in the first place.'

'Just 'cos you did what you did, don't mean we have to think like that,' stormed Kitty. 'We know what went on at Christmas when you was laid up at Mrs Grubb's...'

'Don't you dare say nothing about that,' Nell interrupted in a hiss. 'Ain't my fault I had a miscarriage.'

'Is that right?' Kitty mocked.

Amelia grasped Kitty by the shoulders before she could struggle off the bed and let fly.

'That's nice gratitude after I put you up and ain't asked a penny piece for me trouble.'

'She didn't mean it.' Amelia tried to calm things down. 'Kitty's overwrought after what she's been through.' She didn't like Nell's attitude, but she had been kind letting Kitty stay. Whatever Nell had done, it couldn't have been easy for her. Her voice had trembled when speaking of it.

'Are you lodging with your sister?' asked Kitty.

'Sadie's moved off to north London. A widow is putting me up. Don't know what I would've done without her help.'

'There you are then.' Nell pounced. 'Kind old gel like that won't mind another person kipping down on her sofa.'

'Will she let me stay, d'you think?'

'We can ask,' Amelia answered Kitty's plaintive question. 'If she says no, we'll sort something else out.' Daisy Root had been a godsend but the woman was no fool and wouldn't tolerate liberty-taking.

Kitty took that as invitation enough to struggle off the bed and into her coat with Nell's ready assistance. 'Sorry, for what I said, Nell,' Kitty apologised while cramming her belongings into her carpetbag. 'Amelia's right... everything's got on top of me. Won't ever forget you helped me out.'

'Better not 'n' all. Soon as you're on an even keel you can pay me back,' grumbled Nell.

The drizzle was still falling and Amelia pulled up her collar, wishing she'd worn her hooded cloak. She'd left home in the dry and hadn't intended to go far or to be out for long. Mrs Root would wonder where she'd got to.

As they started down the lane, she took Kitty's carpetbag to save her that burden. When some yards away they heard Nell locking up behind them.

'We'll be all right, won't we?' Kitty rested her head on her friend's shoulder.

"Course we will. I've got a job at the match factory. You can get one too, if you want.' Amelia linked their arms to help Kitty along. 'We'll rent our own little place. Like we planned.'

'Nell used to work at Bryant and May,' Kitty said.

'I guessed so when she said she knew Sadie.'

'Nell started working there at thirteen. She says she keeps packing it in, then going back when she's broke. She hates it there. The money's bad and the guvnors expect you to buy your own tools to finish a job. Cheek of it! They dock your pay, too, for little things... tuppence, fourpence... whatever they say, and you can't do nothing about it.'

'I know they're mean like that,' said Amelia glumly. 'I had a trial and found out they don't like you talking while working. And the machinery and phosphorous is dangerous. You have to watch it. But it's a pay packet, Kitty. It'll have to do for now.'

'Yeah... anything'll do for now to keep a roof over me head,' agreed Kitty.

'Nell's doing a night shift, is she?'

'She's not going to the factory,' said Kitty darkly. 'She does half and half, if you know what I mean.' On noticing Amelia's puzzlement, she explained, 'Half respectable work and half not.

Nell takes gentlemen back to that pigsty. That's why she don't want me around, cramping her style.'

'Can see it must be awkward.' Amelia tried not to sound shocked. She suspected her own sister might have been doing something similar to boost her meagre match girl pay. She tightened her arm around Kitty as she struggled to keep up. 'I could kill that brute for what he's done to you.'

'All agreed on one thing then, ain't we?' Nell Yates came abreast of them speaking over a shoulder as she passed by in long strides. 'John Wolff's a swine.'

19

'Oi, get your hands off me!'

Andrew Bowman received a shove that sent him tottering back on his well-shod heels. In his eagerness to start his search for Amelia and his child, he'd overlooked being given a hostile reception in a seedy part of the East End. He'd found a cheap outfitters that hadn't closed for the day, to purchase a labourer's cap and jacket. Disguising himself as poor rather appealed to him now he was rich. But then he'd spotted his quarry and all that was forgotten. He'd dashed out of the shop into a rumble of thunder, and had hurried around the corner to grab her elbow.

Only it wasn't Amelia.

The shapely blonde had swung about and he'd got a proper look at her, black eye and all, beneath a layer of face powder. He thanked the Lord this common-as-muck individual wasn't the mother of his child. She was older and not as pretty as his sweet Amelia. Nevertheless, his loins were stirring in response to a pink tongue tip poking between her lips as she weighed up the situation, and him.

His attitude didn't bother her. Sadie Burley knew from past

experience that West End men despised East End women. Still, some came to Whitechapel for the girls who listened for their carriages, then emerged from the shadows into gaslight, like moths drawn to flame.

He was clearly well-to-do and she was more interested in his wallet than his manners. 'You're an excitable sort, sir...' she purred, holding his arm in case he had second thoughts. It was early to do business but he was youngish and attractive. And she was homeless and down to her last few coppers. 'How can I help you then?'

'I... er... my mistake, madam. I thought you were somebody else.' Andrew wasn't usually tongue-tied with working girls, but her likeness to Amelia had unnerved him, making him stutter.

'I can be whoever you'd like me to be, sir.' She winked and tightened her grip on his sleeve.

He glanced furtively to left and right. Storm clouds had brought a premature dusk and humidity to the atmosphere. But the beads of sweat gathering on his forehead had more to do with the wretched girl knowing her trade than to the weather. She'd come close enough to tease his inner thigh with her fingertips.

'Have you a carriage, sir?'

He shook his head, looking vexed.

She sighed but gave him a game smile. 'Never mind. This way...' She set off, hoping that the girl he had been looking for wasn't about to barge onto the scene and black her other eye for stealing her punter. She quickly headed into Cooper's Alley, praying the rain would hold off for a while.

Lightning whitened a sheet on a washing line as she turned into an empty courtyard. It would be handy for them to hide behind. Not that folk round here would interfere in illicit goings-on as dusk was falling. The sound of an argument was ebbing and flowing behind a broken windowpane patched with newspaper. The nob didn't seem bothered by the noise or the squalor, which told her he wasn't new to this. He'd pulled his hat brim low to conceal his face and was already loosening his trouser buttons.

A few minutes later, he'd thrust cash at her and gone. Sadie dropped her skirt and petticoats then his money, into her pocket. She used her posterior to propel herself off the wall. A glint of metal caught her eye, making her giggle. He'd left his swagger stick in his haste to get away. She examined the silver ram's head top, thinking she'd made a nice little bonus on top of five bob and would visit the pawnshop in the morning.

* * *

Candle in hand, Mrs Root had gone to investigate the commotion in the corridor and received quite a surprise when peering round the edge of the door. 'So, you're back, are you?'

'What if I am?' Sadie had returned to her old lodging in the hope of finding it vacant. She now knew it wasn't after the old misery guts had told her to sling her hook as he was staying put in there.

'You're on yer own, I see, and looking the worse for wear.' A gimlet-eyed Daisy had spotted the girl's shiner. And no prizes for guessing who'd given it to her.

Sadie hadn't wanted a reminder of her husband. Not for the first time, they'd fought after he came in drunk, smelling of cheap perfume. She should have listened to Amelia and taken up her offer to move in together. Her husband had been her weakness and her ruin at fifteen. Years later, nothing had changed. She felt ashamed and frightened; deep down she knew Jimmy Burley would be the death of her.

Mrs Root had got to know both sisters and judged this one to be a parasite. She would feed off her stronger sibling until she'd stiffened her spine enough to move on. 'You're after Amelia, I suppose.'

'Has she been here looking for me, Ma?' Sadie quickly deduced the use of first names meant this woman and her sister were more than acquaintances. It also occurred to her that Mrs Root appeared neater, as though a civilising influence had arrived in her life.

Daisy didn't disclose she had a lodger but followed her instinct to protect Amelia and changed the subject. Something valuable had caught her eye and Daisy liked valuables. 'That's a fancy walking stick you've got there, Mrs Burley. Belongs to your husband, does it? He must be doing well for himself.'

Sadie didn't answer. With shoulders set and chin up, she brazenly swung the cane to sally forth into the stormy street.

'Sadie!' Amelia yelled in delight as she and Kitty burst into the building, glad to have reached shelter. She dashed along the corridor to hug her sister.

Everybody started talking at once then fell quiet when Amelia disappeared inside, having heard her son making his presence known.

Daisy followed her. She had grown fond of Amelia and believed the girl wouldn't say she was going out to one place, intending to sneak off elsewhere. Daisy had been worried enough about her lodger's long absence to nip to the pub to find her. Dupree hadn't seen her, he'd said. He hadn't added anything else but seemed narked. He'd been stood up so had every right to be, Daisy reckoned. In the same way a mother would demand to know what her daughter had been up to, Daisy expected an explanation.

'You didn't get to have your supper at the pub after all,' was her opening shot.

'I didn't... I must say sorry to Mr Dupree in the morning. It was rude to go off without a word.' Amelia was aware she was expected to account for herself. 'I should apologise to you as well for being late back. I was waylaid by somebody who knows my friend from the mission. Have I kept you from selling your dress?'

'You have, and it's too late to go to Poplar now,' said Daisy bluntly. She'd actually decided against going out in a storm. But the girl shouldn't get off scot-free after worrying the life out of her.

'Oh, I am sorry...'

Kitty and Sadie sidled into the room, hoping they wouldn't get their marching orders from Mrs Root.

'Gawd! You did it then?' Sadie had noticed the infant being rocked in her sister's arms. 'Thought you might've come to your senses, Lia.'

'He's beautiful... look...' Amelia proudly brought her son to meet the first of his relatives. 'His name's Joey. And Mrs Root's been a blessing, letting us stay with her.'

'Ain't done nothing much, so don't go buttering me up,' Daisy mumbled, looking secretly pleased.

Sadie continued to gaze at the adorable tot but her wistful smile and her admiration for Amelia's pluck, were fleeting. She saw a millstone and the drudgery of motherhood wrapped up in that knitted shawl. She knew what she would have done in the same situation.

'You're so lucky to have him, Amelia.' Kitty was peering over Sadie's shoulder at the child. 'Can I hold him?'

''Course...' Amelia handed him over.

'Well... I'll put the kettle on then, shall I?' Mrs Root turned up the oil lamp to brighten the room. She was back to her normal self and stood with her arms crossed and a frown on her face. Daisy had lived a fairly solitary existence since being widowed. Inviting Amelia into her home had changed her life... and she had to admit to liking the change.

'Actually, there was something I wanted to ask you, Mrs Root...' Amelia exchanged a glance with Kitty.

'That sounds to me like trouble coming.' Daisy continued setting four china cups, shiny from regular washing since Amelia moved in. 'Let me guess... your friend from the mission needs a place to stay.'

Amelia bit her lip to stop herself smiling at Daisy's ironic tone. 'Would you mind? Won't be for long, promise. As soon as we've both started our jobs at Bryant and May we'll be back on our feet, and out from under yours.'

An expressive roll of her eyes resulted in Daisy sighing, 'Oh, all right then. But you'll have to sort out between yourselves where you sleep.'

'That go for me too?' Sadie sounded uncharacteristically timid.

Practicalities were being addressed now the excitement of the reunion was over. The reason for Sadie's unexpected arrival doubtless came in the shape of the brute she'd married. Amelia had noticed the bruise her sister was trying to conceal from them all. 'Jimmy's clumped you again.'

'I don't look as bad as she does.' Sadie jerked a nod at Kitty.

That was true, but Daisy, swinging a glance between two bashed-up faces, knew which girl she'd sooner have lodging with her. She'd not forgotten Sadie constantly sniping at her. 'You'll have to go, Mrs Burley. Ain't enough room to swing a cat in here; besides, don't want your husband coming looking for you and starting punch-ups. There's a baby to consider.'

Sadie impudently offered the walking stick. 'How about now? You can have this as an advance on me rent, Mrs R. And take it from me, Jimmy knows we're finished.'

'Right-oh. You can join the queue for a bed then, Mrs B.' Daisy accepted the cane and noticed two engraved initials. The owner clearly wasn't Jimmy Burley as the silver bore an entwined A and I. She leaned it against the wall then turned back to make the tea. 'Never been so popular in me life.' She smirked.

* * *

'I'm sorry I didn't turn up last night. I was really looking forward to our supper but something important happened and I want to tell you about it...'

Amelia had spotted Mr Dupree and given chase up the alley that led to the rear of the pub. She emphasised her apology by gripping his hands, but the moment she received a cool look from a pair of silver grey eyes, she let him go. He carried on walking, the wolfhound loping at his side.

'There's no need to be like that. I've offered to explain.' She had spent a restless night, and not wholly due to the cramped sleeping arrangements. She'd been thinking about him, and that kiss he'd almost given her. Yesterday, they'd seemed close to becoming more than friends and this morning a mix of contentment and excitement had seen her hastening towards the tavern to find him. She'd been eager to share with him her news about her reunion with Kitty and Sadie. Seeing Polly Mayhew entering the pub also needed a comment. Amelia had decided not to jump to conclusions, but it seemed he wasn't prepared to be as open-minded.

'There's no need to explain,' he said gruffly. 'I've got the message. I'll stop bothering you now you've started sorting things out.'

She felt deflated... and bewildered; Nicholas Dupree hadn't seemed the sort to be easily offended. She flew after him and tugged on his sleeve. 'Don't you walk away from me! You can bloody well listen now I've made the effort to come to apologise. I couldn't have supper last night because somebody turned up out of the blue and—'

'I know you met up with the boy's father.' He removed her hand from his arm. 'I'm glad things have turned out the way you wanted.'

'What are you talking about?' She gestured impatiently. 'Whatever you've heard, the truth is I had a reunion with my friend from the mission. She's been in a terrible state. She was punished for trying to run off with me and now Sister Evangeline's sent her baby away.' Amelia gave him a challenging stare. 'If you don't believe me, you can come and say hello to Kitty Wheeler right now. And to Sadie. My sister has turned up as well. We're all lodging with Mrs Root.' She'd given him something to think about. And he had given her something to think about.

'What made you think I'd be with Joey's father?'

Nick gazed across the horse at her while tightening its harness. 'A man's been asking after Miss Spencer. I thought he'd caught up with you. Has he?'

'A man? What man?' Amelia demanded hoarsely. 'He wasn't a big chap with a full dark beard, was he? He's the gamekeeper at the mission who chased us the night I escaped. He's beaten Kitty black and blue.'

'He's a toff, not a gamekeeper.' Nick approached and held her in his arms to reassure her. He felt hurt, not vindictive. He truly wanted her to be happy, and had from the moment she'd crept beneath his skin, months ago. He'd deliberately kept things casual between them, knowing this could be how it'd play out in the end. 'Lenny was in a shop yesterday and overheard a fellow asking after a Miss Spencer who'd recently moved to Whitechapel.'

Amelia found it hard to believe that Andrew would come to the East End looking for her. 'There must be loads of Miss Spencers around here. Did Lenny describe him?'

'Light brown hair and aged about thirty. Clean-shaven, clean hands. Well spoken, and well dressed.' He'd allowed himself a glimmer of hope. It had died the moment she turned pale, but he continued anyway to the bitter end. 'He didn't buy anything. Changed his mind and left in a hurry before the outfitter finished writing out his bill. Lenny had a gander at it on the counter... it was in the name of Bowman.'

Amelia pressed her fingers to her mouth in shock.

'It's him, isn't it?' Nick let her go and grunted a mirthless laugh. 'Sorry if I've ruined the surprise reunion.'

This news would have brought great relief not so long ago. But she'd started building her own foundation without Andrew Bowman, and although shaky, it was supporting her and her son. The idea of him barging back into her life was unsettling. Perhaps he intended to ease his conscience by providing for their baby. Yet, he'd called her a schemer and their unborn child a bastard when she'd told him she was pregnant.

'Do you want to meet him?' Nick asked.

'I don't know. He married an heiress and moved up in the world.' She leaned against the wall and stared sightlessly at the ground. 'What could he want?'

'Same as last time, I'd guess.' He regretted being bitter and sarcastic. Nothing could alter the fact that Bowman – unde-serving though he was – had first claim on her.

Nick clicked his fingers at the dog and it leapt aboard the cart. 'You'll be prepared anyway, if he comes back.' Nick sprang up and before the cart moved off he said, 'If things don't work out and he makes a nuisance of himself, let me know.'

Amelia walked back up the lane. Her housemates were grouped outside the lodging, waiting for her.

'I'm going to get me job back at Bryant and May. Kitty's coming with me to see if she can get taken on as well,' said Sadie, straightening her hat.

'I'm off to sell me frock, if I can.' Daisy also outlined her morning's plans. 'Joey's fast asleep in his bed.'

The bed was actually a deep drawer from a bedroom chest, well padded with blankets. Accustomed to the carpetbag's confines, he seemed to like his new nest, and had nodded straight off in it. The iron bed was barely big enough for two adults yet now occupied three and Amelia was scared to have him beside her in case he was rolled on.

'Nick didn't appreciate being left in the lurch then?' Sadie deduced from her sister's preoccupation that things hadn't gone well.

Kitty piped up, 'I can tell him what happened, if it'd help.'

A smile thanked Kitty for the offer but Amelia kept to herself what she'd learned about Joey's father. She'd receive lots of well-meant advice but this decision was hers alone. She wasn't a fool and knew there was a glaring reason a married man would seek out an old flame without the need for it to be spelled out.

'Bryant and May might not pay much but your bosses will expect some standards.' Daisy tapped her cheekbone. 'You two gels need to powder those bruises before turning up asking for work. Right, I'm off...' She started up the road, swinging her bag containing the carefully folded blue brocade dress.

Kitty headed inside to raid Daisy's cupboards for some flour to dab on her face.

'Nick's upset you, hasn't he?' Sadie tilted up her sister's chin.

'Can't blame him for being put out. It was good of him to ask me to supper in the first place.'

'You've fallen for him, haven't you, you daft thing?'

'There's nothing serious between us. We're friends, that's all.' Amelia hoped they were still friends but didn't want to discuss her feelings for Nicholas Dupree. 'What happened to you and Jimmy going into business and making a fresh start?' After a chaotic reunion last night they'd all turned in without an important conversation taking place.

Sadie grimaced. 'We gave it a go but ran up debts buying equipment. Jimmy's working for his uncle's haulage business again.' There was more to it than that: Jimmy's drinking and gambling for a start. Even now Sadie had a stubborn loyalty to her husband, colouring her version of events.

'Are you two really finished this time?' Her sister had said so last night; but Amelia had heard that before.

'He's been messing around with other women.'

'Pot... kettle...' Amelia rolled her eyes.

'That's only business and he nudged me into it anyhow, saying we needed the extra money to get a better place to live.' Sadie didn't deny what she did and defensively tilted her chin. 'When he went to prison I was skint and had no choice in it if I was to keep a roof over me head.'

'Oh, Sadie...' Amelia drew her sister into an embrace.

'It's what we do around here to get by on match worker's wages.' She elbowed herself free.

'We've got one another now,' Amelia said. 'You and me and Kitty and Daisy can be like a family.'

'I'm not settling for living in that dump for long. The neighbours will think Ma Root's running a cathouse. Old gel with three young women who ain't her family, all living under the same roof. I've got plans...'

Sadie didn't want her sister trying to reform her. Their parents had brought them up to be nice and they'd naïvely expected others to be the same. But they weren't. Sadie played men at their own game now. Her duty as a big sister was to make Amelia wise up to the reality of being an unmarried mother. 'You'll need to find somebody to marry you, Lia, now you've got Joey round your neck. And don't go pining for Nick Dupree. Bachelors like him don't take on other men's kids. A widower with youngsters of his own would. That sort aren't choosy. They're after somebody to keep hearth and home together.'

'Thanks a lot...' said Amelia dryly.

She'd missed her supper with Nicholas Dupree and also a chance to find out more about him. But Sadie might know something. 'Daisy told me the Dupree family have run the Anchor for ages.'

'According to Jimmy, Nick took over when he was about twenty-one.'

'I heard he had two sisters...'

'Jennifer was the eldest... nobody knew much about her.' Sadie shrugged. 'Don't try to change the subject. What are you going to do now you've saddled yourself with a baby?'

'More to the point, what are you going to do now you've pinched that fancy walking stick? You'd better tell Daisy it's stolen.'

'It is not!' Sadie sounded indignant. 'I might be a tart but I'm not a thief, you know. Come by it quite by accident. And that's the honest truth.'

Amelia still felt dubious. She hadn't forgotten about losing her savings months ago, or about her sister's phantom pregnancy and a blackmail plot. She suspected Sadie was often economical with the truth. 'You told Lenny you were expecting his baby, didn't you.'

'False alarm, thank God.' Sadie swiftly found another question to ask. 'You never said much about Joey's father. Who was he, other than a piano teacher?'

'Nobody special; Andrew Bowman was just a run-of-the-mill cheat and liar... Here's Kitty.'

'Bloody hell; she looks like a ghost,' snorted Sadie.

Kitty had reappeared with white flour smudges and a grin on her face. She linked arms with Sadie and the pair of them set off up the road towards Bryant and May.

'Good luck!' Amelia called after them then went inside to her son.

20

'This is a nice surprise. You've been quite the stranger recently.'

Mrs Grubb had been expecting to see a pregnant woman begging for shelter. She couldn't have been wider of the mark. She liked the nun. She was a competent and caring midwife despite sometimes saying things to the girls that seemed unfeeling. Mrs Grubb made allowances, imagining her religious beliefs were to blame.

'I must apologise for letting you down when you sent for me, Mrs Grubb. I've not been quite myself for a few weeks.' Sister Evangeline stepped over the threshold.

'I'm sorry to hear it. Nothing serious, I hope?'

'Nothing infectious, thankfully.' Sister Evangeline allayed the woman's fears on that score. She couldn't explain what ailed her. Most people would think her mad in believing what she did. Even her loyal Jack had trouble concealing his scepticism that a very precious boy had been born at the mission. Evangeline hadn't given up hope that he could be found and brought back into her safekeeping. Wolff had wisely said patience and stealth were needed to achieve their goal. The Spencer girl would take fright and bolt otherwise, and then the boy would never be recovered.

'I expect you have been overdoing it.' Mrs Grubb led the way into the parlour. She felt bad for taking offence when Sister Evangeline had declined to attend a difficult birth. An infirmary doctor had been summoned, costing a pretty penny. Before closing the door she instructed an inmate to make a pot of tea.

'I'm seeking somebody and wondered if you might know her whereabouts.'

'I'll help if I can. You certainly need some more trained pairs of hands at the mission.'

'She's a good kitchen maid and Mrs Baxter could do with an assistant.' Sister Evangeline had come to the conclusion that the two runaways would want to be together, and if one could be found so might the other. 'Katherine Wheeler is her name, or Kitty as she likes to be called. She gave birth at the mission but left after her daughter was fostered.'

'Kitty only stayed here a few days,' said Mrs Grubb. 'She wasn't due and I'd no space for her when some urgent cases arrived. I've no idea where she might be now.'

'Well, never mind. I suppose you've no recollection of Amelia Spencer? She also left the mission but wouldn't have returned home. Her parents disowned her.'

'I do recall her because she arrived on the night of the trouble with Nell Yates.' Mrs Grubb sighed heavily. 'Again, I had no room and felt bad turning her away on such a perishing cold Christmas Eve. I sent her to St Pancras workhouse. I wish I hadn't done that.'

'Why was that?' Sister Evangeline was alert to something interesting about to be revealed.

A young woman opened the door for another to enter,

supporting a rattling tray on her pregnant belly. Once they'd left, Mrs Grubb began pouring tea.

'Well, Miss Spencer had gone with you, hadn't she, not to the workhouse as I thought.' Mrs Grubb employed a teaspoon to make her point. 'Of course, I didn't know that until it was too late. A young man came here looking for her, you see. I'd sent him to the wrong place.' She clucked her tongue in annoyance. 'I hope he found her and things came right for them.'

'He was her sweetheart?'

'He didn't actually say so, but I imagine he was. He didn't give much away. Understandable, I suppose... delicate situation.' Mrs Grubb gave a giddy shake of the head that vibrated the lace on her mob cap. 'Very handsome with black hair, and lovely eyes. Polite too. I thought they'd make a lovely couple. She's such a pretty little thing—'

'Did he tell you his name?' Sister Evangeline interrupted.

'He avoided answering that question and I didn't like to insist.' Mrs Grubb sat forward to pat the sister's arm. 'You do look peaky. You take too much on yourself.' She lifted the nun's half-empty teacup. 'Let me refill you with some hot.'

Sister Evangeline quickly rose. 'Thank you, but no. I must get on. Jack is outside waiting to give me a lift back. One of the girls is quite overdue and likely to start contractions today.'

'I think Miss Spencer's young man worked on the river. He arrived on a vehicle and I thought, he must be doing well to have a business wagon. I couldn't make out the name but *Lighterman* was on the side of the cart. It was a winter's evening you see, and dark quite early.'

'Thank you for telling me.' Sister Evangeline went swiftly into the hall and paced impatiently, waiting for the woman to unlock the door.

'I feel rotten sending that poor chap on a wild goose chase. If he'd found Miss Spencer straight away, they might have been a happy family by now. I suppose her baby was fostered, wasn't it?' she said guiltily.

'Thank you for the tea, Mrs Grubb.' Sister Evangeline swiftly descended the steps with the briefest of farewells. She'd rather say nothing at all than be drawn into that conversation.

John Wolff assisted her aboard the cart, then up he bounced and set the animal to a trot. 'What did you find out?' He could tell something had agitated her.

'Bad news, Jack.' Evangeline shot an alarmed look at him. 'Months ago, Mrs Grubb received a visit from a young fellow looking for Miss Spencer. He was almost certainly the baby's father.'

'What's his name?' Jack frowned into the distance.

'He wouldn't say, but she believes he works on the Thames. *Lighterman* was written on the side of his cart.'

Young men rarely had the means to own a horse and cart, so Jack imagined the vehicle had been borrowed from an employer. 'What does he look like?'

'Handsome with black hair, according to Mrs Grubb. She told him she'd sent Miss Spencer to the St Pancras workhouse. I imagine by now they have found one another. They could be married.' Evangeline gripped her hands together in her lap. 'The night I met Amelia she told me the father promised to marry her. Perhaps he decided to after all.'

'It's no virgin birth then...'

Evangeline glared at his rugged profile until he hung his head. 'Sorry, Evie. I was trying to make a joke to cheer you up.'

'You'll cheer me up when you bring back the boy, safe and well.'

'I'll renew my search in the East End with this lead. I won't let you down.'

He regretted having wasted time seeking Sadie Burley in Islington. He had made little headway in his search then came across her husband by chance, vulgar sot that he was. Burley had been bad-mouthing his wife because she'd run off and left him, to scant sympathy from the pub's landlord. Establishing if the girls were sisters no longer seemed important now there was a better lead to follow.

'The child's father will be harder to deal with. We might have lost the boy for good.' Evangeline continued wringing her hands.

'It's not a bad setback, Evie. The lighterman will be a similar character to her sister's husband. Drunken fools are easily dealt with.'

'He might not be that sort. He came to find her, after all. Amelia could attract a decent fellow. She'd been properly educated and had high standards.'

'She'd let them slip though, hadn't she?' he pointed out sourly. 'For him. And she will do so again when they're living in a hovel in Whitechapel. Her handsome lighterman will probably sell you the boy himself for the price of a pint.'

'I know I shouldn't say such a thing... but I hope you are right about him, Jack. My heart aches so terribly I feel it will break in pieces. I pray every night the Lord will forgive me for failing Him. He chose me and I have let Him down.'

'It will be put right. Trust me. I swear on my life I will bring the boy to you safe and well.'

21

'Are you going to do as he says, Sadie?' Amelia was looking at the declaration the foreman had demanded they sign. They'd asked him to leave it with them so they could read it. He'd reluctantly done so but would return soon to collect it. So far there were no signatures on the paper.

'I don't want to be kept slack,' Sadie said evasively.

'What does that mean?' Kitty frowned.

'It means I need me wages,' Sadie snapped.

Nell Yates chipped in, 'You two ain't been here long but me 'n' Sadie have and we know all their tricks. Being kept slack means you don't get no work. And no work means no pay. It's how the management force us to do what we're told.'

'If I could get by with no wages, I wouldn't be working in this dump in the first place.' Sadie took the pencil from the bench and signed her name.

Amelia looked astounded. 'Are you saying that we'll get the sack if we don't agree with something that's untrue.'

'Yes...' chorused Sadie and Nell in unison.

Nell followed suit in putting her name on the paper.

'Bloody hell,' said an anxious Kitty. She looked at Amelia with an apologetic expression then also signed her name.

'I'm not signing it,' Amelia said firmly. She stabbed a finger on the paper. 'Mrs Besant has told the truth and I'm not signing this to say she hasn't when we all know that the working conditions in this factory are awful.' She was fired up with indignation over the unfairness of it all. 'We should be grateful to Mrs Besant and getting behind her, not going against her.'

'She's posh and ain't got a clue,' said Nell chippily. 'She ain't one of us. We're just her pets until something else comes along for her to push her nose into to make a name for herself.'

Annie Besant was an activist who had published a report about the dreadful conditions endured by the low-paid Bryant and May factory workers. Amelia was grateful she had done so but not everybody agreed. The Bryant and May management in particular were livid, and so were their shareholders. But some match workers who needed their pay more than their rights didn't want the boat to be rocked either.

'Mrs Besant's been good to us. I'm glad she's broadcast that we get paid slave wages and work in rotten conditions that make us ill.'

'Well, you do what you want, Miss High and Mighty,' said Nell. 'You'll soon change yer tune when you've got no rent money to give to your landlady and she kicks you out.' With that she stomped off back to her own workbench.

The other three young women remained gathered about Amelia's bench. Kitty sighed and put a hand on her friend's shoulder. 'You was always braver than me, love. I know we all get treated like muck here, but it is a job and I need one. If I'm ever to get Louise back I'll have to prove I can afford to put a roof over her head and feed her.' Kitty went back to work, looking over her shoulder with a hangdog expression.

'Sign it,' Sadie told her sister, before walking off to start work. 'Principles are all very well, but they're not for the likes of us, Lia.'

'They were once,' called Amelia and pushed the paper away from her. 'He can have that back as it is. I won't ever say that Mrs Besant has made up stories about what goes on here.' She was aware of the foreman standing with his hands on his hips watching her. She felt like sticking up two fingers at him but simply turned her back. A moment later he came up behind her.

'What's this?' he demanded and pointed to the bench. 'You'll be fined for having burnts on an untidy table, Spencer.'

Amelia turned around and gazed in amazement at several blackened matchsticks. 'How did those get there? My station was clean.'

'It isn't now and that's tuppence fine. Now clear it up.' He picked up the paper and studied the three signatures. 'Your name's missing.'

'And that's how it'll stay.' Amelia suspected the 'burnts' – as matches that spontaneously ignited were called – were his doing. Debris on the workbench wasn't allowed and workers were fined for that and a host of other minor misdemeanours, including needing to use the toilet. And talking, as she'd already found out. He'd put the scorched wood there to have a reason to fine her. He hadn't liked her from the start when he'd called her insolent.

She watched him marching away looking pleased with himself. She didn't feel cowed. She felt angry and justified in refusing to sign the declaration against Mrs Besant.

* * *

'Have you heard?' Kitty trotted up to Amelia who was waiting at the factory gate to walk home with her.

'Heard what?'

'Girl's been sacked. She wouldn't sign the paper, like you.'

'Who is it?' Amelia frowned in consternation.

'Not sure of her name but the foreman asked her to fill the matchboxes differently to stop them firing and she didn't. So she's sacked. Just like that.'

'Why would she go against an order when we all know we get fined for burnts?' Amelia gave an angry sigh. 'I reckon they've made an example of her. It's nothing to do with filling the boxes. The bosses are warning us to knuckle down.'

Kitty agreed with that theory and was worried for her friend. 'You might be next, love. If you sign, they'll leave you alone.'

'No. I won't bloody sign. Come on...' Amelia linked arms with Kitty. 'Let's go home and forget about this place for a while.'

The next day Amelia arrived for her shift to find a group of women gossiping by the entrance to the factory. She stopped to enquire what was going on.

'Our colleagues in the Victoria building reckon they're stopping work until the gel that got laid off gets taken back.'

'You'll all get sacked, won't you?' Amelia said.

The woman nodded grimly. 'Reckon so. Some want to withdraw labour. Others don't. People are scared of consequences. We wasn't all agreed on it.' She looked at Amelia. 'Did you sign against Mrs Besant?'

'No... and I still won't,' said Amelia. She wasn't sure which side this woman was on until she saw her gap-toothed smile and received a pat on the shoulder.

'Me neither,' the woman said. 'I reckon we should stop work and come out.'

'If you do, I'll be right behind you,' said Amelia and walked through the open gates to clock on.

* * *

'Slumming it, are you, old man?'

Andrew Bowman had been striding along when he heard a goading remark. To be civil, he slowed down, allowing an old friend to catch up.

'Not run into you for a while.' Gideon Lomax's face was sweaty from his dash across the road.

'Still got your nose to the grindstone at that factory over there, Lomax?' Andrew liked to rub it in that he had risen in status through marriage and no longer needed to earn a salary. Since being cut off by his father for misbehaviour, Gideon Lomax was forced to earn a crust.

'I've a directorship lined up. Next year I'll have a seat on the Bryant and May board and we won't have any more of this blasted nonsense.' He jerked his head at a crowd around the factory gates.

Andrew cocked an indolent eyebrow. 'What the deuce is going on? This won't please the shareholders. I've a holding in Bryant and May myself.'

The throng consisted mainly of shabbily dressed women but a few men and children were also blocking the pavement, and part of the road. Their number was being swelled by others filing out from the various factory buildings that made up the Fairfield Road works. 'Has there been an accident in there, Lomax?' Factories were known to be dangerous places and such an incident would stir up the workers.

'Nothing so simple, I'm afraid. Damned troublemakers are trying to write their own rules. We know who the ringleaders are and they'll not get away with it.' Gideon smirked. 'A lot of the women have roots in the Emerald Isle. We've plans to put the cat among the pigeons: bring factory hands down from our plant in Scotland. Set them at one another's throats.'

'What... you mean those women are on *strike*?' Andrew burst out laughing. Men rarely risked going on an all-out strike that shut down a factory; for women it was virtually unheard of.

'Not for long I'd say.' Andrew threw a contemptuous glance across the road. 'They'll soon find their senses and get back to work when their bellies are empty. Women like that should know their place.'

Andrew muttered an agreement. Even his docile wife had rather too much to say for herself lately. In anticipation of her being damned inquisitive he'd come to the East End today, hoping to put something right. He'd been trawling the area searching for the little minx who'd stolen his walking stick. Being a gift from Ivy, she was likely to question its absence.

'Not feeling quite the ticket, old chap?' Gideon had noticed his companion had gone a rather odd colour.

Keeping his face lowered Andrew watched from beneath his hat brim as his quarry was joined by a redhead and a large woman with brown ringlets. Then a slender blonde turned up and he choked in astonishment.

'Steady on, Bowman.' Lomax thumped his back. 'Take yourself off home, man. You look sickly.' He glanced left and right for a break in the traffic to scoot back across the road. 'Meeting to attend...' he muttered.

Andrew jerked on his arm to halt him and get some information. 'That group of girls...' He jabbed his finger. 'The blonde... I think I know her father.' He came out with the first thing he could think of.

'An acquaintance of yours lets his daughter work here?' Lomax spluttered. 'Surely not.'

'She looks like somebody I know.' Andrew sounded flustered. 'What's her name? The good-looking girl.'

'Oh, you mean Amelia Spencer. Says she's a widow.' He poked Andrew's ribs with an elbow. 'They all say that when they've a sprog and no husband.'

'She's a mother?'

'She has a son and does short hours to care for him.' Lomax added nastily, 'We've got our eyes on her as one of the ringleaders. She's been stirring the troops along with others with too much to say for themselves. Well, if they don't get back to work we'll sack the whole damn lot of 'em.'

'It's not who I thought... Don't know her.' Andrew couldn't let this man see his excitement at knowing he had a son.

'Perhaps you recognise her sister,' Lomax said slyly. 'Sadie Burley's her name. She's the one looking over at us.'

Andrew quickly turned away, his face as white as his shirt collar. 'Time I was heading home to tea with my wife.' He shook Lomax's hand, then backed away, curbing an impulse to break into a run.

* * *

'If I'd known this was going to happen, I would've stuck it out in Islington with Jimmy. We'll all be out of work after this. Even those of us who didn't want to come out on strike.' Sadie glanced furtively across the road and breathed a sigh of relief to see the posh fellow had gone. She prodded her sister to get her attention. 'I said, I might as well go home to Jimmy.'

'He's no good for you, Sadie,' said Amelia with a frown.

'Neither's this poxy strike,' retorted Sadie. 'People like you have got us all into trouble. I need wages or I'll lose that room I've got me eye on. Once the landlord finds out about this, he'll let it to somebody else.'

'The directors will give us what we want. We've hit them where it hurts.'

Sadie snorted. 'You don't think that lot have consciences, do you?'

'I meant their pockets,' said Amelia, rolling her eyes. 'Bryant and May shareholders will create merry hell to see the factory shut down.'

Amelia was aware that no wages and no job would put her right back where she'd started. But others were worse off. She'd not been a match worker for long. Some women had put years of their life into this place and lost their health to it as well. 'There's talk of a strike fund. Mrs Besant's not the only person speaking out against Bryant and May. There are others who agree with her and will support us if the strike drags on.'

'Well, I should hope so, too,' Sadie huffed. 'Mrs Besant stuck her oar in so the least she and her friends can do is drum up donations from rich people.'

'I don't like the idea of accepting charity. But how else will we get a fair deal?'

'It's all right for you...' Sadie said crossly. 'You've got Ma Root wound round your finger. Not to mention Nick Dupree.'

'I've not seen him in ages,' said Amelia.

No argument had taken place between them but a cold hole had opened up where their friendship had once been. And it seemed Nicholas Dupree had no intention of trying to repair it. Amelia wasn't yet sure how to approach things with the ghost of Andrew Bowman in the background. She'd reasoned it might be best to leave things as they were for now. This strike had changed things. She understood the concerns of people like

Sadie but if they didn't make a stand, nothing would ever change for them or for the people who came after them.

'You joining the protest march to the park, Miss Spencer?' Amelia turned around to find a youth she recognised but hadn't seen for a long while.

'I am marching to the park. What brings you here, young man? Are you polishing our bosses' shoes?' It occurred to her then that Charlie Webb, or Spider as he preferred to be known, wasn't wearing his shoeblack brigade outfit.

'Lost me job on the brigade. Needed money so sold me brushes and polish and got in real trouble over it. I've been working here for a few months now. Hate it though.'

He'd jerked his head at the factory and as his hair swung Amelia noticed his bald patch. She'd seen other children and young women who'd had hair rubbed away by constantly ferrying heavy boxes of merchandise on their heads.

'I asked Mr Dupree if he'd give me a job as a potman in the pub. He said he'd think about it.' The boy frowned. 'Hope he does take me on 'cos me mum's gonna go mad when she finds out we're on strike and I ain't got nothing to give her.'

'It'll be tough for all of us.' Amelia put a hand of encouragement on his shoulder. 'Changes need to be made, and now we've taken the first step, we must all stick together and then we'll win.'

22

'I've been hoping to bump into you. You've been avoiding me, haven't you?'

'I haven't,' Amelia blurted, unprepared for this ambush. 'It's only... I wasn't sure you'd want to see me. I have been avoiding you.' She owned up on a sigh.

'He's a bonny little love. Nick said he's called Joey.' Mary Tanner gazed at the infant cradled in its mother's arms. 'Can I hold him?'

'Of course... if you want to.' Amelia felt awkward, as though she'd been rude in not seeking to have this conversation sooner. There was more to it, though, than not wanting to upset a bereaved mother: Sadie was back and Mary Tanner had every right to feel bitter about that bad penny turning up. 'I'm so sorry you lost your baby, Mary.'

'I know you are,' said Mary. 'He's teething early,' she said knowledgeably.

'Mrs Root thinks so too.' Amelia jogged her son on her forearm to quieten him. 'I wish I knew more about these things.'

'You can ask me. I've had two kids... almost three. Has Joey got a teething ring?'

'Not yet. I'll get him one.' Amelia didn't like to say that she couldn't afford one. Every farthing counted now she was on strike. Mrs Root shouldn't be expected to feed all her jobless lodgers, or to buy teething rings.

'Teddy's finished with his. You're welcome to it and a few other bits and pieces, if you'd like them.'

'Oh, I would, if you're sure...' Amelia eagerly accepted.

'Can't be easy for you lot at Bryant and May.' Mary, like everybody else, knew the match workers were out on strike. 'Why don't you speak to Nick about a job?'

'I'm not sure he wants to speak to me now,' said Amelia. 'Things are different between us. We seem to have fallen out... over nothing, too. It's bloody daft.'

'He's jealous. Lenny told me a stranger's been asking around after you. I can guess who he is.' Mary crossed her arms. 'From your expression, I gather Joey's father's not offering a wedding ring.'

'He's married.'

'Well, I'll say this then: Nick likes you a lot and I reckon you like him.'

'I do,' said Amelia wistfully.

'I don't usually interfere in his affairs 'cos I don't want him sticking his nose into mine. But between me 'n' you, Polly Mayhew's had one husband and Nick's made it clear she'll need to look elsewhere if she wants another.' Mary chuckled. 'My brother's a straight talker with women. He's popular, but not a Casanova. Now I've sung his praises, I'll tell you I don't see eye to eye with him on everything.' She sighed. 'Lenny's not perfect but I married him, for better or for worse. It's my job to keep him in line. I don't need Nick to do it for me.'

'He's only thinking of you.' Amelia stuck up for him, as she always did. 'He speaks highly of you and wants to protect you.'

'I feel the same way about him,' said Mary. 'But some things we have to sort out for ourselves.'

'You must've been like a mum to him, bringing him up from when he was little...'

'Told you that did he?' Mary interrupted with a frown.

Amelia shook her head. 'We've never really had a proper talk about his past.'

'I'd heard she was back.' Mary curled her top lip as Sadie appeared on the street.

'She's broken up with Jimmy. Again. She's going to see about renting her own room. We can't all pack into Mrs Root's place for much longer. Tempers are fraying.'

'Didn't look to me like those two had broken up when I saw them yesterday.'

'You've seen Jimmy hanging around here? With Sadie?'

'Indeed I have... and they were getting along just fine.' Mary puffed in disgust. 'In broad daylight, too. Up an alley. Suits me though, her cosying up to her own husband. If I see her sniffing around mine again I'll have her eyes out. No offence, you being her sister 'n' all.'

'None taken,' Amelia muttered, watching Sadie disappear.

Mary picked up the mats she'd been shaking out when she'd noticed Amelia strolling up and down with her baby. 'Come and get the teething ring when you've a minute,' she called over her shoulder.

Amelia waved and headed back inside. She would never again want to live permanently with Sadie. Sharing a bedroom at home, giggling together after lights out had been good times. But they weren't those children now. They were growing further apart. Her sister thought her stupid to have saddled herself with a baby. Amelia thought Sadie stupid to have squandered her youth and looks on a man who seemed intent on moulding her into his own coarse image.

To keep Joey safe she might have to cut her big sister from her life. His aunt Sadie, part-time prostitute, and his uncle Jimmy, full-time thug, were likely to be a bad influence for a growing boy to be around.

A few minutes after Amelia entered the lodging, Kitty trudged in.

'No luck?' Amelia finished washing up their breakfast things and dried her hands on her pinafore. Her friend's dejection indicated an unsuccessful job hunt.

'I nearly got a chance to be a cook's assistant. Until the woman interviewing me found out I didn't have a reference.' Kitty flopped morosely onto the settee. 'She said I wouldn't get employment without one. Miss Hoity-Toity tore up me application.' Kitty covered her face with her hands. 'I just crept out of her office in case she laughed at me again.'

'I'm so sorry, love.' Amelia was incensed that her friend had been ridiculed.

'I can't hang about waiting for the strike to be over. It might be months and months. Or they might shut the factory down.'

'They won't do that. They get too much profit out of us lot.' Despite sounding optimistic, Amelia was also worried about their future prospects.

'I need a job now or I'll never get Louise back. We can't live off the strike fund. It's less than our wages.'

'I know. But thank goodness for those decent people who are helping us.'

'Yeah... we should be grateful, I know.' Kitty sighed. 'Where is everybody?' She glanced around, taking in the unusually peaceful atmosphere.

'Sadie's looking at a room in Bow and Mrs Root's pegging out nappies. Joey's asleep at last.' Amelia sat down beside Kitty. 'We'll have to get you a reference somehow. You can slap it on the snooty so-and-so's desk.' She settled back into the settee's saggy cushions and remained quiet for a few thoughtful seconds. 'How about a reference from working in a pub kitchen. Would that do?'

'Probably, but...'

'Mary Tanner's a cook and I've just had a nice chat with her.' Amelia slid her friend a mischievous glance.

'Would she do something like that for me?' Kitty's voice quavered in hope.

'No harm in asking. I'll nip down the road and see what she says.'

* * *

'You're off out, are you?' Daisy had come in from the backyard to see Amelia pulling on her coat.

'Mary Tanner's got a teething ring for Joey.' Daisy wasn't nearly as amiable as she'd been when just the two of them lodged together. Amelia didn't blame her for feeling fed up now her home had been taken over by people she barely knew, and was feeding from her own pocket. Even before the strike worsened things, the strain had been showing on them all.

Daisy snatched the swagger stick that had remained leaning against the wall since she'd acquired it. 'S'pose it's a trip to the pawnbroker's for me. I'll bring something in for tea and don't want no complaints about bread 'n' jam.'

'The strike committee is meeting soon. As soon as they distribute money from the fund I'll pay you some rent.' Amelia knew it was the least she could do.

'With any luck, I'll be off to me new kitchen job,' piped up Kitty. 'I'll let you have something from me first pay packet, Mrs Root. You've been kinder to me than me own mum.'

'Oh, you've been no trouble, dear. Neither's Amelia.' Daisy appeared chastened. 'You two are good company. Sadie's the pain in my posterior. She'd better take the room she's looking at. I won't have her here no more.'

* * *

'A lighterman? Take your pick, my friend. Any of those yonder might help you.' Bill Potts had been having a drink in the Crown public house on the waterfront when a bearded stranger appeared beside him at the bar and struck up a conversation.

John Wolff gulped beer and surreptitiously scrutinised the group indicated to him by the fellow's jerked thumb. Not one of the men appeared under thirty-five years of age, or could be labelled black-haired and handsome.

Potts peered along his nose at his unexpected companion. He had been hoping a pal might join him for a drink this evening, but nobody had shown up, so he was amenable to some company.

'The fellow I'm after is youngish with black hair. I'm guessing he's under thirty.'

Bill Potts gave a shrug to indicate such a description could fit a multitude of river workers.

'He knows a woman called Amelia Spencer.' John Wolff hadn't wanted to use her name in case she got wind of the fact he was seeking her. So far, he'd got nowhere in his enquiries and was desperate to be able to tell Evie he'd made some progress.

Potts swallowed noisily and slammed down his tankard. He hadn't forgotten about the trouble that girl had caused him.

'*Now* I know who you mean.' He slapped a flat palm against the bar. 'That cow turned a trick on me that cost me four bob.'

'You saying she's a brass?'

'I know she is. Two florins that dishonest tart took.' Bill had sunk several pints and they'd oiled his tongue or he wouldn't have admitted to being made a fool of to a stranger.

Wolff felt no satisfaction in discovering he'd been right to think the Spencer girl a common drab. He had to report back to Evie and the news would upset her.

'I know where Nick Dupree's to be found,' said Potts. 'I reckon he's the one you're after. Confused me, you did. He ain't only a lighterman, you see. He's got fingers in pies and is a successful businessman. He don't usually mess around with tarts but she hooked him.'

'Some men are damn fools. Married her, did he?'

Potts shrugged. 'Ask him yerself, if you catch up with him.'

Wolff swigged beer. 'Drink in here, does he?'

'Him? He don't need to stay this side of the bar. He's got his own boozer. Anchor tavern in Whitechapel.' Bill winked and tapped his nose. 'Like I said... fingers in pies.'

John Wolff smiled slyly into his empty tankard. 'Lucky so 'n' so.' He clapped Potts on the shoulder in farewell.

'Ain't gonna buy me a drink then? Who are you, anyway? And what you after Dupree for? Business deal, is it?'

Wolff didn't answer, or turn around.

A smirking Bill Potts watched the big fellow nearing the door. He reckoned Nick Dupree was in trouble, and was gleefully anticipating his nemesis being taken down a peg or two by that bearded bruiser. He hadn't forgotten being humiliated by Dupree twice. First, in the street in front of the girl when he'd ended up on his backside in the gutter, and then in front of his pals when Dupree had taken money off him with no trouble at all.

'If you could get me florins back while you're at it, I'd be obliged. Bill Potts is me name, and you'll find me here most evenings,' he cheekily called over a shoulder to a closing door, before mooning into his beer.

23

Amelia's first impression of the Anchor tavern's public bar was that the yeasty, smoky atmosphere was pleasant. The craggy ceiling and wall beams embedded in distempered plaster reminded her of the attic room she'd slept in upstairs, months ago. Sunlight spearing through mullioned windows found floating dust motes and brightened tables ringed with spillages. Adding to the cosy feel was a rather nice patterned rug adorning the blackened boards. That seemed a waste as it was sure to have drink slopped on it.

'It belongs in the back parlour.' Mary had noticed the carpet receiving attention. 'I washed it earlier and left it there to dry off in the sun.' She carried on sorting baby clothes. 'Look what I've found.' A teething ring and a toy rattle were put onto the stack of wool and cotton on the bar. 'Teddy's grown out of these. Everything's clean; I washed it all before putting it away in the bottom drawer.'

There were baby gowns and knitted bonnets and jackets. Bootees and mittens, too, with ribbon laces. Joey's few garments were washed and dried quickly in front of the stove so he could be dressed in them again. But family lore died hard. Blanche Spencer would have dressed her kids in patched rags rather than accept handouts from a neighbour and never live it down.

'I shan't need these again,' said Mary. 'Doctor reckons I'm battered about inside and no more babies for me.' The neat stack of clothes was pushed towards Amelia. 'I'd sooner Joey made use of them than the moths.' Mary rolled her eyes. 'Pearl reckons she's too old for kid's stuff now and wants Joey to have her doll. Teddy shows no interest in playing with it, so here it is.' A fair-haired doll dressed in knitted clothes joined the other things on the counter.

'That's very sweet of her,' said Amelia although the toy was far too big for Joey to get to grips with for quite a while. 'I wish I could pay you for such lovely things.'

'Wouldn't let you,' said Mary in her forthright way.

'I know I've got a cheek after you've already been kind, but would you do me another favour, Mary?'

'Spit it out then and I'll let you know.'

'My friend's found a job in a kitchen. But she needs a reference so she can get taken on. I wondered if you'd oblige.' Amelia paused for Mary's reaction, but the woman still looked puzzled. 'Would you make out she worked in the kitchen here? I can vouch for her being a good cook and she's had a rotten time of it lately. Her baby's been sent away to be fostered and she's heartbroken. She badly needs some good luck and a fresh start. I love Kitty like a sister. I'll do anything to help her, even take liberties like this.'

'Ah, I see.' Mary clucked her tongue in enlightenment. 'I would write it for her, if I could, love. But I didn't have much schooling. Kitty wanted to keep her baby, did she?'

Amelia nodded. The memory of that night, dashing over frosty grass with a burning throat and Joey bundled up in her bag, was only ever a nightmare away. She would wake in the early hours in a cold sweat with her heart pounding. Her frantic hand would seek her son, sleeping in the drawer by the side of the bed.

'I was kept home more often than not to help Mum out. I didn't mind as I preferred cooking to lessons.'

'Mrs Root told me you helped your mum run this place.'

'Did she now? What else she tell you?'

'Nothing really... just that your mum was widowed and that she never knew your sister.'

'Well, she didn't miss much there. And sorry I can't help with the reference.'

'I didn't mean to speak out of turn.' Amelia wished now she'd kept her conversation with Mrs Root out of it. It was the second time Mary had been prickly about the Duprees' history.

'I don't like our family being gossiped about.'

'Don't blame Mrs Root. I was being inquisitive, trying to find out a bit about your brother. Daisy told me to speak to him, not her. I intended to but...' Amelia's words tailed off into a sigh.

'It's not too late to try again. I bet he wants a heart-to-heart as much as you do.' Mary drummed her fingers on the polished bar top, considering matters. 'You could break the ice and ask Nick about doing the reference. He's brainier than me.'

'Would he, d'you think?'

'Now's your chance to find out.' Mary nodded at the window as a horse and cart passed by.

The wolfhound appeared first in the bar. It loped to Amelia's side, wagging its shaggy tail.

'That's a good start,' Mary said with a wink. 'Jet don't take to everyone. Well, I'll just see if I can find some paper to wrap the clothes.' She diplomatically disappeared as her brother strolled in.

Amelia was aware of the closing door and of a spark in the atmosphere in the ensuing quiet. They'd not exchanged a word since the day he'd told her Andrew was looking for her.

'I've come to see Mary. She's been kind and given me some things for Joey.' She knew she'd sounded nervous. Conversation – especially the heated sort – had flowed naturally between them before.

'How is he?'

'Crying a lot. Mary gave me a teething ring to soothe him.' Amelia plunged on, keen to keep things moving. 'How have you been, Mr Dupree?'

'Not bad...' Nick took off his cap and jacket and dropped them on a table. 'Be better still if we drop the formalities.'

'Pardon?'

'My name's Nick; think we know each other well enough now for you to use it.'

'Oh... right then...' She bit her lip. It was a light-hearted rebuke, nevertheless it felt like a setback on a good start.

'How have you been, Amelia?'

She overlooked his teasing tone. 'I've had things on my mind.'

'Bowman's taking his time showing up on his white horse – is that it?'

'No, it is not.' Mary was right then: he was jealous and unable to conceal it.

He went behind the bar, found a bottle of beer and swigged from it. 'Drink?'

'No... thanks...'

'I know it's early, before you tell me.'

'I wasn't going to say anything.'

'Right...'

'There's something I'd like to ask you, Nick,' she rattled off before the friction building turned from good to bad.

'Ask away, Amelia.'

'It's serious. *I'm* serious.'

'As am I...' He gestured with the bottle at a table. 'Let's sit down then. Have a proper talk.' He pulled out a chair for her and took the one opposite. 'Cuppa tea?' he offered.

'I won't, thanks all the same. I can't stop long.' Amelia would have liked to linger over tea and his company but she didn't want to test Daisy's good nature with another long absence. She speedily launched into her request for a reference. Before she'd finished, she knew she'd surprised him despite his expression giving little away.

'All right. If you want me to.'

'Really? You will do it?' The hand he'd rested on the table received a squeeze.

'Why not?' He chuckled and upended the beer. 'Got my first job with a fake reference.'

'Did you?' She mocked him with a headshake. 'You villain.'

'Yeah... 'fraid I am...'

'What was your first job?'

'Apprentice barge lighterman. Took years to earn me stripes.'

'My dad told me a bit about lighters. They're not easy to skipper.'

'Your dad's right about that.'

'You followed in your dad's footsteps then, working on a boat.'

He drank from the bottle again and the silence stretched.

'Maybe... never knew him, so can't say. Did Mary tell you my dad was a sailor?'

'No... Mrs Root said Victor Dupree was a merchant seaman.'

Again, there was a pause, then he said, 'He was.'

'And Hannah was his wife and ran the pub with young Mary's help as he was away a lot. You were just a tot then, weren't you?'

'I was.'

'It's sad you didn't get to know him. Has your mum passed away as well?'

He dropped his chin and rubbed the back of his neck as though considering his reply to that question.

She'd made full use of this opportunity to find out a bit about him, but maybe had overstepped the mark. 'Don't mean to be nosy. It's only... I don't know much about you.'

'D'you want to know much about me?'

'Yes,' she said, her guileless honesty making him smile as he got to his feet.

'Has Bowman caught up with you yet?'

'No. And I hope it stays that way.'

'What will you do if he does find you?'

'Tell him to clear off and leave me alone.' She paid attention to the sprawling hound to avoid a gleam in his eyes making her blush. 'He looks comfortable and he's being good, staying off the clean carpet.'

'He knows it's wet, that's why.' Nick stretched, looking content himself. 'You're all on strike at the factory.'

She nodded glumly.

'Are you looking for other work?'

'All the time. I want wages so I can pay my way with Mrs Root. She's been so kind to me. The match factory is a horrible place. But this unrest is allowing us workers to have a say at last.'

He smiled. 'You're quite the shop steward, I've heard.'

'I don't want to be. Others have more of a grievance, having been there far longer. I just want what's fair for all of us.'

'You deserve what's fair, Amelia,' he said quietly. 'In everything in life. Not only factory work.'

She smiled. 'Thank you.'

'There's a lot I should have told you before now,' he said in a husky tone. 'First off, I'll say there's a job here for you, if you want it.'

'I do want it.' An expectant pause followed. 'Don't want to step on any toes though.'

'You won't.'

Amelia considered her next move. She'd had Mary's reassurance that her brother and Polly Mayhew weren't seriously involved, but she'd rather hear that from him. And judge the truth in it for herself. 'There was more to me not showing up for supper than my friend needing me. I saw Polly come in here that evening so I turned around.'

'Why? I invited you, not her.'

'I thought I'd save you the trouble of breaking up a fight.'

'You didn't need my help last time,' he ruefully observed.

'I admit I behaved badly towards her, but Joey could've got hurt. I'll never let anybody hurt him.'

'The boy'll be proud of you as he grows.'

His quiet compliment was as sincere as it was unexpected, making her eyes prickle with tears. 'You and your sister and Mrs Root have all been good to me,' she said huskily. 'I've been lucky to meet generous people, but I know there'll be hard years to come.' She pushed a speck of fluff on the table with a fingernail. 'Sadie thinks I'm bonkers to burden myself with a child. Sister Evangeline called me wicked and said I'll be damned for denying him his destiny.'

'You don't have to listen to what that nun says.' Nick swiftly came to crouch beside her chair and comfort her. 'She's the wicked one to talk like that.'

'It was selfish to keep Joey when I've no proper home or means to support us both. I can't live off charity forever and neither do I want to. If I'd left him behind he would have had a life I can never provide. But I couldn't—'

'A lot of girls would've grabbed the chance to give up their kid for an easier ride. You didn't. You deserve the luck you've had.' He took one of her hands, brushed his thumb then briefly his lips on the back of it before letting her go. 'This place can be your home and your work. Move in here and help me run the pub. Will you?'

'What about Polly?'

'I wasn't expecting her that evening, but it was an opportunity to set her straight on a few things.' He stood up. 'I told her I want you and me to become more than friends. She's taken her wages and quit working here. I've not seen her since that evening. And I've not really missed her either. That's the truth, Amelia.' He ran a hand through his hair. 'S'pose that makes me seem callous... but that's how it is. I've been thinking about you, not her.' He propped himself against the bar. 'I wanted us to have this conversation sooner, but after Bowman came looking for you, didn't seem much point bringing any of it up.' His grey gaze was solemnly demanding she be frank with him. 'I expect you'll want to take things slowly; I know it's complicated and you've been hurt. All I ask is that you keep me in the picture about Bowman. It'd be understandable if you went with him, being as he's Joey's father. So what I'm saying is, you can have a live-in job... no strings attached. See how it goes.'

It was hard to admit to him of all people that she felt dirty and used for having slept with a womaniser who'd had no real feelings for her. Mary had said her brother played fair with women. Amelia's intuition had already led her to conclude that

Nicholas Dupree wouldn't stoop to trick her into bed in the way her son's father had.

'At one time I would have gladly married Andrew,' she said. 'Now I'm relieved it didn't happen. I don't want him. Or his money. Or his apology, if easing his conscience has brought him to the East End to find me. His wife's welcome to him.' She paused. 'But he is Joey's father.'

'I know. Will you move in here and help run this place?'

She nodded.

'Do you want your old room back upstairs? It's up to you...'

'I liked that attic room, so that would be fine, and... let's see how it goes.' She echoed his words. 'Joey cries all night sometimes. I hope he won't keep everybody awake.'

'I've got used to having kids about the place.'

The reality of coping with a screaming infant in the early hours had come as a shock to Amelia. If, in time, she joined him in his room, it would be a lot to ask a man to put up with when the child wasn't even his.

Aware Mary was hovering just out of sight, waiting to parcel up Joey's things, Amelia decided to finish this conversation at another time. Kitty's problem wouldn't wait though. 'Will you have time to write that reference today? My friend wants to go straight back to the employment agency with it in case she loses out.'

'You've worked in service and know better than me what words to use. You write it and I'll sign it.' Nick took a bowl of water from the bar and placed it onto the floor for the dog to lap at.

'Oh, thanks so much.' On impulse Amelia jumped up and rushed to peck his cheek. She willingly stayed by him when his fingers manacled her wrist to keep her close.

'I've missed you...' he said huskily.

'I've missed you.' She leaned against him, knowing he wanted her to raise her face so he could kiss her; she rested her forehead against his shoulder instead. It wasn't just shyness from knowing Mary could barge in at any moment. That kiss would seal things, take her from being his friend to his lover. Take her from her attic sanctuary to the master bedroom. It would change everything. She hoped to soon be ready for that. But such bridges once burned couldn't be built back. She had in him somebody as dear to her as Kitty and such a friendship was too precious to lose.

Amelia locked her small fingers into his larger ones then raised their coupled fist, kissing his rough skin before slipping free. 'I should get back now; Kitty will be so pleased that you'll do it for her.'

He drained the bottle of beer then swung it between thumb and forefinger. 'I'm doing it for you. As you well know.'

'Why d'you like me?' she asked quietly. 'I'm spoiled goods, Sadie says, and she's not the only one. I've heard Daisy defending me to the neighbours, especially him next door.'

'Makes no difference to me what any of them say. Actually, it does. If Daisy can't shut them up, I will.'

'There's no need for either of you to get involved. I can fight my own battles.'

'That's true...' A subtle smile accompanied the observation.

'I'd understand... wouldn't blame you at all... if you don't think you'll want me here for long.' She searched his face for a hint of his uncertainty. 'You can tell me the truth. I don't want any more lies from a man.'

'Do I think it will last?' He wryly questioned himself. 'It's been eight months already for me with next to nothing keeping the fires alight. So, yeah, this is real enough. And you don't need to tell me there'll be obstacles along the way.' He braced his hands against the bar and watched the hound sniffing for crumbs, while remembering the winter months when it had started. 'I wanted to come back for you at Christmas after dropping you off in Hackney. I didn't; I knew I'd make things worse. I thought your mum 'n' dad would let you stay with them... I honestly did. Nobody should turn their back on a girl like you.'

He paused. 'I know he's a good man, but I had to stop meself shouting at your dad when I found out you'd been sent to a refuge. You weren't there, though, or at the workhouse. You seemed to have disappeared. I thought Bowman must have come back into your life. I told myself it was the best thing; I never believed it.' Nick approached her, trailing his callused fingers on her cheek. 'In the end you found me and since you've been back in Whitechapel I've never stopped thinking about you and wanting things to go right for you. That's the honest truth.' He smiled ruefully. 'It's gone past being horny.' He lowered his head closer to hers on feeling her stiffen. 'Listen, you asked why, and this is it. I told you ages ago that I want you. That's not changed, but you're different or it wouldn't twist my guts every time I think of what you've been through on your own. I don't know why you make me feel like this, Amelia, so don't ask me to put it into words... not until I've read some poetry first, anyhow.'

She looked up into his warm grey eyes. 'I thought about you a lot when I was at the mission. I imagined you'd not want the trouble of a baby but I couldn't ever give Joey up. I was desperate to escape and you were the only person I knew who might shelter us. But I was worried you'd be disappointed to see me.'

'Disappointed? Finding you in a dark room in your petticoat?'

She punched his arm. 'I think you know Joey's nappy leaked on me. I had to dry my dress.'

'Stay with me, Amelia. I'll look after you both, promise.'

A cough announced Mary's intention to break cover. She put paper and string on the counter then briskly walked past with a wink for Amelia. 'Look alive, Pearl, and give me a hand with rolling up the rug.' Her daughter had followed her into the bar to pet the dog and make him roll about. 'Let's get these things wrapped up before the men arrive and make a mess of it all.' Mary started folding paper neatly around the baby clothes.

Amelia helped with the wrapping, but she watched Nick as he went to stare outside. She had also heard the door creak, and seen it swinging from being disturbed.

Nick strode onto the step to swiftly look left and right. He couldn't say why the hairs on his nape were prickling. There'd been no more than a shadow blocking the light for a few seconds and a flow of air on his face to alert him to somebody about to enter the pub. He continued walking up the road and glimpsed, close to the corner, a running man's dark-clad figure. A dog... possibly a mastiff... was loping alongside. Instinctively, he gave chase, covering a good distance before accepting they had too much of a head start on him. Soon man and hound had disappeared from sight.

He retraced his steps, brooding on whether he might have overreacted to a stranger changing his mind about wanting a beer.

'Somebody scarpered without paying, have they?' Lenny had been approaching from the opposite direction when a smile was put on his face by the sight of his brother-in-law sprinting up the road. Nick Dupree wasn't usually unsettled but recently that had changed. 'Who was you after?' Lenny asked, thinking it might have been the Bowman fellow. Nick had seemed worked up on hearing his name.

'Nobody...' Nick said and went back inside the pub.

24

The cottage door had been left ajar and Sister Evangeline burst straight in without knocking. They didn't observe proprieties when alone. As youngsters she and John Wolff had fished in streams, raced through meadows and swum naked in rivers together. Then adolescence – and a youth called Rory Dean – had put a stop to their close friendship for many years.

Evangeline had been delivering a baby when Mrs Baxter stomped up the mission's stairs with a pan of hot water, and a message that the gamekeeper had called to speak to her. Once mother and new-born were resting in their respective beds, Evangeline had hurried away to find him.

'What news?' she demanded breathlessly.

'Very good news, Evie.' A half-butchered brace of hare was abandoned with the knife and he turned to her with a satisfied smirk. 'I've found them.' He paused to let that sink in. 'I've seen them together.'

Evangeline's eyes sparkled in excitement. 'You saw the child?'

'I did not, but he would have been somewhere close by. The Spencer girl and her lighterman were in a tavern. Another woman was present – Dupree's relative I think; also dark-haired.'

'Are they a couple?' Sister Evangeline demanded.

'I think so, but what matter? I'll get the boy back now I know where he is.'

'There's no time to lose. She might not return to this tavern.'

'I know how to do this, Evie: slowly, slowly catchee monkey.'

'Slowly, slowly will get us nowhere,' she scoffed, stamping a booted foot. 'What is the name of this tavern? I'm not afraid to rescue him myself. If I wait for you, the child will be in long trousers, and corrupted beyond redemption.'

'No... you mustn't do that!' He thoughtlessly grabbed her hands to detain her. 'A nun will stick out like a sore thumb in Whitechapel. Spencer will get wind of it and take flight.'

'You're more likely to give her the jitters.' Sister Evangeline grimaced at her slimy fingers.

'I didn't mean to get blood on your hands.' He began wiping away the mess with a cloth. 'I know how to move among those sorts of people without being noticed. I've learned things about Spencer that won't please you. I spoke to a fellow she'd robbed. A dishonest tart is what he called her.'

'Well then, it is even harder to bear that our saviour is still in her keeping.' Impatient with his gentle ministrations, Evangeline snatched the cloth to scrub herself clean. She headed for the door with him following her.

'Don't act rashly, Evie, or you'll set us back.' He barred her exit. 'I'll steal the boy as soon as I know the lie of the land at the tavern.'

'Steal him?' Evangeline gave him an indignant frown. 'We're saving him and bringing him back where he belongs.'

He inclined his head in solemn agreement.

'Very well... I'll allow you to get him but you must be quick and don't bungle it.' She sighed. 'Tell me more about Dupree.'

'He is the landlord of the Anchor tavern...'

'I thought he worked on the river,' Evangeline immediately interrupted.

'He does. His married sister runs the pub. I imagine she was the older woman I saw with them.' He scratched his bristly cheek while ruminating on tactics. 'A woman in charge during the day will make that the best time to strike. Cover of darkness will be lost, though.'

'The child mustn't be harmed.' Evangeline grabbed his beard, giving him a warning shake. 'How do you know all this about Dupree's family? You've not been indiscreet, I hope.'

'I'm always careful with my questions. Dupree has "fingers in pies", according to one fellow I spoke to.'

'Are you saying he's crooked?'

'I believe so, which is helpful. He won't want his dealings exposed.'

'Blackmail him, you mean, to give up the child?' She prowled, considering the wisdom in it. 'I don't know about that, Jack. What more do you know about his character?'

'Dupree seems to be generally respected if not liked by everyone.' Wolff had reconsidered his opinion of the man he was up against. He wasn't a pushover, of that he was sure. 'He has done well for himself. Clever, I'd say. But he's got involved with a harlot.'

'Amelia is lovely... men go for blondes...' Her voice was as sour as her expression.

'That wastrel wasn't worth your tears, Evie.' He came closer to gaze into her large brown eyes. 'You are the most beautiful girl in the world to me.'

'You're an old flatterer. And I'm hardly a girl, Jack.' For a few seconds she became coquettish. 'Well, I can't stop any longer. I must check on the new mother and infant.' She stepped outside and he followed her into a gloomy August afternoon. The summer weather had been disappointing and the landscape, usually gilded with light at this time of the year, looked uninspiring. 'You will go back and rescue the child very soon, won't you, my dear?'

'You can rely on me, Evie.'

'I know I can...' She raised her pale hand to rub against his black-bristled cheek. 'What would I do without my loyal Jack?'

* * *

'That's the reporter from the *Star*,' said Kitty, indicating a youngish fellow holding a notebook and pencil. 'Nell said he's after speaking to the ringleaders. And he's brought a photographer.' She nudged Amelia. 'Reckon you qualify. You was one of the first to refuse to sign the declaration. You should say your piece and get your photograph in the paper. You'll be famous.'

'Don't want to be, thanks,' said Amelia. The last thing she wanted was to broadcast her whereabouts either to Sister Evangeline or to Andrew Bowman for that matter. 'Anyway, he seems busy with the girls from the Victoria building.' Amelia recognised the woman she'd spoken to outside the factory. The young match girl who had been sacked and started the strike was also there. The two of them were gesticulating as they outlined their grievances. 'I'm not a ringleader. I won't claim credit that's not my due. Those women brought about this action and helped to set up a committee and our strike fund. We all owe them our thanks.'

'Thick as thieves with Mrs Besant and her cronies, aren't

they, the Victoria gels?' Nell had overheard Amelia and Kitty talking. She counted her strike money and pocketed it.

'This won't go far,' complained Sadie who had also been checking her cash. She sighed, thinking the small payment wouldn't satisfy her landlord and her husband.

'It's better than nothing,' said Amelia who would give most of her payment to Mrs Root.

They were at Charrington's Hall on the Mile End Road. The hall was crowded with people: Mrs Besant was present with some influential friends. They sat behind a trestle table to distribute the strike fund to the throng of match workers waiting in line for their money and their names to be crossed off the list.

'I'm getting off home.' Sadie saw no further reason to hang about. 'Jimmy'll be waiting.'

'I'll walk with you,' said Nell.

'I'm going to speak to Spider before I go,' said Amelia. 'Will you wait a moment, Kitty?' Having received a nod, Amelia went over to the boy. 'Did you get your job as a potman at the Anchor?' she asked.

He grinned. 'Sort of. Mr Dupree said I can have work on Saturday and see how it goes.'

'I've got a job there too so we'll be colleagues again.' She patted his shoulder and as he trotted to keep his place in the queue she went back to Kitty.

Outside, the July sun was hidden behind clouds and the air felt humid.

'What's up with that lot?' Kitty pointed to a group of hecklers.

As people were emerging from the hall with their fund money they were being catcalled by a group of women and teenage girls. Among their number was a young street seller with a tray around her neck containing matchboxes. Although shod in a pair of decrepit boots she put Amelia in mind of the barefoot child she'd seen on her first day in the East End. She'd been searching for Sadie and filled with anxiety about what the future held for her and her unborn child. It seemed an age ago.

'Those are the matchbox makers who do piece work at home,' said Amelia sadly. 'They're kept slack but won't get anything from the fund.'

'You selfish bleeders,' called one of the women and shook her fist.

'You don't give us a thought, do you?' called another of the group. 'We're Bryant and May match gels 'n' all. How are we supposed to feed our kids now you're on strike at the factory?'

Amelia slowed down. Digging in a pocket she took out her money.

'You ain't gonna give it up!' Kitty exclaimed.

'I'll pay Mrs Root her rent from my pub wages. Mary's nice. She'll understand and give me a sub.' Amelia looked at the gaunt-faced women, some with babes in arms, others with toddlers clinging to their skirts. 'It's not fair, Kitty. It shouldn't be like this.'

'Here... take that with you then.' Kitty sighed and handed over a coin. 'It's only a bob. I'll have to keep the rest 'cos I don't know when I might get a pay packet.'

Amelia took the shilling. 'You've got a good heart, Kitty. D'you reckon Sadie and Nell offered anything up? They must've seen them.'

Kitty's snort was answer enough.

* * *

Gideon Lomax hadn't forgotten the conversation he'd had with his old school chum. It had reminded him that in many respects they were alike but Andrew had improved his luck by marrying well. Gideon ground his teeth every time he remembered having inadvertently tipped off Bowman about an heiress he had his eye on. Before he'd made his own move, Bowman had nipped in with an engagement ring.

He continued striding towards the match factory, fuming over the turn of events at Bryant and May. The company directors had backed down to the strikers, giving a bunch of scruffy women a humiliating victory over their betters.

He'd already passed the pawnbroker's window when it registered that he'd spotted something familiar. He retraced his steps and came to a halt. Thrusting his hands into his pockets, he peered at the fancy cane wedged in the corner with some silver tankards displayed either side. It looked very much like the ebony walking stick he had admired propped against Bowman's armchair in their club.

Gideon tilted his head to read the initials of A and I scrolled into the silver top. A smirk lifted a corner of his mouth. It was Bowman's, and the fellow had disposed of it in the East End. He pulled a handful of coins from his pocket to count some out and then exited the shop several minutes later, congratulating himself on having struck a good deal. The tale the merchant had related about how he had acquired the stick was also making him smile. A local hag, rumoured to be running a bawdy house, had brought it in. The pawnbroker had tapped his nose and winked at Gideon before voicing his opinion that a gentleman had exchanged it for services rendered. Gideon set off towards the factory, whistling, and making good use of his new purchase.

He'd forgotten about being bored, twiddling his thumbs in his office beside silent factory buildings. With no menials to boss about he'd only thunder-faced bosses to pacify. And their sulks were their own fault.

His thoughts were now elsewhere: a plan was hatching in his mind on a way to get his own back on Bowman for stealing Ivy from under his nose.

25

'Oh, Sadie, love. Why'd you go back to him? You must've known this would happen.'

'He swore he'd not do it again.' Sadie trudged inside, cradling her bruised jaw.

'He always tells you that.' Amelia sounded defeated rather than angry as she bolted the door. She hurried her sister along the corridor towards the pub's kitchen.

Seated at the kitchen table was Mary Tanner. She was chopping onions by the light of oil lamps and dropping them into the pan of beef for overnight stewing to fill tomorrow's pies. Wiping her hands on her apron, she stared at her enemy without malice or satisfaction. It was hard to feel anything but pity for a beaten woman. Mary had cause to complain about her husband, but at least he'd never raised a hand to her.

Sadie tilted her bloody chin and gave Lenny's wife a challenging look. In response, Mary took a clean rag from a drawer. 'You'd better smarten yourself up then get off home.'

'Not going home.' Sadie caught the cloth tossed at her.

'Well, you ain't staying here.' Mary turned to Amelia. 'I'll check on the kids. By the time I come downstairs your sister better be gone.'

Sadie sank onto the chair Mary had vacated, gingerly touching her torn lip.

'What happened this time?' Amelia began dabbing crusty blood from her sister's face.

'Jimmy's in debt and in trouble. A bloke said he'll kill him if he doesn't pay up by tomorrow.' She winced as Amelia continued to clean her face. 'He knows we got a rise after the strike. But it weren't much and I can't hand over every penny of me wages. I need money for rent or else...' The explanation tailed off.

Amelia knew her sister had been about to add that she'd go back streetwalking to pay her way.

'Where's Nick?'

'Serving behind the bar with Lenny.' On cue came the crash of a chair toppling over. Some shouting followed as the landlord read the riot act to the customers. Since moving into the pub a month ago, Amelia had discovered that not every commotion ended in bad trouble. Nick had told her these men considered a bit of pushing and shoving as playfulness. Amelia's father wouldn't dream of behaving in such a way. But this wasn't the better side of Hackney. And it certainly wasn't Mayfair.

She wouldn't have it any other way; she was happy living and working in a pub with Nick Dupree and his family.

'Fallen on your feet here, eh, Lia?' Sadie sounded envious, and inhaled the wholesome kitchen aroma. 'Plenty of grub, booze on tap and Nick Dupree to keep you warm at night. You have seen Polly off, haven't you?'

'Never mind about that; what are you going to do? Shall I ask Mrs Root if you can stay with her...'

'I'll sort meself out,' interrupted Sadie. 'You've taken to being a barmaid, have you?'

'Don't go in there much. I do the cleaning. Mary's a much better cook than me, but I'm learning not to burn the eggs.'

'You get on with Mary, then?'

'She's nice and very hardworking.'

'Quite a part of the family, aren't you?' Sadie tried not to sound sour. 'I saw Spider this morning at Bryant and May. He told me he's a potman here most evenings. When he's fifteen he reckons he's going to sea.'

'He's a nice lad... artful... but I think with a good heart. Fancy a cup of tea?'

Sadie shook her head. 'Don't get hitched, Lia; once you're his wife with a brood of kids round your ankles, he'll be chasing women... ah, I see, you're hoping he will propose.' Sadie had read her sister's expression.

'Nick's not like that.'

'They're all like that. You of all people should know that after your toff left you high 'n' dry.' Sadie gestured an apology. 'Don't mind me, I'm just feeling browned off.'

Amelia reached for her sister's hands to comfort her but Sadie pulled back. 'Any vacancies going here?' she asked chirpily.

'Even if there were, Mary wouldn't have it after that business with Lenny.'

Sadie gazed up at the ceiling. 'I should've gone with Kitty to Cambridge. Could've turned over a new leaf out in the sticks where nobody knew me and Jimmy couldn't find me.'

'I had a letter from Kitty.' Amelia was glad the conversation had turned to Kitty's fresh start. She'd secured a kitchen job in a country house with her fake reference. 'I miss her but I'm glad she's happy. She's saving every penny to try and get Louise back then take her away from London and all the bad memories.'

'What's the place like where she works?'

'The farm is huge and surrounded by fields full of cows and sheep as far as the eye can see,' Amelia said.

'Air must stink of manure.'

'How's Nell Yates?' Amelia had another go at being cheerful.

'Nell's handing in her notice next week even though things have turned our way. We're not only getting better pay but have been promised a proper canteen to eat our dinners in away from the workbenches and the phosphorous.' She chuckled, briefly displaying the gap where a tooth had been lost to Jimmy's fist a few weeks' ago. 'I'll believe it when I see it. Same goes for Nell quitting. She's always saying that.' Sadie put her elbows on the table and rested her aching face in her hands. 'Perhaps she will, though, now she's expecting again and wants to keep it. She's moving in with her new feller to care for his kids now his wife's left him.'

'Fingers crossed for her then. Let's have a cup of tea.' Amelia rose from the table to fill the kettle.

'I won't, thanks all the same.' Sadie pushed herself to her feet. 'I'd better be off. Don't want to outstay me welcome and catch a right-hander off Mary. Not up to having another scrap this evening.'

'Where will you go?'

Sadie shrugged that she hadn't yet decided.

'Mrs Root will put you up for the night. She'll be glad of some company. I took Joey over to see her the other day and she said it felt odd living on her own again.' Amelia started replacing her slippers with shoes in readiness to go out. 'I'll come with you and have a word—'

'I'm not going back to Daisy's.' Sadie straightened her hat

and set her shoulders. 'I found that room in Bow all by myself and I'm keeping it.' She hugged her sister. 'Don't worry about me, Lia. Jimmy won't hit me again.'

Amelia felt uneasy and sought for a delaying tactic. 'Are you hungry? There's a steak and kidney pie left from dinner time.' She took the pie off a rack on top of the stove then searched in a drawer for paper to wrap it in.

The moment Amelia's back was turned, Sadie took the knife Mary had been using and pocketed it. Jimmy had threatened to stripe her earlier if she disobeyed him. It wouldn't be the last time he'd do that now the barrier had been crossed. If he did it again she'd threaten him right back. She took the offered pie and pecked Amelia's cheek.

Out in the corridor, Mary could be heard singing the opening bars of 'My Bonnie Lies over the Ocean', to the accompaniment of tankards being thumped on the bar. When they reached the side door Sadie fiercely embraced Amelia.

'I'm pleased for you, Lia. Marry him if he asks. You'll be happy with Nick Dupree; he is different to the others.'

'You'll be happy again, once Jimmy's off your back. Nick will warn him off.'

Loyal to the last Sadie sharply said, 'Jimmy and me can sort this out ourselves.'

'You can't. He's a brute. Look at you.' Amelia felt a pang of uneasiness strengthening. 'Stay with Daisy, just for tonight. Please.' She was reluctant to let her sister go and clasped her by the shoulders.

'If you see Mum and Dad, will you tell them I'm sorry about everything? Tell them I love them.'

'You can tell them yourself once Jimmy's gone. I'll come as well. I want them to know I've got a job and a decent place to stay. Then we'll all be back together as a family.'

'Just tell them what I said.' Sadie removed her sister's hands from her arms and backed away. 'Swear it.'

'I will, I promise. Now come back inside. It's too late to be out on your own. You can stay with me in my room. Sleep on it, then deal with Jimmy in the morning.'

'I can't wait. I want it over and done with.' The words drifted over Sadie's shoulder as she hurried away up the alley, past the gas lamp and into the blackness on the other side.

* * *

After Sadie left Amelia went to bed, but was unable to sleep for fretting about her sister. Half an hour later a tap on the door brought her quickly to it. She was hoping Sadie had returned and asked to see her.

'Mary told me you seemed upset earlier.'

Nick had a hand braced against the wall and a troubled look in his candlelit eyes.

'She told you Sadie turned up.'

'Looking a mess, according to Mary.'

'It's true... Jimmy's beaten her.'

'Do you want to talk about it?'

Amelia nodded and sat on the bed with her knees drawn up and her arms clasping them tight to her chest.

He closed the door and put the candle on the washstand. 'Sadie could have stayed here tonight.' He was keeping his voice low, conscious of the sleeping boy in his cot.

'I asked her to...' Amelia smothered a sob by burying her face against her knees. 'She looked dreadful. I offered to take her over to Mrs Root but she refused. I told her to stay here.' She glanced at him. 'Sadie's my sister and I won't turn my back on her.'

'I wouldn't want you to. You think she's gone home for round two – is that it?'

'Jimmy might knock out another one of her teeth or break her bones. She's scared but won't admit it. She knows he could put her in hospital... or in her coffin.' Amelia lowered her face and started to quietly weep.

'I'll go after her. I might be able to get to her before he does and bring her back.'

She scrambled off the bed and rushed to stop him leaving. 'I don't want you to go. Jimmy's sure to be drunk and he'll pull a knife. It's not your trouble. You don't deserve this.'

Nick drew her against him, crushing her in a hungry embrace.

'Stay with me tonight,' she said. 'I want you to. I don't want to be on my own. Not tonight.' She wiped the heel of her hand over her wet eyes and felt his lips caress her forehead. A moment later he'd eased free with a muttered curse.

Amelia had been aware of rowdiness below but the roaring drunks often jigged and sang their way home from the Anchor tavern.

He came back to her, kissing her with slow patience until she relaxed and slid her arms around his neck. 'Come to my room with me, Amelia.'

She knew why he'd asked: her bed was hardly big enough for one. 'If I disturb Joey he'll not settle again.'

'Get into bed then; we'll manage...' His voice was rough with amusement but he gave her another sweet-as-honey kiss.

Amelia pulled the covers to her chin, watching him as he sat on the edge of the mattress to unlace his boots. The sound of shattering glass brought him upright again.

'Is it Jimmy?' Amelia was soon at the window next to him. 'He might think Sadie's here.'

'It's not him. Lenny's started a fight. One of the crew in earlier took a shine to Mary. He wasn't happy about it.'

Foul language and more breaking glass was heard, then Lenny was seen blundering out of the pub to be immediately knocked down.

Nick cursed in frustration and Joey also vented his annoyance at the disturbance.

'I'll have to go down and sort it out or the coppers will turn up.' He cupped her face in his hands. 'Try again tomorrow?' he suggested wryly as she nursed her son.

She gave him a poignant smile and kissed him softly on the lips. 'At least it wasn't Jimmy.'

'Yeah... at least it wasn't him. I'll go and see your sister first thing in the morning. He'll get a taste of his own medicine if he's hit her again.'

* * *

'I've been looking for you.'

Sadie twisted around, squinting into the gloom as heavy footsteps brought the man beneath a street lantern. A glimpse of his snarling face sent her dashing away but she was soon caught and dragged back by her hair.

The moment he let her go, she straightened her hat and used the back of her hand to remove greasy crumbs from her mouth. 'I'm not working tonight so clear off, you pig.' She was furious to have dropped her pie in the scuffle. This toff had treated her rougher than a docker would.

'I'll be off after you return my property,' growled Andrew Bowman. 'Where's my ebony cane, you rotten thief?'

'Don't know what you're on about. See an ebony cane, do you?' She waved her empty hands in his face.

'Your ponce is swaggering about with it, I suppose. Or you've pawned it.'

'It's only a bloody walking stick...'

He was close enough to see the marks on her face and didn't hide his contempt. Sadie was vain enough not to want a man to be disgusted by her looks. At the age of sixteen she'd been able to draw the admiring eyes of everybody in a room.

He'd startled her; nonetheless, she hadn't forgotten a growing concern. She'd not had a customer since him, and more often than not her drunken husband would roll off her, unable to finish what he'd started. Jimmy didn't yet know she was expecting but would assume a baby to be his. If she ever told him about it. She couldn't make up her mind whether to get rid of it or allow a hope that a child would civilise him. This unexpected meeting might have presented her with another option.

From the start this punter acted as though she reminded him of somebody whose space she could fill. He had a violent side but so did her husband. At least he was a bully with benefits. He was wealthy for a start, and cleanly shaven with a hint of cologne on his skin. She imagined he could eat a meal with his mouth closed and without belching.

Jimmy's rough appeal had once entranced her. After years of him blowing hot and cold, delivering kisses or punches at random, Sadie had grown up. Since Amelia had been back in her life she'd glimpsed the girl she had once been. The person she could be again if she shed the bad habits picked up from Jimmy Burley.

Snaring a sugar daddy would allow her to feather her nest and have a child to love. By the time her looks faded she'd have savings. She'd be a respectable woman of means, no man required. All she needed to do was hook her meal ticket...

If he'd known her thoughts, Bowman would have laughed in

her battered face. He slapped her fingers off his thigh. She persevered, putting his hand on her breast. 'You've got lovely soft fingers, sir, just right for stroking a girl's body.'

'I'd sooner stroke piano keys than a scabby whore. And to think I once mistook you for...' He clammed up and pushed her away.

'Who? Who is it I remind you of?' she jibed, coming close enough to pat his cheek. 'Wife? Mistress? Not your sister I hope.'

His startled expression gave him away, and Sadie did some quick thinking.

'It's not *your* sister, is it?' she murmured in enlightenment. 'It's mine.' Her eyes darted to his long, pale fingers. 'Stroked piano keys, did you? At the Campbells' house, I'll bet! Gawdalmighty! You're Joey's father.'

He'd accosted her in the street believing her to be Amelia, not a harlot. Outside the match factory, he'd not been staring at her, but at Amelia. He'd come to Whitechapel looking for the housemaid he'd impregnated and found her sister instead. Sadie hooted in amusement, aware she'd gained the upper hand. He looked as jumpy as a cornered cat. 'That walking stick was engraved with an A and I. What's your wife's name? Irene, is it, Andrew?'

'I don't know what you're talking about,' he mumbled hoarsely.

'Oh, yes you do. Don't worry, I'll keep quiet about what happened between us. For my sister's sake, not yours. Not that she wants you now.' She dropped his hand on to her belly. 'I've got another one here for you.'

'You're insane...' He was so shocked by the turn of events that he couldn't utter a coherent defence. 'Lomax was right about you lot. You match girls need crushing beneath a man's shoe. I'll make sure he sacks you, you thief.' He was desperate to escape and gain time to think what to do. This harlot could ruin his life and reputation. She'd said she'd keep quiet, but she'd got valuable information to exploit.

Sadie felt humiliated by his rejection... and vengeful. He'd called her a scabby whore but she didn't regard herself as a common prostitute; she was a factory girl who dabbled in the profession on the side. She and her fellow workers had shown the world that they weren't inconsequential drabs. They were people to be reckoned with who'd taken on the Bryant and May bosses and won.

She set off after him as he hurried away. She wouldn't let him get her sacked. Two could play at threats and insults.

'I didn't steal your cane; you left it behind. Anyhow, I can lay me hands on it,' she said. 'I'll bring it to your house. If I bump into your wife, I won't let on what we was doing to make you forgetful.'

'You impertinent bitch,' he exploded. 'Try to blackmail me, would you?' He started shaking her to and fro by the neck.

The more she gasped and tried to plead with him to let her go, the fiercer the glitter in his eyes became. His lips had disappeared in a weird grin that displayed a set of clamped teeth. She raked her nails under his chin, unable to reach his face now he held her rigidly at arm's length. She fumbled for the knife in her pocket and stabbed him in the thigh to make him free her. With a yelp of pain, he let go to grab his bleeding wound. Sadie buckled at the knees, wheezing and coughing while fighting him for possession of the knife. In her weakened state it was a battle soon over. The hateful triumph in his eyes was imprinted on her mind as she collapsed to the ground with him hunched over her.

26

'What have you been up to? I went to Brooks's to find you but you hadn't been there. You're a cheat and a liar. You're not fit to be a father to our baby.' The door was rattled some more. 'My mother warned me about you. Let me in, I say...'

'I'm going to bed. And so should you. We'll talk in the morning when you're over your hysterics.' He scrambled to his feet the moment he heard her slippered feet shuffling away and their housekeeper's voice comforting her.

Andrew had been hunched behind his bedchamber door on the parquet to avoid staining the rug. His clothes and his hands were still covered in Sadie Burley's blood.

His escape had first been made on foot. Only when miles away from the scene of the crime had he hailed a cab in case a driver remembered picking up a fare in Whitechapel. This particular night wouldn't be forgotten; he had no doubt of that.

Muffled in his black cloak, and with his hat low upon his head, he had swept past his elderly manservant creaking out of his hall chair. Before the yawning fellow found the wits to bid him a goodnight, Andrew was halfway up the stairs, feeling thankful to have got to his bedroom unobserved.

His wife had been waiting to interrogate him but with a second to spare he'd managed to lock her out. But for her blasted nagging he wouldn't have gone to find the cane with terrible consequences. Women were the bane of his life, always being a damnable nuisance in one way or another. Even his sweet Amelia presented him with problems.

From the moment he'd sprung up from Sadie Burley's lifeless body, he had been in the grip of strong tremors that were only now easing. He went to the dressing chest and turned up the lamp before gazing at his reflection in the mirror. No horns had sprouted from his forehead but his eyes were unnaturally bright. He'd not been fornicating as his wife believed but what he'd done had excited him. A tingling in his groin remained, filling him with dread. He pulled the knife from his pocket. He'd wanted to rid himself of it as he rushed away yet couldn't part with it.

He upended the pitcher into the bowl, then he dropped the gory trophy into the water before plunging in his hands. He wetted a flannel, scrubbing it over his face until it was clean. His clothes were stripped off and he examined his cut thigh.

The wound was not deep and had already stopped bleeding. He dabbed away the crusted blood and surveyed the scene. The crimson washing water could be flushed away in the lavatory. And thank God he had borne the expense of Thomas Crapper's plumbers installing his and Ivy's ablution facilities. From the start of their marriage he had known he wanted to sleep and bathe separately from the woman he found distasteful in every way. But now she was pregnant he must tread carefully until his heir was born.

His bloodstained clothing was a problem. He perched his

bare buttocks on the edge of the bed and stared at the embers in the grate. He could build that up into a useful furnace. He supported his face in his hands and thought about what might be unfolding in Whitechapel. A hunt would start for the murderer when the body was discovered.

He screwed up his eyes but found it impossible to block from his mind the horror on Sadie Burley's face as the light in her eyes dimmed and she realised what he'd done. He rushed again to the mirror to study how he looked. A well-styled cravat would cover scratches from her fingernails. He scraped his fingers through his hair, satisfied he didn't look capable of slitting a woman's throat. He was the sort of upstanding individual who'd work to rid the streets of London of thieves and prostitutes.

* * *

'That lad looks like the hounds of hell are after him.' Daisy Root had stopped chatting to gawp after Spider. He had raced past, chin up and arms pumping, neither looking to left nor right. On reaching the pub he struck a hand against the wall, holding his ribs with the other, before bursting inside.

'I'd better go and see what that's all about then.' Amelia raised her eyebrows. 'Mary's gone shopping but Pearl's home. She's off school with bellyache.' Amelia got a better grip on her lively son. At five months old Joey was starting to crawl and was always wriggling to gain his independence.

'Don't forget to collect your dress later in the week. You do look a treat in it, dear.'

From the moment Daisy realised Amelia liked the blue brocade dress, and Nick Dupree liked her, the gown had been wrapped up and put away. Daisy guessed the girl might soon require a special outfit. An hour ago Amelia had tried it on, with a matching velvet hat that Daisy had also acquired from her totter friend. The dress hardly needed any alterations. The sight of Amelia twirling in her finery had brought a lump to Daisy's throat. She was a beauty in match girl's clothes; in a classy second-hand Harrods gown and a velvet hat, Amelia Spencer could give a society lady a run for her money.

'Thanks so much. I will pay you...' Amelia began.

'You won't,' Daisy bluntly differed. 'It's my gift to wish you good luck in your new life.'

Amelia affectionately pecked Daisy's wrinkly cheek. 'You're very kind.'

'You can tell me later what the commotion's about.' Daisy tapped her nose.

On entering the pub, Amelia found Spider sitting on the floor with his back against the bar. Pearl had been trying to comfort him but straightened up with a shrug to show she'd no clue what the trouble was.

An agitated Spider struggled to his feet. 'Where's Mr Dupree? I want to speak to him, not you.'

'He's at work. What's happened to upset you like this?'

'Can't tell you, only him.' Spider snorted back a sob. 'Got to find Mr Dupree.'

'You're being silly.' Amelia suspected he wasn't being silly but was frightened of distressing her. Joey had sensed the tension and started to whimper. 'Would you take him upstairs for me?' She hoped Spider might open up with Pearl out of the room.

Amelia drew Spider towards a table to sit down. 'Has something happened to your family?'

He shook his head, his big hazel eyes fixed on her face. 'I just come from the factory. Mr Lomax sent me 'cos he knows you're

Mrs Burley's sister...' He swallowed noisily then hid his face on his clasped arms, resting on the table.

Amelia barely noticed the larger bald patch on his scalp from carrying crates of matchboxes. She stood up and thought about last night's events with Sadie that had sent Nick out at dawn. He'd returned quickly to say neither Sadie nor Jimmy were in.

Amelia had felt reassured and given Nick a grateful hug before he left for work. He'd given her a kiss and a promise that they'd talk later about everything. She knew he'd meant her move from the attic to his bedroom.

But he was back early, and it looked as though romance was the last thing on his mind. He'd flung open the door then stopped for a second before stepping inside and allowing it to swing shut behind him.

'Has Spider already told you?' His voice was almost too hoarse to hear.

'Told me what?' She put a hand on the chair-back to steady herself. The first day of autumn had arrived. The flow of air felt mild... yet she felt cold as ice. 'What's happened to Sadie?'

He couldn't immediately answer, but in two strides he'd reached her and pulled her into his arms.

* * *

Nick had offered to come alone to do this and she'd been tempted to accept the coward's way out. She loved and admired him the more for his courage. But it wasn't right to shirk this duty. She couldn't allow her family to hear about Sadie from a stranger, and Nick was to them a stranger. Neither should the police or a newspaper headline inform her parents of their eldest daughter's sordid end in a backstreet. Amelia owed it to all of them – especially to Sadie – to be here first. She'd promised to pass on a message.

Amelia would never know whether saying or doing something differently, might have saved Sadie. There had been a moment last night when they'd talked and had sensed doom approaching. Amelia had chosen Nick over her sister and had stopped him searching for her. She should have let him leave. She should have made Sadie stay. She should have offered a bribe of money or alcohol or both to lure her sister upstairs to sleep safely in a bed and wake to another day.

If only she'd done one of those things... all of those things... she might have come to Hackney today to bring her mum and dad news of how happy and blessed she was to have met Nicholas Dupree.

He had been first to tell her. Gossip had spread like wildfire and had reached the docks very quickly. Then had come the constable. He had been an officious sort, lacking in sympathy. There would be more of his attitude to come: Sadie Burley was a match girl and part-time prostitute, associating with bad men. She'd been inviting trouble and was partly to blame for what had happened to her.

The desolation she felt today was far greater than the last time she'd come here on Christmas Eve. But she'd stay strong and tell them, although it would break their battered and bruised hearts all over again.

'You won't take him with you then?' Nick settled the baby on the seat and tucked the warm blanket more firmly about his sturdy little limbs.

'Today's not the day for them to meet you or Joey. That should be a happy time. Now's for grieving.' Amelia carefully wiped her face with her handkerchief then moved closer to the edge of the cart. Nick got down and helped her to the pavement.

'We'll be waiting right here for you,' he said.

* * *

'Oh, it's you. I thought it was my friend from school.'

'Let me in, Becky. I've come to speak to Mum and Dad.'

'What's wrong?' Rebecca peered at her sister's white face and bloodshot eyes.

Amelia couldn't answer but edged inside, wiping away fresh tears.

'Mum's in there.' Rebecca sounded apprehensive as she indicated the front parlour.

For some seconds, Mrs Spencer remained unaware her youngest girl wasn't alone. Blanche appeared comfortable in the armchair, counting knitting stitches. She looked up, blinked in disbelief then put aside the needles and wool and got to her feet. 'I said not to come back here.'

'Is Dad at home?'

The sorrow conveyed in Amelia's voice and her black-clad presence was being digested by Mrs Spencer. 'He's not well. In bed. You mustn't disturb him.'

'Is Tom at home?'

'At school. What is it, Amelia?' Mrs Spencer's voice was sharp with anxiety.

'I've news about Sadie.' There wasn't an easy way to tell them but Amelia knew not to come straight out with it. Her mother might want Rebecca out of the way first, although it was probably too late to send her upstairs now her curiosity had been pricked. The girl was almost fourteen, soon out to work. The age Sadie had been when she first caught Jimmy Burley's eye.

'What about Sadie?' Blanche whispered.

'I wanted to be the one to tell you.' Amelia tried, and failed, to force out the right words. What had emerged sounded suffocated and shaky.

'Is she dead?' Blanche croaked in shock.

Amelia nodded vigorously, relieved she'd been spared uttering the worst of it.

'Why? Why's she dead?' Rebecca demanded to know with youthful logic.

'It's him, isn't it?' Blanche was dazed but dry-eyed, and had immediately leapt to the conclusion Amelia had.

'Jimmy Burley didn't kill her.' Amelia calmed herself to repeat what she'd been told. 'A constable said Jimmy's been questioned. He admitted they'd had a fight yesterday but he wasn't with her later. He was gambling and has an alibi.' She paused. 'The constable said Jimmy collapsed when he found out.'

'It was an accident then?' A pathetic note of hopefulness was in Mrs Spencer's voice.

Amelia was conscious of the force of two pairs of wide staring eyes on her. 'Sadie was murdered, Mum.'

'Who murdered her?' Rebecca sounded outraged.

Amelia hurried to catch her mother as she saw her start to sway. She helped her to sit down then crouched beside her, chafing her hands. 'The police don't know who did it. They have to investigate. I'm so sorry to bring this news, Mum.'

'I thought I heard somebody at the door. What's all this about?'

Wilfred Spencer was on the threshold, in his dressing gown. He hurried in to pat his anguished wife's shoulder while looking from one chalk-white face to another.

'Sadie's dead,' Rebecca blurted. She dashed from the room, clasping her mouth as though she might be sick.

'Why's Becky acting daft, saying things like that?'

'Sadie has... been... murdered,' his wife expelled the words between wails.

Wilfred's sharp intake of breath sent him into a coughing fit. Amelia attempted to embrace her father in comfort but his jerking ribs shook off her arms. 'Sit down, Dad. I'll tell you as much as I know.' Amelia sank down onto her knees in a spot midway between the pair of fireside chairs.

She couldn't tell these two dear people everything; she abbreviated the constable's report of Sadie's throat being cut to saying a knife had been involved. They didn't interrupt but listened intently while making small, anguished noises. When she'd finished, her father drooped into his chair, gripping its arms with fingers that showed bone. Her mother hung her head towards her chest and howled.

Amelia pushed herself up and opened the sideboard, hoping some Christmas drink might be left over. The brandy had gone but half a bottle of sherry was in there. She poured two glasses and offered them one each.

'Take it, Blanche,' Wilfred urged when she turned her face away. He took his own glass and gulped it all down. 'There was gossip about Sadie being a streetwalker. Is it true?'

Amelia nodded and took the sherry from her mother's trembling hand to stop it slopping everywhere. She placed the glass on the hearth, then she sat again on the rug. 'I saw Sadie yesterday; she asked me to pass a message to you.' Amelia paused to bring her voice under control for this precious task. 'She said she loves you and that she was sorry for hurting you. She made me promise to tell you.'

Sadie's goodbye increased the volume of Blanche's sobs and Wilfred clutched his ribs. He was first to raise his head and dry his eyes. 'She comes home,' he raggedly announced. 'Her coffin will rest on the table in the front parlour.'

Blanche had also heard the rumours about Sadie. She hadn't told him what the neighbours were saying; he hadn't mentioned to her that men at the Ind Coope brewery talked about his eldest girl behind his back. 'I don't know if that's wise; we've the younger ones to consider...'

'It's too late to be wise,' Wilfred cut across her. 'We should have kept Sadie close. We should have kept them both close.' He looked at Amelia, her cheek resting on her drawn-up knees as she sat between them, quietly weeping. 'Sadie says sorry to us from the grave. *I'm* sorry.'

'Jimmy Burley is her next of kin; the police say he isn't involved. He might arrange his wife's funeral,' Blanche said.

Amelia was listening but feeling too drained to contribute. Her mother had made a valid point but Jimmy would doubtless be happy to allow others to bear any cost. He was in debt and in trouble, Sadie had said.

'The hearse will come here to collect her,' said Wilfred. 'We will all walk behind it with our heads high. Sadie will be properly laid to rest with only us... her family... about her. It makes no difference whether Burley struck out with a knife that night, or not. He used to beat her. Everybody knew it. This is his fault.' Wilfred lowered his shaking fist and used it on the chair arm to assist himself to his feet. 'And so are we guilty, for turning our backs on her. Now, I'm getting dressed then I'll go to the undertakers to make some arrangements.' He paused. 'If it's the last thing I'm able to do, I'll do this for that child.'

* * *

'Are you certain this unfortunate woman was Miss Spencer's sister?' Evangeline smothered a gasp on receiving a nod.

Wolff had appeared in the house several times throughout

the day, sending her significant looks. She had been too busy to stop then. Two births had been imminent. One patient had gone on to safely deliver a girl. The other baby was taking its time arriving. The expectant mother and the other inmates had settled down for the night. The mission house was dark and quiet. In this room candles were lit and an urgent whispered conversation was taking place.

He had roused Evangeline from her bed to read the newspaper he'd brought with him. It remained open at the grisly report of Sadie Burley's killing.

'Surely, you recall I looked for Sadie Burley in Islington?'

'I do. But you didn't find her. You can't be absolutely sure they were kin. I hope they are not since you have publicly shown an interest in her. That wasn't wise.'

'They were sisters, Evie. Somebody confirmed it.'

'Somebody trustworthy?'

He nodded. 'And there was a family likeness.'

'I wish you hadn't asked questions about a woman who's been found murdered.'

'Don't fret so. I was passing the match factory and spotted a woman I thought at first was Miss Spencer.' John Wolff had been loitering close to the factory gates, in the hope of ambushing Nell Yates and questioning her about girls she'd known at the mission. He'd struck unexpected gold finding Sadie Burley there.

Nell had spotted him and tried to run off, but he'd nabbed her. She'd reluctantly confirmed that Sadie Burley had a sister called Amelia.

'If you fall under suspicion we will never get the child. Whitechapel is a hellish place for him to be.' She brought the candle closer to the newspaper to reread a paragraph. 'It says the victim was a prostitute.' Evangeline nibbled her thumbnail, seeing trouble ahead.

'I won't be a suspect, Evie. I was with you in the chapel that very night.'

'True. I will vouch for you, Jack, if the police come.' She rubbed her aching forehead.

'Kneel by the bed, Evie; let us pray. It will ease you.' He turned her about and after picking up the cross on the table, hung the chain around her neck. His hands covered it, pressed it against her bosom.

'We should pray for the poor woman's salvation.' Evangeline sank down with her nightdress billowing about her. When on her knees, she rested her forehead on the edge of the bed. Before he had time to settle down behind her and draw her hips between his parted thighs, footsteps were heard. He straightened up at the same moment the door was rattled.

'Sister... Sister Evangeline... are you awake?' hissed a querulous female voice. 'It's Eliza Aitkin, Sister... her baby is coming again. She sent me to get you 'cos she's wet the bed, and she's crying.' The banging on the door increased in volume.

Before the message was concluded John Wolff was helping Evangeline up.

'Stop your shouting or you'll wake everybody,' Evangeline said firmly. 'Go back to Aitkin and stay with her until I come. I'll be there in a few minutes.' She turned to Wolff. 'The mother's waters have broken. I must say goodnight, Jack.'

'Goodnight, Evie.' He glanced moodily at her as he left. She had forgotten about him and was collecting her nun's habit to put it on.

On his way down the stairs he met the cook coming up. Mrs Baxter, in her night robe, held a candle in one hand and a pan of hot water in the other, having been alerted to the emergency by an inmate.

She didn't like John Wolff and she knew he didn't like her right back... because she'd got his number. The one that confused her was Sister Evangeline. Mrs Baxter found it bewildering that the nun had any time for this man, but then there was no accounting for taste... or for urges.

'Not your lucky night, is it, John Wolff,' she said sourly as they passed.

27

'What's your poison, squire?'

'Half of bitter.'

'Not seen you in here before.'

'Just passing. Looked like a good place to stop.'

'It is. You won't find better ale or grub round here.'

'Dupree's the name above the door outside. That's you, is it?'

'That's me.'

'Must be doing all right. Young fellow like you, having this place. Unusual name you've got.'

'Huguenots to blame. My lot come over from France and settled in the East End, way back.'

'Your dog's a mongrel, I reckon.' The stranger jerked a nod at the wolfhound stretched out behind the bar. Jet had one watching eye open.

'Yeah... nothing pure about him... or me. Now you know my business, what's yours? Doing all right yourself, are you, Mr...?'

'You ask a lot of questions, landlord.'

'Would have said you was a butcher... something like that.'

'Why's that then?'

'Blood underneath your fingernails. Certain smell. Can always tell an abattoir worker... gamekeeper... when he comes in.'

'Observant fellow, aren't you?' Coins were tossed down for the beer.

Nick pushed the tankard across the bar with a genial smile. He palmed the money and moved on to serve the next customer. But he continued brooding on the bearded man who'd swooped on his drink and carried it to a table in the corner. The stranger was also keeping a crafty eye on him while drinking. Nick looked elsewhere when those black eyes slewed his way. He continued to banter with a jolly woman and her loud-mouthed friends. He joined in as they began to warble 'The Boy I Love is up in the Gallery'. The inebriated women were chucking Spider under the chin. He was playing up to them, jigging along, then dodging away to collect up the empties. Nick dropped out of the choir and spoke to Lenny.

'Be gone a few minutes.' He left his brother-in-law serving, with Spider as backup.

He stopped in the corridor to light a cigarette and lean against the wall. He was certain he'd just spoken to the stocky man he'd seen a month or more ago, running with a dog at his side. The fellow hadn't ventured inside the pub on that occasion. Perhaps because Amelia had been there and would have recognised him.

Another slashed body had been found a week after Sadie was murdered. There was talk of setting up a local Vigilance Committee. The East End was a dangerous place at the best of times, but panic was spreading that the similar deaths indicated a maniac was on the loose, slaughtering streetwalkers. Knowing Sadie hadn't been as badly mutilated as the later victim was a mean consolation for the Spencer family.

Nick took the stairs two at a time and entered the attic bedroom. Amelia was in her nightgown, lying on her side with Joey lightly enclosed by a protective arm curled over his body. Both were sleeping, their breathing barely moving their chests.

She'd not recently mentioned the mother and baby home or Sister Evangeline's sidekick, John Wolff. She'd been too distressed to talk or do anything much at all. But Nick knew she hadn't forgotten that place. And he hadn't forgotten her description of the gamekeeper, or how he'd tried to stop her leaving. She'd believed Wolff would search for her, to steal her son for the nun. Nick had thought that far-fetched. He didn't now.

Since Sadie's funeral had taken place a few weeks ago Amelia had settled into a profound grief and guilt. She blamed herself for stopping him searching for Sadie that night. Nothing Nick said to ease her torment seemed to be of use. The funeral had only been attended by her family. Jimmy hadn't found the gumption to show his face, pleading the agony of it would kill him. If Nick had believed that cock-and-bull story, he would have dragged the bastard to the cemetery himself.

He tenderly smoothed a flaxen tress from her cheek that bore some dried tear salt, hoping she slept peacefully.

Jet had followed him from the bar to guard the foot of the stairs. The dog rose, but his wagging tail stiffened and his hackles rose.

The corridor was dimly lit by a single gaslight but Nick could make out the bulky figure of a man standing in the shadows. He descended the last treads and walked towards him. 'Private back here. No customers.'

'Looking for the privy.' John Wolff propped an indolent arm against the wall.

'Won't find it here. Outside, use the gutters.'

Jet's growling intensified and Nick clicked his fingers to quieten the dog. 'Don't think he likes you, pal.'

'Might be able to smell a dog on me.'

'He smells blood. Puts him on edge. We're all on edge round here after what's gone on. Expect you've heard about the murders.'

'I have.'

'People could think a stranger with blood under his finger-nails was up to no good.'

'Obliged for the warning.'

The pulse in the quiet atmosphere intensified as a baby's crying drifted down from the bedroom. Then came a gentle voice singing a lullaby.

'That sounds sweeter than the caterwauling in there,' said John Wolff as the choir in the saloon bar burst into action.

'Customers here like it rowdy. I'd say this isn't the place for you. There's the way out.' Nick jerked his head at the exit.

John Wolff smiled, and a soft tuneless whistle emerged from between his teeth as he strolled away. 'Good ale, landlord. Reckon I'll be back again... give it another try.'

'I'll be waiting for you then,' said Nick.

* * *

'You're looking peaky, love. Not pregnant, are you?' asked Mary.

'What? No! 'Course not.' Amelia's complexion had turned fiery but she continued rolling pastry.

'Just my crafty way of finding out how things are between you and Nick.' Mary was stirring scrambled eggs while talking over her shoulder. 'Bet you think I'm a nosy so-and-so, but I think we should have a talk, woman to woman.'

Amelia hadn't expected to have this conversation with Mary.

With Nick perhaps, but he'd been treating her with kid gloves. She did feel like crumbling at times and was grateful he understood that a need for love and romance had withered after her sister was murdered. She just wanted his comfort and he willingly gave it.

Mary propped her hands on the floury table where Amelia was seated. 'Wanted or not, here's my advice: I know you're grieving for your sister, but don't forget about the other important people, or the better times to come. Or maybe they won't come.' She sat down in the chair facing Amelia. 'I'm not saying Nick's given up on you but I know what men are like if they're without their oats.'

'Has he said something?' Amelia interrupted. 'Does he want me to leave?'

'No! Nothing like that.' Mary paused. 'I can see how he feels about you; if he thinks you don't feel the same... well he's got his pride. Is Joey's father still on your mind, making you hesitate?'

'I've been over him for a long while.' Amelia sighed. 'I can't get over what happened to Sadie and to my family. We're all broken apart like bits of useless china.'

'It's a terrible tragedy for any family to bear.' Mary paused. 'I made no secret of having an axe to grind with Sadie. I'd've cheerfully throttled her at times. But never would I have wished this on her. You do know that, don't you?'

Amelia nodded. 'I know you and Lenny were shocked and upset when you heard.'

'We honestly were. You couldn't protect her, you know,' said Mary. 'You couldn't change her, either. Sadie... well, that gel was her own person. I admired her in a way. Sounds daft, after what she did, but it's true.' Mary shook her head. 'Takes guts to live like that. And if it's any consolation, I reckon she went down fighting. She marked the monster that did it. That's what I think.'

'When we were growing up, she was a smashing sister,' Amelia's voice was soft with nostalgia. 'We had some real larks, the two of us.'

'I'll bet...' Mary snorted a chuckle and returned to the scrambled eggs, cussing beneath her breath while scraping at the bits stuck to the bottom of the pan. 'You've got a lovely little lad and a man who thinks the world of you.'

'I liked him, and trusted him from the start when he was kind and let me stay here.' Amelia cocked her head while reflecting on the first night she'd met him. 'Thought him handsome, too,' she added with a self-conscious smile.

'You're not the first to say that,' said Mary. 'So, why not tell him before Polly chances her luck again...' She broke off, muttering to herself, 'Why can't I keep me big mouth shut?'

'Has she been back?' Amelia stopped pushing the rolling pin.

'You was upstairs getting ready for the funeral. Nick didn't have much to say to her but he was polite. Thanked her for coming to pay her condolences. That's all there was to it.'

Amelia gave Polly Mayhew the benefit of the doubt. A few pub customers already knew of Amelia's connection to the first victim; others had recently found out. Most people expressed sincere sympathy but there had been some ghoulish curiosity.

'Did Nick ask you to keep quiet about Polly's visit?'

'You've been grieving, Amelia. He's only thinking of you...'

'Did he?'

'He did, 'cos he didn't want you hurting any more than you already are.' Mary read the emotion in the girl's eyes. 'Don't be jealous. It'll burrow into your common sense and rip it to shreds. Believe me, I know.'

'I trust Nick. He'd tell me if he and Polly...' She made a small gesture rather than accuse him of trying to cover this up.

Mary had reason to sound sour now Lenny's affair with Sadie had been picked over in public. That particular liaison had been common knowledge and Sadie's past friends and lovers were in the spotlight. The newspaper reporters hanging around were fuelling gossip among people already speculating wildly about the motives for such dreadful crimes.

'I wonder if the second victim knew the brute's identity and was going to tell the police. So he killed her.'

Mary shuddered. 'No more talking about it, please.' She started dishing up eggs onto plates. 'After this lot's cleared away I'll light the copper and get the sheets washed.'

'I'll lend a hand.'

'I wish that bloody dog would give it a rest,' said Mary.

Amelia had also been aware of Jet's constant barking in the background. Mary had put him into his kennel earlier when he wouldn't stop prowling the empty corridor, sniffing and growling. Amelia determinedly rolled out pastry and cut it to shape for pies. Nick had gone down to the river as usual but when he'd said goodbye she'd sensed something was playing on his mind. Polly Mayhew's visit perhaps, and a reminder of missing his oats, as Mary called it.

Lately, he had seemed to be frequently preoccupied.

His sister was right about the worm of jealousy driving a person mad. She mustn't let it though.

28

'A gentleman caller is waiting in the hall, ma'am.'

Ivy wasn't expecting a visitor, yet it was rather a nice surprise to have one. Her friends and family had fallen away since she'd married. She understood why that was. She didn't like her husband either. Nevertheless, she was jealous and obsessed with knowing what he was up to.

'Who is it?' The question emerged through the napkin removing cake crumbs from her lips.

'It's a Mr Gideon Lomax,' informed the elderly housekeeper. 'He came to see Mr Bowman but will speak to you as the master is out.'

After memory searching, Ivy recalled her father had sat on the board of a charitable institution with a Lord Lomax. It was unlikely that lofty fellow would call on them. Perhaps a lowly relative moved in Andrew's circle and might be able to shed light on her husband's increasingly strange behaviour.

'Shall I send him away?' The housekeeper prompted her mistress for a reply.

'Oh, no. Please, show him in here.'

Once Mrs Murray had gone, Ivy put her plate of half-finished cake on the tea tray then rearranged some ornaments in front of it. Deciding that wasn't enough to hide her gluttony – as her husband called it – she threw the napkin on top of the crockery so the cake and dish of bonbons were hidden.

She was settling back down when a fair-haired fellow sauntered in smiling. She studied him, thinking that despite his bad skin he was rather a nice looking young man.

'Mrs Bowman, how are you?'

'I'm very well, thank you.'

'Well... please do sit down Mr Lomax,' she said, thinking him charming. Then she noticed he was holding Andrew's walking stick, or its twin.

'Ah, you have guessed what brings me here.' He presented the cane with a flourish, propping it against the side of her chair. 'Your husband's, I believe. I thought he might like it back.'

Ivy was too astonished to immediately comment. 'How did you come by it, sir?' She examined the engraving to be sure it was the one she'd bought.

'Well, I expect your husband told you it had been stolen. I can't account for it being in a Whitechapel pawnshop otherwise. By chance, I recognised it in the window.'

'Thank you for retrieving it for us. I gave it to Andrew as a wedding gift.'

'I imagined that might be the case when I saw the inscription. I knew I must buy it and return it. Especially after being told about the person who'd had it in her grubby possession.'

'The thief was a woman?'

'Possibly. The pawnbroker related an unsavoury account of how the cane turned up there.'

'Now you have whetted my curiosity, you must tell me,' urged Ivy when he seemed shy of concluding the tale.

'It would be indelicate of me...'

'Oh, never mind that.' She moved an impatient hand.

He leaned closer and she copied his pose. 'The pawnbroker acquired it from a woman of dubious character,' he whispered. 'The cane had been exchanged for services rendered was his take on the situation.' Gideon noticed her lips tightening. 'Naturally, I rebuked the fellow for finding it funny that a gentleman's property had been so misused.'

Ivy sat up straight. 'My husband will be glad of its return.'

'And I'm glad to be of service. I'm sorry to have missed him and bothered you with this.' That was a lie; he'd kept out of sight until he saw Andrew leave the house. He'd heard rumours that all was not harmonious, Chez Bowman. Ivy had barged into Brooks's demanding to speak to her husband. He'd not been there and neither had been the ebony cane she'd been fussed about finding.

Andrew wouldn't be the first jaded society gentleman to visit a Whitechapel brothel and get fleeced. Gideon kept a tight hold on his wallet when frequenting such places. He'd avoided them since Sadie Burley's murder for fear of suspicious looks falling on him. Gideon had liked brazen Sadie, and the shock of what had happened to her had been the final straw for him as far as the East End was concerned. Impulsively, he'd resigned his position at Bryant and May after the management were made to look foolish over the strike. Since his father had cut him off, he needed another job and an influential friend.

He glanced at Ivy twice in quick succession, making her blush.

'Are you related to Lord Lomax?' she asked.

'A humble younger son.' Gideon gave her a boyish smile.

'Ah... I see. My husband is the youngest child. A difficult position for a boy to be in.'

'Indeed...' sighed Gideon. 'We attended school together.'

'He's not mentioned you.' She liked having some company and wanted him to stop for a drink with her. 'Will you have some tea... no, let's have something stronger. A whisky?'

'That's kind of you, Mrs Bowman. But I shan't outstay my welcome.'

'You could not, sir.' She turned crimson beneath his intense stare, sure he was flirting with her.

'I'm very pleased to have met you, Mrs Bowman. Your husband is a lucky man.' He sighed. 'But now I must get along.'

'Before you go, you must let me reimburse you. What do I owe you for the cane?' She eased her pregnant figure out of the chair, prompting him to jump to his feet.

'I wouldn't dream of taking payment for doing you a good turn.'

'I'm indebted to you then... Gideon.'

'My pleasure, ma'am...'

'Ivy... please...'

'Ivy...' he purred.

She could definitely detect flirtation in his nice blue eyes. Andrew had looked at her like that in the early days. He never did any more.

'Are you sure you won't have a whisky, before you leave? One for the road, as my papa would say.'

'I would like to but alas, I've an appointment with Montague Hawthorne at his office in the Strand. I have to make a good impression as I want a job.'

'My late father knew Sir Montague. They were friends.'

'Your father was a highly respected fellow.'

Since he'd brought his need of employment to her attention, Ivy had noticed his frayed cuffs and a missing button on his jacket. He was taller than Andrew and broader in the body, too.

More her sort of size. Gideon Lomax appeared debonair despite his shabby attire. He had a presence with his fair hair and ample girth that her husband lacked. Andrew's mousy hair and weedy stature rendered him rather nondescript, now she came to think of it. Neither was he attentive nor considerate since putting a ring on her finger. It was good of Gideon Lomax to have spent money on the cane when it was obvious he could ill afford to.

'When I see Sir Montague I'll mention having been in your company recently and how much we enjoyed talking. He'll like to know his old friend's charming daughter is looking quite radiant.' Gideon placed his lips on her pudgy knuckles in farewell. He would have liked to stay and have that whisky but was conscious that Bowman might return and find him cosying up to his wife. He'd done as much as he could. Inferring a close friendship with Ivy Bowman might sway Sir Montague to overlook his past misdemeanours and give him a job at Barings Bank.

He left the house and, crossing the road, glanced back. She was watching him from the window. Gideon turned and gave Ivy a lingering stare that made her quickly drop the curtain back into place. He chuckled and carried on across the road, feeling rather wistful. He could have been first to court her. Their marriage would have solved all his problems. She was no beauty but they might have rubbed along quite nicely as man and wife.

Too late now though.

* * *

'It's too late to say sorry, you evil wretch. You've got a bloomin' cheek to show your face back here. You'd be dead and buried alongside your poor baby but for Sister Evangeline's care.'

'I've made a mistake but I don't want charity. I can cook and clean and help you with the other girls until it's my turn.'

'Made a *mistake*? Your *turn*? Don't tell me you're expecting again!' Mrs Grubb spat a tsk of disgust. 'You've learned nothing from it, have you? I'd've had the police after you, you baby murderer.'

'I swear I won't be no trouble. I'm homeless and need a place to stay till the baby's born.'

'Well, you won't find one here,' declared Mrs Grubb and, blowing out the candle, shut the door in Nell Yates' face.

'You old cow. You wouldn't be so high and mighty if you knew more about the nun you praise to the skies.' Nell pulled and pushed the big brass doorknob but the bolts were slid home.

With a dejected sigh Nell perched on the step, pulling her hat down on her brow and turning up her collar to cover her drooping ringlets. It wasn't a particularly cold autumn evening, neither was Nell bothered about being recognised. She was hunched up so nobody could see her crying. She put up a hard front but she'd had one knock too many lately. Sadie Burley had been a friend and her murder had badly upset Nell. The second killing had jolted her into taking stock of her life. The improved pay and conditions at the match factory were all very well, but had come too late for her. After being employed by Bryant and May for so long, eating her dinner at a workbench with fingers covered in phosphorous, the rot had already set in. She rubbed her palm over her chin to check its changing shape. She'd been persuading herself gingivitis from holding washing pegs in her mouth had loosened her teeth and made her gums bleed. She wasn't feeling optimistic now. Phossy jaw was taking hold of her and a few extra pennies a week and a dinnertime canteen, wouldn't stop her bones crumbling.

Nell had packed up work to care for her boyfriend's family but then he'd gone back with his wife. His kids had never stopped crying for their mother so Nell hadn't put up much of a fight. She'd pinned her hopes on Mrs Grubb and a foster home for her unborn baby. Then she wanted a fresh start, like Kitty Wheeler. First, she needed a helping hand to straighten herself out.

A hound loped out of the gloom on the opposite side of the road and settled into padding obediently at its master's heels. The fellow's long dark coat made him appear to be a moving black shadow. He'd probably noticed a woman's figure perched on Mrs Grubb's step, but that wasn't an unusual sight when passing this property.

Nell watched John Wolff from beneath the brim of her hat, glad he hadn't recognised her. He frightened her but a meeting with him could prove useful. He was a violent bully and depraved with it; not a man to cross without a backup plan. When he was a safe distance away she brushed herself down and followed him.

She couldn't lose sight of him now she'd hit on a scheme to force him to help her. Nell hastened around the corner but before she'd covered half the alley's length she let out a shriek that was silenced by brutal fingers pinching her nose and mouth.

'Thinking to rob me... Oh, it's only you.' Wolff lowered the knife that had been whipped to within a whisker of Nell's throat. 'I'm not after business tonight, so clear off.' He pushed her away.

She tottered on her heels, panting, 'You scared the bleedin' life outta me.' She crossed her arms over her heaving chest. 'I'm a nervous wreck after what happened to Sadie Burley.'

'Don't go creeping up on me then, you fool,' he snarled, and dropped the knife back into his pocket. He'd been aware of being shadowed and had expected a desperate young footpad to brave the hound and chance an attack.

In her agitation, Nell had come straight out with Sadie's name rather than building up to it. She thought she might as well carry on and get this over with. 'I was following you for your own good,' she burst out. 'The coppers know I was friends with Sadie. They've been asking questions about the men she knew. I kept your name out of it. Didn't say nuthin' about you asking after her and her sister that day you stopped me outside the factory.'

Wolff detected a threat in what Nell was presenting as a good deed. He brought his face closer to hers and his brawny hand again squeezed her face. 'Make sure you do keep me out of it.'

'I will... swear...' She jerked her aching jaw free. 'Need a favour back, that's all.'

'What sort of favour?'

'I'm knocked up again and got nowhere to stay. If you put in a good word for me, Sister Evangeline might take me into the mission.' He didn't comment but stared at her with an odd expression. 'You owe me, John Wolff.' She was unnerved by his silence and kept babbling when staying quiet would have been wise. 'I never said a word to Sister Evangeline about you making me pregnant, or about what you made me do to get rid of it even though I was called all sorts of names by her and Mrs Grubb.' The more she brought the nun into it the more she sensed him stiffening in rage. She ploughed on, though; he owed her a good deal. 'I could've dropped you in it with the coppers over Sadie Burley. I didn't, even though you've treated me like dirt.'

'I wasn't in Whitechapel. I've got an alibi for that night.'

'Oh... in the chapel, with the sister, was you? Pretending to be a Christian.' He'd easily trumped one of her aces, and her temper had made her reckless. 'Why can't you do me that one favour, now I've done you lots?'

'What do you know about me and the sister in the chapel?'

'Nothing...' She avoided his eyes and took a step back. She knew all right. She'd been an inmate at Our Saviour's Mission, pregnant with his baby when she'd snooped on them one night. Jealous of his closeness to the nun, she'd crept from her bed and gone to the chapel. She'd watched them from the doorway, on their knees, him behind her and his hand slipping beneath the skirt of her habit. The moaning Nell had heard hadn't sounded religious.

She'd had to wait until he was out of the way on a hunting trip before applying for a place at the mission. When he returned with the deer, he'd looked at Nell as though he wanted to kill her too. He was looking at her that way now through a veil of misty gaslight. He hadn't let her have her baby. He'd told her to leave the mission and to use the knitting needles on herself, or he would.

'I said, what d'you know about me and the sister in the chapel?'

From past experience, she knew the softer his voice, the more savage he'd be. She'd been beaten... and worse... by him. Kitty Wheeler also knew how he used a crucifix to put the fear of God into bad girls.

'You spied on us in the chapel, didn't you, you no-good whore.'

Nell was angry but too scared to carry on blackmailing him. 'I saw you all right,' she shouted as she turned and fled. 'That's how I know that nun's as much of a whore as I am.'

Wolff gave the dog a signal. It sprang into action, penning Nell before she reached the end of the alley. Her scream was cut off and within seconds all was quiet again.

29

Amelia had watched from her bedroom window for the cart to turn the corner before settling her son in his cot and coming downstairs for the important talk she was determined to have with Nick. 'This is the third time this week you've been late home from work.'

'I told you I've been busy at the warehouse.'

'Must be a lot to do there,' she said spikily.

'You don't trust me?' He came closer. 'Don't you trust me, Amelia?'

She looked away. 'You've been different lately.'

'So have you.' He drew her against him. 'Look, I know what you're going through and I've tried to protect you or you'll never get over what's happened to your family.'

'I know we're not a proper couple, but even so I think you should tell me if you're seeing Polly Mayhew.'

'That's my answer then. You don't trust me.' He stepped away from her with a mirthless laugh. 'D'you think that's the sort of man I am?' He paused to allow her to speak but she avoided his eyes. 'Well do you?' he insisted on having an answer. 'Why would you even think I'm interested in her when I thought we were a proper couple? I can wait for you, Amelia, but there's no point, is there, if this is how you feel.'

Amelia's stomach had tied itself in knots. She wanted to hug him, say she was sorry for doubting him. Say she was a fool for even thinking bad things when he had been good to her and Joey. He treated her son as a father would, with patience and affection. She should agree she must be imagining things. She was overwrought from trying to cope with knowing her sister had been horribly murdered and her whole family was sinking beneath its grief. But... even when challenging him and receiving his assurances, she knew he was holding something back from her. And so had Mary sensed a change in him. Perhaps he hadn't strayed yet, and perhaps he wasn't lying, but there was a secret he couldn't or wouldn't share.

From the moment they had met on that winter's night she had recognised her soulmate. She loved Nicholas Dupree; unconsummated, pure love and friendship that bound her to him. Even if he had been with Polly, and told her so, she might still love him. The fear of having misjudged his character was terrifying. So was the idea of losing him. But something had happened to steal his time and thoughts away from her. And if he wouldn't tell her what it was then he was right; there was no point to this... no future for them.

'I don't believe there's nothing going on. There is something you've not told me.'

He rubbed his chin, blew a sigh between his teeth. 'All right,' he said hoarsely. 'Something's happened and I've kept it to myself because I know it will worry you and I don't want that. You're a strong girl, but you've been to hell and back lately. I can deal with it alone. I swear it's nothing to do with Polly Mayhew. I don't want her. I want you. D'you believe me, Amelia?'

She nodded and quickly approached to cup his solemn face between her palms. 'What is it? Tell me what's wrong... You're frightening me.'

He took her fingers from his face and held them tightly. 'A man came into the pub the other night...'

'You giving me a hand in there?' Lenny had flung open the kitchen door, looking irate. 'I've been behind the bar on me own. The crew off the merchantman just piled in. You two must be deaf if you can't hear the racket they're making.'

'I'll be there! Just give us a minute.' Nick's barked response spoke of his frustration at the interruption.

'Let's talk later, when we're alone.' Amelia didn't want a quick garbled account. 'Promise you'll tell me later, at bedtime?'

'Promise. And you have to promise me you'll keep yourself and Joey out of sight. Stay in the back. I'll lock up early tonight.'

* * *

'Your mum thinks you're asleep upstairs.' Amelia wagged a warning finger.

Pearl had slipped out to meet an older boy she liked who lived close to Mrs Root's lodging. Being fourteen and at work, he was allowed to stay out late whereas Pearl was confined to the house after dark since the murders.

'If your mum finds out from someone else that you've been disobedient she'll go mad at you.' She urged Pearl towards the sound of sea shanties and tankards used as percussion. 'I'll call your mum out of the bar so you can own up. I'll vouch for you not being gone very long.' Amelia was closer in age to Pearl than to Mary and remembered being stranded in that awkward, in-between age when childhood seemed left behind but adulthood remained out of reach.

'You'll never guess who I just saw.' Pearl had thought of a distraction. 'Your friend with the red hair who used to work at the match factory. She was talking to Mrs Root.'

'Kitty Wheeler?' Amelia shook her head. 'You're mistaken; she's moved out of London.'

'I'm not making it up, honest. It was her.'

'Kitty's back here?' Amelia sped to the window but it was impossible to identify the people who passed the mouth of the alley, yards away.

'If you want to go and see her, I'll keep an eye on Joey until you get back,' said Pearl.

Amelia had promised to stay out of sight, but she wasn't going far and wouldn't be away for long. While scrubbing pots and plates in the relative calm of the kitchen, she'd filled in the missing bits of the tale Nick hadn't finished. A man had come into the pub, he'd said, about to tell her that Andrew was still looking for her. Andrew Bowman meant nothing to her. And if he was loitering about out there, she'd tell him so.

Amelia quickly took off her apron, pulled on her coat and left by the side door. She hurried into the lodging house and banged on Mrs Root's door.

'Didn't take you long to find out I've got a visitor then.' A grinning Daisy ushered Amelia inside.

Kitty was indeed in Whitechapel, drinking a cup of tea on Daisy's saggy settee. With a whoop of delight she deposited the cup on the floor to rush into Amelia's waiting embrace.

'I thought Pearl was having me on when she said she'd seen you.'

'That girl's mother needs to keep an eye on her,' said Daisy.

'I've spoken to Pearl; she knows she's due a ticking-off.'

The friends broke apart and both started talking. 'You go first,' said Amelia.

'I had to come as soon as I read about Sadie in the paper.' Kitty shook her head. 'Couldn't believe it at first. I cried me eyes out when it all sunk in. I liked Sadie.'

'I know you did...' Amelia said tearfully.

'Now buck up, you too,' said a gruff Daisy. 'They'll catch him soon, you wait 'n' see.'

A quiet settled on the room as they mulled over the developments since the second victim was found. Some men had been arrested then released when found to have alibis, or when no proper evidence could be gathered against them. The Vigilance Committee regularly patrolled the streets and was possibly proving effective as no more gruesomely murdered women had been discovered in the past weeks.

'I can only stay a day or two. Told lies to get away.' Kitty grimaced her regret. 'The housekeeper's nice and allowed me to visit me sick mum.' Kitty pulled a face. 'Me mum's probably feeling better than I am. She won't reply to me letters although I wrote about not having a child to embarrass her.' She paused. 'I wish I'd fought to get Louise back. I've met a kind old soul in Cambridge who takes on widows with kids as domestics. I could've made out I'd lost me husband, like you did at the match factory.'

'No good crying over spilled milk,' said Daisy briskly to cheer the atmosphere.

'Now Bryant and May are offering a better deal I might come back and try again. I'll make a bloody fuss, and I don't care if John Wolff is there and tries to stop me.'

'Let's talk about it in the morning.' Amelia sounded a caution. She didn't want her friend taking another beating. 'I have to get back to the pub and I expect you're tired after the journey.' She stood up. 'The Anchor's packed to the rafters. Pearl promised to keep an eye on Joey but she's probably asleep by now.'

She left feeling buoyant. Her good mood evaporated the moment she spotted somebody she'd hoped never to clap eyes on again.

Fresh from prison, Jimmy Burley had been skinny and shorn of hair. He was still thin but now had a tangled dark mane that appeared as unkempt as the rest of him. Before she could slip away unnoticed, he drunkenly yelled her name. Amelia was tempted to ignore him but he was beloved Sadie's widower.

'So, iss you,' he slurred, forcing her to step back to escape his alcoholic breath. 'Iss down to you I've loss' me wife,' he carried on. 'We was all right together before you come to Whitechapel 'n' poked yer nose in.'

'That's not true, and you know it,' said Amelia. 'Sadie had run off before I turned up.'

'Me wife was lonely when I was in gaol. Thass why she did a flit. She loved me, like I loved 'er...'

'You bullied her and beat her up.'

'You made her disobedient so I had to bring her in line. You turned her against me.' He started to snivel. 'She shouldn't have been over here that night. She should have been safe at 'ome wi' me...'

He was a pathetic wreck without his wife by his side, but Amelia wasn't fooled by his self-pity. 'Sadie wasn't safe with you; that's why she came to me. And you weren't at home. You hit her then went gambling and drinking with money you stole from her.'

He swayed and swiped his wet face with a sleeve. 'Your lot in 'ackney should've treated us better, then none of this would've 'appened.' He turned and set off up the road, careering from one side of the pavement to the other. 'I've lost me wife. Spencers owe me summat.'

Relieved to see the back of him, it took her a minute to realise he intended to go and threaten her parents. She turned around and raced after him, apprehending him just around the corner.

Having a goal in mind, had helped Jimmy sober up. He shook her hand off his arm, remaining steady on his feet this time.

'Don't you bother my family, or ask them for money. If you need help, go to your own mother for it.'

'Piss off...' He shoved her away. 'Or you'll get a taste o' this an' Gawd knows you deserve it.' He shook a clenched fist in her face then started off again.

'Nick will come after you,' she shouted in desperation. 'So you leave all of us alone.'

He carried on marching in a reasonably straight line, and Amelia gave up. She had to. She'd already been out too long. The pub would still be filled with customers and noise, and Joey might be crying, unheard by a sleeping Pearl. Picking up her skirts she began to trot back the way she'd come. She felt her arm tugged before turning the corner and twisted around, prepared to thump Jimmy back if he got violent.

'Amelia... it's really you, isn't it? Oh, at last, I have found you,' said Andrew Bowman, pulling her into his arms. 'I know this is a shock, my love... You thought I'd forgotten you. I never did, I swear.' He was desperately holding on to her as she wriggled and slapped at his hands.

Finally free of him, she straightened her coat but didn't back away, she stepped closer. She remained calm while looking him over. Not so long ago, this meeting would have made her joyous, but now she felt nothing of the sort. Neither was she angry. She stared apathetically at the man who'd fathered her son and broken her heart. What did occur to her was that Andrew Bowman seemed different, yet she couldn't put her finger on why that was. His looks and build were more or less the same, although his face – what she could see of it, muffled up as he was in a scarf – appeared ghostly pale.

Never a striking fellow, he seemed small and insipid to her now. She had a tall and darkly handsome man in her life and the comparison was stark. But that wasn't the reason; it was Andrew Bowman's meanness towards her that had shrivelled him and made him ugly in her eyes.

'I've missed you dreadfully. I never stopped loving you, Amelia.' He tried to charm her, adjusting his scarf so she glimpsed his smile.

'I know you've been looking for me in Whitechapel. I didn't want to see you again but at least I can tell you never to come here again. I know you're married. I've found somebody else, too. I'm happy now, and greatly relieved that it's over between us.'

'Over?' he spluttered. He'd not expected to be rejected and his astonishment transformed to wrath. 'I think you forget yourself, you little hussy. You have my son. Where is he?'

Amelia's stomach lurched. So he'd found out she'd given birth to a boy. 'He's being well cared for.'

'Yet, you're out on the streets after dark. Are you no better than your sister?' He regretted letting that slip.

'What do you know about my sister?' Amelia repeated the question when he didn't answer her.

'Everybody who can read a newspaper knows about your sister,' he blustered. 'Fetch my son; I'll not allow him to be reared in a cesspit such as this. I'll take him with me.'

'Take him where?' Her fierce maternal instinct brought her fists up, ready to attack him. She'd escaped from a mad nun and her sadistic gamekeeper. She'd outwit a lecherous trickster; it made no difference to her who she stood against when fighting for Joey. 'Will you take him home and introduce your wife to a housemaid's bastard? That's what you called him, didn't you?'

'You've no need to be jealous of her. It's no love match and I can handle that side of things.' He slipped back into the role of smooth-talking Romeo. 'I shall buy us a place of our own, my dear, and some of the time we can live as a family. My wife will never know about you or him.'

'Your wife will know, because if you don't leave us alone, I shall tell her all about your lies. I would never live with you, or want my son to be corrupted by you. You're no good, and I'm ashamed that I didn't see the devil in you before now.'

His eyes seemed unnaturally bright and were constantly shifting, betraying an inner agitation that had been present even when he'd believed she'd snatch at what he offered.

She felt uneasy and backed away from him. 'Don't come here again or you'll be sorry.'

'Dare to threaten me, would you? I should've known you two were alike in more ways than one.'

He lunged at her but she dodged away and bolted. His running footsteps were close behind but suddenly halted. Then she heard her name shouted out and she pelted around the corner and into Nick's arms.

Without a word he grabbed her wrist and hurried her down the road towards home.

Amelia knew he was furious with her. She deserved a tongue-lashing but he seemed unable or unwilling to speak to her. She was angry with herself for taking risks, even though her drunken brother-in-law and a worthless liar were the worst people she'd encountered.

She clung to his hand with stiff fingers and glanced back just once at a street that was becoming deserted.

30

Wolff stepped over Nell's lifeless body and allowed his hands to be licked clean of gore. Moments later he was on his way with the mastiff loping at his side.

He'd used his head, copying what had been reported of the previous victims' mutilation to make it seem the murderer had struck again.

He wasn't squeamish; from the age of eight, when his mother died, he'd assisted his father to hunt and butcher for the table. He'd liked being an only child and even now hated his stillborn sister for killing his mother. On Wolff Senior's passing, he'd inherited the position of steward to Evangeline's family.

From a boy he'd wanted her. But a gamekeeper wasn't a suitable match for a squire's daughter, no matter how devoted to her he was.

Her fiancé was of equal status but had eloped with his pregnant mistress. Within a few months they were both dead: he fell from his horse and broke his neck. She swallowed arsenic before the baby was born. Evangeline had wished them dead and believed she'd invoked the devil and needed to repent. John

Wolff didn't see himself as the devil, rather her avenging angel. He was untroubled by his conscience and waited for her to come back to him. After twelve years she left the convent as a trained nurse to claim her inheritance. Her father had died and she used the bequest to set up a shelter for unmarried mothers, continuing to atone in a practical way.

Her fiancé and Nell Yates had repaid her goodness with betrayal. Unchecked, either of them could have destroyed her bond with the man who unconditionally adored her. Evangeline would never return his feelings. But she had put all her trust in her loyal Jack. He was the one who could destroy her. Her fiancé had awoken her to lust but no longer eased her body's torment. Wolff did.

He'd no wish for a wife; Evangeline was his partner and he bought his own relief on the streets of the East End. Which brought him back to Nell and his mistaken belief that she'd be too timid to blackmail him...

A sound of footsteps jerked him out of brooding on underestimating Nell. The darkness was too thick with autumn mist for him to see who approached. The length of stride indicated it wasn't a female, yet Wolff sensed he wasn't the only one deliberately keeping to the shadows. He brought the mastiff to heel with a growled command.

The shape of a cloaked man gradually emerged on the opposite side of the road. A beaver hat was pulled low on his brow, his face barely visible. Drawing abreast, the men slanted glances at one another as they passed.

* * *

Andrew Bowman threw off his bloodstained cloak. Each time he'd returned in this state he'd felt sickened yet invigorated. A fellow walking his dog had almost caught him at it. He'd never go back there. He'd control the demon if it killed him.

He blamed his run-in with Amelia Spencer for his increased frenzy. He'd almost given up searching for her and his son, then fate dealt him a bad hand. He was the fiend she'd branded him. He should leave the child alone or risked corrupting his own flesh and blood...

A creaking floorboard brought him hastily onto his feet. 'What in damnation... how did you get in here?' He was shaking violently and failed to quickly cover his bloodstained shirt with his cape.

'Good grief! What's happened to you, Andrew? Are you hurt?' Ivy dropped the ebony cane onto the bed and tried to fuss at his clothes.

'Why are you spying on me?' he screamed, knocking her to her knees. 'How did you get in here?'

He stood over her menacingly, and she scuttled away on all fours. He'd never before delivered a blow and she was scared as well as angry. 'Tomorrow I'm seeing a solicitor,' she panted, struggling to her feet with the aid of the bed frame. 'I'm divorcing you. You will see nothing of our child. My mother will give me every penny I need to fight you in the courts.' She tottered to unlock the door, one hand nursing her slapped cheek and the other brandishing the ebony cane. He'd left the key in the escutcheon and she turned it and stumbled outside.

'Ivy... please, we must talk.' He wanted his heir and a divorce would ruin him, but he had more on his mind than that.

'Stay away from me.' She jabbed the cane at him to keep him back. 'I know all about how you gave my wedding gift to a trollop.'

'No... you're mistaken. Forgive me, I didn't mean to lash out. But you made me do it; you had no right to break into my room.'

He tried to pacify her while wondering how much she'd seen. His bureaux were always locked. He had burned every incriminating item of clothing, other than what he had on. The room was cleaned but only at times when he was home to keep an eye on the housekeeper. Tomorrow, Ivy would open the newspaper and read of a murder in Whitechapel. She'd seen him bloodied and would start to wonder…

She was close to the top of the stairs, undecided whether to send for a policeman or a physician. She had considered before that her husband might be suffering a brain sickness that made him seem two different people. The thought of the scandal and the shame that would ensue from either course of action, made her hesitate and loathe him even more.

'How did you break in, my dear?'

'I had no need to break in; you left this in a coat you gave to Murray to hang up.'

He gazed at the key she held, furious at the elementary slip-up.

His contorted features sent Ivy rushing onwards, intending to summon help, and embarrassment be damned. Andrew seemed deranged this evening.

Realising she was about to scream, he lunged at her with a ferocious growl. The cane was brought down on his head, propelling him into a dazed run, arms flailing. Ivy skittered aside to avoid him crashing into her.

He made an attempt to save himself but couldn't find his balance and pitched forward, grabbing wildly for banisters just beyond his fingertips. He hurtled, bouncing and rolling, to the hallway and lay still.

Ivy supported her pregnant belly while her stout legs pounded down the stairs. She dropped breathlessly to her knees, staring at his motionless, half-closed eyelids. She darted a glance to the door that led to the servants' quarters. The Murrays would have retired to their beds down there. All remained quiet. Nobody came to investigate. She gave thanks that her husband's meanness allowed only two hard-of-hearing old retainers to share accommodation with them.

Gingerly, she disturbed his hair to peer at the wound. The blood flowed fast, pooling on the flagged floor. She knew the injury had been inflicted by the cane rather than the fall. Nobody need know that. She could clear up the worst of the mess on the floor and on him.

Andrew would want his reputation and his unborn child to be protected. Its father had died in a bad accident but the circumstances needed to be acceptable, for all their sakes. He often drank more than was wise. As did many an upstanding fellow barely able to clamber into a carriage to get himself home. A stronger whiff of whisky about him was necessary. It must seem he'd lost his step at the head of the stairs, had broken his neck while squiffy, and stained his clothes in blood. Feeling calmer she grabbed the newel post to hoist herself up. She padded in the direction of his study to find a decanter and make a start on covering their tracks.

* * *

Once back at the Anchor, Amelia had said goodnight to the Tanners then raced upstairs to check on Joey. Thankfully, she'd found him to be sleeping soundly. Nick had seen off the pub's reluctant home-goers, then locked up and joined her in her bedroom. There was a lot to be said, but after the door had been closed, a silence ensued. A customary fiery spark of excitement was lacking from the atmosphere, as was a natural ease at being in each other's company.

She'd already apologised and there seemed no point in repeating herself. She had her pride and wouldn't grovel. It broke her heart, though, to see him looking so weary in body and mind. He was losing patience with her, and resenting all the problems she'd brought to his door. She knew their bond was loosening and might completely unravel.

'I know I shouldn't have gone out. I was excited to see Kitty.' Amelia broke the ice by going over old ground after all.

'You're back safe and that's all that matters,' he eventually replied.

She knew he didn't mean he wasn't cross. She watched him gazing down into the street, one arm braced on the window frame.

'I feel ashamed for worrying the life out of you.' She got off the bed and went to him, slipping her arms about his waist and resting her forehead on his broad back. She breathed in the tarry tavern scent of him, willing him to still love her. 'I did see him... quite by accident. And I know you might not think so, but it was for the best. I had a chance to tell him to stay away and never come back. He knows he can't have my son.'

Nick turned around and gripped her shoulders. 'You just ran into John Wolff out there?'

Amelia blinked in confusion. 'No... Andrew Bowman ambushed me. You were going to warn me he'd come into the pub, weren't you?'

'So, he's still after you as well.'

'What do you mean... as well?'

'John Wolff came into the Anchor...'

Amelia's fingers covered her mouth in shock, then just as swiftly dropped away. 'Are you certain it was him?'

'Heavyset with dark hair and beard. A while back, I'd seen the same man with a bull mastiff at the top of the road.'

'It is him... he does have a dog.' Amelia's eyes grew round in apprehension.

'He bought a drink and later I caught him skulking in the corridor, having a look around. He heard you singing to Joey and said you sounded sweet.' Nick dragged his fingers through his hair. 'He was smug. Said he'd be back. He knows you're here, Amelia. That's what I've been keeping to myself.' It was Nick's turn to sound apologetic when saying, 'I should've told you. You wouldn't have risked going out alone, if I'd warned you he's been prowling about.' He embraced her tightly. 'I was frantic when Pearl said you weren't at home and should have been back ages ago.'

Amelia perched on the edge of her mattress, chewing frantically on her thumbnail while digesting this news. He hunkered down in front of her. 'I'll keep you safe... Joey too... I swear. But you must take care. Don't go out on your own at night. I can't be around all the time to protect you.'

'If you hadn't disturbed him, do you think he would've come upstairs?'

'I do...' Nick said hoarsely. 'He will come back.' He stood up and paced the room while she went to the cot.

Her son was peacefully sleeping, his chubby fist curled by his mouth. She wouldn't disturb him despite her urge to scoop him up and cuddle him tightly.

'What did Bowman have to say?'

'He knows I had a baby boy. I told him to stay away or I'd tell his wife what he did to me. He didn't like that. I hope it's enough to make him leave me alone.'

'If he comes back, I'll deal with him.'

'I'd never have bumped into him if I hadn't stopped to speak to Jimmy.' Before coming upstairs she'd told Nick about that meeting, and that Pearl had broken the news of Kitty's unexpected visit. It had seemed best to leave the worst bit until now. She'd not known the worst bit, though. 'We should go to the police and report Wolff,' she burst out.

'And accuse him of what? He came in for a drink and got lost in the corridor, he'll say.' Nick plunged his hands into his pockets. 'He's done nothing wrong yet.' He reckoned Wolff had done wrong in the past, but had covered his tracks. Much as he had done himself. The gamekeeper would be no easy opponent when the battle came.

Amelia knew Nick was right; with a serial killer at large the police would be too busy to take their complaint seriously. Her thoughts turned to her family and Jimmy's threats to bother them for money. 'Shall we go and see my parents tomorrow and take Joey? Enough time has passed since the funeral.' Amelia crossed herself. 'I pray the murderer will be caught soon and put an end to it.'

'Amen to that.'

She recognised the frustration in his voice. His family and his business had been dragged into this calamity, through her. 'I would never have come here if I'd known I'd bring such troubles to your door. I'm so sorry...'

'Don't say that. I want you here.'

'John Wolff and Andrew Bowman, even Sadie and Jimmy Burley... all my problems, not yours.' She paused. 'Yet you've not complained and you've offered to deal with it.'

'And I will.'

'Andrew had read about Sadie's murder and knew we were sisters. He said we were alike... to be insulting. I don't remember my name being mentioned in the paper, though.'

Nick watched her taking ribbon and pins from her fair hair then brushing it out. 'He probably picked that up from gossip, same as Polly did.' He paused. 'Do you believe me about her?'

'Yes... I'm sorry... I was feeling jealous...'

A soft tap on the door halted him halfway towards her. He opened up and Lenny began talking in a fast, furious hiss then he was gone, his footsteps clattering back down the stairs.

'What's happened?' She threw down her brush and repeated anxiously, 'What's happened, Nick?'

'Old Mr Jenkins has knocked for a bed for the night.' He'd named one of the Anchor's regular patrons. 'Jenkins said police are crawling all over Flower and Dean Street. Seems another body's been found.'

Amelia stifled a sob of despair.

'It might be unrelated to the others. Could be natural causes... a drunk... we'll know more tomorrow.' He came to her, stroked away her tears with his thumbs. 'Go to bed, Amelia. Try to sleep. I'm going to see what I can find out then we'll talk in the morning.'

* * *

By midday, when the news that not one, but two, bodies had been found, Kitty needed little persuasion from her friends to return to the safety of Cambridgeshire. She bid Mrs Root and Amelia a tearful farewell before heading for the railway station.

Outside on the streets, shocked and angry people were gathering. Some of the Vigilance Committee members were shouting from soapboxes about the lack of police action. A brick had been lobbed through the window of Leman Street police station. The mob had refused to disperse; everybody thought it was high time the murderer was caught.

Then came the whispers about the dead women. A horrified Amelia realised that one of them was somebody else she knew.

Nell Yates hadn't been her close friend, but her sister had

known her well as they had been work colleagues on and off over the years. Respectable women were reassuring themselves that the killer would only pick on prostitutes. Amelia didn't think anybody was safe after this.

She decided not to visit her parents; this double murder would soon make newspaper headlines and bring it all back for them. Seeing her would make it worse. She knew she reminded them of Sadie, and the shame the two of them had brought down on the family.

Nick was still out late in the evenings. At the warehouse, he said, and she wouldn't challenge him again. Mary avoided talking about him and seemed embarrassed, due to having her own suspicions, Amelia guessed. Mary and Lenny were doing the lion's share of the work, running the Anchor and Amelia kept herself busy behind the scenes, cooking and cleaning. She suspected things would soon come to a head and would rather go of her own accord than be asked to leave.

31

'Sister Evangeline says you must come straight away. She's in the front parlour and it's urgent.'

Eliza Aitkin had drawn the short straw and been sent to fetch John Wolff. She'd heard the chop of his butchering tools before poking her head around the open door. The sight of the lifeless rabbits on a bloody table was making her feel sick. Chore done, she sped away from his cottage despite her abdomen being still tender from her recent labour. That man gave her the shivers. And not in a nice way. The drama unfolding in the front parlour was another reason for Eliza's haste; she didn't want to miss any of it.

Evangeline knew the girls were eavesdropping while crouching behind the banisters. Any other day, she wouldn't have tolerated it, but observing a normal routine after this seemed in bad taste.

'You must drink some tea, Mrs Grubb; the sugar in it will settle your nerves.' Evangeline exchanged a look with Mrs Baxter. The cook remained hovering by the door in case something stronger needed fetching to calm the hysterical woman.

'I cannot, Sister. I feel so queasy,' moaned Mrs Grubb, pushing away the cup. 'If I'd known what might happen to the poor wretch, I would have taken her in there and then.'

'How could you have known, though?' Sister Evangeline offered the smelling salts instead. Mrs Grubb snorted at the bottle just as John Wolff appeared on the threshold. The cook curled her lip and went out.

'Mrs Grubb has brought some dreadful news, John.' Evangeline shook her head. 'Perhaps you don't remember Nell Yates who was once a resident here... well, it seems she has been murdered. And another body has also been discovered. Both women are believed to be victims of the serial killer.'

'Two victims?' Wolff remained by the door.

'It's hard to take in, isn't it? Maybe that's a mistake. The papers will report the details, anyway.'

'I will never forgive myself for turning her away,' whimpered Mrs Grubb.

'Had she come here, I expect I would have done the same,' Sister Evangeline admitted on a sigh. 'Mrs Grubb thinks you might have some information, John.' Knowing him as well as she did, Evangeline saw a fleeting change in his expression.

'Me?' He shifted position and crossed his arms.

'You see, after I barred Nell, I watched her from the window because I knew she'd sit on the step. I was worried she'd make a nuisance of herself.' Mrs Grubb pressed her handkerchief to her lips. 'Then you went by with your dog, and shortly afterwards Nell got up and headed off in the same direction. Did you see her, sir? Might you know where she went, or who she met?' Mrs Grubb shakily gained her feet. 'Any information might help the police to catch the beast, and ease my conscience.'

He shrugged. 'I can't help.' He glanced at Evangeline.

'Thank you, John. You can return to your work now.'

He was aware of whispering and scuffling at the top of the stairs as he crossed the hallway. At any other time, he would have stopped and stared to let the little harlots know he was on to them. He didn't lose pace or give them a glance and was soon striding out of the house.

Mrs Grubb left soon after with Eliza accompanying her, in case she had a fit of the vapours en route. Evangeline left the house and headed in a different direction.

'Did you notice Nell? Did she speak to you?' She gazed determinedly at Wolff. 'I know these women are shameless and will accost any fellow they see. Don't be frightened to own up.'

'Nothing frightens me, Evie.' It was confidently said yet not strictly true. Losing this woman's friendship and affection terrified him. Yet he'd done what he'd done to protect her as well as himself.

It was unfortunate that the serial killer had operated again when he'd been in the East End himself. Wolff wiped his hands on his leather apron, remembering the fellow he'd passed. Others, similarly muffled in scarves, had been out on the wintry streets; only one had stuck in Wolff's mind. He might be remembered in return: the man with the dog.

'I think you know more about Nell Yates than you admit, Jack. I won't be cross that you talked to her.'

'I ignore the creatures that come here. The Spencer girl is different, but only for being a thorn in our sides. I went to Whitechapel to try to snatch the child. Somebody was sitting on Mrs Grubb's step when I passed. I took no notice; I never do.' Wolff knew not even the Whitechapel murders could distract Evangeline from yearning for the boy.

'What happened at the tavern?' she asked eagerly. 'Will you be able to outwit Dupree soon?'

'He's a clever fellow and I couldn't chance anything last

night; the Anchor was rowdy with navvies. If a fight had broken out the coppers might have turned up.'

'That was indeed wise. But too much time has been lost already.' Evangeline sighed impatiently. 'I shall go and confront the girl. I'll tell her she's being selfish keeping the boy when he is destined to be our saviour.'

'She will laugh at you and say you are mad, Evie.' He could see his honesty annoyed her. His heavy hands massaged her shoulders. 'I will succeed by stealth. But the boy can't stay here for long. This is the first place they will come for him.'

Evangeline frowned but couldn't disagree. Dullards and heathens wouldn't understand that she did none of it for personal gain but for mankind. 'He will be sitting up now. Soon he will be talking. I long to see him and hear his voice.' She shrugged out of Wolff's caress and approached the door to breathe in sweeter air than was in this abattoir.

'I heard him crying upstairs in the tavern. She was singing to soothe him.' He'd managed to delay her departure with that snippet of information.

'I trust her to care for him. But she will never adore him as I do.' Evangeline's shining eyes clouded as she turned her thoughts to the recent drama. 'Mrs Grubb will talk to the police... your name will crop up. My reputation is everything in my work. Tittle-tattle about the mission could be ruinous.'

'We were at prayers when those other murders took place. Let the coppers come; I'll tell them the truth.' He was confident that nobody saw him with Nell. 'When we're in the chapel later I'll swear on the Bible, if you like.' He gave her a smile. 'We won't have trouble, Evie.'

* * *

'I know who you mean.' The landlord of the Prospect of Whitby was leaning on the bar having a gossip with Bill Potts about the double murder that had taken place a few weeks ago. 'Dark-haired fellow... bearded. He did know Nell Yates. He had a drink with her in here and came back again looking for her.' The landlord pushed a full tankard towards Bill.

'Sounds like the same cove, all right,' said Potts. 'Never used to see much of him but since summer he's been hanging around the area more. Sometimes brings a dog with him.'

'He's not been in here with a dog,' the landlord said.

'Struck up a conversation with me, he did, and started asking about Nick Dupree. Now, Sadie Burley was first to be killed and her sister is shacked up at the Anchor with Dupree. How's that for a coincidence?' Bill hiked his eyebrows and swallowed beer. 'That big fellow's got a connection to two of them dead gels. And I heard that he's a gamekeeper, works for a nun who takes in fallen women.'

'Well, that is queer. I recall he said he'd look over north London for Sadie Burley. I warned him her husband would lay him out.' The landlord inclined closer. 'Could be you should tell the coppers your thoughts.'

Bill Potts shrank back. 'You tell 'em! I ain't pointing a finger. Just sayin' there could be something needs lookin' into.' He finished his beer, slapped on his cap and made for the door.

There hadn't been a killing for weeks and people were praying that it was really over with now. Nobody had been brought to justice and traumatised locals hadn't put the atrocities from their minds; in fact, the lapse had provided the time for speculation to mount.

Bill Potts had his own theories and had purposely brought them somewhere public to air them. He had been one of Nell Yates' punters. He was praying nobody knew about that. He imagined there were plenty of other fellows on tenterhooks, trying to recall if they'd been indiscreet in their dealings with any of the victims.

The landlord here had a big mouth. It wouldn't take long for their conversation to be repeated. Bill reckoned he'd done his best to shift any attention away from himself and onto somebody else.

* * *

Mrs Grubb sent girls she couldn't accommodate to the mission, and Evangeline didn't want such recommendations to dry up, as well they might if rumours continued to swirl around.

Evangeline hurried up to John Wolff, leading the horse into the stable adjacent to his cottage.

'A policeman came while you were out,' she announced. 'I expect he'll come back to speak to you. This is too much, Jack. The girls suspect something. I've heard them whispering.' She followed him into the cottage, annoyed by his silence. Her livelihood was at stake. His too. In the past, when they'd spoken about this he would immediately attempt to pacify her; he didn't this time and appeared more dour than usual.

Parts of his shotgun were laid out neatly on the table beneath which the dog was sprawled. The animal stood up and padded over as his master started assembling the gun he'd recently cleaned.

'Why would a policeman want to speak to us again? I've already told them you were with me on all but that dreadful night when there were two victims.'

'You've no cause to fret, Evie. Gossip's going round. I work for you as a gamekeeper and you take in bad girls. Fools put two and two together and make five.'

Evangeline stared indignantly at him. 'Are you implying it's *my* fault the police came?'

'You're too charitable for your own good. You took pity on Nell Yates and we're both paying for that mistake.' Wolff had noticed that when he was out, people had started crossing the road to avoid him. He wasn't overly worried about coming under suspicion; it was assumed a single killer was responsible for murdering the Whitechapel women. On other significant times he'd been in the company of a nun who had already vouched for him.

'The double murder is sticking in people's minds. Once the perpetrator strikes again, attention will shift away from Nell and her acquaintances.' She sighed. 'Nell was trouble but she didn't deserve such a dreadful end.'

'She was trouble, right enough,' he muttered. 'You think there will be another killing, do you?'

'Well, I hope not, of course... although that doesn't help our cause. It leaves us in the spotlight. I have been thinking, it would be best if you moved away until this calms down.'

'Away?' He threw the gun onto the table in a clatter. 'And go where?'

'I don't know... find a lodging somewhere. It might not be for long if they arrest somebody soon. The mission can't be black-listed or the girls won't come.'

'You seem to care more about those whores than you do me.' He turned away from her. 'If I leave here you will never have the boy. Making a fuss will get you nowhere; Dupree will set the law on you. The coppers will be back for you, not for me.'

Evangeline felt flustered. They never had cross words. Even as children they'd not argued. She'd grown used to his hero worship and to him holding his tongue. He'd grown used to her keeping a roof over his head and cash in his pocket. Dangerous times had unsettled them. And the birth of a baby boy on Easter Day. Momentous things had happened that couldn't be undone to allow them a way back to harmony.

'If you still want the boy, I'll get him. I said I would and I will. After that... neither of us can remain here.' Wolff jerked his head at the mission house. 'Think carefully what you choose to do, for they will come after us, Evie. Not just Dupree... the authorities as well.'

'I'll never give up my work here.' Evangeline calculated the risks. 'You told me Dupree is a dodgy sort; he won't want the police involved in case they turn their attention to him. The child will be put out of sight in the countryside with a trusted foster mother. I will visit him there.' She smiled, satisfied. 'Things will die down; Amelia Spencer is young and healthy. She and her handsome man will have other babies to love... six or seven, perhaps. She can't be allowed to be selfish and deny me the one child the Lord gave to me.'

32

'Are you leaving me?'

'Yes.'

'Why?'

'I have to.' Amelia put down the clothes she'd been folding and perched on the edge of the bed. The movement in the mattress rolled Joey over. She sat him up and he clapped his hands, enjoying the game. Her heart was breaking, her eyes scalded by tears, but her happy little boy made her smile.

'Why?' Nick closed the door and came into the bedroom. 'Mary sent for me when she realised you were packing.'

'I wish she hadn't done that.'

'You wanted me to come back later and find you gone – is that it?' He stared at her then gave a harsh laugh. 'You're going to Bowman, after all, aren't you?'

'If I was stupid enough to want to, I'd be too late.' She picked up a letter from the blanket. 'A colleague at Campbell House wrote to let me know Andrew died in an accident at home. He broke his neck on the stairs while drunk. Lorna Smith thought I should know and sent this to my parents to forward. Read it, if you want to.'

His tarry fingers took the letter and started to unfold it. He let the smudged paper drift to the bed. 'I don't need to read it. I'm not going to say I'm sorry he's gone.'

'Neither am I. But he's Joey's father and it's hard to believe somebody else I know has died.'

'Where are you going?'

'To Cambridge. Kitty told me about a woman who'll accept a domestic with a child. I can't stay here any longer.'

Nick leaned back against the door, and closed his eyes. 'Look... I know it's been tough lately.' A self-mocking gesture acknowledged the understatement.

Another murder had taken place just a couple of days' ago. So gruesome a sight was the victim's mutilated body that it was said a constable had swooned outside the lodging house where it had been discovered.

'You shouldn't be burdened with my troubles,' said Amelia. 'I want to be with you. But we both know we're already drifting apart.' She paused. 'I don't blame you for missing the life you had before I barged in and turned everything upside down.'

'I won't pretend it's been easy. But I want you to stay with me, Amelia. I love you and Joey.'

She'd longed to hear him say that and now it was too late. 'Perhaps you do. But you resent us as well. So how long will love last?'

'That's not true. I don't regret getting involved with you, if that's what you mean.'

'I suppose I mean that I understand why you stay away so much from your own home. And I know this awful business with the murders, and with John Wolff, isn't over. In a few months' time when it's weighing even more heavily on us, there'll be no more love or friendship. I want us to part as friends. Then, perhaps in the future, there'll be another chance for us.'

'Are you running away from me or from John Wolff?'

'Both of you. For different reasons.' She put another garment neatly into the carpetbag, and kept talking. 'We've never had a proper heart-to-heart... or anything else really. Before I go, I'd like you to trust me with an honest answer about something. I trusted you on that first night we met when you guessed I was pregnant and homeless and hoping somebody would help me.' She stood up and faced him. 'You said to me: "So tell me if I've got this right..." and went on to sum up my life in a few seconds. You know a lot about me and my family.' She gazed soulfully at him. 'All I know about your folk are their names and the little Mary's said. I've had plenty of time to think about you, though. Cooking and cleaning have some benefits.'

He gestured a wordless invitation.

'Jennifer Dupree isn't your sister, she's your mother. She was seduced, in the same way I was, and had a son.' A rueful twitch of his lips was confirmation enough. 'Did your nan throw her out when she got pregnant?'

'She tried to make her stay. Jennifer ran off.'

Amelia considered that, thinking Jennifer lucky and foolish. 'What happened?'

'My grandfather tracked her down. She was seventeen, living with an escaped convict. There was a fight.'

'Were you with your mother then?'

'I was born in a workhouse and left there. My grandmother got me out and brought me here. I was about a year old by then.'

'I'm so glad you came home.' Amelia's voice was thick with emotion. 'Where's your mum now?'

He shrugged. 'Could be anywhere. She didn't want me. I

always thought of Hannah as my mum and Mary as my sister. That's how I grew up. Mary's my aunt but refers to me as her brother. We're close in age and nobody knew any different. Apart from perhaps old-timers like Daisy Root.'

'If she knows, she keeps it to herself,' Amelia said, thankful of her friend's decency. A hard and bitter life awaited a child known as a bastard. 'Do you know where your father is?'

'Pauper's grave. He died in the fight with Victor Dupree.'

Amelia thought about that while subduing her shock. 'Did your grandfather go to sea to avoid being arrested?'

'Given a chance he would've; it was self-defence but he didn't escape a prison sentence. Jennifer spoke for her father in court, said he'd not started the fight. Made no difference. He was incarcerated on one of the prison hulks at Woolwich.'

'How long before he was released?' Amelia had heard of the floating hells, anchored just off the banks of the Thames. They took convicts that couldn't be housed in overflowing gaols. Her father had told stories of seeing gangs of shuffling men chained together on the towpaths.

'He never was released,' Nick said after a short silence. 'He didn't die while sailing the seven seas. That's a myth started by my grandmother to throw gossips off the scent. He was a merchant seaman but he died of cholera on a stinking prison ship.' He choked a sour laugh. 'Apparently, it was the same one my father – if that's who he was – had escaped from. Could be another myth...'

'I'm so sorry,' Amelia said husky-voiced. 'Did your nan tell you all of this?'

'Some of it. Mary filled in the rest after Hannah died.' He gazed up at the ceiling. 'Prisoners on the hulks were put to work dredging the river. My nan would go to Woolwich to watch him. Once or twice she managed to get close enough to give him some food. He was buried on the banks of the Thames... lots of those convicts were. She'd go from time to time to pick the red nettles that grow there. Convicts' flowers, they're called. Mary says her dad gave her mum cholera, picked up from the Thames mud, because he wanted them to be together again.' He fell quiet but Amelia didn't fill the silence. 'That finished the pub off for a while. People stayed away, frightened of catching it. Mary told everybody a ship's crew came in carrying it.'

It was a tragic family story to rival her own. 'Not a lucky lot, are we, the Duprees and the Spencers?'

'We've got to make our own luck, Amelia.'

She knew he was asking her to change her mind and stay. But she wouldn't. 'Dreadful things started to happen after I came here. I have awful dreams about it.' She picked up Joey's teething ring and gave it to him as he mewled.

'I know you have nightmares,' he said gently. 'Those will pass. You're still grieving.'

'It's real to me. This feeling I have that I'm responsible somehow.'

'For the deaths? Don't be daft.' He was by her side in a single stride, tilting up her lowered chin.

'Sometimes Sadie comes to me when I'm asleep, then when I wake, the urge to leave here is so strong. I think she knew her murderer... She's warning me he's coming for me.'

'Hush,' Nick urged her to sit on the bed and crouched down by her side. 'The size of it all is making you ill. That letter about Bowman is the final straw. He was important, being Joey's father. It's another loss.'

'Everything's all mixed up, going round and round in my head, sending me mad.' A sob tore from her throat and he held her, stroking her hair and murmuring of his love until she quietened. Amelia wiped her eyes on her wrist. 'I've even been thinking Joey shouldn't have been born.' Her beautiful little boy bounced, flapping his hands, responding to his name. 'Other times, I think I should have left him behind at the mission. Sister Evangeline still wants him or Wolff wouldn't be prowling about. She must love Joey. There's something bad at that place, though; that's why I ran away in the first place.'

Nick reached to comfort her again but she caught his hand, brought it to rub a caress against her damp cheek.

'I feel guiltier about Joey than anything else... even hurting my mum and dad. I'll risk everything for him, including losing you. I'm taking him away to protect him. There's something evil in Whitechapel.'

'We'll go together.'

She jerked up her face. 'No... you can't leave. You have your work and this place and your family.'

He drew her up to face him. 'You're my family. You and Joey. I'll give it all up for you. I love you.'

'But... the pub...'

'I knew this day was coming. Ever since Wolff turned up, I knew. I'm not quite ready for it, though. I've been selling everything up to buy a sailing boat. That's why I've been late home. I hoped I'd be ready by the time Wolff showed his hand. I got the boat yesterday. Things need doing, but it's seaworthy. It's not perfect timing, but we'll have to make do.' He paused, preparing to reveal more. 'There's something else you should know. I'm a crook. Have been for years.'

'What sort of crook?'

'You're not surprised,' he said dryly.

'Sadie told me, long ago, that you made her Jimmy look like a saint by comparison. I'd've worked it out anyway. It's unusual for a man to have his own pub at a young age.'

'My family lost the Anchor for a while, after all the trouble.

Living and working in the pub was all Mary knew. She was still a kid when she started baking pies and filling tankards. She used to sing and dance on the bar.' He chuckled. 'Punters loved it. After Hannah got sick, Mary was on her own with me. I was too young to be much help so she got laundry work and shop work, anything she could. Then she married Lenny Tanner at sixteen so she could keep me with her and I didn't end up back in the workhouse.'

'Did Lenny do you that fake reference for your first job?'

'An old navy pal of my grandfather's did it. He had connections with the right people. He'd kept in touch with Mary after her parents died... felt sorry for her. He was one of the few that knew our history.' He paused. 'He gave good advice to a bitter thirteen-year-old orphan boy. Old Father Thames is a cruel master, but you can make him work for you, he said.'

She knew he was talking of taking revenge for the wrong done to his grandfather.

'Victor Dupree died after rotting for a year on that prison hulk. I never got to know him. My nan was gone too soon as well. By the time I was fourteen I was unloading ships packed with booze, tobacco, beef... all the things that a publican needed.' He paused. 'Mary deserved to have her home back. Old Father Thames owed her more than he owed me. I didn't intend to be a criminal for long... only until the pub was up and running again. It's been over ten years. Long enough. Dues are paid.'

Amelia was torn between shock and fascination. She admired rather condemned him for what he'd done. The good girl from Hackney believed anything could and should be done to protect family. 'You weren't caught?'

'It pays to be shrewd. And to know the underground passages... the hidey-holes. I always moved things on quickly.

There's nothing left. Warehouse... cellars... all empty. I'm done.'

'Are you done with the Anchor tavern, too?'

'Mary can have it. She's earned it ten times over. Lenny's pulling his weight. Seems he can be trusted at last. I think losing the baby shocked him into being the man she needed. I've not said anything to them but I know they'll be happy to take it over lock, stock and barrel. When we're gone, they'll need help. Spider wants a full-time job.' He brushed Amelia's cheek with his finger. 'You deserve a home of your own choosing. I know you've felt you've been treading on Mary's toes at times.'

'I was happy here at first, before everything bad happened...'

'I know. Finish packing your things; I'll go down and tell them we're leaving.'

'You'll come with me today?'

'This evening. Catch tonight's tide and head towards Kent. I've some ideas for the future. Still half-baked, though.' He paused. 'Are you ready for a leap of faith with me, Amelia, and to be my wife?'

'I'm ready,' she said. 'Have been since the moment I jumped off the mission wall with Joey in my bag. I was terrified. I just kept telling myself it would be all right because you'd be there.'

He rested his forehead against hers. 'I swear I will look after you both. We're in it together now, whatever life brings. Man and wife and son.'

'We are.' She kissed his stubbly cheek with its scent of river brine. 'I must see my parents one last time though. I'll go this afternoon. Tell them we're going away to be married and to make a fresh start.'

'Leave Joey with me. He'll be safe.'

'You feel it, too, don't you?'

He nodded. 'Don't be gone long. Be back before dark.'

* * *

Joey was missing his mother. Nick went to look out of the window again with the baby wriggling in his arms. Twilight had descended but the lamplighters hadn't yet started work. He'd told Amelia to return quickly and was trying to find reasons for why she hadn't. She was keen to leave tonight, so something unexpected had delayed her. If she wasn't back soon, he'd go and find her. He stiffened, making Joey protest at his tighter grip.

The man he feared might have ambushed Amelia was right here beneath his nose. Greatly relieved to see him, he stepped back from view, in case Wolff looked up and realised he'd been spotted trespassing.

Jet would be growling downstairs. The faintest of sounds or scents infiltrating an open shutter would put him on guard. Nick closed his eyes in silent prayer. He knew this was it. No more time left to prepare, only to act. And do it fast and smart; there'd be no second chance.

Spider had lit some oil lamps and was polishing tankards, ready for opening time. He gave his boss a wide grin and tickled Joey under the chin to stop his grizzles. He knew he'd been promoted and could quit the match factory now. He'd sooner work for Mr Dupree than Mrs Tanner but Spider had high hopes that this fellow would be back once his honeymoon was over.

'Where's my sister?'

'Gone up the road to find the lad sniffin' around Pearl.' Spider shrugged. 'I offered to deck him but Mrs Tanner said she could do it herself. She's got the nipper with her and taken Pearl 'n' all.' He rolled his eyes to show trouble was brewing.

Nick knew his brother-in-law wouldn't be back from the market yet and that left Spider as his only accomplice.

'Got a job for you, Spider, and you'd better not mess it up, d'you hear me?'

Spider nodded, licking his lips nervously, having picked up on his boss's mood.

Nick put the baby into Spider's clumsy hold. Only minutes later, he was heading towards the side alley.

'Still looking for that privy, eh?' He positioned himself in the centre of the pathway, blocking Wolff in.

'Waiting for opening time. Told you I'd be back.'

'You did. But my dog still don't like you, or the mutt you've brought with you. You're not welcome.' Jet had trotted to take up position, coat bristling and a growl vibrating in his craw. The mastiff reacted to the challenge with bared fangs.

'Free country.'

'You're trespassing on my land. I reckon you was trying to break into my pub.'

Wolff snorted derision. 'Your ale's watered down. I've tasted better. I'll drink elsewhere.' He shoved past. As he turned into the street, Spider hared past and disappeared inside the Anchor.

Wolff had watched Amelia Spencer go out alone. He had also seen the regular barmaid marching up the road, carrying a toddler and dragging a girl by the hand. He was banking on them all being gone for a while. Dupree would be busy with only the youth as backup. There wouldn't be another such chance to snatch the baby.

Evangeline might insist he leave the mission even after she'd got what she wanted. He would, but he'd take the boy with him, confident she'd follow to safeguard her little messiah.

From his vantage point in a courtyard across the road, he watched Dupree come out of the pub and take a look around. He went back inside, but reappeared, cradling the shawled child. The pot boy was with him and handed him another blanket. Once the baby was wrapped up, Dupree set off in the direction of the docks with his wolfhound padding in his wake.

Wolff followed, seeking the shadows lent by dark walls and hedges, making sure he and the mastiff stayed out of sight of the man who at intervals searched over his shoulder in case of pursuit.

33

He was outranked. What he lacked in brawn he'd need to make up for with youth and speed. His adversary would also be weighing up odds and tactics. Nicholas Dupree continued to prepare for a fight to the death while assembling his armoury.

Wolff was older. He wouldn't possess the stamina and agility of a man half his age. He'd be intending to trap his opponent in his powerful gamekeeper arms; then it would be a wrestling match, hard for Nick to win. Or, perhaps, Wolff had no intention of exerting himself. A hunter would be skilled in bringing down his quarry with knife or shotgun.

The weight of his own blade was dragging on his pocket and Nick withdrew it by the hilt. He'd had plenty of dirty fights, won most. He'd not killed a man before. This was different though. His future – and Amelia's and Joey's – depended on what happened next. He reckoned Wolff had an advantage there: he hadn't only stalked and killed game.

Having mulled over what Amelia had said, he found he agreed with a lot of it, hard though it was to believe that even a depraved lunatic would butcher five women as a smokescreen to abduct a baby. If Wolff were the culprit, the killings would stop after his death. Nick needed to survive beyond tonight to find out.

He'd purposely lured his enemy here. This was his home ground. He knew where every crowbar and chain was stowed, even in darkness. His senses were on high alert, yet he could detect only shadows and the creaking of aged timbers harmonising with Jet's warning growl. His foe had stopped circling the warehouse and was now inside.

'Thought I'd find this place full of contraband booze and baccy,' said a disembodied voice. Wolff stepped out from behind pallets and was silhouetted by a naphtha flare on the jetty.

'If you're buying, I'll find you some; don't worry about that.'

'Funny... very funny. Got that pub on the back of smuggling, I reckon. Might as well own up to it. Time to confess your sins.'

'If I tell you me secrets, mate, I'll have to kill you.'

'You could try... that's all you could do, boy. You're a criminal, I reckon, Dupree.'

'So, arrest me.'

'Ain't here to arrest you. You know what I want, so no games need playing. Give me the Spencer boy. Then it'll be over. Nobody gets hurt.'

'You mean this? Think it's a girl, mate. But, here, it's yours.' Nick took Pearl's doll from beneath the bulky shawls and hurled it at Wolff, then sprinted in behind it. The mastiff sprang but was met in mid-air by Jet attacking from the side and bringing the dog down.

Nick grabbed the chain he'd lined up minutes earlier and swung it at Wolff's head, sending him to his knees, but the big man had the knife ready and hurled it. He missed his target: it embedded in Nick's bicep rather than his chest. Nick shouted a curse, dropping his makeshift weapon to yank out the blade and clamp a hand over the wound. He swooped on a crowbar, hidden earlier beneath a pallet, viciously lashing at Wolff's legs to keep him at bay while regaining his feet.

They fought evenly at first, each man driving forward then retreating, ferociously lunging and evading, their knives slicing air. The only sound in the warehouse was hard, fast breathing and the thud and crack of metal bouncing off wood. Wolff had the advantage of two good arms and a larger blade. He led with the knife, and a short iron pole he'd snatched was his backup.

The dogs had fallen quiet but for occasional yelps.

Nick's right hand was slimy with blood and he knew he had to end this soon. Wolff was still dazed from the blow to his skull, swaying like a drunk, but he'd shake that off before long. Nick fell back, drawing Wolff with him. A boat hook was within reach. He grabbed it then wielded it double-handed with all his remaining strength. The metal pike found a home in Wolff's back, sending him off at a run then onto his knees then down, face front.

Nick sniffed in air, found his knife on the floor, and stood over him. 'Come back again and I'll finish you,' he panted. 'Swear on my son's life I'll finish you.'

'You gave him to the potman to hide, didn't you?' Wolff lifted his head slightly; he had to know how he'd been outwitted.

Nick crouched down and realised the hole pumping blood in Wolff's back looked bad enough to finish him. Even if it didn't, such an injury would prevent him being a danger to anybody from now on. 'Yeah... that's what I did. I saved my son from you with the help of a kid and an old woman up the road.' Nick mockingly patted his opponent's arm in consolation.

Spider had entered into the spirit of the adventure. He'd pulled one side of his big brother's hand-me-down jacket over

Joey then hurried off with his precious cargo to be given into Mrs Root's care.

'Now, you tell me something, 'cos I reckon I know what you've been up to, 'n' all.' He lifted Wolff's head by its hair. 'Did you murder the five Whitechapel women?'

Wolff tried to laugh: a croaky sound that transformed into a cough and spurted blood from his back. 'Fuck off,' he wheezed.

Nick let his head thump down on planking. 'Reckon I will. Got things to do while you go straight to hell, you evil bastard.'

He stood up and went to kneel by Jet. He ran a hand over his warm sticky coat. The wolfhound was already dead, the mastiff getting there more slowly. He put the dog out of its misery, then pulled Jet into his arms. With a groan of exertion, he stood up and with a shout of pain manoeuvred the dog across his shoulders.

He stumbled out of the warehouse and made unsteady progress over stony mud down to the banks of the Thames. He waded in almost up to his waist before the tide rocked him and he halted. He ducked down, and let Jet go then surfaced to watch as the dark river took him seawards.

* * *

'Where have you been? I've been waiting and waiting for you.' Evangeline had entered Wolff's cottage, and glimpsed his bulk occupying an armchair. 'Why haven't you got a fire? Or a lamp? It's cold and dark in here.' She fiddled on the table to find a candle and matches then hurried closer to illuminate his face, making him squint. 'Don't tell me you failed again. Oh, Jack, you vowed this time you would get the boy.' She gave his beard an angry tug. 'Tell me quickly what's gone on. I can't tarry. A girl is in labour. Mrs Baxter is with her. With luck the infant will hang on until morning as the pains have stopped.'

He gripped her wrist to stop her jabbering. The candle flame wavered from being disturbed and it took Evangeline a moment to realise the wet on her skin was blood.

'What's happened to you, Jack?'

'Will you come to the chapel with me, Evie?'

'Not now. I'm too busy.' Evangeline raised the light to peer at his face. She nearly dropped the candlestick in shock on seeing his forehead was cut open beneath a knot of hair. And he was slumped rather than sitting in the chair with his eyes half closed. A coppery odour became significant. She was used to a gamey atmosphere in here. This seemed different: like the smell of fresh blood in a labour ward.

With a groan, Wolff used both hands on the chair arms to push himself upright. 'I must confess my sins and pray for salvation. I'm dying, Evie.'

'What nonsense. Where have you been?' She dodged to block his way as he lumbered towards the exit.

Wolff hung his head and Evangeline heeded that unspoken plea, letting him pass through the open doorway. She rushed after him as his laboured footsteps took him in the direction of the chapel. 'You've been fighting. Dupree beat you, didn't he? That's why you've returned empty-handed. Come to the house and I'll patch you up.'

'You can't nurse this, Evie.'

The inmates had used the chapel earlier and the candles had been left burning after evensong. Twin windows were aglow, like kindly eyes, and he plodded onwards towards the beacon of light, deaf to Evangeline urging him to accompany her to the house.

He sagged to his knees by the altar. In a panic, she came

down beside him, her face as white as his. She had been frantically turning things over in her mind. 'Tell me the truth; have you been fighting with Dupree, or have you done something dreadfully wicked and not made a clean escape this time? Are the police about to turn up for you?'

The silence lengthened and the blood from his gouged back puddled on the floor. 'Only two were my work,' he mumbled. 'I swear it's the truth. I didn't want to kill them. But I had to, to protect you.'

'Protect me?' she whispered and scurried backwards on all fours. From the moment Mrs Grubb had come to question him about Nell Yates, Evangeline had seen guilt in him that nobody else could. She'd hoped and prayed to be mistaken. She'd also beseeched the Lord to have the child safely in her possession before challenging him over these suspicions.

'Nell Yates would've blackmailed us. She spied on us while we were in here together. She called you a whore, Evie.'

Evangeline crawled towards him on the stone floor. 'Blackmail? No! What did she see?'

He raised his head and his black eyes bored into hers, daring her to deny it. 'She saw us as lovers. She would have betrayed us and ruined you. So I stopped her. For your sake.' He sighed. 'The second one... that was bad to do... but another murder would help our cause, you said. A doe for butchering, not a woman, that's how I had to think of her to throw the scent off us.'

'*Us?* I had no part in this,' Evangeline shouted. 'What have you done? *You* have ruined me. I'll be accused of being an accomplice to murder.'

'Your loyal Jack will be dead by morning, and forgotten when the real killer strikes again.'

'He might not strike again; I'll be arrested... strung up like a common criminal. You can't die. You must own up, and tell everybody I'm innocent.' She was gibbering hysterically and tried to rise to her feet but he held on to her with surprising strength left in his grip. 'Let me go, Jack! I'll fetch someone. The authorities must hear your confession and you must say I had no hand in it.' She slapped at him, beat on his chest, wailing and sobbing.

'Everything will be all right, I promise. Stay with me, Evie. I don't want to be alone.' A heavy arm about her shoulders, dragged her to his side.

'Oh, Jack... I cannot be hanged by the neck. It will hurt terribly. I don't deserve torment when the Lord knows I'm innocent.' She clasped her shaking hands on the crucifix and bowed her head towards it.

'Yes, he knows, and you will be at peace with Him in heaven, Evie.' He slipped the knife out of his pocket, and used it without hesitation, as he would on the beautiful woodland creatures he never allowed to hurt. He cuddled her, crooning to her until her jerking limbs became still and she sagged in his arms.

He laid her down carefully, neatening her habit and straightening her wimple, tucking into it her dark brown hair loosened by their struggle.

Supporting himself against the altar he staggered onto his feet then laboriously retraced his steps along the cinder path to the cottage to collect the things he needed.

* * *

Mrs Baxter had asked Eliza Aitkin to keep an eye on the expectant mother while she went to check on the babies in the nursery. Eliza suspected the old girl had gone for a nip of gin as well.

'What in Gawd's name's going on out there?'

The patient lying in bed pushed herself up on her elbows to take an interest. 'What's that you say, Eliza?'

Eliza's mouth dropped open as the grey smoke that had billowed into the night sky, turned orange in colour. She jumped up from the chair and went to fully open the curtains and stare out of the window. 'Bleeding hell! The chapel's caught fire!' She whipped about with a hand clamped to her mouth.

Mrs Baxter came in just as a loud bang startled Eliza into jumping on the spot and shrieking, 'Where's Sister Evangeline?'

'Calm yourself down, Eliza Aitkin. That sounded like his shotgun; that's all, that was. Foxes are at the chickens, I expect.' Having reached the window Mrs Baxter discovered why Eliza had become hysterical. She gawped in disbelief at the blaze in the distance then crossed herself.

'Get yourself dressed for outdoors, Eliza Aitkin,' said a grim Mrs Baxter. 'Then find another girl to accompany you to Mrs Grubb's. We're going to need help.'

Not wanting to miss out, the expectant mother waddled over to see what was causing the excitement.

'When you reach Mrs Grubb's, tell her she must raise the alarm at once.'

'Shouldn't I go and find Sister Evangeline first?' said an anxious Eliza. 'What if she don't know there's a fire?' The girl wasn't keen on going out in pitch-dark even with a companion.

Mrs Baxter carried on staring and grimly shaking her head.

'Where *is* Sister Evangeline?' Eliza asked.

'The sister went looking for John Wolff...' Mrs Baxter turned away, crossing herself again. 'Reckon she found him.'

34

The boat rocked as Amelia stepped on deck. Once confident she'd found her balance, she took her son from Nick and murmured soothingly to the baby. It had been a hectic, strange day for him, too. At almost eight months old, Joey was becoming knowing. Usually, he would be warm in his cot at this hour, not beneath frost-bright stars with sharp briny air on his face.

'Take a seat over there.' Nick swung the lamp to indicate a small-planked bench.

She immediately perched on it, wrapping Joey in his shawl and watching Nick making preparations for the off. Their bags and boxes were loaded while he vaulted nimbly on and off the craft, using ropes and poles to assist. Then, when all their belongings were off the jetty, he stopped to look at her.

'Ready?'

'Yes.'

He came and sat beside her, holding mother and child within his embrace.

Amelia had known bad trouble had started as soon as she found out Mrs Root was caring for Joey. When Nick returned, soaked through and bleeding, it had seemed nothing much compared to her terror that she might never see him again.

They'd had little time to talk. A quick decision had to be made if they were to catch this evening's tide. Nick's wound had been bathed and bandaged and, although it needed stitching, he'd said he would do without.

'It's finished now, isn't it, with Wolff?'

'It is for us, Amelia. He couldn't have been as badly injured as I thought to have dragged himself away.' Nick gazed in the direction of the warehouse. 'The mastiff is still in there. Rats will dispose of him.'

'I'm so sorry about Jet. He was the loveliest dog. I'll miss him.'

'Me too...' Nick said quietly. 'We'll get Joey a pup when he's older. A boy should have a dog.'

'I wish I'd not been so late back; I waited for my dad to come home. He's very poorly.' Her mother hadn't been exaggerating his frailty. In the short time since Sadie's funeral, Wilfred Spencer's grief had shrivelled him. He'd been joyous that she'd waited to see him and they'd had more tea and talked of happier times. 'They asked about you and Joey. That's the first time they've done that.'

'I'd like to meet them. I've spoken to your dad but he probably doesn't remember me.'

'Oh, he does. I said I'd write to them when we're settled somewhere. They could visit us. A holiday by the sea will do my dad good.'

Amelia knew it was a fantasy. There'd be no seaside reunion for the Spencers. Mary and Lenny had said they were coming to see them first chance they got to shut the pub for a few days. It had, of necessity, been a brisk farewell at the Anchor but the Tanners were happy with the new situation.

'This is the first time I've been on a proper boat.'

'Don't worry, we'll make a sailor of you. This is home now until we find a place on dry land.' They gazed at one another, smiling.

'Cast off then, shall I?'

She nodded excitedly.

He placed the lantern on the bench. Before he could step away, she stopped him and kissed him on the mouth. He curved his hand around her nape and kissed her back, hard and sweet. 'I've waited a long time for that from you,' he said when eventually they broke apart.

'You're a good man, Nicholas Dupree... even if you have been bad in the past.'

'I'm a lucky man,' he said. 'And don't just mean 'cos I've got you. There were times when I thought the coppers might barge into the Anchor and arrest me.' He stared at the oily black water that reflected riverbank flares. 'It's as well to bow out before Old Father Thames turns on me.'

'Whatever you've done, I couldn't have wished for a better husband or a better father for Joey. We both love you.' She glanced up at the dark sky. 'No sunset for us to sail into.'

'Too late for sunset. Anyway, we're heading east.'

Joey started to grizzle and punch at his shawl. 'He's tired,' said Amelia. 'Past his bedtime, and mine.'

'Go below.' Nick nodded at a cabin door, then stood up and went to open it. 'Inside is a bunk. You'll find blankets and pillows in the locker.' He came back to her, stroked her face with his roughened thumb, and kissed her warmly goodnight. 'Go and get some rest, Amelia. I'll wake you at sunrise.'

EPILOGUE
MAYFAIR 1889

Mrs Lomax dandled her son upon her knee, smoothing his dark brown hair.

'Shouldn't young Oliver be having his nap?'

She turned her cheek to receive her husband's kiss. 'I'll take him to the nursery.'

'I've come home from my club especially to see you, Mrs Lomax.'

'It's the middle of the afternoon, Gideon.' She giggled. 'We'll scandalise the servants.'

'Never mind them. We've scandalised all of society by marrying so soon after your first husband died.'

'I wish you were my first husband, and this your child.'

Gideon ruffled the boy's dark curls. 'He's a bonny lad to be proud of, in any case,' he said with genuine affection. 'And to all intents and purposes, he is mine.'

Ivy settled the baby in his cot and he was soon yawning. She stared at his placid little face, searching for a sign of his real father in him. Any thought of that man upset her. Yet she felt guilty for suspecting Andrew Bowman could be the

Whitechapel murderer. On the night of his fatal accident, he'd arrived home in a dreadful mess, then the following day the newspapers had broken the news of more women slain. There had been another murder after his burial, attributed to the serial killer, and the hunt went on for that savage. She now believed Andrew had got into a fight, probably with a pimp. It would account for his agitation and his bloodstained clothes that night. The East End was a lawless place and he'd been a fool to allow his addiction to prostitutes to lure him there.

She approached the window and her eyes were caught by a magpie bobbing about on the lawn. She waited for its mate to appear; one for sorrow... two for joy. She softly chanted the superstitious rhyme but stopped, having noticed the bird had hopped around and seemed to be staring at her. With a raucous cackle, it flew off and she shivered. She scolded herself for being silly. Andrew Bowman couldn't mock her from beyond the grave.

'Let's move from this house, Gideon,' Ivy said as her husband opened the door and beckoned to her with a wink. 'I've had enough of this place.'

* * *

Bloomsbury 1889

'You had no idea of Sister Evangeline's intentions?'

'I did not, sir.' Mrs Grubb continued to gawp at the solicitor. His letter had mentioned a bequest; she had anticipated receiving some of the sister's midwifery equipment.

'What a grand surprise then,' said the fellow. He imagined her reluctance to celebrate had much to do with a tragedy having brought her a property worth a substantial sum.

The coroner reported Sister Evangeline's death was, in all likelihood, the result of the brave woman perishing trying to save her manservant. John Wolff had built a funeral pyre of pews, intending it to cremate his remains then shot himself while in an unbalanced state of mind. Little more than ash and bones had remained of the bodies. Wreckage of a shotgun by his side, and a bullet hole in his skull, told its own story. The sister's crucifix had lain amid the debris of her skeleton.

An unbreakable loyalty had existed between the deceased, confirmed by witnesses who blamed the police for badgering Wolff and driving him to it. Sister Evangeline's testimony and alibi should have been enough to prove his innocence. The man once thought a bit queer, was now regarded with pity.

The solicitor pushed a set of keys across the desk, together with some documents. He tapped one. 'This letter expresses Sister Evangeline's wish for the house to continue to be a rescue home for Unfortunates. Please sign to say you have taken possession of the deeds and the keys.'

Mrs Grubb picked up the pen, dipped for ink, and scrawled her name. She glanced at a silent Mrs Baxter, perched on a similar hard chair to hers. The cook had been left ten pounds and didn't appear miffed to get so little in comparison. But she was eager to get away and fidgeted. Finally, her banknotes appeared and were counted out. Again the pen was dipped and Mrs Baxter also signed the paper. She immediately scraped back her chair, and with a nod and a muttered 'good day', took her cash and hastened towards the exit.

Mrs Grubb caught up with her along the road. 'I would like you to continue to work at the mission, if you will.'

'I won't, thanks all the same,' said Mrs Baxter pithily. 'I'll not step foot in there ever again.'

'A dreadful to-do, indeed. But the sister wanted her good work to continue and I will do my best in that to honour her.'

Mrs Baxter snorted. 'Honour? Her? I take a different view on it.'

'What do you mean?' Mrs Grubb wondered if the cook was sour from feeling short-changed, after all.

'I'll say no more, not because there's nothing to say, but because I won't speak ill of the dead.' Mrs Baxter pursed her lips. 'Good day to you.'

'Well, I thought I would offer,' sniffed Mrs Grubb. 'I shall go there tomorrow, and start getting ready for reopening. If you change your mind, do come. Otherwise, good luck to you.'

'I won't change my mind.' Mrs Baxter put the money grasped in her hand, into her pocket. 'And good luck to you. Reckon you'll need it in that godforsaken place.'

* * *

Whitechapel 1889

'What you after then?'

A gruff voice made Rebecca jump and spin away from the window of the Anchor public house. A youth she judged to be older than herself was grinning at her.

She bristled at his amusement, tilting her chin. 'I've come to speak to the landlord.'

'Well, he won't hear you from there. It's a landlady, in any case. Mrs Tanner's her name. Coming in?' He jerked his head and pushed on the door.

Rebecca blushed, unsure if she was ready to brave entering a public house. Yet she really had come for a reason.

'You're too young to get served in a pub.' She played for time to pluck up courage to go with him.

'Been in there more times than you've had hot dinners, miss. Don't get served though. I do the serving. Drinks... grub... whatever the customers want.' He sounded proud of his job. 'Better introduce meself then.' He lifted his cap. 'Charlie Webb... Spider me friends call me.' He took her hand and gave it a shake. 'And who might you be?'

'I'm Miss Spencer and I've come to see if somebody has my sister's new address.'

'Ah... now I see it.' Spider slapped his thigh. 'You look like Amelia, 'n' all.'

Rebecca had heard that before. Mrs Logan – the only neighbour who spoke to her – would sigh and warn Rebecca the likeness to her sisters was growing. 'We had an address in Kent for Amelia but our letters got returned as they'd moved away.'

'France, that's where they went. Mr Dupree's got cousins over there.'

'*France?*' Rebecca's face fell.

'Important, was it, that letter that got returned to you?'

'Our father passed away. Amelia would want to know.' Rebecca blinked back tears at the memory of his funeral with two of his children missing.

'Sorry to hear it.' Spider's cockiness evaporated and he clumsily patted her arm.

There was something else Rebecca wanted Amelia to know; a newspaper cutting about the fire and deaths at the mission where Joey had been born was enclosed with the letter. Her mother had paid little attention to the report, but nothing interested her any more other than Tom. And he didn't deserve mollycoddling. He was always in trouble, making the neighbours gossip and their mother cry. Rebecca stepped away.

'Thanks for telling me where they are. I'd best get off home then.'

'Hold on and I'll get you that French address from Mr Dupree's sister.' Spider returned quickly and handed over a piece of paper. He cocked his head. 'Gonna tell me your first name? You know mine's Charlie...'

Instead of telling him she mumbled a hasty farewell and hurried away up the road. She didn't need to turn around to know he was still watching her.

* * *

Normandy, France, Autumn 1889

Amelia put on a spurt over the sand as her naked son toddled into the gentle waves and lost his balance. She scooped him up, swinging him high into the air, gazing at his laughing face and silver curls, haloed by an azure sky.

'Now you're soaked,' she said, lowering him to kiss his warm cheek. Joey wriggled to get down and she let him run again on the beach. He made an effort to climb over some fishing nets but his sturdy legs got tangled in ropes. Her husband rescued him this time and off the boy went again, stopping at intervals to crouch and collect shells and seaweed.

Nick put a loose arm around Amelia's shoulders and they strolled on along the deserted shore in Joey's wake, while the sun sank closer to the horizon.

'You're very like your mum's family in looks,' she said.

'Handsome bunch, I know.'

She tutted, making him chuckle. She had been welcomed by the Duprees as though she was known to them instead of a stranger from across the sea. Nick, she'd discovered in surprise, was not a stranger to his French family; his illicit dealings had brought him across the Channel on numerous occasions and he spoke French reasonably well. Blond Joey had been doted on by the continental women. 'They're all lovely people and so hospitable...'

'Is a "but" coming?' He slanted a wry look at her.

'They're not my people, Nick.' She came to a halt, holding on to her straw hat as a breeze lifted it on the crown of her head. She gazed at him, bronzed from the sun, muscular from his work hauling fishing nets and boats in and out of the Gallic sea. His hair, not as black as she'd believed, now had russet streaks bleached into it. She loved him so much. 'I want to go back to England. I'm homesick.'

'So am I, if truth be told.' He smiled and kissed her. 'I'm sorry we missed your dad's funeral.' He knew that had been playing on her mind ever since a letter and a newspaper cutting arrived from Rebecca. The deaths at the mission were startling and thought-provoking. The nun's death wouldn't have been accidental, they'd concluded, having talked about it for hours. But whether a suicide pact or a murder had been committed, they couldn't decide.

'It's been a beautiful summer, a lovely long honeymoon. I'll never forget this time for as long as I live. But I want to go home now. I miss them all so much. Kitty too. I'd love to see her again. Letters aren't the same. They get lost. Mum must've thought I'd forgotten about them and gone off not caring how my dad was.'

'They know you too well for that, Amelia.'

'There's another reason I want to go back...' She turned to him, cupping his face between her hands. 'You're going to be a father and we'd both like Joey's brother or sister to be born in England, wouldn't we?'

'Are you sure?' He removed her hands and kissed their palms, blinking his sparkling grey eyes.

'I am.' She knew he considered himself to be a father already but they both knew there was a difference.

'We'll go back at the end of the week.' He gazed out over a calm sea, knowing it could turn cruel with little warning. 'Best set sail before October.'

'Will we go back to Whitechapel and the Anchor?' She was worried they'd be treading on toes if they did.

He raised a stroking hand to her fair hair; it hung in rope-like skeins almost to her waist, thick with salt and shimmering like mother of pearl. Coast and country suited her, and him.

Joey had scampered up, holding fistfuls of shells to show, whimpering in tiredness. Nick crouched and took them with a thank you and put them in his pocket. He lifted the little boy who was rubbing his eyes, unfurling small fingers to wipe away sand. He saw marks on his palms and smoothed them with his thumb. 'He's hurt himself with those shells. Some can be sharp as nails.'

'He's had those marks for a while.'

Amelia reflected on what lay ahead for them in England. 'Will you take over the pub again?'

He put his arm about her and they proceeded towards the anchored boat that soon would take them home. 'Don't think so.' He slanted a roguish look at her. 'Something new... different... I've got a few ideas...'

* * *

MORE FROM KAY BRELLEND

The next instalment in this gripping, emotional historical saga series from Kay Brellend is available to order now here:
https://mybook.to/MatchFactory2BackAd

AUTHOR'S NOTE

Like many people, I have long been fascinated by the Whitechapel murders that occurred during the autumn of 1888.

Five women were slaughtered by an unidentified killer and became known as the 'Canonical Five'. It's commonly thought middle-aged prostitutes were the target, but the fifth victim was in her twenties.

Other theories have the victims as homeless drunks, roaming the streets to find a dosshouse rather than a client. After two killings occurred on the same night speculation started on whether an accomplice or a copycat was involved.

Victorian London was a brutal and dangerous place for a destitute woman. Beatings, murders and misogyny were commonplace in East End slums, and not only contained there. The Bryant & May Match Factory strike during the summer of 1888 saw an unprecedented clash between privileged men and poor working class women. The Bow match workers risked their health to 'phossy jaw', the disease that attacked their bones from handling phosphorous. They were the lowest of the lowly paid, toiling under unfair and inhumane conditions even by Victorian standards. Yet those humble match girls won a landmark victory against their male bosses, forcing them to improve pay and hygiene standards, paving the way for the Great Dock Strike the following year. Their triumph inspired their stevedore husbands and brothers to achieve another workers' victory.

But not everybody liked women getting above themselves and upsetting the status quo. The year 1888 was packed with action in the East End of London, and the summer weather was unseasonably stormy too.

I drew inspiration from those momentous happenings to write *The Match Factory Girls* but the book and characters are fiction and it is not my intention to put forward any theories of how or why the notorious 'Ripper' killings took place.

It is more a case of, what if...

ACKNOWLEDGEMENTS

I would like to thank my editor, Emma Beswetherick, and all the Boldwood team for their enthusiasm and support for the *Match Factory Girls* series.

Also, Louise Raw's *Striking a Light: The Bryant and May Matchwomen and their Place in History*, was of great help when writing the series.

ABOUT THE AUTHOR

Kay Brellend was born in north London, and writes gripping historical sagas. Her early work drew inspiration from her grandmother's childhood in 'the Bunk', as the notorious road was known, where her own mother was born as well. Kay now lives in Hertfordshire and, having worked in various professions, concentrates on writing.

Download your exclusive bonus content from Kay Brellend here:

Visit Kay's website: www.kaybrellend.com

Follow Kay on social media here:

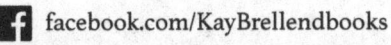 facebook.com/KayBrellendbooks

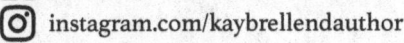 instagram.com/kaybrellendauthor

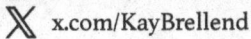 x.com/KayBrellend

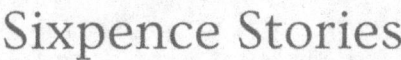

Sixpence Stories

Introducing Sixpence Stories!

Discover page-turning historical novels from your favourite authors, meet new friends and be transported back in time.

Join our book club Facebook group

https://bit.ly/SixpenceGroup

Sign up to our newsletter

https://bit.ly/SixpenceNews

Boldwood

Boldwood Books is an award-winning fiction publishing company seeking out the best stories from around the world.

Find out more at www.boldwoodbooks.com

Join our reader community for brilliant books, competitions and offers!

Follow us
@BoldwoodBooks
@TheBoldBookClub

Sign up to our weekly deals newsletter

https://bit.ly/BoldwoodBNewsletter